More Praise for

"Godwin's riveting and wise story of the slow coalescence of trust and love between a stoic artist and a grieving boy . . . subtly and insightfully explores different forms of haunting and vulnerability, strength and survival . . . Word will spread quickly about Godwin's tender and spellbinding supernatural novel." —*Booklist* (starred review)

"Godwin's forceful prose captivates with the quiet, renewing power of a persistent tide." —*Publishers Weekly* (starred review)

"An exquisite narrative . . . This grace-filled story probes aspects of life and death, isolation and family, and how great pain and loss can ultimately lead to unforeseen transcendence." —*Shelf Awareness* (starred review)

"Godwin . . . explore[s] themes of loss, connection, and growth unfettered by the corporeal world." —*Kirkus Reviews*

"A contemporary *Turn of the Screw.*" —BCC.com, "Ten Books to Read in June"

"*Grief Cottage* concerns an orphan named Marcus and some ghosts, but it's really about how each of us is haunted, even when we don't acknowledge it." —Lit Hub

"Like Henry James' classic *The Turn of the Screw, Grief Cottage* is less a paranormal thriller than an exploration of the psyche's creative tactics to survive trauma . . . Godwin shows she is still at the top of her craft, using the fragile link between living and spirit to illuminate a young man's coming of age in this keenly observed, powerful novel." —*BookPage*

"An absorbing and wise novel." —*Washington Independent Review of Books*

"[A] compelling story of family and loss. Godwin's vivid prose, well-wrought characters and captivating plot will keep readers turning pages to the end." —*The Charleston Post and Courier*

"Godwin again works her magic in a novel at once uplifting and somber . . . *Grief Cottage* melds literary and popular fiction, glows with Godwin's heart and humanity and reflects the wisdom of her years." —*Richmond Times-Dispatch*

"[Godwin] knows how to make the atmosphere tense and make your skin tingle." —*The Raleigh News & Observer*

"Gail Godwin peers into the souls of her characters to find the healing nature of kindness, tolerance and love." —*Minneapolis Star Tribune*

"Brilliant . . . Godwin's perfectly flowing prose reaches that elusive place where reality and fiction collide seamlessly. Her ability to infuse her characters and settings with heartbreaking depth makes this novel unforgettable." —*Woodbury*

"Godwin, a three-time National Book Award finalist, mixes horror and mystery tropes with literary musings on growing up and growing old. The result is a sort of supernatural bildungsroman, less a traditional ghost story and more a cautionary tale about the specter of impermanence . . . Full of curiosity and spectacle . . . The novel succeeds in questioning the uncanny and finding life even in a ghost story." —*The Atlanta Journal-Constitution*

"A stately meditation on loss and longing." —*Arkansas Democrat-Gazette*, "Summer Reads"

"Godwin handles the supernatural deftly. It's up to the reader whether Marcus actually sees something or is letting his imagination run riot." —*Star-News* (Wilmington, NC)

"We've learned to count on certain things in a Godwin novel. Entanglement with the unseen. Grief suppressed and revealed. And those finely wrought paragraphs that make tangible our vaguest feelings and thoughts." —*The Charlotte News & Observer* (Charlotte, NC)

"Whether the ghost is 'real' or the creation of a distressed psyche becomes irrelevant. As in Godwin's favorite story, Henry James' *The Turn of the Screw*, it could go either way, and despite the heat of the South Carolina summer, there is a peculiar chill in the air." —*Alabama Public Radio*

"Can the needs of the living and dead sometimes merge? Eleven-year-old Marcus's desire to believe so leads him, and us, on a harrowing and unforgettable journey toward an answer. *Grief Cottage* further confirms that Gail Godwin is one of our country's very finest novelists." —Ron Rash, author of *The Risen* and *Above the Waterfall*

"No one writes about the psychological weight of the human condition like Gail Godwin. In *Grief Cottage* Godwin is able to conjure on the page what few of us can conjure in our minds: the implications of loss and time and what it means to be haunted by both." —Wiley Cash, *New York Times* bestselling author of *This Dark Road to Mercy* and *A Land More Kind Than Home*

"Gail Godwin brings grace, honesty, and enormous intelligence to every page." —Ann Patchett

BY THE SAME AUTHOR

NOVELS
Flora (2013)
Unfinished Desires (2009)
Queen of the Underworld (2006)
Evenings at Five (2003)
Evensong (1999)
The Good Husband (1994)
Father Melancholy's Daughter (1991)
A Southern Family (1987)
The Finishing School (1984)
A Mother and Two Daughters (1982)
Violet Clay (1978)
The Odd Woman (1974)
Glass People (1972)
The Perfectionists (1970)

STORY COLLECTIONS
Mr. Bedford and the Muses (1983)
Dream Children (1976)

NONFICTION
Publishing: A Writer's Memoir (2015)
The Making of a Writer: Journals, vols. 1 and 2 (2006, 2011)
edited by Rob Neufeld
Heart: A Personal Journey Through Its Myths and Meanings (2001)

Grief Cottage

a novel

GAIL GODWIN

BLOOMSBURY PUBLISHING
NEW YORK · LONDON · OXFORD · NEW DELHI · SYDNEY

Grief Cottage is dedicated
to my three nephews
Trey and Cam Millender
&
Justin Cole

and to my great-nephew
Matthew Millender

BLOOMSBURY PUBLISHING
Bloomsbury Publishing Inc.
1385 Broadway, New York, NY 10018, USA

BLOOMSBURY, BLOOMSBURY PUBLISHING, and the Diana logo are trademarks of
Bloomsbury Publishing Plc

First published in the United States 2017
This paperback edition published 2018

Copyright © Gail Godwin, 2017

All rights reserved. No part of this publication may be reproduced or transmitted
in any form or by any means, electronic or mechanical, including photocopying,
recording, or any information storage or retrieval system, without prior permission
in writing from the publishers.

Bloomsbury Publishing Plc does not have any control over, or responsibility for,
any third-party websites referred to or in this book. All Internet addresses given in
this book were correct at the time of going to press. The author and publisher regret
any inconvenience caused if addresses have changed or sites have ceased to exist,
but can accept no responsibility for any such changes.

ISBN: HB: 978-1-63286-704-9; eBook: 978-1-63286-706-3;
PB: 978-1-63286-705-6

LIBRARY OF CONGRESS CATALOGING-IN-PUBLICATION DATA

Names: Godwin, Gail, author.
Title: Grief cottage : a novel / Gail Godwin.
Description: New York : Bloomsbury USA, an imprint of Bloomsbury Publishing Plc, 2017.
Identifiers: LCCN 2016036527| ISBN 9781632867049 (hardback) |
ISBN 9781632867063 (ebook)
Subjects: | BISAC: FICTION / Literary. | FICTION / Romance / Gothic.
Classification: LCC PS3557.O315 G75 2017 | DDC 813/.54—dc23 LC record
available at https://lccn.loc.gov/2016036527

2 4 6 8 10 9 7 5 3 1

Typeset by RefineCatch Limited, Bungay, Suffolk
Printed and bound in the U.S.A. by Berryville Graphics Inc., Berryville, Virginia

To find out more about our authors and books visit www.bloomsbury.com
and sign up for our newsletters.

Bloomsbury books may be purchased for business or promotional use.
For information on bulk purchases please contact Macmillan Corporate
and Premium Sales Department at specialmarkets@macmillan.com..

Not everybody gets to grow up. First you have to survive your childhood, and then begins the hard work of growing into it.

1.

*O*nce there was a boy who lost his mother. He was eleven years, five months, four days—and would never know how many hours and minutes. The state troopers came to the apartment around midnight, but the accident had happened earlier. A part of him believed that if he had known the exact moment her car slid on a patch of black ice and somersaulted down the embankment, he could have sent her the strength to hold on. Please, Mom, you're all I've got. And she would have heard him and held on. She had gone out to buy them a pizza. They were going to watch one of their favorite old movies on TV, the one where Alec Guinness and his band of thieves pretend to be musicians. They rent a room in a nice old lady's house, shut the door, put a string quartet on the gramophone, and she is never the wiser. Before the movie is over, she is helping them move their stolen goods and she is still none the wiser. The star of this movie had special meaning to the mother and son because they had read an article about how Alec Guinness never knew who his father was because his mother had refused to tell him, but he had still grown up to be famous anyway.

★　★　★

AUNT CHARLOTTE WAS my mother's aunt, which made her my great-aunt. I had only heard tales about her before I went to live with her. Even the tales weren't much. She had run away from home early, married several times, and then gone to live by herself on an island. At some point she had taken up painting and had become a successful local artist. She wasn't a letter writer but whenever Mom wrote to her she sent back a post-card with one of her paintings. I was always mentioned by name. Mom stuck the postcards up on the refrigerator, paint-ings of storm clouds over waves, orangey light on wet surf, a gloomy ruin of an old beach cottage. The paintings had names: *Storm Approaching, Sunset Calm, Abandoned Cottage*. My late grandmother had referred to her as "Crazy Charlotte," or "my Bohemian baby sister." She painted under the name of Charlotte Lee. "It could have been the name of one of her husbands," Mom said. "Or maybe she chose it for herself."

I DID NOT get to Aunt Charlotte's island until late spring. The wheels of the law had to turn first. A person from Social Services stayed with me the rest of that night and helped me pack my things. She asked about my next of kin and I showed her Mom's life insurance policy. "We've got to get you a guardian ad litem quickly," she said. "That's someone who will be your voice in legal matters." When I asked what legal matters, she said, "Determining who will be your permanent guardian and how your estate will be managed." When I asked what estate, she said, "The estate from this insurance policy." Our belongings from the apartment were put into storage and I was sent to live with a foster family and finished seventh grade from their address. I was a year ahead of my age because I had skipped sixth grade. The boy I shared a room with in the foster home had had the left side of his face crushed by his stepfather while his mother was out at work. From his right profile he looked like a normal boy, but from the front and left it looked like his cheek had melted. There was much plastic surgery ahead. At night I could hear him whacking off under the covers.

I liked my guardian ad litem, William. He was the one who got me into the hospital morgue to see my mom and helped me decide on burial arrangements. William was so tall he had to stoop to get through ordinary doorways, and he wore a flowing dark beard. He could have been a stand-in for Abe Lincoln, though he had a shiny bald dome. He had grown up in the high mountains of western North Carolina and had a mountain twang so thick it sounded like it was making fun of itself.

The foster parents had Bible study for us every night. It was called "Parable Party," and they made it a competitive game. Even the little kids could quote chapter and verse from the gospel parables and I soon became a whiz at it myself. I was a fast learner and a good memorizer and I enjoyed a mental challenge. Mom and I had read the King James Bible aloud to each other because she wanted me to be grounded in its stories and language. Sometimes we used it as our augur, opening it at random to see what we should do about something. But it didn't take precedence over everything the way it did in the foster home.

Then one day I was told to pack my things. It was all set up legally and I was going on my first plane ride to live with my great-aunt at her beach cottage in South Carolina. "You are one lucky boy, Marcus," the foster mom said. William stayed with me at the gate until I had a nametag hung around my neck and was escorted onboard by a flight attendant. William's last words to me were, "Live long and prosper," and we gave each other the Spock hand-blessing from *Star Trek*.

Aunt Charlotte was waiting just on the other side of the security gate, a very thin lady in white slacks, loose white shirt, and scuffed brown sandals. She had stern, beaky features and a frosty mannish haircut. At that time she was fifty-seven, but she appeared elderly to me. Though she was my late grandmother's younger sister by six years, she looked at least a generation older than that stylish, coiffed lady who had visited Mom and me several times. The flight attendant who had escorted me checked her papers. Then he handed me over and wished us good luck. I had steeled myself for a theatrical hug like the foster mother's or some display of aunt-ish emotion, but she simply gave me a firm handshake and said, "Well, Marcus, here we are."

While we waited for my suitcases down in baggage claim, she told me "my boxes" had arrived and were stored in her garage, to unpack when I was ready. It took me a minute to realize she meant Mom's and my stuff from our apartment.

We went out into the suffocating heat and she had me heave the suitcases into the trunk of her old Mercedes sedan. The leather seats were boiling, but she said they would cool down in a minute. She wasn't much of a talker. "Are you hungry? Do you like shrimp? We'll go to a place where they serve all the shrimp you can eat."

The shrimp were very small and fried in batter and I ate three helpings. There were also these sweet fried bread balls called hush puppies. Aunt Charlotte picked at her salad and had two glasses of red wine. The waitress kept urging me to go back and refill my plate. Her name was Donna, which was stitched on her uniform, and she smiled a lot. Her teasing-affectionate tone with me reminded me a little of Mom and I went back for the third mostly to make her smile some more. Aunt Charlotte had not smiled once. Looking back on that first day, I realize she must have been as apprehensive as I was. I doubt if I smiled that day, either.

When I threw up in my aunt's car, she pulled over. "No problem, the seats are leather and most of it's on the rubber mat." She set me up with an eight-ounce bottle of spritzer water, a roll of paper towels, and gallon of windshield wiper fluid from her trunk. It rained a lot during this season, she said, so she always carried reserves of wiper fluid. "I'd use the spritzer water for the front of your shirt and the wiper fluid for the rest." Then she withdrew to the grassy embankment and appeared to be studying the traffic. Heat waves rose from the asphalt and made wavery squiggles around her thin white form. The good thing about the heat was that my shirt was dry before I even finished cleaning the car. When we were on the road again I apologized for the smell. "All I smell is wiper fluid," she said.

After we crossed the causeway to the island, she stopped by a store with gas pumps in front and we bought some things for supper. The man at the counter told her the day's shrimp catch had just come in, but she said, "My nephew has already had his fill of shrimp for the day."

11.

Whenever I try to crawl back into the skin of that boy Aunt Charlotte suddenly found invading her precious solitude, a boy who was neither a charming child nor a promising young man, I am surprised that after living alone by choice for so long she was able to tolerate my company as well as she did. She spoke like someone who wasn't used to social talk. She said what needed to be conveyed and stopped. ("Are you hungry? Spray yourself with sunblock even if it's overcast. If it's anything *urgent,* Marcus, you can always knock on my studio door.")

Mom had guessed right about the Lee surname: Aunt Charlotte had made it up. ("It was the obvious choice to take the surname of their hallowed Confederate general, Robert E. Lee. In these parts people still refer to the American Civil War as 'the great unpleasantness' or 'the war of northern aggression.' If I was a 'Lee,' I had a better chance of blending in.")

Aunt Charlotte and Mom had grown up in West Virginia, known to Southerners as the "turncoat state" because it separated from Virginia and joined the Union in the Civil War. Neither of them had any accent other than a mid-Atlantic one, if there was such a thing. Aunt Charlotte's voice was dispassionate and flat compared to my mother's emotional range. Mom could please, tease, or appease, whatever the situation called for, whereas Aunt Charlotte, even when she was in one of her rare good moods or making fun of somebody, stuck to a gruff and matter-of-fact monotone.

After we had established a routine for ourselves that consisted mainly of each mapping thoughtful routes around the other's privacy, she had a serious talk with me about money and my "trust." She invited me into her studio for this. She removed some books and papers from a chair and asked me to sit down. There was the smell of turpentine and oil pigment, a smell that connects me even today with the pleasant idea of someone making something alone. Her studio faced the north end of the beach and had a milky, regulated light, less yellow and warm than the other rooms in the cottage. She also slept in the studio behind a curtain.

It took me longer than it should have to realize she had given up her bedroom to me.

"I have always worked," she began. "Ever since I left home at sixteen, I have held a job. When I married, I supported the first of my no-good husbands and I worked twice as hard as the next two slackers. I will never be rich, but this fluke of a talent has made me safe for the time being. People want paintings of the beach. My style is on the primitive side, but that's an asset, too, don't ask me why. For a large part of my life now I have lived alone and supported myself by my painting and it has suited me." She was perched on a high stool in front of a gigantic paint-spattered easel on wheels. Its large canvas was covered with a cloth. She was looking at me, but actually she was looking through me as she carefully picked her words. "When they contacted me back in February about your mother, they said I was the only living relative. I asked about your father's people, but I was the only name listed on the policy. Did you know she had taken out an insurance policy on her life?"

"It was in case anything happened to her." Mom and I had imagined some fatal illness that would take her away and leave me all alone. We didn't foresee that something as ordinary as driving two miles on a winter night to pick up a pizza could accomplish the same ending.

"I met your mother only once. She was a girl, still in high school. Your grandmother brought her to visit me here. I liked her and I felt she liked me. But it was not a successful visit. Did she ever mention it?"

"She talked about your beach house and how nice it was to lie in bed and hear the ocean so close. She said maybe one day we would go back and visit you. I mean, not stay with you, but in a hotel."

"You would have been welcome to stay here. It was my sister Brenda who spoiled that visit. Always putting everyone down. She couldn't stand my lifestyle. I think that was her reason for bringing your mother to see me; I was to be a warning. But I must remember that Brenda was your grandmother, so you probably loved her. Funny how the same person can be an entirely different entity to various people. Where do you think you'd like to go to school? There's the public school across the causeway and a few of those so-called 'academies.' Or you could go to boarding school. There's enough money. You know that, don't you?"

"It was supposed to be enough to get me through college," I said.

"Then it will be, we'll see to it. Meanwhile, it will pay your expenses until you're old enough to live on your own. And as your guardian I get a nice monthly stipend from the trust. You understand about that, don't you? I want everything to be aboveboard between us."

I said I understood. But her insistence on aboveboard-ness, which would turn out to be one of her sterling qualities, had a bitter effect on me that day. *So it was the money,* I thought, she only took me because of the money. Without that nice stipend she would never have forfeited the solitary life that suited her so well. She went on to explain the trust and how it was set up with a law firm in Charleston that specialized in that sort of thing. There would be monthly statements about how the money was invested and how well it was doing. It seemed that if you had a certain amount of money, you should expect it to make more money out of itself. "And you are welcome to examine these statements anytime you want, Marcus."

"Maybe I'll just leave them to you for now," I said.

It was all I could do to sort out the information arising out of this talk we were having. The revelation about her "nice stipend" had deflated any grand illusions of my being wanted simply because I was me. On the other hand I saw advantages to her scanty information about my past. When she had said, "I asked about your father's people, but I was the only name on the policy," I realized she had assumed that my father was the person whose last name I bore—Harshaw—even though Mom and Mr. Harshaw had parted ways two years before I was born. With my background being so vague to Aunt Charlotte there would be less embarrassing information to worry about her finding out. "Look at it this way, Marcus," Mom had said when I almost killed the grandson of her employer and we had to leave her good job at Forster's furniture factory in the flatlands of North Carolina and move to the mountains. "In a new place we can tell people what we want them to know and that will be our past."

To cover the readjustments going on inside me, I asked Aunt Charlotte what she was painting. After apologizing for it being one of her "bread and butter commissions" she removed the cloth from the large canvas on the easel. So far she had only outlined a substantial-sized beach house and some palmetto trees in dark blue. She explained she was working from a color photo provided by the owners. "I don't paint from life anymore. It's too messy. Sand blows into the pigment and nosy people crowd around and make dumb remarks. If you're interested in seeing the actual house, it's down at the south end of the beach, where they're building the new McMansions. So far it's the only one with three stories. And a fake cupola. For my honest paintings I go to the north end of the island. Those are the old houses, when people built behind the dunes. There's one old house I must have painted at least fifty times. But people keep asking for it. Since I took my business online I can't keep up with the orders for that one house. I paint it from photos now, but they are photos I took myself."

"What's a fake cupola?"

"A cupola is a tower where you can look out at the view. But this one is just stuck up there for show, with no way to get to it."

"Why do people want paintings of that other house?"

"It's a very old cottage, what's left of it. It's a ruin and it has a haunting quality. I'm still trying to do justice to its quality. Walk up there and see it for yourself. It's the very last structure at the north end. It's half gone, but it emanates a powerful mood. The locals call it Grief Cottage. The town commissioners have been dying to tear it down, but the historical society's on their back because it was built in 1804. I need to go up there and get some more photos in case they lose the battle."

"Why do they call it Grief Cottage?"

"A family was lost there in Hurricane Hazel. A boy and his parents. The parents were out desperately searching for him, when all the while he may have been in the cottage. Anyway, none of them were ever found. Some of the locals think the boy may have been hiding in the house somewhere smoking. They thought it might have been a cigarette that started the fire that burned down the south end of the cottage, but they never found a body. Others think that when he realized his parents had gone out searching for him he rushed out searching for them and got swept out to sea. But his body never washed up either."

"Maybe it still could."

"I don't think so. It was fifty years ago. I can show you the last *Grief Cottage* I painted—I mean, on my computer screen. As soon as I get this commission out of the way, I'll give you a tour of my online gallery. But now I must earn my bread and butter while the north light is still strong."

III.

"Walk up there and see for yourself," Aunt Charlotte had said, and I had the rest of the afternoon ahead to do it in. I sprayed myself with sunscreen, marched down the rickety boardwalk that bridged the dunes between the cottage and the beach, descended the wooden stairs, and before heading north stopped for my usual inspection of "our" roped-off hatching site with its big red diamond-shaped warning sign. LOGGERHEAD TURTLE NESTING AREA. EGGS, HATCHLINGS, ADULTS, AND CARCASSES ARE PROTECTED BY FEDERAL AND STATE LAWS.

The eggs buried in our dune had already survived their first catastrophe. Back in mid-May, just before my arrival, the people renting the cottage to the right of Aunt Charlotte's had been negligent about smoothing out the sand at the end of their badminton games, and that night a mother turtle had mistaken the hilly clump for a dune, laid her eggs, and departed. The Turtle Patrol had to dig them out, a "clutch" of 110 eggs, tenderly transfer them into buckets lined with wet sand, and re-bury them in a suitable spot. The patrol knew Aunt Charlotte's way of life and could depend on her boundaries to stay untrammeled and safe.

I kept my sneakers on because my beach walks had taught me you made better progress on sand with rubber soles. Aunt Charlotte hadn't said how far the north end of the island was but surely she wouldn't have said I could walk there if she had judged it too far.

Before I came to live with her I had never seen the ocean. Mom and I had lived first in the North Carolina piedmont, which was a long way from the coast. After she had to leave her job at the furniture factory, we moved west to the mountains, which was even farther from the coast. Although I was a competent swimmer in a pool, I was still nervous of the ocean. After being knocked down about twenty times, getting water up my nose and sand in my eyes, I postponed trying to master the waves and took to walking on the beach. There were new ocean things for me to discover every day, comparisons to be made, conclusions to be drawn. Everything I encountered seemed to be sending me some kind of message. Some of the messages made me feel good, others not so good. The patterns made in the sand by the outgoing wash redrew themselves again and again, different each time, and would continue to do so after I was dead. The stately pelicans flapped in a single line toward their destination, while the skittish gulls zipped and zapped, shrieking at one another and getting diverted. When the tide went out, as it was starting to do now, it left behind these tiny-shelled creatures frantically trying to dig themselves back into the wet sand before the birds ate them. Some made it, some did not. And on top of that, all the birds I saw, plus all the crabs that came out at night, were already programmed to gulp down the tasty defenseless little loggerhead babies when they hatched in mid-July and raced for the sea.

I knew why the tides rose and fell; it had been part of seventh-grade science. I also knew that we were composed of seventy-eight percent water when we were born, though it went down to sixty percent as we got older. Our brains remained eighty percent water, however, and the ancient part of our brain remembered that when we were formed many millennia ago, we swam before we could crawl or walk. Even now we began our lives immersed in the waters of our mothers' wombs.

Children playing in the shallow waves screamed with exaggerated terror while mothers hovered close by. There was this one mother sitting in a low chair near the surf. She wore a straw hat and oversized sunglasses. Her toddler, about three, was carefully transporting a shovel full of water from the receding ocean to pour on her feet. By the time he reached her, the ocean had all spilled out and he emptied a waterless shovel on her painted toenails. But then I saw her raise her eyebrows at him behind the oversized sunglasses. Her glossed lips gave him a special ironic smile, meant for just the two of them. Better luck next time, the look said. Meanwhile, I'm staying right here. There were little eddies of security going back and forth between them and it wrenched my heart.

Yellow trash barrels were placed at regular intervals along the beach border where the grasses and dunes began. To date, I had walked north as far as the fourth yellow barrel beyond Aunt Charlotte's cottage. The barrels stretched ahead of me, getting smaller and smaller in perspective toward the island's north end until I could no longer count them.

But today, even before I reached the third barrel, something horrible happened. It was like I had been turned upside down. Everything was so terrifying it stopped me in my tracks. My heart was pounding a mile a minute and, worse than that, I found I no longer knew how to walk. Somehow I found myself sitting down in the sand—it must have been abrupt because my bottom was stinging. A couple in bathing suits passed by and the man looked over and acknowledged me with a man-to-man wave. After lifting my hand in return, I quickly unlaced a sneaker, pretending there was a pebble inside it and that was why I needed to sit. I turned the sneaker upside down and made a big deal of shaking out the pebble. I put the shoe back on but when it came to tying the laces in a knot I couldn't remember how. The boy whose stepfather had smashed his face in had lost his memory for weeks. "A whole bunch of my life was just wiped out forever," he went around bragging to anybody at the foster home who would listen. Maybe I was going insane. When Mom was still working at the furniture factory, a woman who worked in the sanding department "lost it" one day and never came back. Two men had to carry her from the floor. She had to go to a mental hospital. This sometimes happened to people, Mom said, either because they couldn't endure their life anymore or because, through no fault of their own, something suddenly went haywire in their brains.

I didn't think it was the first reason, because I could endure life at Aunt Charlotte's much better than the foster home, where nothing was private and you never had a moment alone. At Aunt Charlotte's I had plenty of time to myself and didn't have to listen to platitudes about how everything horrible that happens to us is part of "God's plan." I no longer had to share a room with a boy who made noises under the covers. At Aunt Charlotte's I had my own room and could listen to the ocean at night, just as my mother had done as a girl that time she had visited here.

If it was the other thing, and something in my brain had suddenly gone haywire, what would happen to me? At the very worst, I would be discovered insane on the beach, unable to remember anything or tie my shoe, and sent off in an ambulance to a mental hospital. If the brain somehow righted itself and I made it back to the house, what then? If I told Aunt Charlotte about the panic, she would get on the phone and call in another grief counselor, if I was entitled to any more of them—or did you get to start all over in a new state?—or I'd have to go to a therapist and Aunt Charlotte would resent having to drive me there and we would be diminishing the money in the trust.

It took some rude plops of water on my head to remind me that if I was using my brain well enough to figure out possible outcomes of my madness I probably wasn't mad. The skies had opened and people were fleeing the beach or sheltering under umbrellas. The woman in the big sunglasses and her little boy had vanished. I looked at my feet and saw that both sneakers were tied. Walking home in the pouring rain, I decided not to mention anything to Aunt Charlotte.

"THAT'S THE TROUBLE with afternoon walks," said Aunt Charlotte. "In this season you can depend on it to rain. Sorry it spoiled your adventure, but I'm glad you changed clothes. I had a productive afternoon. I've laid in the sky over my McMansion, and tomorrow I'll tackle the shrubbery. It's not there yet in real life, but I'll duplicate what's in the architect's drawing."

"Maybe I'll go the whole way to the cottage tomorrow morning."

"It's a fair walk, but you're young. I haven't done it for a while. The last time I went up there to take some new photos of Grief Cottage I drove north as far as Seashore Road goes, parked in the turnaround, and then fought my way on foot up through the dune grasses and Spanish bayonets."

"What are they?"

"*Very* prickly plants. They look like succulent bayonets sticking up from the ground. You don't want to sit or fall on one."

Supper was the only meal Aunt Charlotte and I ate together. I did not mind this. I liked making my own breakfast and having a sandwich around midday on the porch. Mom and I had never eaten all our meals together because of her jobs and her different shifts. Aunt Charlotte wasn't a cook and didn't aspire to being one. The foster mom made a big deal about her cooking and baking, but everyone had to sit down together for every meal and we had to take turns praying and then we each had to tell what we had learned that day. As soon as I was old enough, Mom and I had shared the cooking. Spaghetti sauce was her masterpiece (her secret was clove powder), and she made a fabulous thick soup from her own combination of cans. I could fry hamburgers and scramble eggs and do pulled pork in our slow-cooker. For the rest, we got our stuff from delis.

Or went out to pick up a pizza.

No wonder Aunt Charlotte was so skinny. All day she snacked on bananas and crackers and little cartons of yogurt, and at supper she picked around the edges of her meal and kept refilling her wineglass. She ordered her wines and had them delivered in cases. The store on our island had a deli with salads and cold meats and kept a spit going that roasted chickens all day long. So far we had not risked shrimp again and I didn't want to be the first to suggest it.

At our shared meals, she gamely dredged up things to talk about. I could feel her reluctance to probe into my past. After downing several glasses of wine, though, she loosened up a little. What had she done when she ate her suppers alone? There was an old TV in the kitchen, she had probably watched it. Or just sat comfortably, enjoying her solitary life and sipping her wine.

She saw me staring at the TV and asked if I would like to order cable. "I can get old movies and the networks, but maybe you and your mother had other favorite channels. Should I look into it? All the neighbors are already hooked up. I'm the last holdout."

"Mom and I never had cable. They had it at the foster home because the state paid for it. There was this two-year-old boy who sat strapped into his little swing-chair and watched it all day long."

"Is that a yes or a no?"

"Only if you want it." As this sounded rude, I added, "I mean, I can do without it if you can." One less expense to take out of the trust.

"Look, Marcus, we're both new at this. If there's anything missing here, something you'd like to have to make the summer go faster, you need to tell me. I won't know otherwise, I'm not a mind reader. Would you like to have a look at those boxes waiting in the garage, or is it still too soon?"

"Maybe it's still a little too soon."

"Well, you set to work on them when you're ready. School starts at the end of August. You'll be with people your own age. These days won't last forever. No days ever do, though sometimes it's hard to convince oneself of that."

111.

At night, the tides washed in and out. I did not think I would ever get tired of that sound. It felt like the watery part of the earth taking regular breaths in your ear. Thud-wash, thud-wash, never stopping, doing its job with the same rhythm as millions of years ago when the little loggerhead turtles were waiting to hatch and begin their race for the sea. ("It's their Normandy," an old-timer on the Turtle Patrol told me, "only in reverse.")

My mother had slept in this room before she was my mother. Her young head, like mine, had been divided from the ancient tides by a mere cottage wall and a few dunes. Where had my critical grandmother ("Brenda") slept? Now that I asked that question, it seemed likely she had shared the bed with my mother while Aunt Charlotte slept in her studio. When Mom used to tell me how nice it had been to lie in bed and hear the ocean so close, I had always imagined her alone in the bed. But maybe she had adapted her memory of that night when telling the memory to me. As someone who had slept all his life with his mother, I could identify with that. Whenever I was telling my best friend, Wheezer, about a dream I'd had, I pictured an alternate vision of myself alone in a bed, the way Wheezer, who slept alone in *his* bed, would naturally be picturing me.

That is, until the unlucky day he came to our apartment and found out the truth.

My shoelaces were tied this morning and like the straight-flying pelicans I had a goal: Grief Cottage. In my backpack I had my lunch and a bottle of spring water. Aunt Charlotte reckoned it would take me about forty minutes each way at a normal pace.

"When I first moved here I was in an ecstasy of freedom. I hardly touched the ground, my first year on this island. I was in my early thirties, which may seem decrepit to you, but I had never had so much energy before in my life. Nobody could tell me how to live anymore; nobody could criticize me or lay a hand on me. I spent all my savings on a beach shack. It was even named Rascal Shack. The young scions would gather here when they wanted to get drunk. It didn't even have an indoor bathroom when I bought it."

"What is a *syon*?"

"Offspring. Usually meaning the offspring of privileged families. You put a 'c' after the 's' when you're writing it. S-C-I-O-N. When I first came here I walked to the north end of the island every day. Forty minutes each way. The walk north was exactly the right distance to make me walk out of myself. And then that desolate cottage at the end, falling in on itself and all its secrets. What better spot for sorting through the debris of my own history?"

"If you walked out of yourself going north, what did you do on the return walk?"

"Enjoyed my emptiness. Or sometimes just congratulated myself for escaping."

"Escaping what, if it's not rude to ask?"

"Escaping the kind of life I'd always felt trapped in. But that's another story. Do you know, Marcus, it was Grief Cottage that started my painting. One day there was someone else in my lonely spot. This person had planted an easel in the sand and was painting the cottage. At first I assumed it was a man but when I got closer it turned out to be a woman in a hat and trousers. She was a cheerful tourist, staying for a short time, and I watched her mix her colors. It was fascinating. It was a competent little painting; I could see it hanging on a wall and pleasing someone, though she had missed the mood of the place. I could do that, I thought. I bought some paints and some canvas board and a book called *A Beginner's Guide to Landscape Painting*. It took me a while to figure out how I could capture the mood she had missed. But first I had to teach myself the most basic painting skills. Later I borrowed books from the library to see how the masters had done their skies. Constable would spend hours sketching clouds and skies. He called this practice his 'skying sessions.'"

"Constable?"

"John Constable, English. Late eighteenth, early nineteenth century. Look at his skies up close—he loves approaching storms—and you realize clouds *don't have outlines*. He works them up from within. Clouds are brushstrokes. Constable is the king of clouds."

TODAY THE RISING tide had covered the spot where I had seen the mother and the little boy yesterday afternoon. By afternoon the waters would have receded again and maybe the happy pair would come back. Perhaps they had their own family routine in one of the beach houses behind the dunes. Was a father with them, or was he somewhere else, or was he one of those secret fathers nobody gets to know about?

I was walking up closer to the dunes because of the incoming tide when a neat white dump truck stopped alongside me. A sunburned man in shorts jumped out and gracefully upended a yellow trash barrel into the truck's bin. "Disgusting!" he called to me over the sound of the waves. "What people will put into these things!" Without waiting for a response, he asked where I was headed. When I said I was walking to the north end of the island he said, "I'd offer you a lift but it's against regulations. I could lose my job."

"That's okay. I want to walk."

"Well, dude," he said, looking me over, "I'd take it easy if I were you till you get back in shape." As he raised his sunburnt arms to swing the empty barrel back onto its concrete platform, a pungent man-smell issued from the wet underarms of his T-shirt. "You have a good day," he called over his shoulder, springing up into the truck and setting off northward to the next yellow barrel.

Already I was tired and hadn't yet reached the spot where I had panicked and turned around yesterday. But I had to keep walking north till the trash-barrel man finished his round and passed me coming back or he'd see how out of shape I really was.

After Mom left her job at the furniture factory and we moved to the mountain town of Jewel, I entered fifth grade. Then at the end of the year the teacher told Mom I was ready to do seventh grade work if she had no objection to my skipping a grade. She didn't—it made her proud because she had helped me study that first lonely year in Jewel. She asked me my opinion and I said it suited me. But the seventh grade kids were more developed and must have looked on me as a freak: here was this kid still built like a child and piping up with the right answer every time the teacher called on him in class. At first they called me Baby Wonk. Then when I began to gain weight, they called me Pudge. ("Boy, Pudge sure makes the most of the Reduced Price Lunch Program, doesn't he?")

Back in Forsterville where the furniture factory was, my best friend had had a nickname: everybody lovingly called him Wheezer, because he suffered from bad asthma. But to Wheezer, whose real name was Shelby, I was never anything but Marcus.

Just the right distance to make me walk out of myself, Aunt Charlotte had said. I wished I knew what she was trying to walk out of, what kind of debris in her history she needed to sort out. If she came to the island when she was in her thirties, did she have three times as much debris as I had?

One foot and then the other. Remember, each time the water inches closer, you are closer to your goal.

Is it a mirage, that tiny white truck bouncing toward me? No, that's him, heading south. His sunburnt salute. Way to go, dude. Tide swirling closer now. Pride saved.

Oh no, surely *that* couldn't be Aunt Charlotte's famous cottage, rearing up all broken and ugly in front of me. But it had to be because the island ended here. The town commissioners had been right to want to remove such an eyesore from their ocean view. When Aunt Charlotte first came here, it couldn't have looked this bad. After all, some cheery tourist had been painting it. And then Aunt Charlotte taught herself to paint and painted it over and over until it became the kind of picturesque ruin people paid money for.

If a house could be a zombie, this grim husk, guarded by those evil-sharp bayonet cactuses Aunt Charlotte warned about and fenced by sagging wire posted with CONDEMNED and KEEP OUT: DANGER signs, would qualify as one. And more than fifty people had paid money to have Aunt Charlotte paint this zombie house to hang on their walls at home! The porch on the south side had been sheared off and some shingles were nailed up against a replacement wall. Had that been the porch where he left a cigarette while his parents were out desperately searching for him?

When I got closer I could view the rest of the house from the front. The noon sun boiled down on its crumpled roof, mercilessly entering a doorway without a door and the gaping window holes on either side. Maybe at dark this place would pass as a picturesque ruin. But the cottage would have to be almost a silhouette to make you want to hang it on your wall.

I was hot and very thirsty. The zombie house offered the only shade in sight, so I wriggled under the wire fence with the KEEP OUT warnings, snagging my backpack and scratching my arm. I cautiously climbed the rotting steps to the front porch, which slanted downward. At least it was cool under the crumpled roof and I could report to Aunt Charlotte that I had "almost" been inside.

I made a kind of lounge for myself on the slanty porch. As its slope inclined toward the ocean, it was like being teasingly tilted forward, just short of getting tossed overboard. Sweat drying on my shirt, I drank my water, then slowly ate my sandwiches, the high tide crashing around me. I would not be ashamed for the sunburnt man to see me now, though in his official capacity he would probably have to order me off the condemned property. ("Because otherwise, dude, I could lose my job.")

I folded the empty lunch wrappings and stuffed them inside my backpack, which I plumped into a pillow for myself. It was the backpack I had taken to school when Mom was still alive and I sniffed it to see if there were any traces of our old life together in the apartment. There was a faint bread-y smell, but that was probably from today's sandwiches. The porch beneath the backpack had its own smell of salt and old timber and decay. The ocean was so close I could feel the spray and I felt myself sliding into a nap. Which was okay, I had earned my tiredness. I would rest up before heading back to Aunt Charlotte's. She was only in the middle of her day and would expect me to be in the middle of mine.

WHEN I AWOKE, it was out of a dream in which the sunburnt man had been standing in the doorless doorway of the cottage. He leaned lightly against its frame, watching me sleep. I knew not to turn and look toward the door because I would wake completely and I wanted to prolong the way I felt him watching over me. Also, a dialogue was going on between us, though neither of us spoke aloud. We could read each other's minds. I asked him if he had been inside the cottage and he said yes, he sometimes checked things out to see how bad they were getting. I asked how bad were they, and he said bad enough for this place to come down. When I asked if I could have a look inside, he said that is exactly why I am here, to forbid you to go inside. But why? I wanted to know. Because, Marcus, people who go in don't always come out. I asked how he knew my name. Because I needed to know it, he said.

★   ★   ★

NOW THE TIDE was going out, the sound of the waves more distant. How long had I been curled up on the porch, completely awake? It seemed a while ago that the sunburnt man had been watching over me.

But *something still was.* I felt its presence by the electric prickles all down my back and by my serious reluctance to move a muscle. Then the reluctance turned to cold fear. There was no way in the world I could muster the courage to roll over and see what was in that doorway.

Whatever was behind me was not watching over me like the sunburnt man. It was more like I was being *appraised* the way I might appraise some alien creature that had wandered into my scope of vision and curled up with his back to me. I felt no big-brotherly protectiveness coming from this watcher, only an intense, almost affronted, curiosity. Whatever was looking down at me seemed to be waiting to see what I would do next.

I'm not sure how much time I remained sitting there with my back to the watcher. It might have been only a couple of minutes but it felt like the clock had stopped and I was trapped in a timeless state of fright. What I did do next was somehow force myself to sit upright on the slanty porch. My heart was thrashing, louder than the ocean. My back, still feeling the prickles trained on it, stayed rigidly turned to the doorway. My knees were shaking so much it was an effort to stand. Snatching up my backpack, I took a flying leap over the rotting steps.

Even after I had crawled under the fence with the CONDEMNED and KEEP OUT signs and started walking south, my neck felt fused forward on my shoulders. I knew it was beyond my powers to swivel it around and risk seeing whether I was still being kept in sight.

*L*ast time you were there, did it have the fence with all those 'condemned' and 'keep off' signs?"

"Those have been up for a while," said Aunt Charlotte. "The fence is in my photographs, but I transformed it into an erosion fence—those picturesque wooden fences you see in so many beach paintings. How did the cottage look?"

"It's in terrible shape. It has to be a lot worse than when you last saw it. It's more of a *zombie house*. Did anybody ever say anything about it being haunted?"

"Not that I've heard. Why?"

"You said they started calling it Grief Cottage. I thought maybe—"

"You mean, the parents coming back to see if the boy ever returned home? Their spirits unable to rest, that sort of thing? No, all I've heard are the stories about how they were all lost."

"Or maybe the *boy*."

"What about the boy?"

"*His* spirit being unable to rest."

"I'll have to check. I have two books about the history of the island. Grief Cottage is mentioned in one of them, but I forget which one. I've never been able to read either of them all the way though. Every time I try, I get angry. Did *you* feel any spirits when you were there?"

"I only went on the porch."

"You shouldn't even have been on the porch. But what boy could resist?"

"Why do you get angry?"

"About those books? Where to start? With the sea turtle eggs, probably. But I need to back up a little. The ladies who wrote these books are from families who have been coming to the island for a zillion years. I don't know which gets my goat more. Their cozy assumption of entitlement, or their cruel ignorance about anything outside themselves and their family histories. The sea turtle eggs are a case in point. You know how sacred the whole egg-laying thing is now. We have to turn off our porch lights after dark so the mothers can come up to the dunes and lay their eggs in peace. And then the whole count-down period—well, you know. We have our very own 'clutch' of eggs with the red fence and warning sign. So I'm paging through this book—I forget which one—and the lady's saying how much fun it was back in the good old days to go out in the morning and find some turtle eggs buried in the dunes and bring them inside and eat them for breakfast. So delicious. The size of ping-pong balls, and even better, the yolks don't get hard even after you boil them, so you can suck the yellow out. A real gourmet treat for the privileged few."

"That was in *a book*?"

"Yes, and more. Of course, both these books were published back in the nineteen-seventies, before the turtle patrols got going. But I'll turn them over to you and you can look up the stories about people lost in hurricanes. As for ghosts, there's this man in gray who appears on the beach before a hurricane. Some say he wears a Confederate uniform, others say just gray clothes. If he looks straight at your house, it won't get washed away. If he avoids looking at it, you'd better evacuate."

"And people have seen him?"

"That you'll have to decide for yourself, Marcus. People see what they want to see. Or imagine they saw. And others *say* they saw something in order to sound psychic or special. I'm not big on ghosts. There are enough horrors in the real world to worry about."

That night Aunt Charlotte gave me the promised art tour of her website. We sat side by side in front of her laptop at the kitchen table and she clicked on the different paintings and then we enlarged them. I was mostly interested in the Grief Cottage painting, which I recognized as the "Abandoned Cottage" post-card Mom and I had received.

It was the place I had seen today but it was also something else. If this painting hung on my wall, it would make me feel sad and spooked every time I walked past it. But I would walk past it again and again just because it made me feel this way. Surprisingly, given its dark mood, Aunt Charlotte's painting wasn't a night scene. Above the derelict cottage was a soft blue sky with innocent clouds. The sand dunes, though heavily populated with sea grasses and Spanish bayonets, were white and pure. The marked contrast made the picture even more unsettling. It was an anterior view of the cottage, though you could figure out it had lost its south side. The front of the cottage, including the slanted porch where I had slept earlier, had sunshine breaking into its shadows. It was the middle of the day in the painting, the light fell much as it had today, but somehow, the way Aunt Charlotte had painted it, the picture reminded you of the impermanence of everything and the treacheries awaiting you even on a nice day.

"You really captured its mood," I said.

"What kind of mood?"

I hunted for a good word. "Well, *forlorn.*"

"*Forlorn,* I like that. Too bad you can't really see my brush-work on the computer screen. It intensifies the forlornness." Pleasure softened her gruff voice. "The actual painting is small, only eight by ten. Nestled in a deep frame under the right lighting, the effect is even stronger."

THE DAY AFTER my trip to the cottage, the rain began. "I'm surprised it didn't come sooner," remarked Aunt Charlotte at the end of the second day. "June is always the wettest month. I hope you'll be able to amuse yourself, Marcus."

The first two days of the downpour were a gift. I wasn't ready to repeat that walk to the cottage. And it was a relief to have some indoor time when I wasn't expected to act like a boy pleased to be at the beach. All I had to do was give the appearance of amusing myself. This turned out to be easy. I could lie in the hammock on the covered porch and watch the tides going in and out. I liked the aches all down my legs from the day before. I doubted I had ever walked that far in my life. The aches were a reminder that I had made it. I liked to go back over the moment when the sunburnt man, bouncing south in his little white truck, gave me a thumbs-up. During the rainy days, I was to see the white truck bouncing up and down the beach but couldn't tell if it was him inside. When it rained, there probably wasn't as much trash in the yellow barrels. I wondered whether he thought of me. But then I had to remind myself that he knew nothing about me, except that I had set out to walk north that day, that I was out of shape, and that I was later seen still walking north—probably farther than he had thought me capable of walking. He didn't know I lived here full time: for all he knew I was a one-day visitor with a backpack.

I had Aunt Charlotte's two books by the local ladies. One was called *Chronicles of a Legendary Island* and the other *Our Island Then and Now*. I kept both books with me in the hammock so I could be seen looking into them on Aunt Charlotte's sporadic trips to the bathroom or to the refrigerator to grab a yogurt or uncork a fresh bottle of wine. Though my back was to the house, I was conscious of her checking on me through the window. Just as when I lay turned away on the porch of Grief Cottage and had been conscious of something checking me out from behind. The only difference was: one was an everyday occurrence, the other implausible—maybe just a lonely boy imagining something "in order to sound psychic or special."

First I leafed through the books looking for illustrations. In both there were lots of old maps and reproductions of records and deeds in old-fashioned handwriting, mostly dating from the 1800s. Transfers of property dated as far back as 1791. There were rough line-drawings of the island with the names of owners printed out on little numbered squares representing the lots where the first houses were built. Both ladies' books had this same map, labeled *Courtesy of the South Carolina Historical Society*.

The first numbered square at the north tip of the island had belonged to a family called Hassel. Then, some pages later in the *Then and Now* book, there was a map where the squares bore the names of later owners. #1 Hassel was later sold to Wortham, who later sold to Barbour. But there was a star next to #1, which led to a footnote saying that since Hurricane Hazel, this property was now the site of a ruin "slated for demolition." The *Then and Now,* published in the 1970s, said the demolition was already being announced. Aunt Charlotte had come to the island in the late seventies. Neither book contained a photograph of Grief Cottage, though some other old houses were often included as a backdrop for blurred family pictures: a group of women picking shrimp on the porch of "Sunrise Cottage"; men in hats standing beside a Model-T; women with bathing suits like dresses and men in costumes like long johns setting out for the beach. At frequent intervals there would be a posed snapshot of a black person in apron or overalls looking up from work to grin at the camera.

The only mention of "Grief Cottage" was at the end of the "Fierce Storms" chapter in the *Legendary Island* book. After pages of blow-by-blow descriptions of houses floating out to sea and entire families and their servants dropping one by one from trees into the engulfing waves of the 1822 and 1893 hurricanes, a single paragraph was devoted to Hurricane Hazel ("the most devastating storm since 1893"), which struck with merciless fury in 1954, "the year before the island got telephones." But due to an efficient neighbor warning system, most of the islanders made hurried escapes to safe places on the mainland. The only missing people had been a fourteen-year-old boy and his parents, an out-of-state family staying in the Barbour cottage after the summer season. No one knew their fates for sure because their bodies were never found. It had been a sad tale of out-of-state people underestimating hurricanes, the book said: the parents having gone out in the storm to search for the boy and the boy possibly having gone out in search of the parents.

The house itself, the oldest on the island and tucked safely behind its dunes, withstood the tempest, all except the south porch, which was destroyed by fire before or during the hurricane. Since then the cottage had remained empty and been allowed to fall into ruin. Islanders had taken to calling it "Grief Cottage."

I was glad to be able to report my findings to Aunt Charlotte. "It was an out-of-state family, but it didn't give their names or mention anything about a cigarette."

"I must have heard that part from the locals, then. Did both books mention this out-of-state family?"

"No, just the one. The same one that had that story about the turtle eggs."

"I'll bet the Confederate ghost made both of the books."

"Yeah, they had the same painting of him walking along the beach."

"That painting has become an industry all by itself. You can order it in a variety of sizes, either as a framed print, a metal print, or a canvas print."

"What's a metal print?"

"When the painting is reproduced on a thin sheet of aluminum. It gives a very high gloss effect. Looks good on large walls in offices."

"But they don't get to have originals. The artist doesn't paint it fresh, over and over again, like you."

"He can't. He died in the 1930s, shortly after he painted it. His heirs are still raking in the bucks from that one picture. He was an excellent landscape painter. I saw a local retrospective once. That painting was the only time he ever put in a human figure. What would he think if he knew his one gray guy would make him famous?"

"Do you ever think about being famous?"

"As I said, Marcus, I'm thankful to have this fluke of a talent. It's my livelihood and I enjoy it. When you're painting you don't dwell on old miseries. There's something about the smell of pigment and the way time becomes meaningless when you're painting."

As the rain continued to fall, those boxes from my old life stacked in the garage nagged at me. I didn't want Aunt Charlotte to think I was at loose ends. If she found me hanging about, she might worry she wasn't doing enough for me and start feeling guilty and then the guilt would turn into resentment. I had watched my mom fight this progression in herself after we had moved from Forsterville to the mountains and had been cooped up for too long in our miserable upstairs apartment in Jewel while our life went from bad to worse.

Mom and I had always shared a bedroom and a bed. I had never given this a second thought until the day I brought Wheezer to our apartment back in Forsterville. It was a far better apartment than the one we were to have in Jewel, but there was only the single bedroom. I invited him home with me reluctantly—it was much nicer to go to his house, where he had his own room and his grandmother, who ran the household, made us special treats. His father traveled around the state selling Forster's furniture, and his mother—they had long been "estranged"—lived in Palm Beach, organizing women's golf tournaments. Wheezer had confided to me that he had been "an accident." His mother had been eager for his big brother, Drew, to leave for college, "but then when Drew turned eighteen, she and Daddy messed up and I was the result." Drew, who worked for an accounting firm in Charlotte, was old enough to be Wheezer's father. He came home frequently on weekends, tanning himself in the backyard if it was warm enough and shut up in his bedroom listening to jazz and blues except for mealtimes. He treated Wheezer and me with a grumpy, bemused forbearance.

Wheezer was fascinated by my closeness with my mom. He was also curious—perhaps too curious—about the "socio-economic" differences between us. It would be safer, I thought, for him to go on romanticizing my home life as frugal but noble, like the homes of the poor in Dickens. But he persisted in digging for details about how we lived until Mom said to ask him over one Saturday when she wasn't working at the furniture factory. She would go out and get pizza for our lunch. (This was to be the first time her going out to get pizza would precede a disaster.) She said it was only right that we return his hospitality when I spent so much time at his grandmother's house. How different our life might have been if I had not invited Wheezer over that Saturday!

"Wait a minute," he said when I was showing him our bedroom. "You sleep in the same bed with your mom?" "Where else would I sleep?" I flashed back. "Some poor families sleep four to a bed." That shut him up until I made the fatal mistake of showing him the picture of a man I was never supposed to show anyone. Mom kept this small framed photo in a tin box at the bottom of a drawer, and said she would tell me more about him when the time was right. But after Wheezer's remark about our sleeping arrangements, I was desperate to divert him with a new mystery. Without a word, I walked over to the bureau, opened the bottom drawer, opened the tin box, and took out the photograph. "This is my real dad," I said, "but you can't tell anyone. He's dead now, but when I'm older she's going to explain everything." In his eagerness, he snatched the photograph out of my hand. He examined it, turned it sideways, shook it in its frame, scrutinized it some more, and then handed it back to me. "This is something that's been cut out of a book," he said, giving me a hostile look. "This person could be anybody. You and your mom are both crazy. I need to leave." Those were the last words he ever spoke directly to me. By the time Mom got back to our apartment with the pizza, he was gone. I told her he'd felt an asthma attack coming on and rushed home for his medication.

At recess on Monday he had waited until I was in hearing range and then announced to the other boys. "Guess what? Marcus sleeps with his mom. He's his mother's own little husband."

And then I did go crazy. I grabbed a hunk of his beautiful salon-cut hair and banged his head backward against a rock wall until there was blood on the wall. The asthmatic boy gasped and gagged and then stopped breathing altogether. Everyone including me thought he had died. But I went on punching that neat little face until others pulled me away. He almost lost the sight in one eye. Mom gave up her job, and as soon as my sessions with the psychiatrist came to an end we moved away. I had felt thankful when I heard the eye was out of danger. But deep down, below the level where right and wrong stayed separate, I was awed at myself for being able to summon such wrath.

When the psychiatrist had asked what I had felt when I was attacking Wheezer, I said I had "blanked out." But even as I lied I knew that to bloody Wheezer's head and crush his face and stop his breathing had been my supreme task. And as I saw this being accomplished before my eyes I was filled with elation. I felt that I was driving out the badness from my life through my fists and feet. But I had been wise enough to keep this from the psychiatrist. He would have judged that anyone admitting to such things needed to be in an institution. Yet I had also been able to tell him, in all truth, that I had been sickened and appalled when I heard how badly my friend had been hurt. It was as though Wheezer had been in a terrible accident and I was hearing about it afterward.

Aunt Charlotte had not mentioned the boxes again, but as the rain hadn't let up I got the first one from the garage and carried it to my room. After a quick glance inside, I fetched a black trash bag from the pantry. The slow-cooker could stay; I could impress Aunt Charlotte with my pulled pork. The rest—aspirin, Q-tips, even our old toothbrushes, for God's sake, and two pathetic chipped mugs—into the black bag. Some social-worker-in-training had probably packed these boxes. "This boy lost his mother and had to go into foster care," the supervisor would have said. "Pack everything even if it seems worthless. There are always lawsuits to consider."

U.

During the rainy spell I dreamed that the sunburnt man picked me up on a motorcycle. The dump truck was in the shop, he said, so our job was to ride up and down the beach on the motorcycle and *check the levels* of the yellow trash cans. Riding behind him felt wonderful. I was the one who had to hop off and inspect each can. He laughed so hard I could feel his back shaking when I said, leaning against him as we rode straight into the wind: "Yuck, you wouldn't want to know what was in that last can." When we got to the trash can in front of Grief Cottage, I said, "I guess we won't need to check that one."

"Why not?"

"Because. Nobody has been in there since Hurricane Hazel."

"That's what you think," he said. "I'll check this one out myself."

"Just as I expected," he said when he returned. "Remember what I told you, Marcus. Do not go in that house."

"But what was in the can?"

"I could tell you," he said, laughing, "but then I'd have to kill you."

★ ★ ★

THE RAIN BEATING down on Aunt Charlotte's tin roof shut out
the sound of the ocean. At supper a few evenings back, she had
announced that she was within days of completing the McMansion
painting. I told her I had made a start with the boxes. "Then this
rain has been good for something," she said. In the bathroom I
always rinsed the sink after using it and wiped it dry with my
towel. Mom had taught me this when she had to take a second
job cleaning houses. It was the little touches, she said, that pleased
people. Dry sinks and soap dishes, shiny taps. A single hair in the
tub could ruin the whole effect. And I always made sure the seat
was back down on the toilet. So far, I had erred only once, and
Aunt Charlotte had let it go with a dry comment about sharing a
bathroom with a man.

I brought in a second box only to shrink back as soon
as I had taken a sneak preview. This box contained a different
set of sorrows. Underneath some childhood books (*Goodnight
Moon*, *Mrs. Ticklefeather*, *Winnie the Pooh*, and *The House at Pooh
Corner*) were my mother's winter coat, her sweatpants and
tops she wore at home, her shoes, nightgowns, underwear,
elastic stockings (which held in her varicose veins from
standing at work), her laminated badge ("Section Manager")
that she had proudly worn at Forster's furniture factory, her
makeup and moisturizers, a box, half empty, of super-sized
Tampax. Had the social-worker-in-training made a phone
call to his or her superior? "Listen, should I go ahead and
throw some of the really personal items out, or what? I mean,
Goodwill would take the winter coat, though it's sort of shabby,
but the other stuff?" And the superior must have repeated the
lawsuit spiel.

The whole of that box, even the coat (let Goodwill find its own shabby coats!) went into the black trash bag. After paging nostalgically through *Goodnight Moon* and feeling sad, I tossed the books. Then remorse overcame me and I rescued the Pooh books. Mom had been so proud of herself for finding them at a library sale. ("They're like new, except a child crayoned over a few pages in *Pooh Corner.*") Best to pace myself with these boxes. What if they were going to get incrementally worse, each one harder to take than the one before?

It was a relief to return to the books by the privileged ladies with their cruel ignorance about anything outside their own history. When I was out on the porch in the hammock, the ocean noises drowned out the softer patter of the rain. I watched the Turtle Patrol, clad in slickers and rain hats, make regular visits to our clutch. And from Aunt Charlotte's porch there was always the chance of spotting the little white truck bouncing north or south.

I went back to the "Fierce Storms" chapter in *Chronicles of a Legendary Island,* remembering how I had aced my research paper at the mountain school where I was Baby Wonk and Pudge who had skipped a grade. Our teacher, who liked me so much she often looked at me while she was addressing the class (which didn't lessen my freak reputation), said that instead of rushing to start writing your paper you should read your material through several times and treat it like *clues in a mystery.* Because each time you read through something, the more things you would realize that you had missed the time before. What clues like in a mystery could I extract from the single paragraph that dealt with Hurricane Hazel at the end of the "Fierce Storms" chapter?

In the early parts of that chapter, which had recounted lost lives in the bad hurricanes of 1822 and 1893, all the drowned family members and their drowned servants were named. Even visitors and strangers had been diligently listed by name, even if only part of a name. ("Also drowned on that fearful night, a century and a half ago, were Mr. Warren Botsford's nephew, Botsford Channing; Captain Wise, a visiting architect; a Dr. Venn from Charlotte, N.C.; a Miss Satterwhite and a Mr. de Vere . . .")

Yet the only missing people after Hurricane Hazel hit on October 15, 1954, were not named. There weren't yet telephones on the island in 1954, but due to an "efficient neighbor warning system," most of the islanders made hurried evacuations to safe places on the mainland.

The only people who could not be accounted for were the fourteen-year-old boy and his parents, the out-of-state family staying in the Barbour cottage after the summer season. It was an unfortunate chain of circumstances, the out-of-state family most likely being unfamiliar with hurricanes, and underestimating the force of this one. One evacuating islander, Mr. Art Honeywell, reported having been stopped in his truck on Seashore Road by the desperate parents searching on foot for their son, but the boy had not been seen by anyone. It was later surmised that he had set off in another direction in search of the parents. As their bodies were never found, it is assumed that all three were washed out to sea. The house itself, the oldest on the island, withstood the tempest, all except the south porch, which had been mysteriously destroyed by fire during the hurricane. Afterward the cottage was sold and the new owners allowed it to remain empty and fall into ruin. Because of its sad fate, islanders took to calling it "Grief Cottage."

★ ★ ★

WHAT EXACTLY WAS the "efficient neighbor warning system"? Did it mean only your neighbors got warned? What about strangers? Especially out-of-state strangers unfamiliar with hurricanes, who underestimated their force? Why hadn't Mr. Art Honeywell in his truck said to the parents, "Climb in and we'll search for your son together?" Where did the "age fourteen" come from? Had the parents told Mr. Honeywell, "We are out looking for our son, who is fourteen . . ."? Why hadn't the boy been in school? And what kind of family stays in a beach cottage in October, "after the season"? Most likely a family who needed to take advantage of reduced rates. If Mom and I had ever gone to the beach we would have had to wait for after the season.

I was almost sorry this wasn't a school assignment. I knew exactly how I would go about making the most of the material from the privileged lady's storm chapter. Baby Wonk would have aced that assignment and earned more contempt.

I would have called my paper "Who Is My Neighbor?" after the story in the Bible where that "gotcha" lawyer tried to pin Jesus down by asking, "Who is my neighbor?" Jesus had trounced him with the story of the Good Samaritan. ("Luke ten, twenty-nine!" the little kids at the foster home would have shouted wildly.)

Last year Mom had started imagining a future for us. In this future, she would pass the high school equivalency exam and we would "start college at the same time." The more excited she got about this plan, the more conflicted I became. I began counting the years ahead of us: seventh grade through twelfth. I saw myself turning into my mother's "own little husband," as Wheezer had called me at school in front of our friends.

Mom would often say, "I may not be able to afford the best, but I do know what the best is." And where I was concerned she did go for the best: the best dental treatment at a clinic free to children, but not open to adults (while sadly neglecting her own teeth), the best life insurance for $24 a month (a stretch when you're making less than $24,000 a year). I kept hoping I would have an important dream about her. I had seen her in several dreams, but she was not at all like herself or else hurrying away in order to avoid me.

The weird thing was I regularly dreamed of Wheezer, who still lived in Forsterville. In the dreams I called him by his birth name, Shelby, and he was very much like himself. Occasionally he wore a patch over one eye. ("See what you did, you devil?") In the patch dreams he really had lost sight in that eye but he had forgiven me. In the dreams we were closer than ever, learning about the world and growing up together.

III.

The Aunt Charlotte I went to live with when I was eleven could have qualified as a hermit. She made use of modern conveniences, but lived the life of a solitary. And even after I came, she maintained most of her solitary ways. She called out on her land phone to order things but never picked up incoming calls. The caller was transferred to voice mail and could leave a message—or not. She often let days go by without checking her messages. She used the laptop computer that lay sleek and closed on the kitchen counter to look up information and weather and "to see if the world still existed," as she put it. Much of her business was conducted online, between her website and potential customers. She also had linkups to local and online art galleries who liaised between her and potential buyers and charged finders' fees. As I didn't pine for it, she continued not to have cable television. So far, I had not seen her turn her old TV on. She usually retired soon after we'd had supper, taking her wineglass and the unfinished bottle to her studio with its sleeping quarters behind a curtain.

She could rise to most household emergencies: change a fuse, replace a washer on a leaky faucet, fix a misbehaving toilet, rewire electrical switches, unstop a gutter, replace rotting boards. Near the ocean, boards were always rotting. After buying her "beach shack," she had required the services of professionals to add rooms (her studio and her bedroom, which was now mine, and an indoor bathroom) but she had done most of the finish work, teaching herself from books the way she had taught herself the basics of landscape painting. She could even do rudimentary carpentry and had built shelves and trestle tables to hold her art supplies.

She had no official religion and didn't call on God or Jesus, either for help or as an oath. I think painting was the closest to any religion she had. For proof that she practiced charity, you had to look no further than myself. Of course there was the "nice stipend" attached to my person that she had been so "aboveboard" about at the start, but I soon dropped any notion that she had taken me only because of the money. If my mom hadn't bought that policy, I believe that Aunt Charlotte, once aware that she was my only kin, would have welcomed me under her tin roof no matter what.

When I first laid eyes on her at the airport, she wore her wiry white hair in a very short brush cut. But in 2004 the shorn look was becoming fashionable for women, because of feminism or because they were cancer patients or because they wanted to announce to the world they were lesbians or because it made them look more dramatic. It made Aunt Charlotte look like a Roman centurion and emphasized her well-shaped skull. She cut it herself.

She had no love interests of either sex. Had the three good-for-nothing husbands in a row soured her on relationships altogether, or had there been intimacies during the earlier island years, when she was always in the company of carpenters and plumbers and electricians? After all, she had been in her early thirties when she moved here. My mother was already twenty-eight when I was born and was asked out by men until she died eleven years (five months and four days) later. Mom never went out with anyone more than a few times, but she would report on what she called her "dates" when she got home. "Never again," she might say. Or, "He's kind. When you get to my age kindness becomes a major attraction." But no one lasted very long because, as she said, she could recognize the best and she had loved the best. The mere memory of my father would always outclass all living suitors. There was a quote she liked: "Better to have loved and lost than never to have loved at all." It was from a long poem Tennyson had written after the death of his beloved friend. It took the poet seventeen years to put down all the thoughts and emotions he felt about the loss of this friend.

After the remodeling of her house was finished, Aunt Charlotte had continued to work with men: first as a receptionist for a veterinarian on the island and then as a receptionist at a foreign car repair shop on the mainland. ("I also changed the oil and did other unladylike repairs when the customers weren't present.") Later she and the foreign-car man, a local old "scion" named Lachicotte Hayes (pronounced "LASH-i-cott") became partners in a taxi service. They took turns picking up people in vintage cars. ("For a while we were driving a 1935 Rolls-Royce, until Lash got an offer for it we couldn't refuse.") Eventually, they sold their taxi business for a profit. ("My half provided me with an income until my paintings started to sell.")

On the first day we had clear skies again, Aunt Charlotte finished her big McMansion painting. "Good timing," she said. "Now I can examine it in natural light. Come into the studio, Marcus, I want your opinion."

"Oh," I said, when I stood in front of it.

"Oh, what?"

"It's different from how I expected it to be."

"And how was that?"

"You said it was a bread and butter commission, not one of your honest paintings. This looks pretty honest to me."

She was standing right behind me, so I couldn't read her face. But I could hear her indrawn breath and sniff the ferment-y smell of the red wine she sipped all through the day. I sensed that she really was anxious to have my opinion. The painting *was* different from what I had expected. It had the qualities of the ones I liked the most on her website. Actually, I thought it was wonderful, but *wonderful* was such a used-up word. "It has your mood," I said.

"My mood?" she coaxed.

"It's in your sky. It's in the house, too. I mean, it's more than just a painting of a McMansion. It's saying something about how life is. I wish I could express myself better."

"You're doing fine. How is life in this painting?"

"You know the way you painted Grief Cottage? When you look at it, you think right away of the overall sadness of life. But your McMansion house's sadness creeps up on you. The way you've painted it, you can feel it thinking. 'I'm new and too big, and if I have a message it's a shallow message. But I can't change what I am.'"

My aunt's hand gripped my shoulder, and then quickly let go. She wasn't a toucher.

"Well," she said, moving into my sight line, "I hope the Steckworths won't see all that in my painting, but I'm obliged to you, Marcus. I especially like the sky in this painting. It came out just right. I agree with you, the McMansion does have its own quality of sadness. A hint of impermanence for those who wish to see it."

"Could they turn it down and not pay you?"

"I've never had that happen, but I suppose it could. On the commissioned ones I always take a deposit. Nonrefundable. And this is a very big canvas. It costs money to buy enough pigment simply to cover a canvas this large. And I have another kind of protection, too. It's called 'hard to get' or 'what if she turns me down?' or 'waiting list.' By now I'm known well enough for people to want a Charlotte Lee and be willing to wait for it. Oh, hang it, I have to clean the house before they come. People expect *some* occupational clutter in an artist's studio, but I've let things go too far."

"I can help. I know how to clean."

"Yes, I've noticed you don't leave the bathroom a mess. Your mother raised you well."

"My mom cleaned houses. I mean, that's one of the things she did to supplement our income. She taught me some tricks people like."

"Well, I hope you will teach me those tricks."

"SHE MUST HAVE been a gutsy woman, your mom," Aunt Charlotte said the next day while we were doing the kitchen together. "It's not easy to be a single mother. I'm sure I would have got on with her. We might have had things in common. I liked her that time your grandmother brought her to visit when she was a teenager. Too bad we never got to know each other better. Though Brenda would probably have ruined it, warned your mom off the hippie aunt. Not that I ever thought of myself as a hippie. I have worked nonstop all my life and will go on working till I drop."

"You had things in common," I said. "You both ran away from home when you were young. Mom ran away before she finished high school."

"Now that I didn't know. Why did she run away from Brenda?"

"It was Brenda's father. He was coming to live with them and Mom said she'd rather die than live under the same roof with him."

"Her grandfather was my father. I ran off at sixteen to get out from under his roof. Isn't it just bloody amazing how defilement can become a family tradition? Why on earth did Brenda ask that monster to come and live with her?"

"She needed him to help her run the lumber mill after my grandfather died. When Mom heard about it, she ran away with an older man who was a foreman at the mill. She talked him into marrying her. The two of them moved to North Carolina and got jobs in a furniture factory. Mom said he was kind and a good worker and she felt safe with him. It broke her heart not to get her high school diploma, but she had to escape a worse situation."

"Damn right." She dropped to her knees on the kitchen floor. "Always escape a worse situation, even if escaping it is going to rob you of an education and ruin your life. Hand me that scrub brush, Marcus."

"But I'm not tired yet."

"Just hand it over. I need to scrub something within an inch of its life. It's either that or kill someone."

She snatched the brush from me and began making angry circles of soap foam on the tiles. "Why don't you go down to the beach?

"But—"

"Just *go*, Marcus! Don't make me ask you again."

Ulli.

I would have liked to hang out in my room or the hammock until suppertime, but Aunt Charlotte had ordered me from her house, and it wasn't raining anymore, so I went to the beach. What had I done to turn her off? We had been getting along so well; she had even gripped my shoulder when I said something good about her painting. Then I had told her what cleaning products she needed and we had driven to the island store and I found them for her on the shelves. We had been dusting and polishing and scrubbing as a team, saving the tiled kitchen floor for last so it would gleam for the Steckworths the next day.

Had I said something wrong? We had been talking about my mother and how Aunt Charlotte and she might have been friends. It was the first time I had heard my mom described as a gutsy woman and it made me proud to think of her like that. Everything had been going so well.

I stopped to check on the dune that held the protected loggerhead eggs. All was quiet and untrammeled. *Caretta caretta* was their Latin name: the world's largest hard-shelled turtle. Fully grown they ranged from almost a yard to a hundred inches long and weighed anywhere from three hundred to a thousand pounds. They could live until the age of a hundred, but they didn't reach sexual maturity until they were in their thirties. "Which, when you think of it, isn't such a bad idea," said the old guy who had compared the hatchlings' dash for the sea to "Normandy in reverse." His name was Ed Bolton and he said these turtles had been doing their thing for forty million years, whereas modern *Homo sapiens* had appeared on the scene a mere two hundred thousand years ago.

I walked down to the surf and studied the patterns the outgoing tide was sketching in the sand. But the shrieking children all around me only intensified my agitation. It was too late in the day to look for the sunburnt man. The little white truck was gone from the beach by noon. What did he do for the rest of the day? Did he have other trash routes on the island or did he go to a second job?

What would happen if Aunt Charlotte's tolerance for human company were to run out? ("Listen, I've given it a try, but I've been a solitary too long. He's a nice boy, but I'm too set in my ways.") Would she send me somewhere else? ("He was a nice helpful boy and the stipend that came with him was nice, but I have worked nonstop all my life and will go on working till I drop. And I have my painting. I'm known well enough for people to want a Charlotte Lee and be willing to wait for it.")

I would go as far as the fourth yellow barrel and then head back slowly and sit on the steps leading up to her boardwalk. I would keep company with the turtle eggs for a while. Funny, I usually thought of Aunt Charlotte as a self-sufficient older person, but when she had dropped to the floor like that and started that desperate scrubbing, I had glimpsed a scared and angry girl.

It was too late for the white truck, but I could create my own dialogue with the sunburnt man as I walked north.

He would be surprised to see me still on the island.

"You? Still here at the beach?"

"I live here. With my great-aunt."

"Whereabouts?"

"Back there. It's the gray shingle house with the dark blue trim. It was just a shack when she bought it, but she added on. She's a painter."

"A house painter or the artist kind?"

"Artist. She's pretty well known. She does paintings of the beach and of people's houses. All the local galleries show them. She has a website, too. There's this one painting people keep asking for. She must have painted it fifty times. You know that old cottage at the north end of the island? That zombie house they call Grief Cottage?"

" 'Zombie House' is the perfect name for it! That place is waiting for a major accident. Why they haven't torn it down beats me."

"It's pretty bad. I ate my lunch on its porch. But I didn't go inside."

"Don't even go on that porch again. The whole structure is rotten through and through."

"A boy and his family disappeared from that cottage. They were staying there after the season was over, and they didn't know about hurricanes, and Hazel came and washed them all away. But their bodies were never found."

"That was a long time ago," says the sunburnt man. *"Long before my time and even longer before yours. Look, dude, it's one thing to be interested in history, but you want to stay away from that house. Because people who go in don't always come out."*

IX.

I had never met people like the Steckworths. They were half an hour late, which got Aunt Charlotte's bristles up.

"Now we'll wait to hear what their excuse is," she said, pacing up and down the scrubbed and gleaming kitchen floor. "You can tell a lot about people from their excuses."

"How?"

"Nice people simply apologize. Others, the sort who want to impress you, give you a story about how something *really* important came up. To put you in your place."

"What would something 'really important' be?"

"Oh, our good friend the governor dropped by—or my uncle the senator. Or, the plumbers who are installing our ninety-foot hot tub showed up unexpectedly. That sort of thing."

It was hard for Aunt Charlotte and me to keep a straight face when the Steckworths had hardly stepped through the door before announcing that they were late because the tree company putting in the thirty-foot mature palmetto trees around their Olympic swimming pool had dropped by unexpectedly to check measurements.

The Steckworths—Ron and Rita—were suntanned the color of mahogany and both wore heavy gold chains around their necks. They lingered just inside the front door, which opened into the kitchen, and treated us to a blow-by-blow chronicle of the building of their McMansion—though naturally they didn't call it that. The two of them made it into a kind of duet, Ron vocalizing the measurements of rooms and staircases and trees, and Rita chiming in with the frustrations of having to deal with architects and contractors and landscapers. "Not to mention the decorators," wailed Rita.

This was my aunt's cue to say, "Well, let's go into my studio and have a look at your forty-two by fifty-six painting."

I watched from the doorway, nervous. What if they took one look and said in chorus, "Oh, this is not what we wanted at all!" Aunt Charlotte would be stuck with only the non-refundable down payment. Or what if one of them asked a stupid question and earned a caustic retort from my aunt which would humiliate them, make them feel obliged to retaliate in some way—perhaps to quibble over the agreed-on price, or ask for changes in the painting?

"Oh, look, Ronnie!" was Rita Steckworth's first reaction. "All our palmettos are already in!"

"If only life was that simple," said Ron Steckworth, winking at my aunt. "Have you ever painted one this large before, Mrs. Lee?"

"No," said Aunt Charlotte. "Ordinarily I prefer to work on a smaller scale."

"*How* small?" asked Ron.

"Oh, sixteen by eighteen, twelve by sixteen. I have a particular fondness for four by sixes, about the size of my palm." She held up a palm.

"A sixteen by eighteen would be completely swallowed by our mantelpiece," said Ron.

"That's why we agreed on a forty-two by fifty-six," my aunt replied.

"Wait, is that *yellow* paint I'm seeing up there in the sky?" Rita asked, standing so close to the painting that her nose almost touched it.

"Very observant," said my aunt. "It's cadmium yellow. If you'll step back a bit, you'll see it disappearing into the blueness. Someone standing at the proper distance when it's hung in your house will see a richer blue sky than if I had used blue pigments alone."

"Oh, *richer*," Rita Steckworth echoed, obediently stepping back. "Yes, you're right."

"Turner used yellow in his skies a lot," Aunt Charlotte said. "And Sisley. I learned the trick from Sisley."

"Sisley? Now where does he——?"

"We'll Google him when we get home," Ron cut her off. Sauntering around to the rear of the big studio easel mounted on wheels, he examined the reverse side of the canvas. "What will you do back here?" he asked.

"Do *back here*?" inquired Aunt Charlotte.

"I mean, you gonna put something back here? Or do you leave it open like that?"

"Most professionals leave it open. An oil painting never completely dries. If you were to cover the back, it couldn't breathe and condensation would set in . . . followed by mold."

"Euw, mold!" cried Rita.

"Your framer may want to finish off the back with a sheet of porous brown paper so the air can circulate," Aunt Charlotte said. "But the paper is mostly for looks."

"We were thinking gold for the frame," said Rita, "but what would *you* suggest?"

"If it were me, I'd keep it simple. You don't want the frame to distract from the painting. I'd suggest a simple molding. No more than an inch. And I would go for chrome or silver rather than gold."

"Maybe just a *thin* gold molding?" Rita Steckworth entreated.

"Well, if you keep it very thin," said Aunt Charlotte.

X.

*A*fter Ron Steckworth had written his check with a flourish, and Aunt Charlotte had given loading directions to the strapping handyman waiting outside with a van to transfer the forty-two by fifty-six safely to the Steckworths' McMansion ("No, do *not* cover it, let it breathe during its short ride. And please be careful of those impasto areas where the paint is thickest . . ."), my aunt, sighing and looking inconvenienced, said she ought to drive over to the mainland to the bank. "I don't like keeping a check this large in the house. If I should drop dead tonight, Marcus, it would make things difficult for you." She asked if I wanted to accompany her and when I said an enthusiastic yes— I had not left the island since the day I arrived—I thought I saw a flicker of annoyance on her face. Too late I realized that she probably looked forward to going somewhere all by herself again.

However, she had brightened by the time we were rattling over the causeway. It was early afternoon and some black men with fishing rods were leaning over its railings. Aunt Charlotte replayed some choice Steckworthian utterances (Rita's "Look, Ronnie, our palmettos are already in!" and Ronnie's "What will you do *back here*?").

Then she floored me by announcing she was going to buy me a really nice beach bike out of her cash cow. Struck dumb by her offer I let the moment go by during which a proper boy would be voicing his excitement and gratitude. Moreover, I couldn't yet ride in her Mercedes without recalling the shrimp vomit from our first day. Did a whiff still linger?

When we got to the bank she merely said, "I'll be right back," not asking if I wanted to go inside the bank with her. What had she meant about dropping dead when the check was still in the house? Why would that make it difficult for me? Why had she said such a thing in the first place? It seemed insensitive given that the only other person in my life had just died.

Back on the island again we stopped at the store and bought a chicken roasted on the spit, various cold cuts and salads, and more bananas and yogurt for Aunt Charlotte. "I'm going to collapse," she announced as soon as we got home. "If I'm not up by suppertime, go ahead without me and I'll see you tomorrow." Off she went to her studio/bedroom carrying an unopened bottle of red wine and the corkscrew.

I put away the things and ate a banana with a cheese sandwich and drank a glass of milk. The chicken, still warm from the spit, called out to me, but I imagined her getting up late in the afternoon and finding one of its legs hacked away. ("Couldn't the boy have waited for me?")

Soon it would be the longest day. I had hours more daylight to get through. I could leave a note and walk to the north end of the island and back and the sun would still be strong. Checking myself in the bathroom mirror that cut me off at the collarbone, I marveled that my aunt could exist without a full-length mirror. At our poorest, Mom had always had a full-length mirror. A woman had to know how she looked from behind, she said. A hem could be crooked, a heel worn down, or something hanging that wasn't meant to show. But Aunt Charlotte seemed to get along fine without knowing how the rest of her looked. She cut her hair in front of the mirror above the sink and that must have been as far down as her grooming concerned her. As she wore only pants and shirts and sandals, there were no skirts or heels or slips to worry about.

I missed seeing my whole self. It would soon be half a year since I had been able to stand in front of a long mirror and see myself from top to bottom, dressed or undressed. I was aware of changes going on below where Aunt Charlotte's mirror stopped, but I couldn't judge the whole picture for myself.

I was in a sacrificial frame of mind as I headed north on the beach. I was not meant to enjoy the march, not to look forward to seeing little white trucks or discover meaningful patterns in nature. I simply set myself on automatic to march to the north tip of the island and back, where Aunt Charlotte would probably sleep through the night just to have some time all to herself. The march was something I had to do to keep my mood from getting any worse. If only I could walk until I was empty, like Aunt Charlotte used to do.

Since coming here back in May, I had taken it for granted that I would live with my aunt until I went off to college—though she had mentioned boarding school, if I wanted. Now I was wondering if I should take her up on the boarding school before she got really sick of me. Yet I saw myself doing better if I stayed on the island, going to public school with the children of the ordinary working folks who lived here year-round. If I were to go away to a boarding school, there would be snotty questions about family and fathers. I would have a better chance at passing with the local kids.

Passing for *what*?

Here I tried not to think my next thought, because I knew it would make me feel horrible. But have you ever tried not to think your next thought? Which was *that I would be more respected coming from Aunt Charlotte's house.* Artists could get away with living as they pleased. And Aunt Charlotte was a woman solitary by choice who had a website and a waiting list. My mom had been a single mother who worked minimum wage jobs to support herself and her child. How unfair for Mom that there was plenty of money for Aunt Charlotte and me because of the high-quality insurance plan she had chosen while she lived. I had been the spoiler of my mother's life.

And here came a worse thought: though I loved her and felt it was unfair that she hadn't had an easier time, I had been ashamed of her in life as I would never be ashamed of Aunt Charlotte.

My sacrificial march moved me past the yellow trash barrels at a smart clip. I had hardly noticed anything or anybody along the way, although I was aware that the tide was going out. A perverse plan was taking shape: in this punishment mode I would go right up on the porch of Grief Cottage and stand facing the door and confront whatever had scared me there. What was the biggest thing I could lose? Myself. And how bad would it be to empty the world of Marcus? The idea thrilled me. Too bad it wasn't hurricane season so I would have a better chance of being destroyed. ("Marcus knew better than to go out in that storm. He'd read those books about people drowned and washed out to sea. I'll never forgive myself for letting him slip out like that.")

If I got destroyed, what would happen to the insurance money that came with me? Would Aunt Charlotte get it, or did it stop when the beneficiary was dead? If it was nontransferable, she would be sorry, but then she would hate herself for even thinking about money when she should be concentrating on her grief.

Lost in my fantasy I was totally unprepared for the Grief Cottage I saw ahead of me. Last time it had been an eyesore. Today the dazzling afternoon light had transformed it. Before its downfall it must have looked like this to walkers approaching from the south. In the golden haze of five o'clock sun, it shimmered like a mirage.

In school we had learned that light was just a wavelength that made you think you saw colors. It all had to do with the light sensing cells in your retina. They activated a chemical reaction that sent an electrical impulse through your nerves to the brain. And then your brain had to decide what to call the wavelength you were seeing. ("Oh, that's a *yellow* trash barrel; a *golden* light has magically transformed the zombie cottage.") Technically there was no such thing as yellow or golden light. That was just your psychological name for it. First the physiological eye-brain system had to do its job, and then what they called the psychological distinctions kicked in.

Keeping to my forced-march agenda, I wriggled under the wire fence more expertly than last time, and noisily stomped up the unsteady stairs to the sloping porch. I *wanted* to be heard approaching. As soon as I was on the porch, I "announced myself" by grunting and exhaling loudly the way people do to express their relief at arriving.

This afternoon there was no backpack, no lunch to eat, no nap to sink into, no dream of the sunburnt man standing in the doorway to watch over me. Today I sat on the edge of the slanted porch, my feet on the next-to-top step, but still keeping my back to the house. As I had been climbing the stairs I braved a single glance at the gaping doorway, enough to see that the golden haze filled the room inside. I decided that if something was watching from within that haze, it would be a good plan to *sit with my back to it* so its curiosity could feast on me.

I don't know how long I sat with my back to the door before I felt a change in the air that caused me to tense up. The tension was close to fear, but not the usual kind of fear. This was a brand-new sensation. The longer I sat there straining to stay alert, the stronger the sensation became, until it felt like something was coming closer. Then something made me stand up, as though I was being challenged to show more of myself. Still keeping my back to the house, I pulled myself up by the wooden railing and stood on the next-to-top stair where I had been resting my feet. I could hear my heart knocking in my chest. But then whatever was behind me wanted more. It wanted me to step up on the porch *and show my full height.* This I did, my knees shaking, my back still to the house.

At that point I realized that if something actually *did* touch me from behind, I would pass out. Drawing on what little courage I had left, I forced myself to turn around and look straight at the gaping doorway. I could hardly breathe as I stood and offered my full body and full face to be seen.

And was met by the violent realization that someone was also showing himself to me. Pale and gaunt, the boy slouched against the frame of the doorway, wearing a faded red shirt and jeans and boots. Because his back was against the light his face was in shadow. But I could make out its lean contours and the flat unsmiling mouth and the hungry dark pools of his eyes. He seemed *posted* there in a rigid stillness, having perhaps made an effort as strenuous as mine to confront the creature facing him.

Countless times since then I have replayed that scene, trying to imagine what else might have happened if I could have endured the tension between us for a little longer.

But before I even registered what I was doing, I was flying off the porch, scraping knees and elbows in the sand, crawling under the wire fence, and running south, the late sun blinding my vision.

XI.

Aunt Charlotte had answered my note that told her I was going for a long walk. ("Got some more wine and went back to bed. I always crash after finishing a painting. Tomorrow we'll find you a bike.")

Now that she had made the first move on the chicken, I ripped off the remaining drumstick, laid it on some squares of paper towel, poured a glass of milk, and headed outside for the hammock. I needed to hear the close sound of the real ocean and feel the ropes of a real hammock against my body and try to find a place in my scheme of things for what had happened at Grief Cottage.

Recalling it now, minus the fear, it seemed as though we had somehow been trapped together in a net of golden light charged with energy. Using what science I knew, I worked out that if technically there was no such thing as "golden light," no colors at all, only *the electrical impulses* that made you give names to wavelengths, then maybe the same theory could apply to ghosts. An electrical impulse caused by some unusual wavelength produced an image in your brain and over the centuries people had given that wavelength the name "ghost."

From the safety of Aunt Charlotte's hammock (I was relieved that she had crashed for the rest of the day!) I pursued my speculations. I knew a lot about how nature worked. But I was also one of those people willing to accept that uncanny things might turn out to be aspects of the natural world.

Before it got dark the moon rose from the northerly direction of Grief Cottage. It was a large, round moon, first the color of butterscotch, then tangerine, as it climbed higher. Its light would be shining directly over his cottage now.

Maybe I would get a pillow and a blanket and spend the night out here in the hammock, close to the ocean, watched over by the moon that watched over him. I was comforted by the ocean's thud and wash, thud and wash. Not everyone would have seen him; perhaps no one else. He appeared because I had prepared for him, because I sensed the presence of him before he showed himself.

Now the moon changed color again. It was Aunt Charlotte's cadmium yellow and it had grown larger, a super-moon advancing southward and ascending higher until it was directly in front of me, lighting Aunt Charlotte's porch and my own face if I could see it. For *him* the main moonlight would now be past.

Even from this distance, I felt that charge between us—his curiosity coming to meet mine, mine going north toward him.

I wished I knew his name—for all I knew it could be Marcus. I wished I knew if he could think about me when I was not there, as I was thinking about him. I didn't know whether ghosts could keep track of what was going on in the living world, imagine what could be happening, or be likely to happen, by comparing it with what had gone before. Or were they like animals in not being able to project or imagine the future?

It struck me that he might need me to keep faith that he was still there. He had been waiting all this time, fifty years Aunt Charlotte had said, for someone to *wonder where he was*—to miss him after he was gone.

★   ★   ★

I DID GO inside after it was completely dark and bring out a pillow and a blanket. I felt safer outside in the darkness; in the house, there were more possibilities of my doing something wrong. I fell asleep in the hammock and had dreams that seemed to be knitting opposing things together—something about embarking on an important mission that was accompanied by almost unbearable fear. But all details were lost when I was awakened by a thud that shook the house, followed by a smashing of glass.

A halting outburst of obscenities followed, like someone experimenting with profanity. After that came a groan, and then "Stupid, stupid, stupid!" Followed by a final, crisp "Shit!"

I found Aunt Charlotte lying on the kitchen floor, her body curled around a table leg, her right hand, in an awkward position, still clutching the neck of a beheaded wine bottle whose dark red contents were spreading across the tiles.

She groaned. "I fell."

"Are you hurt?"

"I don't know."

My mom had fallen in the snow once. But before she'd let me touch her she systematically ran her hands up and down her body. Then she said, making light of it, "Nothing's broken. You can help me up."

"Do you think anything's broken?" I asked Aunt Charlotte.

"My ankle hurts. And my *wrist*, oh hell my wrist! Marcus, can you *very gently* loosen my fingers from around this bottle?"

I knelt beside her, but she screamed when I unclutched her fingers from the jagged bottle top.

"Shouldn't I call 911?"

"Call the Island Rescue Squad, they come faster. The number's at the top of the tide chart on the wall. No, wait. Put that phone down. First we need to clean up this mess."

"But shouldn't I call the number first?"

"*Do what I say, Marcus.*"

It seemed the wrong way to do things, but I got the dustpan and the sponge mop and the bucket and swept up all the glass and mopped the tiles while Aunt Charlotte lay curled around the table leg, alternating her *stupid, stupid, stupids* with moans of pain.

"Can you smell anything?" she asked when I had rinsed the tiles and put everything away.

When I said all I smelled was Mr. Clean, she allowed me to call the number. While washing the floor I had been planning what to say and when a man picked up I told him my aunt had fallen and hurt herself. He wanted to know if she was conscious and if her breathing passages were clear and if she was an elderly woman. I said yes to all, glad she hadn't heard the questions. He took down the address and told me not to let her move and to keep her calm.

When I sat beside her on the floor she became chatty. "The Rescue Squad pride themselves on efficiency. They like to say they can be anywhere on the island in seven minutes. Of course the island is only three miles long and two-tenths of a mile wide. Which is why I wanted to tidy up first. Everybody knows everybody's business on this island. I don't socialize much, but the locals can tell you when I came here and what I do and then they invent the rest. But I don't intend to give them any new material for their inventions."

While the rescue men were wrapping Aunt Charlotte's left leg and right arm in stabilizing tubes and plying her with questions as they worked, I stood above watching and feeling guilty for looking forward to the ride to the hospital in an ambulance. The two responders reminded me of my sunburnt man; they were around his age and spoke with his kind of drawl.

"You're lucky it wasn't a hip," said one curtly while they were easing her onto the stretcher.

"But I'm right-handed! I make my living painting pictures!"

"Maybe it won't be so bad," the other consoled her. "It might be just a light sprain. How did you manage to twist yourself around like that?"

"My foot caught against the table leg and I put out my hand to break the fall."

"You'd be surprised how often people do that," said the curt one. "Break the fall and break something else. You need to bend your knees and try to roll over on your butt. Keep your hands out of it."

"I'll try to remember that, next time I fall," said Aunt Charlotte.

"Should we lock up the house?" I asked my aunt.

"You'll stay inside and lock up after us."

"But aren't I going with you to the hospital?"

"No, Marcus. You'd be—you'd be bored to death."

"I wouldn't!"

"Please, Marcus. Don't argue. This is the way I want it."

They lifted her up, one in front, the other in back, commenting on how light she was. ("Bet *you* never had to diet, ma'am.")

Aunt Charlotte's undamaged left arm wafted toward me in a conciliatory gesture. "Be a good boy," she said, making it sound like I was about six years old. "And be sure and lock up, front and back. I'll be in touch as soon as I know what's what."

"Don't worry, son, we'll take good care of her," the nice one said.

I locked the front door after them, but rebelled by leaving the back door unlocked.

This is the way I want it—as they were carrying her out on a stretcher. She was dying to go somewhere without me—even if it was to the hospital in an ambulance. Just as earlier today she had not invited me to go inside the bank with her. And before that, the annoyance that flickered across her face when she had asked if I wanted to accompany her to the mainland and I'd said yes. And I knew what she'd stopped herself from saying before she changed it to "You'd be bored to death."

You'd be in the way. For a large part of my life I have lived alone . . . and it has suited me very well.

Disappointed and angry that I didn't get to ride in the ambulance, I returned to the oceanside porch. The night had moved on. When I lay down in the hammock the moon was no longer in my face. I was in the same darkness as *he* was, up at the north end of the island. I wished he could be here with me, but probably he could only stay where he was. A further idea arose: if a dead person could make himself known to a living person, then why wouldn't the reverse apply? Couldn't it be equally possible that I was haunting him?

Too much had happened today. The Steckworths and the trip to the mainland in the morning, the encounter at Grief Cottage this afternoon, rounded off by Aunt Charlotte being carried away in the night on a stretcher.

Though she was at this moment being safely conveyed by ambulance to receive hospital care for non-life-threatening injuries, the incident dragged me back into the winter night not six months ago when I waited for someone who never returned. *Where was she*, why was she taking so long? Ordinary delays, a road closed, or maybe the place had run out of pizza dough and they had to send out for more. Then on to imagining car break-down (our Honda had 125,000 miles on it)—or a car *accident*—then feeling hungry and eating cereal, then resenting her taking so long to get our pizza and making me ruin my appetite. We had been going to watch that movie we liked on Turner Classics, and I watched it anyway and let her existence slip my mind for chunks of time: *The Ladykillers*—the crooks posing as musicians and renting a room from a clueless old lady, who ends up, still clueless, picking up sixty-thousand pounds for them in a suit-case at the railway station. I laughed and cackled just as I had done with her the last time we watched it together. We loved Alec Guinness. He never knew who his father was, but lived a successful life all the same.

If he couldn't come south to me and share my porch, I would try to send an emanation of myself north to share his. Down the boardwalk to the beach, the tide coming in. All alone, except for the moonlight, and the little turtle eggs maturing as fast as they could in their protected dune. And then the next ordeal of breaking out of their shells and crawling on their little legs as fast as they could, down a vast stretch of beach to the safety of the waves. Some would make it, some would not.

Since I was sending an emanation of myself, I could order time and space as I pleased. I didn't have to wait forty minutes, I could be at the wire fence immediately, crawl under it, climb the rotting steps to the porch—and stand facing the doorway.

Then, heart knocking against ribs, I approached him through the darkness, not running away this time.

You came back, a voice says, as if speaking from underwater. Despite its hollow tone, I can hear pleasure. I keep on moving toward him, though it's too dark to see his shape. I know without seeing that he stands in the doorframe, no longer slouching against it, but upright and welcoming. The energy charge between us is still there. Though I can't see him, I feel his outstretched arms. I walk forward into them. There's no going back now.

XII.

A persistent knocking yanked me out of a sleep so profound that I couldn't recall where I was or who I was. The nearby crash of the waves against the surf brought me back to Aunt Charlotte's island and then I remembered my mom had died, and something else bad had happened more recently. It was morning though I had no memory of going to my room the night before, but obviously I had left the hammock, changed into my pajamas, and crawled into bed.

I was remembering Aunt Charlotte's fall only as I opened the front door to a stranger, an elderly man, built like a bantamweight wrestler gone to seed, with shaggy white hair and white stubble all over his face. The only things neat about him were his clothes: a freshly ironed short-sleeved shirt with small red and white checks, khakis with the crease still in them, white socks, and docksiders.

"Good morning, Marcus," he said, though what I actually heard was *mawnin, Mah-kus.* "I'm Lachicotte Hayes, a friend of your Aunt Charlotte's. She wanted me to check on you. May I come in?"

I hadn't found my voice yet, but I stood aside to indicate he was welcome.

"First things first," he said. (*Fust things fust.*) "Your aunt is going to be okay, though she's vexed because her arm's in a soft cast and she won't be able to paint for a while—her wrist wasn't broken but she tore a ligament. They're releasing her at noon and I'll be bringing her home."

"What about her ankle?"

"Well, it's broken. Clean break in the fibula. It's in a cast, too, which poses another problem. She can't do crutches with one arm so she has to make her choice between a walker and a wheelchair. I told her I'd opt for the wheelchair, but if I know your aunt she'll prefer to hop around on one leg in order to retain some control. Have you had your breakfast yet?"

"I just woke up."

"And I woke you. May I make amends by cooking your breakfast? I'm a good cook. My third wife said she married me for my cooking."

Both of them had been married three times, I was thinking. Had they ever had sex? It was hard to imagine, when people were so old. As it seemed polite to say something back, I asked if he was still married to his third wife, which made him laugh, exposing a mouthful of small, brownish teeth.

"Oh, she had enough of me a long time ago. These days, I'm taking a page from your Aunt Charlotte's book, though I'm a speck more sociable than she is. How about breakfast?"

As the house opened directly into the kitchen, he was already en route to the refrigerator. "Uh-oh," he said, after examining its contents. "No eggs, no bacon, no butter (*buttah*). What do you all have for your breakfast?"

"We don't eat breakfast together. Usually she has a banana and microwaves some coffee in the middle of the morning."

"I see nothing's changed there, except she used not to have the microwave. What do you eat?"

"I usually have a bowl of cereal and a glass of milk. That's really all I want."

"Well . . . ," scratching the shaggy head. "I guess you better have that, then. I'll join you in a cup of tea." He opened a cabinet above the sink. "There used to be a nice tea caddy in here, from Queen Elizabeth's coronation . . ."

"A red tin box with a lion and a unicorn on it?"

"That's the one."

"It's in her studio. She keeps her brushes in it."

"Oh, my, isn't that just—" He cut himself off midsentence and patted the upper shelves until he seized a plastic container filled with tea bags. "At least she saved my Typhoo."

And so I sat down across the table from Lachicotte, as he asked me to call him. It was the first time since coming to live with Aunt Charlotte that I had faced another person at breakfast. He took milk in his tea and settled for two packets of sweetener after unsuccessfully digging at the rock-hard substance in Aunt Charlotte's sugar bowl.

"I've been commissioned to go shopping with you for a bike," he said. "I know a place."

"You mean now?"

"Sure. It's only half past nine. We can't pick her up until noon, after the doc has checked her out. If you don't absolutely have to have a new one, they've got some prize vintage models at this place. I'm partial to vintage models when it comes to cars, but it's completely up to you."

"But won't it seem thoughtless?"

He looked perplexed. "Come again?"

"I mean to shop for a bike the same day she's coming home in two casts."

"That's very thoughtful, but the sooner we get you some wheels, Marcus, the better for her. She won't be able to drive for some time. You'll be running errands, doing the grocery shopping. We'll get you a roomy basket to go on the back, and you're going to need a helmet. Until she phoned last night from the hospital, I didn't know she had anyone living with her. I offered to come over right away, but she said you were a mature young man and had locked all the doors and would be fine. We haven't been regularly in touch, your aunt and I, though she knows she can always count on me. And I feel the same about her."

I had never set eyes on a car like the one waiting outside Aunt Charlotte's house. A dazzling creamy white with a long swooping back and a majestic hood in front crowned with silver wings. Its upholstery was buff-colored leather, the dashboard a highly polished wood, and the steering wheel was on the wrong side.

"It smells good" was all I could think to say once I settled in the passenger seat.

"It's the leather cleaner I use. They ought to make it into an aftershave. This is a 1954 Bentley Sports Saloon. It was built in England, which is why the steering is on the right. You should have seen it when it came on the lot, it would have made you cry. Restoring these old beauties is my passion, like your aunt's passion is painting. I love this automobile. Pray God nobody makes me an offer I can't refuse. Fasten your seat belt. I was required to install them if I planned to drive in traffic. When I was your age, Marcus, nobody dreamed of seat belts in cars. We expected them on airplanes but that was it." He keyed on the ignition and pulled away from the curb. The engine sound was a discreet, obedient murmur.

As we were driving across the causeway he said, "I'm very sorry about your mother." (*muh-thah*) "Charlotte told me about it. But your aunt's a good person. You can trust her. That doesn't mean she can't be provoking sometimes, but we all have our warts. I used to provoke her on a regular basis."

"How, if it's not rude to ask?"

"She said I tried to repair people like I do cars. And I nagged her about—certain of her habits. Like not ever picking up the phone. And some other things. Are you looking forward to school?"

"Some parts of it."

"Which parts are those?"

"Well, I really like studying and learning things. Making friends is the hard part. I had a best friend at my old school, but then Mom and I had to move away and I never found anybody at my next school."

"What grade will you be in?"

"I'll be in eighth. I skipped a grade."

"You'll like our middle school. My second wife's daughter went there. She loved it. The kids are friendly. It's too bad you had to leave your best friend, but my guess is that a new one is already waiting in the wings for you to show up."

"What happened was, Mom worked in this furniture factory in North Carolina. Then we moved across the state to the mountains and she worked for a small outfit that made custom furniture for people. It was time for us to make a change." That had been Mom's and my story after we moved away and I thought it sounded very credible as I told it to Lachicotte Hayes.

"I've always been partial to the mountains myself," he said.

"After I got older and could be on my own, Mom was planning to take the high school equivalency exam and go on to college. She wanted to make something of herself."

Lachicotte Hayes took some time to mull this over. "I would say she had already made a great deal of herself by bringing you up so well."

XIII.

*I*t was a subdued Aunt Charlotte that Lachicotte Hayes and I helped into the passenger seat of the Bentley. Gone was her edginess, her gritty independence. It was as though she had hired a stand-in to represent her in the role of the humble invalid who was grateful for any help offered to her by fully-mobile people until she could resume her self-sufficient remoteness.

She had been stoically awaiting us in a chair in her hospital room, dressed in last night's clothes and sheathed in two serious-looking casts. She looked smaller and defeated. In the other bed was a lady watching a game show with the sound turned up much too loud. But for all that, Aunt Charlotte might have been deaf. *I am not actually here,* her face said. When the nurse came with the wheelchair, which was "policy," she allowed herself to be folded into it and wheeled out to Lachicotte's car. I carried the shiny new walker she had been issued, stowing it beside me on the backseat. By the time Lachicotte got her settled into the Bentley, she had mumbled several half-audible thank-yous without appearing particularly glad to see either of us, though she did call me by name once. Lachicotte didn't get even that: she called him "you" and I saw her roll her eyes at him once when he attempted to say something optimistic. He helped her fasten her seat belt and told me to fasten mine, and off we went with a swish of tires. In the backseat it sounded like I was riding inside the wind. Lachicotte told Aunt Charlotte we had found me a bike and it would be delivered to the house, along with its accoutrements, later today. "Repay you" was her barely audible reply. These were her only words on the trip home.

Just before we reached the causeway, Lachicotte announced he was going to take a "teeny *shoaht*-cut" in order to drive by the middle school I would be going to. He cruised slowly around its circular driveway, the Bentley's reserved engine ticking over, and pointed out where the school bus would unload me. "I used to pick up my second wife's little daughter from this school and take her to my shop on the days her mother had classes: she was studying to be a psychologist." The school was a single-story brick building that had been added onto. Its grounds were well kept and there were bright shrubs in bloom. Though Lachicotte had meant well, I felt queasy at the thought of school buses and classrooms and recesses, the whole thing starting over.

"Some days, if I happened to get there a little early," Lachicotte said, "I would go inside and wander the halls. There's a school smell that carries you right back: floor polish, metal lockers, chewing gum. I loved my one year in middle school, only back then they called it junior high."

"Why did you have just the one year?"

"My folks sent me off to boarding school. It was the customary thing. My sister had to go, too, when the time came. She loved her school in Virginia. I about froze to death in New

Hampshire. I ended up going to four boarding schools, but each one was farther south so at least I got warmer."

"Then did you go to college?" I asked.

"I lasted half a year at the College of Charleston. Then I embarked upon my true calling as grease monkey."

Aunt Charlotte uttered a scornful *humpf.*

When we got home, I unfolded the walker and with Lachicotte's assistance she made it up the front stairs and into the kitchen, where she planted herself in a chair and announced she was perfectly all right. "It's not as though I've been permanently damaged," she said, as if we had inferred she was.

"You might want to consider getting someone in," suggested Lachicotte. "I could rustle up some names for you, if you like."

"Marcus and I will manage on our own," she said firmly. "But thank you, Lash." It sounded like she was dismissing him and he must have picked up on it because he left, saying to call him if we needed anything.

When he was gone, she said, "Listen, Marcus. I want us to go on as before. You'll have to put up with the annoyance of my *hopping* around the house, but other than that things won't be all that different—except I can't paint! I may be symmetrically challenged, but I still have a working right leg and left arm. I can dress and undress myself; I can also get myself from one room to another and open and close the refrigerator door."

"But I *want* to help. Are you in pain?"

"The painkillers haven't worn off and I have the rest of the container and a prescription for more if I want them. But I'll probably tear it up."

"No, don't do that."

"I don't want to become an addict or anything. Of course you can help, Marcus, but I don't want you to feel trapped." Then she laughed, which I thought was a promising sign. "But since you're here, could you bring me a bottle of wine and a glass? You'll have to open a new one. I can't manage the corkscrew. And while you're at it, you'd better uncork an extra bottle. I think I'll sleep away the afternoon. Maybe when I wake up, I'll discover all of this has been a bad dream."

How far back did her "all this" cover? As far back as before her fall in the kitchen? Or as far back as before I arrived?

All was silent in her studio/bedroom by the time they delivered the bike, a vintage 1954 beach cruiser, suitable for riding on sand. In addition to the helmet, Lachicotte had purchased a large rear basket, which could be attached to the fender when I went to the island grocery store, and a saddle pack for small items that fitted beneath the seat.

I would have liked to inaugurate my bike on the beach, but high tide was rolling in. So I set off north on Seashore Road, which ran parallel to the beach. This was the road Aunt Charlotte used when she carried too much painting equipment for walking to Grief Cottage, even if she had to climb over the prickly dunes at the end. It was the same road on which Mr. Art Honeywell in his truck, fleeing Hurricane Hazel, met up with the nameless parents "on foot," desperately searching for their nameless boy.

There had been an awful moment on the track behind the bike shop when Lachicotte and the shop owner stood by dotingly to watch me "test drive" the beach cruiser I had chosen. But what if I had somehow forgotten how to ride and fell off? Lachicotte would be so embarrassed. Every boy in the world could ride a bike, though it had taken me a while to learn on Wheezer's older brother's bike. "Your trouble, Marcus, is you're *thinking* about falling off," Wheezer said. "Stop thinking and just ride."

I wished Wheezer could see me on this beauty. How odd that he felt like the dead one, though he was still living in Forsterville, doing his old things—whereas the nameless dead boy in Grief Cottage was so alive.

When Lachicotte and I had been doing some emergency grocery shopping, leaving Aunt Charlotte in the car, he had given me his business card with work and cell phone numbers. "Call me if you need me, doesn't matter what time of day or night," he said. "It may get depressing for her. She won't be able to paint for a while and she hates being beholden to anyone. We've got to try and keep her from *festering*."

When Mom had the flu really bad once, I did everything for her. I made sure there were always liquids beside the bed and that she took her medications when she was supposed to. I changed her sheets and pillowcases sometimes twice a day and made simple things for her to get down (Jell-O, chicken noodle soup from a packet) when she didn't want to eat. I slept on the sofa and cleaned house and did the laundry and still kept up with my homework. Aunt Charlotte wasn't actually sick. She was, as she said, "symmetrically challenged" and couldn't paint for a while, and our job was to keep her from festering, though I wasn't entirely sure what Lachicotte had meant by that.

But one thing I did know: until I turned eighteen, she was all that stood between me and foster care.

My bike tires made an exciting thrum on the paved road. On my left side was what they called "the creek," where people fished and crabbed, but it looked wide enough to be a river. Whatever they called it, it needed a causeway over it between the island and the mainland. On my right side were high dunes, which allowed passing glimpses of the ocean from the driveways cut into the dunes. The driveways led to the beach houses, a few spiffy ones with sprinklers going on lawns and bright shrubs in bloom, others varying from needful maintenance to shabbiness. Most of the houses had names carved on lintels or displayed on boards. Rossignol House, No Saints, Pryor's Folly. Had my aunt chosen not to name her house, or simply not bothered to? The house to the left of Aunt Charlotte's, facing the ocean, belonged to an old lady named Mrs. Upchurch. Its name, Seacastle, was carved deeply into a driftwood signpost. Though it stayed empty most of the year, except when the old lady came with her caregiver from July through October, the house was faithfully maintained by a local service. There was also, Aunt Charlotte said, a middle-aged son who lived in Washington and visited for short periods. The house on Aunt Charlotte's right, facing the ocean, was one of the shabbier rentals with no name, hardly visible behind its dunes and tall grasses, from which we often caught bursts of rock music between the roar of the waves. It was some renters in that house who had forgotten to smooth down the sand after their badminton games and caused the mother turtle to mistake the humps for a dune.

After she told me about old Mrs. Upchurch, I imagined a very old Aunt Charlotte with a caregiver and myself as a middle-aged man coming to visit. But it didn't feel like something that would ever happen. What I could imagine quite well was a very old Aunt Charlotte, wheeled out on the porch and telling someone, "My great-nephew lived with me for a while. He was a thoughtful boy and I liked having him around. He was so helpful that time when I hurt myself and was laid up. I often sit here listening to the waves and wonder what he would have been like as an adult."

The bike's momentum gave me a sense of power. With my own speed I was creating a breeze. A fishy smell rose up from the creek. The sky had wisps of clouds with strokes of purple. Aunt Charlotte and her skies. How was she going to get through the days without her paints? The Steckworths had happened only yesterday! I had seen the boy in the doorway only yesterday. Then later came the moon shining on the hammock and the thud and the smash of the bottle, followed by the ambulance men and then the new bike today and seeing the middle school where it would all start up again.

Was Aunt Charlotte still sleeping? She ordered her wines in cases from a discount store in Myrtle Beach and had them delivered to the island. ("They have a much better selection than locally, and nobody around here needs to know my business.")

"I can show you how to take care of your bike," Lachicotte had offered rather shyly. Wheezer had been right, why not just ride and stop thinking? But that was easier said than done. "You are a deep thinker," Mom would say. "You get it from his side. I'll tell you all about it when you're a little older. All you need to know for now is that we loved each other, and he would have loved you if he had lived. When you're old enough to understand, I'll try and answer all your questions."

Did he even know you were going to have me before he died?

I had told Wheezer he was dead and showed him the picture I was not supposed to show, the man she kept in a tin box in the bottom drawer. It was a small posed black-and-white photo, just the frowning face.

"This was before I met him," Mom said. "He was younger then. But it was the only picture he had to give. When that picture was taken he wasn't in a place he wanted to be. When he did choose to smile, he could light up your world."

XIV.

I had reached the end of the road, where Aunt Charlotte had to park the car when she brought her heavier painting equipment. Hiding Grief Cottage from sight were the tall dunes that she'd had to climb, negotiating her way around the Spanish bayonets.

What I had been intending to do suddenly seemed completely insane. I had been planning on showing him my new bike. ("This bike frame is from a 1954 design that has become a classic. You might have been riding a bike like this if Hurricane Hazel hadn't happened.") But there were two levels of reality I had completely left out. Why would it please him, even if he were alive, to see another boy with a bike he probably couldn't afford? And beyond that, the more serious level: why would a dead boy, trapped in his rotting cottage for fifty years, unknown and uncared about by everyone in the world, wish to celebrate my new bike?

I needed to keep the different parts of myself in their proper places or I could go insane. Aunt Charlotte would be in her rights to send me to an institution.

Yesterday afternoon, at just about this hour, I had seen him slouching in the doorway. I had seen him with my daytime eyes and though his face had been in shadow, he was gazing straight at me. We were in some kind of electric time warp. In the moonlit hammock last night, I had fantasized sending myself north to be with him at Grief Cottage because he could not come to me. And, although this was in my willed imagination, as I walked into his outstretched arms there had been actual physical rapture, which had left results on my body and on my clothes. These results were nothing new. They had been happening for years in my sleep. Mom said it was perfectly normal for little boys. "What about little girls?" I had asked her. "They have those episodes, too," she said, "only with little girls it happens inside them and there isn't any evidence."

If I hid my new bike in the tall grasses, would it be safe from thieves, or had I better drag it with me up through the dunes? I was still headed for Grief Cottage, though not to show off the bike. I would leave it outside the wire with the CONDEMNED and KEEP OUT signs and go up on the porch and simply show myself to him. It was important, I felt, for me to come every day so he wouldn't think I had forgotten him.

But just as the roof of the cottage showed itself above the dunes, I heard men's voices fading in and out against the sound of the ocean. And sure enough, when I reached the top and looked down, there were two middle-aged men standing outside the wire fence, one in sunglasses and khakis with a polo shirt and docksiders like Lachicotte's, but without socks, and the other looking hot and out of place in a dark suit and tie. Not far away in the sand was parked a strange two-seated vehicle with fat wheels and an open frame. The man in the suit was writing in a small notebook but the other man looked up and spotted me and called out. I called back that I couldn't hear and slid down the dunes dragging my bike.

"I said I hope you weren't planning on breaking into this place."

"Oh, no sir, I—"

"Because it's about to fall in all by itself, and we wouldn't want anyone to be inside when that happens." He spoke with Lachicotte's accent.

But there is somebody inside.

"I'm supposed to take photographs of the cottage for my aunt to paint from. She just broke her ankle, so I said I would ride up here and take some new shots of the cottage."

"Well, son, you better get cracking. It's going to have to be leveled pretty soon."

"But it's the oldest house on the island."

"Eighteen-oh-four, to be precise.. The Historical Society never loses a chance to drum that date into me."

"Eighteen-oh-four?" inquired the man in the suit, still writing in his notebook. "They might want to put that in the brochure. 'The Old—' Does the house have a name?"

"Grief Cottage," I said, earning a sharp look from the local man.

"You'd want to call it the old Hassel House," he told the other. "That's the family that built it. Rice-planters who came here in summer to avoid the cholera. Back then the cypress was hewn on the mainland. They chiseled numbers on the pieces so the house could be assembled on the island. Then the timber was conveyed by horse-drawn—"

"But why 'Grief Cottage'?" the man in the suit asked.

"Oh, it's just a name that sprang up after Hurricane Hazel hit the island in 1954," the man with no socks replied. "There were some folks staying in the cottage and they were swept out to sea. They weren't even *in* the cottage. No bodies were ever found. If they *had* stayed inside, they'd have probably survived. These tough old houses withstood the storm because they were built so high off the ground on solid brick pilings. Plus the dunes protected them. This house would still be usable today if its successive owners hadn't let it fall to pieces."

"Why doesn't anybody bother to know the name of that family?" I heard myself asking belligerently.

"What family is that, son?"

"The people who *died* in that hurricane. The family that was in the cottage."

"Well, I expect their names are known by somebody. It surely would have been in the papers."

"My aunt has two books about the island's history and neither of them said a name. Just that it was an out-of-state family, the parents and a boy. And yet they were the only ones lost in that hurricane."

"Maybe someone should look into it," said the man in the suit. "It could make interesting copy for the brochure— like that gray ghost you told me about that wanders the beach before storms."

"I'll look into it," said the man with Lachicotte's accent. He had regarded me coldly since my outburst. I was probably considered a threat to his transaction with the other man. "If you want to take pictures, son, you'd best get on with it."

"Oh, today I was only scouting out possible angles," I said. "My camera's back at my aunt's house. To tell the truth, I wanted to try out this new bike."

"It's handsome. Vintage beach cruiser, isn't it. You get it locally?"

I named the bike shop. "Lachicotte Hayes helped me choose it."

The atmosphere warmed. "If *Lash* helped you choose it you can be sure it was the best bike in that shop. My name's Charlie Coggins." He bounded forward and thrust out his hand. "And this is Mr. Sampson from Chicago."

Mr. Sampson nodded me into existence and resumed his note-taking.

"You see that vehicle over there?" Charlie Coggins pointed toward the strange contraption on fat tires. "That's what is called an amphibian. You can drive it through water, up and down dunes—it's ideal for my line of work. I thought I knew everything about assembling things, so I sent for this kit. When it arrived I couldn't make head or tail of the directions, so I had the parts trucked over to Lash and he helped me put it together. Lash could put together a space shuttle if he had all the parts. Well, we better get on with our work, Mr. Sampson has a plane to catch this evening. Nice meeting you. Say hello to Lachicotte for me."

Producing a metal tape measure, he knelt down and shot it across the sand, calling out dimensions. The Chicago man wrote them down. Once he interrupted Charlie Coggins to ask, "Won't that be too long for the property?" "Not at all," said Charlie. "You've got to remember that this property sits on two lots." They appeared to be designing a long terrace, where people could dine out above the sea. Understanding I had been dismissed, I mumbled a goodbye and prepared to drag my bike back up the dunes.

Before I turned to go, I stared hard at the cottage door. It was lit up, like yesterday at this time, but there was no figure in the doorway staring back at me. What had I expected? For him to be lounging there watching the men who had come to destroy his house? Yet in case he was looking out from some unknown spot, I leveled a powerful gaze at the cottage which I hoped would send the message that I knew he was there, and that I would be back, and that I had by no means forsaken him.

But as I was pedaling home I realized he might not have recognized me in the new bike helmet.

XU.

*L*ooking back on that period Aunt Charlotte referred to as her "house arrest," I am touched by my faith in my young powers. I felt pretty sure that I could take charge of any problem that arose. And who is to say that this confidence, even though founded on the heroism of inexperience, didn't make a difference? Riding my bike home from its first outing to Grief Cottage, I was already deep into ways of helping Aunt Charlotte get through her laid-up spell without hating herself for being *beholden*, to use Lachicotte's word. My job was to keep her spirits from *festering*—another of Lachicotte's words.

For a start, I knew she was going to be another kind of patient from my mom. Mom had a completely different temperament. Mom was the kind of person who tried to fit in with the situation, always ready to admit she was at fault, and grateful—too grateful, sometimes—for attentions shown to her. You might say Mom's major tactic for enduring (though Mom was hardly a tactician) was appeasement. After stowing my bike in the garage, I was surprised and a little crestfallen to find a very in-charge-looking Aunt Charlotte presiding at the kitchen table with a banana and a glass of wine before her. Wearing fresh clothes, she announced that she had just taken "a bath of sorts" by perching at an angle on the rim of the tub. "I left the floor wet, but other than that it was a success. It will be easier next time."

"I'll run the mop over it."

"Sit down first and tell me about your bike ride."

"I went up to Grief Cottage on the road—the tide was too high to ride on the beach. There were these two men up there talking about tearing it down."

"Who were they?"

"One was a real estate man named Charlie Coggins. He knows Lachicotte."

"Yes, Coggins sold me my shack. Not him, but his father. Back then it was the only real estate firm. Who was the other?"

"He was from Chicago, a Mr. Sampson. I think he was a representative for some buyer. They're planning on building something bigger because the property has two lots."

"Ah, I wanted to take more photos, and here I am grounded."

"I'll take them for you. I already told them I was going to. All I need is your camera and for you to show me how to use it."

"You're very thoughtful, Marcus. Unlike most boys your age. Not that I know any boys your age except you."

"Mom had to work, so I did the things at home."

The swervy way she guided the wineglass to her lips showed how new she was at using her left hand. "Did you like the look of your new school?"

"It looked okay. I think Lachicotte is very nice."

"Well of course he's nice. Tiresome sometimes."

"How is he tiresome?"

"He nags too much. He means well, it's just his way. He wants to fix things. Rehabilitate them, smooth out their kinks, polish them up. But people aren't cars. And it does wear a little thin, his aw-shucks-grease-monkey routine. His family is older than God, at least in these parts, and he has tossed away more advantages than most people ever dream of having. Marcus, since you're here, would you mind peeling this banana for me?"

For the first few days of Aunt Charlotte's house arrest, things went smoothly. We had established our routine. She slept later into the morning because she wasn't painting. She hated hopping along behind her walker and soon dispensed with it, preferring to hop on her own steam, steadying herself against walls and furniture with her left hand. I got used to hearing her hop down our hall and shut herself into the bathroom, which was next to my room. She would mutter to herself while taking her "bath of sorts." I kept the bathroom super-clean, leaving supplies of fresh towels and washcloths and extra rolls of toilet paper in easy reach. Whenever I finished in there, I made sure the floor was dry, the sink had no hairs in it, and the toilet seat was down. Now she asked me to open four bottles of red wine at a time. I was to put two of them, lightly re-corked, in her studio, and the other two on a kitchen shelf in easy reach. She stayed in her studio all day, with the door closed. I heard her hopping about intermittently, muttering and moving things around, and then long periods of silence. Our one meal together continued to be supper.

She was still in her quarters when I set out on my early morning bike rides. From six to eight the beach was wonderful. Dogs were allowed to run without leashes during those hours, and there was an entirely different kind of beachgoer. There were the dog owners, of course, and the very old, with hats and sleeves, who needed to avoid the stronger sun. The bird life was louder and bolder down at the surf before the children cluttered it up with their shrieks and toys. There were also the runners and the exercisers and a few bike riders like me. This one old man had his black poodle tied to the back of his bike, which distressed me until I saw that the poodle seemed proud to be trotting along and showing off his obedience. I couldn't believe how much faster biking was than walking. I could bike from Aunt Charlotte's to Grief Cottage in less than fifteen minutes.

I hadn't seen the ghost-boy again, but, like with Aunt Charlotte and me, he and I had a routine of sorts. I would sit on the top stair with my back to the open door and talk to him. I kept it safe and casual, the way you might turn away and pretend to be talking to yourself to put a nervous animal at ease. I had thought about warning him they were planning to demolish the cottage, but then decided it would be cruel. Besides, what alternative dwelling could *I* offer him? Also, he might connect the bad news with the person who brought it. Of course, it was possible that he knew already, that he had seen and heard the men—or absorbed it in some ghostly manner unknown to me.

There was so much I didn't know about relationships between the dead and the living. Whenever we had indulged in one of our ghost story binges, my former best friend, Wheezer, would grumble, "There ought to be a *rule book* on how to behave with ghosts!" He improvised a few rules for us to follow if we ever met a ghost, but so far none of his rules fit the situation with my ghost.

At first I limited my talk to nature, the ocean, and the surroundings we shared. I remarked on the sunrises and the tides and I worried aloud about the fate of the baby turtles, which had been much on my mind. ("They need to get out to those ocean currents fast because the coastal waters are thick with predators and the babies are defenseless and very tasty." And when I felt a knot of sadness behind me, like the gathering of someone's woe, I quickly reassured him: "Don't worry, they are born knowing what they have to do. They have been doing it for forty million years.")

It was hard work courting a ghost, requiring constant exertions of empathy. Some subjects left him cold. For instance, I had thought I would initiate personal topics by filling him in on what the islanders thought had happened to him and his family during Hurricane Hazel. But I'd barely begun when I felt his withdrawal. I was a crazy boy talking aloud to an empty porch.

I recalled how stealthily I had courted Wheezer back in first grade. At the beginning I observed him from a cautious remove. He was a delight to watch—a complete little man, everything about him defined and sharp: his precise and finicky modes of movement and speech; his lovely floppy roan-colored hair, cut often at a salon in the style of an old-fashioned boy, like Christopher Robin dragging Pooh down the stairs. He had a soft, reedy, hoarse voice and employed his own phrases for keeping aloof from the mob. "Come on, people," he would say, or "behave yourself, people." When his friends displeased him, he called them "people," which crushed them. But when someone impressed or surprised him he would reward you with an "Outstanding!" in his hoarse little voice that was a side effect of his asthma.

For the whole first half of first grade, I watched and listened and kept my distance. Besides being a natural leader, he was a keen placer of people. Aware that I would be seen by him as an outsider, I decided to play up my outsider-ness. I had studied him long enough to guess that the way to his heart was to be as unlike his friends as possible. I could see that they bored him with their lack of imagination, their likeness to one another. The phrase "single mom" was just coming into popular usage and I told him that's what my mom was. His grandfather owned the furniture factory where Mom worked as section manager in the polishing and packing department.

Wheezer was fascinated by anything to do with the paranormal and was always devising tests to see how extrasensory we were. (I was more developed than he was, he concluded.) He did a brisk business on eBay, acquiring old issues of *Weird Tales* dating back to the thirties. He introduced me to the stories of Roald Dahl, Harlan Ellison, and Ray Bradbury.

He loved gossip and hearsay, the more shocking the better, stories about the extreme things people had done, true things that made one lower one's voice in the telling. ("Tell me a *true*, Marcus," he would command.) I was always on the lookout for the kind of trues that would appeal to him. ("Did you know that Van Gogh the artist cut off his ear after a fight with his friend Gauguin? He wrapped it in a handkerchief and on the way to the hospital he handed the ear to a prostitute and she fainted.")

Wheezer also had trues to offer, including a dramatic one from his own family. His father's older brother, the brilliant Uncle Henry, who could read Greek and Latin, dropped out of Harvard to return home and become a heroin addict. ("His IQ was off the charts, it almost killed Granny to watch her favorite son disintegrate in front of her eyes. When Grandpa finally kicked him out, he moved into a rusty trailer with rats and died in bed shooting up.")

As long as it wasn't about himself, my Grief Cottage friend also quickened at the lure of a true. As soon as I began, "I'm eleven, and I'm an orphan," I could feel the air behind me snap to attention. "My mom was killed in a car accident last winter and my dad died before I was born. She never told me who he was but when I'm older I'm going to try to find out."

But if I got too digressive or laid on too many details, the frequency between us faded. Like Wheezer, the listener in the space behind me was a sensationalist. He liked me to head straight for the extremes.

Commuting between Aunt Charlotte and the boy in Grief Cottage, I felt torn. I had specific duties at each place and I told myself my mental health wasn't in danger as long as I remembered the *differences* between those duties. It was a matter of keeping separate realities separate and steadying myself inside an awareness that seemed to be expanding too fast. Some days my balancing act felt wobbly or downright precarious and I feared I was on the slippery slope to insanity. If only I had somebody I could ask! But what exactly would I ask them? ("Do you think if your consciousness starts growing too fast it could be just as frightening as the beginnings of insanity? Maybe you could even confuse it with insanity.")

One morning as I was returning to Aunt Charlotte's after my hour with my back to the inhabitant of Grief Cottage, I passed the sunburnt man in his white dump truck heading north. I waved enthusiastically, and he waved back. But I could see that he didn't recognize me. How could he? I was wearing my helmet and riding a bike. In a flash of insight I understood how it felt to be the ghost-boy, who knew others could not ordinarily see him. For a moment I looked forward to sharing this parallel experience with him until I remembered that references to him had so far earned me a cold withdrawal.

XVI.

Aunt Charlotte's mood was deteriorating. And at supper one evening I made it deteriorate further with a stupid question meant to cheer her up.

She had confided to me that she had been attempting to paint with her left hand. ("I thought why not try for mood expressed through color? Just those two things: mood and color. Well, maybe a few shapes.") That morning she had squeezed out her colors and chosen a big flat brush and started to work. ("I was going to do a minimalist version of Grief Cottage. After all, I know the proportions, having painted them so many times. What could be so hard about laying in some sky color and some brushy Constable-like clouds and then roughing in a dark broken shape at the bottom? Who knows, I thought, these restrictions might lead to something exciting.")

But her left hand had refused to go where she wanted it. When she tried to hold it steady it started shaking. She got more and more frustrated, then depressed, then gave up in disgust. She drank a bottle of red wine and slept the rest of the day.

After Aunt Charlotte finished telling me this, I got my dumb inspiration. I asked her what she had done with her days on the island *before* she started painting. Thinking this would give her ideas on how to while away the time until her wrist healed.

She stared at me incredulously, as though I had switched to an alien language. "Well," she said bitterly, "let me see. For one thing I could *walk*. I walked a lot. Up and down the beach. I walked until I got tired. And I went over and over my rotten past and gave myself credit for finally breaking free. I walked until I walked out of myself. Then, as I told you, I had jobs. I worked for the vet and then with Lachicotte. And, as you know from your mother, a job fills up your days. And then I saw that woman painting Grief Cottage and I thought, 'I can do that.' And I could.

"Now, however, I can't walk and I can't paint, and there's— well, I have other responsibilities. And I'm twenty-five years older. This mishap is like a preview of old age. It's a foretaste. I can see myself like Mrs. Upchurch in her wheelchair next door. And what's the point in living on for that?"

By "other responsibilities" she had meant me. Her ominous follow-up question was even worse. How could I get us onto safer ground?

"But even if you were old and in a wheelchair," I reminded her, "you'd still be able to paint."

"One Grandma Moses is enough for this world."

"Who is Grandma Moses?"

"An old woman who started painting in her seventies because her arthritis was too bad for her to embroider anymore. She lived to be a hundred and one and there's a postage stamp in her honor."

"What kind of paintings?"

"Oh, nostalgic country scenes that made people feel *safe*."

She pronounced "safe" in such a sneering way that I thought it wise to drop my safer-ground plan. I could have simply shut up, or cleared the table, but something egged me on. Since I had already done the opposite of cheering her up, since her future in the wheelchair was getting us nowhere, why not go for her rotten past?

"Why was it rotten?" I asked.

"What?"

"You're always mentioning your rotten past."

"I wasn't aware I was always mentioning it. I'll try to curb myself."

"But I'm *interested*. We're from the same family and I don't know anything about anyone in it! Mom kept things to herself, and the few times my grandma visited us she didn't want to talk about the family, either."

"Ha. I can well imagine. So what did my sister—your grandmother—talk about?"

"What Mom and I were doing wrong and how we could improve ourselves. And how well she had done for herself. After she left, Mom always cried for a few days. She never said why, but I don't think it was because she was sorry to see Grandma leave."

"I don't think so, either. How is it that some people can make us feel worthless even when we know we're seeing ourselves through their eyes? Certain humans are poison. If I had to sum up my past in a few words, I would say: 'Beginning at age five I was poisoned.' End of story. But I can see from your face that's not enough. Well, here's a shrink-wrapped follow-up. There are very few family stories in this world. My family story consists of a useless cowardly mother, a poison fiend of a father, and an older sister who chose to pretend there was no poison in the house. Take your pick of the variations, down through the ages, of the good old family horror story. Try the Greeks, try the Bible, try Shakespeare, or choose from the abundant pity-memoirs on your local bookstore racks. When you are able to shrink-wrap your family story down to a few words, Marcus, maybe we will exchange further notes."

Aunt Charlotte's screed appeared to have converted her despair into an angry energy. I was congratulating myself for the turnaround, but then she asked me to uncork more bottles of red wine because she had run through all the open ones. I must have displayed some qualm because she harshly added, "This is a bad patch, Marcus. Just do it."

A day or so later, more cases arrived from the Myrtle Beach wine shop. She must have made the phone call while I was out on my bike. The delivery man carried the cases in and I later unpacked and stored them, continuing to uncork them as stipulated. But the number of bottles for me to leave in her studio had now increased to three. It was then that I started wondering if it was time to make a phone call to Lachicotte. But Aunt Charlotte would hear me if I made it on the house phone, and this was in the first years of the new millennium, before everyone carried a cell phone. I would have to wait until my next bike trip to the island grocery store, which had a pay phone.

But would a phone call to Lachicotte qualify as disloyalty—going behind her back—joining forces with "the nag"? I was starting to have an idea about what Lachicotte's nagging had addressed. I had unpacked some more boxes from my former life and looked up *fester* in my dictionary. "To form pus to fight off a foreign body." For there to be pus there had to be some foreign body that needed to be fought off. Mentally, that foreign body was her depression. Physically it was alcohol. Though I wasn't exactly sure how that worked. Alcohol was supposed to numb your pain. Wheezer had told me how in the Civil War they poured whisky into a soldier before amputating his leg. But though alcohol-numbed pain, could it cause another kind of festering underneath the pain?

I tried to find a disloyalty comparison from my life with Mom. If a phone call to Lachicotte to snitch on my aunt's drinking was a disloyalty, what were the ways my loyalty had been challenged when I was living with Mom? Well, Mom wasn't a drinker for a start. She could hardly move when she got home. Her feet and lower back hurt. I gave her massages. (The thought of giving Aunt Charlotte a massage seemed not only improper but bizarre. I didn't want to imagine what she would say if I were to offer such a thing.)

The weak spots in my loyalty to Mom concerned anything in our life that would reinforce Wheezer's taunt that I was my mother's little husband. In those last years with her, I was always torn between wanting to give her what comforts I was capable of giving (my last Christmas present to her had been a drugstore kit of massage oils) and feeling shame when the comforts recalled Wheezer's unforgiveable assessment of my home life. Whereas with Aunt Charlotte the loyalty conflict was between what would be best for her and how much I would sink in her estimation if I went behind her back and reported on her to Lachicotte Hayes.

While I continued to fret over these options, Lachicotte dropped by one afternoon bearing an oyster pie.

"These are farm oysters, the season's over (*ovah*), but they work perfectly (*pufectly*) well in a pie."

He'd had a haircut since I last saw him and seemed altogether more spiffed up. He smelled like someone just out of the shower, and I could smell the pie as well.

"If I could make crust like you, Lash," said Aunt Charlotte, who had taken an urgent hopping trip to the bathroom following his arrival, "maybe I would start baking pies." Now Aunt Charlotte smelled of mouthwash. "I'm sure Marcus must miss his mother's pies."

I let this go by rather than say our pies were from the frozen section of the supermarket.

"It just came out of the oven," said Lachicotte, setting down the pie dish on the kitchen counter. "I'd advise you all to have it for supper. It tastes better before it's refrigerated. I hope you like oysters, Marcus."

"Oh, yes." Though I'd only had cans of oyster stew.

"There's nothing to making crust," he said to Aunt Charlotte. "All you need to remember is that bowl of ice water for keeping your fingers cold."

"Maybe I'll try it when I have ten fingers again," she said.

"Marcus, I bring you a message from Charlie Coggins. He stopped by my shop yesterday. You made quite an impression on him. He wanted to know how old you were and when I said eleven he wouldn't believe it."

"Will you sit down, Lash?" Aunt Charlotte had remembered her manners.

"What was the message?" I asked when we three were seated at the kitchen table. Lachicotte had turned down my offer of a cup of tea because he was meeting a potential buyer for his 1962 Rolls-Royce Silver Cloud at five.

"It was about that family who got swept away during Hurricane Hazel. Charlie said to tell you he checked the firm's listings for 1954 and it wasn't a Coggins rental. It must have been a private transaction by the owners. In fifty-four that cottage still belonged to the Barbours, but they sold it soon after

Hurricane Hazel. What was it you were interested in knowing, Marcus?"

"I just think it's strange that nobody remembers their *names*. In those two ladies' books about the island, the man in the truck who talked to them when they were out looking for their son—*he* gets named, but not the only people on the island who were lost. It's like they didn't *count*."

"Marcus feels the pain of others," said Aunt Charlotte, "even when they're dead and gone."

"Well, we can surely find out," said Lachicotte. "We can track them through microfilms of local newspapers at the library (*li-bry*). I'll take you there tomorrow if you like, Marcus. Then you'll be able to bike over there whenever you want."

"Speaking of which," said Aunt Charlotte. "I need to reimburse you for his bike and all those extras. Marcus, would you bring my checkbook from my purse? I've been practicing my left-handed signature. I called the bank to alert them to expect the scribble of a five-year-old child and they said no problem. But you'll have to fill in the rest."

Lachicotte insisted there was no hurry and Aunt Charlotte insisted there was, and they almost had a fight before the check finally got written. Then we all played at writing left-handed signatures on Aunt Charlotte's note pad. Lachicotte's clumsy attempts got a snort out of Aunt Charlotte. My efforts recalled to me how shaky my early right-handed attempts had been when I was a child. How quickly you forgot how hard it had been to control your fingers when you first started! Aunt Charlotte's left-handed signature was far better than either of ours, which lifted her mood. "Though of course I've had all day to practice," she said, almost gaily for her.

"Well, your neighbor Coral Upchurch will be arriving right after the fourth," said Lachicotte.

"How is it you always remember such things, Lash?"

"It's just this little thing that I do." He laughed. "My first wife used to call me her walking anniversary book."

After Lachicotte left, I asked Aunt Charlotte if she knew why he'd had three wives. "Did he leave them, or did they leave him?"

"They left him. Lash is the kind of man who lets women walk all over him. I was just the opposite: I always sought out the kind of men I could depend on to hurt me. Then I left them when I'd had enough."

"I wonder how many times I'll get married."

"Oh, Marcus, you make me want to laugh and cry at the same time."

XVII.

When Aunt Charlotte told Lachicotte I felt the pain of others even when they were dead, I worried that I had been talking in my sleep. But thinking it over I decided she was simply referring to the interest I had expressed about the nameless boy and his parents and to my sensitivity on their behalf.

Though he was the most compelling presence in my life, I knew better than to tell anyone about our connection, and certainly not that I had *seen* him. I was drawing from the same fund of wisdom I had called on when the social services psychiatrist kept asking what I had felt while beating up Wheezer and I kept replying that I had "blanked out."

Funny enough, of all the people in my life, past or present, it was Wheezer alone I would have loved to tell about the dead boy. How he would hang on to my every word. His favorite thing was the occult. He would insist on going over every detail.

"Now Marcus, tell me again, what *exactly* did you see?"

"He was there in the door frame, facing me."

"What door frame?"

"It was the front door leading out to the porch. I mean there's no door, but he was slouching against the frame."

"You're sure the whole thing wasn't a trick of the light or something?"

"I'm sure. He was thin and had a sharp jaw and . . ."

"Was he tall or short?"

"More like tall. But very skinny. And he wore a faded red shirt and jeans and boots. He was somebody specific. And I not only saw him, I felt him."

"How do you mean you felt him?"

"The way you feel people when they're standing right in front of you. I felt I was being looked *back* at. I felt his curiosity. He was as interested in me as I was in him. The whole thing was as real as you and me facing each other right now."

"What kind of faded red shirt? Polo?"

"No, it buttoned down the front and it looked a little small for him. It had short sleeves—or maybe they had been cut off."

"What were the boots like? Why would someone be wearing boots at the beach?"

"I'm not sure. The whole thing was pretty intense while it was happening."

"Oh, God," he would have cried out with envy. "Why couldn't this have happened to *me*?"

I LIKED TO keep to my schedule of the early morning bike ride to the north end of the island, but Lachicotte was picking me up from Aunt Charlotte's at nine-thirty to go to the library, and I didn't want to seem rushed while I was at Grief Cottage. When you visited someone they could sense if you were in a hurry or had to be somewhere else after you left them. I would go in the late afternoon. After all, it was the late afternoon when I had seen him that one time.

Lachicotte brought Aunt Charlotte a lettuce and two cucumbers from his garden and some rolls, still warm, that he had baked. I had peeled two bananas for her and sealed them into plastic quart bags. The requisite uncorked bottles were ready in her studio, the ones in the kitchen discreetly out of sight. As she did not come out to say hello, I told Lachicotte I thought she was still sleeping.

"How's she doing, in your opinion?" He asked this before the Bentley had pulled away from the curb.

"Okay, I think."

He appeared to be pondering my stingy reply as we drove down Seashore Road. He was still pondering as he drove us across the causeway. He was expecting more, but what could I loyally add?

"She tried to paint with her left hand," I said. "It didn't work too well. She couldn't control the brush and she gave up."

"What did she do after that?"

"She slept for the rest of the day."

He pondered some more. Though I tried not to I could hear his thoughts.

I kept quiet until we were on the causeway, passing the people fishing over the railings. "What kind of fish are they fishing for?" I asked.

"Catfish mostly. It's also an opportunity to socialize." A resignation in his voice indicated that he was not going to pry any further. I had let him down.

"Look, I'm not sure I can—" I had to stop; I was choking up. I looked out my window so he wouldn't see. "I'm not sure I can keep her from fermenting."

As soon as it came out I realized my stupid mistake. In terms of loyalty to Aunt Charlotte, it was probably the most ill-chosen word I could have hit on. "I meant to say festering," I corrected myself. "I don't know why I said the other."

"They both have a certain applicability," he remarked and left it at that.

"Did you sell the 1965 Rolls-Royce yesterday?"

"Ah, no. The minute he laid eyes on my beauty here, he fell out of love with poor Silver Cloud."

"But you can't sell the Bentley. You said you loved it."

"He made me a handsome offer, but I haven't decided. It doesn't do to get too attached to things. But as I say, I haven't decided yet."

Like the middle school, the mainland library was a well-kept one-story building with extensions added on, surrounded by bright bushes in bloom. In one of the extensions there were a lot of glass windows and they were open and you could hear the commotion of children and a woman's voice telling them to settle down.

"That's my niece Althea in there," Lachicotte said. "I recognize her voice. She runs the summer pre-K for the little kids. You're going to be surprised, Marcus, at how up to date we are in our gadget room. We have the very latest in microfiche."

The computer and microfilm room was in one of the new extensions. On the wall to the right as you entered was a large bronze plaque that read THE MARGERY LACHICOTTE HAYES WING. 1994.

"Is that one of your relatives?" I asked.

"My mother. Our family has always been passionate about libraries. I'm glad she lived to see this wing finished."

A smiling lady in a crisp pantsuit hurried forward to meet us. "This is Mrs. Daniels, our librarian," said Lachicotte. "Lucy, this is Marcus Harshaw, who's interested in Hurricane Hazel."

"I'm very happy to meet you, Marcus. We are all so proud of your aunt. We have one of her wonderful paintings above our front desk. Lash, I have all the envelopes ready. I got them out after you phoned yesterday."

"We're much obliged, Lucy."

"No trouble at all, they were close at hand. Being as this summer is Hazel's fiftieth anniversary, we've had a right many calls on those old newspapers. And I've got a new magazine for Marcus as well. This month's *State Magazine* is featuring stories by people who lived through Hazel. Marcus, I expect you'll want some help setting up the scanner and printer?"

"No, thank you. I used one like this when I was writing my research paper at school. I just need a user's card to stick in that slot."

The librarian was impressed and I think Lachicotte was, too. They hovered over me until I had taken the first fiche out of its envelope—being careful not to leave fingerprints on the film—and slid it into the tray, and started reading the screen. Then Lachicotte said that since I seemed to know what I was about, he and Mrs. Daniels would go and print me out a library card. "Would you like your middle name on it or a middle initial?" he asked. I said Marcus Harshaw would be enough. I didn't have a middle name.

Left alone with my research, I became impatient then indignant at the skimpy information found on the screen. Here were the microfiches from *three* state papers of fifty years ago reporting on the aftereffects of Hurricane Hazel, and not one of them rendered up anything as useful as the *one* state paper I had pored over from *a hundred and fifty* years ago while researching my seventh-grade school project back in Jewel about a nearby North Carolina mountain town that had been split in half by the Civil War. One side was Confederate and the other Union and the two sides slaughtered each other.

The South Carolina state papers of fifty years ago offered plenty of nonhuman information about Hazel. The hurricane had hit on the day of October's full moon high tide, the highest lunar tide of the year, which meant the most water damage. Hazel left Haiti as only a Category 2, but kept gathering strength as it headed up the Atlantic coast. When it hit north of Myrtle Beach on the morning of the fifteenth, it was a Category 4. The newspapers reported wind velocities and estimated the millions of dollars of property damage it left in its wake. There were some eyewitness evacuation stories, but they all ended safely. All told, Hazel left nineteen fatalities along the coast of North Carolina and one fatality in South Carolina—but there were *no names*. Where were the names? I scanned the film until my head began to hurt and I still never found a single name. If even the accounted-for fatalities didn't rate getting their names in the papers, what hope for you if your body was never found?

I gave up on the fiches and paged through the "old-timer" stories in the fiftieth anniversary state magazine the librarian had left for me. Their Hazel recollections were the kind that began "Mamma and I were driving to the island to see her sister, who was a year-round resident. But when we got to the causeway, we were stopped by a highway patrolman who told us we had to turn around, everyone was evacuating . . ." Or "A week after the storm, when J. W. McLauren of Charleston finally crossed to the island, he found his family's hundred-year-old island cottage with all its tongue-and-groove joints miraculously intact, only the waters had moved the house a hundred yards down the beach."

There were a few vivid descriptions—winds snapping trees like chicken bones and a family hunkered down in a truck bed with salt water filling their noses, but the eyewitnesses of those scenes had lived into safe old age and gotten interviewed by this shiny magazine fifty years later.

I left everything in a neat pile for Mrs. Daniels. She was not around, so I returned the user's key for the fiche machine to the woman behind the front desk. Involved in her own work, she barely looked up from her computer to acknowledge me, so I was able to study the painting that hung over her desk in peace. I recognized it from one of those postcard reproductions Aunt Charlotte had sent to Mom. It was a long, wide painting of the island's shoreline at dusk, just the sand patterns and shallows at low tide, not a single breaking wave, not a living thing in sight, not even a single shore bird, everything glowing and peaceful in a soft orange end-of-day light. It made you feel glad you lived close to such beauty. I made a mental note to tell Aunt Charlotte how well I thought the painting graced the library wall, setting the tone for the whole place.

Then I went to find Lachicotte, who was in the pre-K room, sitting at a table beside a gray-haired lady, their backs to the open door. Below them on the floor, the children were finger-painting on sheets of paper. I had never seen children wearing kid-size latex gloves to finger-paint, but it seemed like a very practical idea. Moving closer I saw that Lachicotte and the gray-haired lady, who must be his niece, were making small finger-paintings of their own at their table. They, too, wore latex gloves, and were so wrapped up in what they were doing that I hung back in the doorway, not wanting to disturb the scene. The gray-haired niece was painting a still life of the jar of yellow roses placed in front of her on the table. Aunt Charlotte would have judged it "a competent little painting." Lachicotte, hunched forward raptly, swirled vigorous circles of dark blue paint behind what looked like either a lopsided mountain or a crouching white beast. I would have stood there longer if a watchful little girl hadn't broken the spell. "Why is that man over there *spying* on us?" she cried.

XLIII.

*L*achicotte's painting of the lopsided mountain or crouching white beast turned out to be his "farewell portrait" of his 1954 Bentley R-Type Continental. "Even while I was painting her—or trying to, I'm no artist—I knew our time together was over" (*togethah, ovah*). He told me this as we ambled around downtown Charleston while Aunt Charlotte underwent her wrist surgery at the medical center.

Her "sprain" had been a misdiagnosis. The first x-ray taken weeks ago at the local hospital had missed the lesion and now everything had to be done all over again, with a projected twelve more weeks in a new cast. What she had was an "occult fracture of the scaphoid bone"—I tried not to read any messages into the *occult* word beyond its medical meaning of a hidden injury. The break was found in her follow-up x-ray, which also revealed a loose piece of bone fragment that had to be excised. So now the ligament and the scaphoid bone were being properly reconnected and "fixated" with a metal screw. The surgery was being done under general anesthesia, after which she would spend a further hour in the recovery room before we could take her back to the island. Lachicotte was driving her car now, the old Mercedes sedan, while the mandatory seat belts were being installed in the Silver Cloud Rolls-Royce, which the buyer hadn't wanted after he laid eyes on Lachicotte's beloved Bentley.

"Were you sad when you saw your Bentley driving away?"

"You might say I felt an elegiac pang. But then I turned my mind to all I could do with the proceeds."

"Was it a lot of money, or is that rude to ask?"

"It was a fair amount because it's a rarity and he had to have it. I can buy my niece a waterfront condo and donate a much-needed new roof to my church."

"You must really like your niece."

"Althea has gone through some rough passages, but she's kept her humanity intact. Which is admirable in itself."

"What kind of rough passages?"

"Well, she was fifteen when she lost both parents. Her mother was my sister. They were flying up to see Althea at her school and my brother-in-law's Cessna crashed in a fog."

"That was your sister who loved her boarding school in Virginia?"

"You remembered that. Yes, I had only the one sibling. When Althea was in her late teens she hit some turbulence. She blamed herself for her parents' death because they had been coming to see *her*—but we got her through that, Mother and I. But then as soon as she turned twenty-one, she eloped with a deep-dyed scoundrel who had been waiting in the wings. After he'd run through her money, he decamped and left her with all his debts and a broken heart."

"Did she have any children?" I wondered whether Althea's story would meet Aunt Charlotte's standards for a shrink-wrapped tale of family woe.

"One daughter. Unfortunately their temperaments clash. But Althea adores her little granddaughter, who I'm afraid was that child at the library who accused you of being a spy."

We went to the art supply store because Lachicotte wanted to buy Althea a paint set. "When we were finger-painting with the kids while you were busy at the fiche machine, my niece said to me, 'You know, Uncle Buddy, I haven't had so much fun in years. Isn't it a shame that grown-ups forget how to play?'"

While Lachicotte consulted with the saleslady about what kind of paint set to buy for his niece, I wandered around inspecting the lavish displays of paints and crafts. This was the temple of Aunt Charlotte's vocation, and not only was she not here with us to inhale the smells of her art and be tempted by new brushes and pigments, but she was lying anesthetized on a table while an orthopedic surgeon cut and clamped and probed and "fixated" her painting hand. He would do his best, he told Lachicotte, but he couldn't guarantee total return of flexibility. We would just have to wait and see. There would be months of physical therapy to help, of course. The new x-rays had shown some arthritis, and we had to remember Mrs. Lee wasn't a ten-year-old skateboarder with miraculously supple bones. No, Lachicotte had told him, she's only a gifted and successful painter at the peak of her talent and her earning ability, and you are the head of wrists and hands over here, so we're counting on you to do your utmost. They knew each other, of course. Lachicotte seemed to know everybody.

There was something I needed to consult with Lachicotte about. I had been preparing how to ask it in the art store and as we were walking back to the medical center I took the plunge.

"Don't you think it would be a good idea if I went off to boarding school?"

Lachicotte came to a full stop on the sidewalk, clasping his gift-parcel to his breast. "What has given you this idea?"

"I'd be out of the way. Aunt Charlotte could have her solitude back, except for when I came home for holidays."

"Wait a minute. Help me think this through, Marcus. What would be the advantages for her?"

"She wouldn't have the burden of being my guardian nonstop."

"What makes you think it's a burden?" He commenced walking again.

"Because I'm always *there*. When people are cooped up together too long they get—"

This wasn't going so well. What was it about Lachicotte that made me choke up when I was trying to say something important? "I mean, even back with Mom, we sometimes got on each other's nerves. And Mom was out at work most of the time. But Aunt Charlotte's always in the house with me. And now she's going to be in the house more than ever."

"So you're saying if you weren't there she'd have her solitude back. How else would it be an advantage to her, not having you around?"

"I don't mean *right now*. I know I can be useful right now while she's in her casts and has a hard time, well, you know, filling her days without being able to paint. But I think . . ." Here came the choking-up danger again. "I think if I went away to school for most of the year it would be better in the long run."

"What do you mean by the long run?"

"Until I'm eighteen and don't need to have a guardian anymore. When I'm eighteen she'll be free of me. I mean, I know she gets a stipend for being my guardian and all, but I really think she'd prefer going back to her old lifestyle."

"Has it occurred to you there are ways you might be *her* guardian?"

I said it hadn't.

"Well, you might want to take a little time to consider it. However, let's look at this proposition from another angle. What would be the advantages for *you* if you went away to boarding school?"

"The main advantage is I wouldn't wear out my welcome with Aunt Charlotte. The disadvantage would be that at a boarding school they might be more curious about genealogy and that kind of thing. Whereas at the local school, they'd know who I was *now*. The thing is, I don't know much about my father's side. What I mean is, I don't know *anything*, not even who he was. Mom was going to tell me when I was old enough to understand."

We walked on in silence. Lachicotte appeared to have sunk into one of his pondering states and I had time to wonder whether my disclosure had been more than Lachicotte wanted to hear.

"You know, Marcus, I was delighted when your Aunt Charlotte discovered she could paint. It was just what was needed. Nothing better in the world could have showed up in her life at that time. And now I'll tell you something else. The day you and I met, when I came to the house that morning (*maw'nin*)—it took me only a few hours in your company to feel the same delight again. Nothing better in the world could have showed up in her life. You were just what was needed."

XIX.

*A*unt Charlotte's mood underwent a further change as she began her extended convalescence. Strangely enough, she had been more annoyed and despondent when she had believed she was facing only a matter of weeks with her arm in a soft cast and then a return to painting. Now she seemed to have entered a state of passive indifference, spending hours in a chair on the screened porch gazing out to sea, her right arm in a more serious cast resting on the chair arm, her left foot in its cast propped on a stool. I had felt more at home with her old combative self.

In this new phase she spent less time shut away in her studio/bedroom. For a while I was required to uncork fewer bottles of red wine. She was in pain after the surgery and condescended to take the Percocet the doctor had prescribed. That may have decreased her desire to drink, or maybe she was simply taking seriously the dire warnings on the bottle about mixing opioids with alcohol. She had expressed a horror of "turning into a dope fiend" and made me keep the bottle hidden in my room and dole out the pills as needed.

Lachicotte's suggestion that I was also her guardian had sunk in, and I swung between pride in this responsibility and resentment at some of the restraints it imposed.

The worst restraint was the sacrifice of my late afternoon bike ride to the north end of the island. Aunt Charlotte seemed to appreciate my company particularly in the late afternoon. Of course, I continued to go faithfully to Grief Cottage every morning, via the road or the beach, depending on the tides, while she was still asleep, but those morning visits had become sterile. There was no longer the sense that he was somewhere just behind me. He might be inside the cottage but he was no longer available to me, even as an unseen listener. I felt I was being punished for dividing my attentions. Now whenever I spoke aloud with my back to the door, I was more than ever the crazy boy talking to himself on the top step of a ruined cottage.

After I got my own card, I had biked over to the library a few times. In my saddlebags I brought home promising books that either fulfilled my hopes or didn't. I tried *The Count of Monte Cristo,* which I had started back in Jewel, but then had to return to the school library because someone else was waiting. Now even opening the book made me sad and a little queasy and I returned it on my next trip. I took out Ray Bradbury's *Fahrenheit 451* and read it straight through. Bradbury always reminded me of Wheezer, who had introduced me to him. I had hopes for a horror writer's thick omnibus of his "favorite scary stories," but found I had read many of them already.

On one trip I hauled home three art books for Aunt Charlotte. I picked a heavy book of English landscape paintings, making sure Constable was included. Mrs. Daniels, the librarian, had recommended my other choice: a slip-cased two-volume collection of Paul Klee's drawings and paintings. "Your aunt Charlotte might find him an inspiration while she's recovering. He can be playful and quite philosophical. And it has his notes about what he's doing. These volumes aren't really supposed to go out of the library, but since it's your aunt . . ." Aunt Charlotte was touched when I showed her the books. She made me lug them off to her studio. What she did with them after that, I didn't ask. It would be like asking someone if they were enjoying your gift. When it was time to return the books, she remarked how thoughtful I always was; she said Klee could be a hoot and it was nice to see all her English friends together in one book.

She was at her most sociable on our porch around the time the pelicans were flying home in their straight line from their day's fishing. She seemed to enjoy whatever I had to say.

"Well, Marcus, what do you have to report?" She would ask this while gazing at the ocean, not turning her head to look at me. This freed me to talk more easily. I remembered how, in my old life, after Mom and I had moved to the mountains and we didn't know anybody, I had wished for someone to "report to." Mom mostly came home too exhausted to make more than a dutiful inquiry into my day. Aunt Charlotte, facing out to sea as if she could accept whatever arose in my mind, was the ideal listener. Like the ghost-boy, and like Wheezer before him, she harkened to a good "true." As with them, I could feel her interest quicken when I was on the right track. She liked hearing about my first trip to the library with Lachicotte.

"I'm sorry you didn't have better luck," she said when I complained about the slim pickings on the microfiche and in the fiftieth anniversary magazine. "I know you were hoping to find something about that family, the boy in particular. I can see why he would capture your imagination."

That's when I came close to telling her about the ghost-boy. Not dangerously close, but closer than I had ever come to telling Mom about showing Wheezer the forbidden photograph and about why I beat him up the next day. I had learned during my sessions with the psychiatrist that certain experiences must be kept to myself—perhaps forever. So all I finally said to Aunt Charlotte was that it made me mad that a whole family could be wiped out of human memory as though they'd never existed. Her reply was that billions of people had suffered that fate and billions more were destined to be forgotten as though they never existed. ("That is, if we don't all destroy this planet first.") She sounded satisfied with the prospect.

The finger-painting part of the library story made her snort with laughter. She wanted to hear again how I had first thought Lachicotte had been painting a white mountain and then a white beast, and didn't know till he told me later that it had been a farewell portrait of his Bentley. Then she wanted my assessment of the niece's painting of the yellow roses. I told her she would have judged it a competent little painting, "like you said about that woman's painting of Grief Cottage that started you painting."

"Really?"

"Well, I never saw that woman's painting, but the niece's roses were something you might want to frame, or at least tape up on a wall, especially if you knew the artist. The roses in a jar had a nice—I don't know the art word for it, but the way the paint sticks up from the paper sort of imitates the way the artist painted it."

"I think you mean impasto, if it was thick. Was it thick?"

"Yeah, it stuck up in little whorls. Of course, she was pinching it up with her fingers."

"Or you could say 'brushwork.' 'Fingerwork' in this case. You describe paintings very well, Marcus."

"She told Lachicotte she hadn't enjoyed herself so much in years. She said adults forgot how to play. That's why he bought her that paint set while you were having your surgery."

"What kind of paints did he get?"

"I think he said water-based. But they weren't just kids' finger paints."

"'Water-based' covers a large choice. And they all wore gloves?"

"Those thin latex gloves. The kids had little kid-size gloves."

"I can see the advantage of gloves when you've got a roomful of pre-kindergarteners, but I would think gloves would deaden your tactile advantages. I don't know. I've never finger-painted."

DURING OUR AFTERNOON porch talks, Aunt Charlotte extracted more of my history. Some information I volunteered; other disclosures escaped as a sort of overflow. Since I had already spilled the beans to Lachicotte about my secret father, I figured I might as well admit to my only living relative that I had no idea who he was. I had been unpacking more boxes from the old apartment life. It made me increasingly sad that so many of the contents, things Mom and I had formerly liked or needed—or were even proud of—went straight into the black bags. I showed Aunt Charlotte the small photo in the silver frame that had ended my friendship with Wheezer. Like Wheezer, she turned the picture sideways and shook it.

"Could we open this frame?" she asked, making me wonder why I had never thought of this myself. She handed it over to me and as I was folding back the four metal clips that held it in place, I let myself imagine there would be a name of somebody on the back of the picture. But it turned out to be a glossy photo cut out of a book, most likely a yearbook Aunt Charlotte said, because there was a photo of another man, posed the same way, on the back.

"Well, that's that," I said angrily.

"What do you mean, 'that's that'?"

"I'll never know who my father was because there's nobody left to tell me."

"Well, he's a nice-looking man," she said. "He has your wide-apart eyes and quizzical eyebrows, and I definitely see a likeness in the set of the mouth when something annoys you."

"You know the actor Alec Guinness?"

"Not personally, but I know who he is," said Aunt Charlotte with a welcome return to her old dryness.

"His mother never told him who his father was, either. She died without telling him and he never found out. He wrote about it in his autobiography. Mom said this photo was taken before she knew my father, when he was a lot younger."

"So you did talk about him."

"Not much. She said he would have been proud of me if he had lived to know me and that I would be proud of him. But she wanted to wait until I was a little older before she said any more. The reason I have Mr. Harshaw's name is because people at the factory remembered him, though he had moved away by then. So Mom could get away with saying that they had tried for a reconciliation and it hadn't worked and I was the result. Mr. Forster, the factory owner, was one of those—what's the word for someone who owns the business but wants it to seem like everybody's just one big family?"

"Feudal? Paternalistic? I know what you mean."

"Somebody once told Mom Mr. Forster was a patriarch in socialist's clothing. I think the person meant it as a joke, but I'm not sure."

"It's a provocative remark, however it was meant."

"But Mom liked the way Forster's factory took care of its workers. They even had a free nursery so the workers could visit their babies at lunchtime. She said long before I was thought of she used to pass the nursery and think how nice it would be to have a little somebody she could pop in and see."

"Did she and Mr. Harshaw ever think of having children? They were married for a long time, weren't they?"

"She ran away with him at sixteen and they split up when she was twenty-six. So that's ten years. He was a lot older than her and had been married before. He didn't have kids in that marriage either, so maybe he couldn't. The reason he and Mom decided to separate was because he was sick of doing what he called 'fancy side work.' He wanted to go back to logs and own a sawmill. The sad thing is he did get his sawmill and was crushed by a log falling off one of his trucks. But Mom loved Forster's. When they made her supervisor of finish work there wasn't much of a raise, but she said she felt appreciated. And even when we had to leave, Mr. Forster wrote her a recommendation to a custom furniture maker he knew in the mountains and that's why we went there. But Mom only worked at that place for a short time because he went out of business and she had to start looking for other jobs."

"Did you ever tell me why you and your mother had to leave Forster's?"

"It was my fault. I beat up a boy so bad he stopped breathing and almost lost an eye. He was my best friend. He was also

Mr. Forster's grandson. His family had settled the town and pretty much ran everything. The name of the town itself was Forsterville."

"It doesn't sound like you, Marcus. Did he do something?"

"He said something really horrible and they say I went crazy."

"My word," Aunt Charlotte said, pressing her left hand flat against her heart.

"After that I had to go to a psychiatrist for some mandatory sessions and when those were over we packed up our things and drove to the mountains to start a new life."

"Well, Marcus, if you ever want to tell me more about it, I'm here. And if you don't want to, that's fine, too." She repositioned her left leg in its cast on the stool in front of her. "I'm sorry you didn't get to know who your father was before your mother died. But from the little you've told me, he sounds like someone who would have loved you and been proud of you. I did know who my father was, for all the good it did me. It turned out he was the devil incarnate."

"How would a person know that their father is the devil incarnate?"

"You wouldn't at the time. It would be later, when you were safe enough to look back. At the time all you would feel at first would be a misgiving, that something wasn't as it should be. Later on, it may grow into a full-blown sense of wrong. But it's a wrong you're part of. You can't do anything about it because you're a child and you have no way to compare your life to other people's lives. Your foremost need is to stay safe within the only life you know."

The only specific past history she had offered in our porch talks were some caustic anecdotes about her no-good husbands and more information about her former jobs. She and my mom would have had so much to talk about. Aunt Charlotte had stocked shelves at a Home Depot ("I loved riding around on the forklift cart"), mixed drinks in a bar, seated people at a Howard Johnson's restaurant, been secretary to a funeral home director ("I also did the makeup on the stiffs, undercover, of course") and a "Jill of all trades"—house cleaning, yard work, care-taking, and pet sitting—her third husband serving as the titular and mostly useless "Jack" of their short-lived enterprise. ("We lived from hand to mouth, most of the time.")

"Where did you get the money to buy this house, if it isn't rude to ask?"

"I won a lottery. No, I did, really. Actually I won two lotteries. Every week I bought one of those cheap scratch-off tickets. Without fail, every week, tongue in cheek. The first time I won thirty-five dollars. The second time I won ten thou-sand. Just enough to get out of West Virginia and buy a beach shack in South Carolina."

"What about your husband? Didn't he want his share?"

"Luckily, we were divorced by then, or he would have wanted it all. At the time of my lottery windfall I was bartending at night and I was still in a state of ecstasy to be free at last. You have no idea."

"So that was the beginning of your solitary life?"

"Yes, I guess it was. You're good company, Marcus. You listen and put things together."

XX.

While being good company for my aunt, I was also thinking about the ghost-boy who waited for me at Grief Cottage. Did he feel slighted that I had cut down my daily visits to the single morning ones? Did he wonder what he had done wrong, or was I pushing my human tendencies onto him? In my afternoon talks with Aunt Charlotte, I felt disloyal about neglecting him. Or maybe I should start thinking of him as the ghost-*man*. After all, Lachicotte's niece's little grand-daughter had mistaken me for a man. ("Who is that man *spying* on us?")

But stop, I would warn myself: What sane person would be equating one's loyalty to a great-aunt with one's loyalty to a ghost? What, after all, was the figure I had seen once in a dazzle of afternoon light? How could I consider it a relationship when the person I thought I saw had been dead fifty years? The truth was, I felt love for him the way someone feels love for another living person.

I went back and tried to track the whole thing from the beginning, as you would trace on a map a route taken. When had it started, our strange relationship? Well, with Aunt

Charlotte's story about Grief Cottage—the history of the place itself—and, following that, the story about what that derelict cottage meant to her, what it stood for, when she walked up there in her first days of freedom on the island. It had reminded her of the debris in her past, but then also it had started her painting.

Having heard her say it had a haunting quality and a powerful mood, my first view of the actual thing had been a letdown: what an eyesore, the sooner it's leveled the better. And then I had crawled under the wire fence and eaten my lunch on the porch and fallen asleep and dreamed that the sunburnt man was standing in the broken doorway behind me, watching over me while I slept. And then I woke up and was scared to turn around and face the doorway. I sensed something watching me from behind and I felt its motives were not as friendly or protective as the sunburnt man's had been. But then, *what were they?* And I had caved and fled.

And then the rains had come and I'd read the two ladies' books and felt anger on the part of the boy. He and I had things in common, except that he was dead and couldn't stand up for his rights, or even how truly or falsely people remembered him. And then Aunt Charlotte finished her big McMansion painting for the Steckworths, and later that afternoon I had walked to Grief Cottage and actually seen him. And that same night, I lay in the hammock and watched the moon rise and concentrated on sending my spirit north. And then, without my ever leaving the hammock, there was the embrace and the rapture. From that point on, I couldn't account for it in literal or sane terms. We were connected: he was always with me.

I used to cringe with embarrassment when the foster mother talked about how Jesus followed her around the house, always a few steps behind her, just out of her line of sight. He is always with me, even in my most private places, she told us. I had imagined what private places she meant and cringed some more. But how was my connection with the ghost-boy any less embarrassing than hers with Jesus?

Sometimes I resurrected the psychiatrist back in Forsterville who had grilled me so patiently and professionally about what my feelings were while beating up my friend. I imagined sitting down in his office once again and explaining to him, this time without holding anything back, my relationship with the ghost-boy. What questions would the psychiatrist have asked? What diagnosis would he have given? So far this exercise had not been very fruitful. I could hear the psychiatrist asking the first thing Wheezer would have asked: was I absolutely sure what I saw wasn't just a trick of the light? Then he might ask me to describe the onset of the fascination, what had triggered it, how long had it been going on? He would end up prescribing medication, "just for a while, to see how it goes."

At the end of our final session, the psychiatrist in Forsterville had given Mom a prescription for me—"If needed"—but after we left his office she said, "I don't think we need to cash this in, do you, Marcus?" and she had torn it up and thrown the pieces into a trash can on the sidewalk. "Let's make a completely fresh start in this place where we're going," she had added, with forced courage in her voice.

Unlike Aunt Charlotte, Mom never said it was "up to me" whether or not I wanted to reveal what Wheezer had said to make me fly at him. I had told Mom that Wheezer had said something about the way we lived. And I told her this only after we left Forsterville. I never told the psychiatrist even that much, because I knew he would pass it on to her.

Naturally I never explained to Mom why Wheezer left our apartment. That would have meant admitting I had gone into the tin box and showed the secret photo to someone else. After she came back with the pizza for our lunch, when I told her he had felt an asthma attack coming on and had bicycled home, she had said, "Oh dear, I hope it wasn't something in our apartment that set it off."

But right up until the night she died, she would wait for moments when we were close and then tilt her head wistfully and spring it on me afresh: "I wish you'd *tell* me what he said about how we lived, Marcus. After all, I am your mother. Whatever it was, it might not be as bad as you think."

Oh yes it was.

★ ★ ★

THE FOURTH OF July came and went, much to the relief of the island's Turtle Patrol, whose members had set up NO FIREWORKS! zones up and down the entire length of the beach and had taken turns, in twos and threes, guarding the nest sites of the logger-head babies, due to hatch soon and make their live-or-die dash for the sea. I had made friends with the retiree on the Turtle Patrol. After he became aware of how often I checked the site below Aunt Charlotte's boardwalk, he gave me his beeper number on a laminated card so I could call him from our cottage, whatever the hour, if I spotted any threat or change in the protected dune. ("I always carry my beeper, when I'm out on the beach or working on my jeep in the garage.") This was his beloved wartime 1944 Wilys Jeep, with its original camou-flage paint, which he drove up and down the beach to check on the nests. He also lent me one of the patrol's infrared flashlights.

Soon we would be in countdown mode, he said, and proceeded to explain ways we would be able to tell when the hatchlings were going to crawl up through the sand and "boil out" of their nest, usually a few hours after sunset. ("Last year we rigged up a microphone and amplifier and installed it next to the site. We'll do it again this year when we get close to hatching time. You can actually hear the hatchlings as they crawl up through the sand. It's a rattling sound, like pebbles being thrown against a metal roof. The first time I heard the amplified sound of those little fellows I had to wipe away tears, it was so affecting.") His name was Ed Bolton, a retired high school science teacher from Columbia. He'd lost his son, a helicopter medic, in the Viet Nam war. After he retired, he and his wife moved full-time to their beach cottage. "It's one of the real oldies, with the brick footing columns and the tongue-in-groove joints. But we've modernized it a lot, of course."

He knew the story of Grief Cottage, though Hurricane Hazel was long past before he and his family started coming here. He belonged to the faction of locals who wished it had been leveled decades ago. ("It's one more disaster waiting to happen.")

I had not gone to Grief Cottage on the Fourth, which fell on a Sunday that year. All day long the beach had been thick with tourists, and I knew from Mr. Bolton that the north tip of the island was a traditional spot for serious firework displays, with preparations starting early in the day. With so many people milling around, I would surely be seen defying the CONDEMNED and KEEP OUT signs as I crawled under the wire fence. I might become the agent of immediate demolition. ("If that boy is crawling under that fence with us watching, isn't it time we get moving on the safety measures and level that thing to the ground?") I tried to imagine how the ghost-boy marked such occasions. Did he enjoy watching the spectacle, or did he hide out from the noise in some safe corner?

But here I was crossing a line again. Hadn't I reached the limits of imagining what he could do without me? By now I had more or less accepted that we worked in tandem: to a great extent he was dependent on my awareness of him. Since ghosts didn't have living brains, the work must be done by the living person. The living person had to offer his brain as the dwelling place for the ghost. Once again I reminded myself how imperative it was to my mental health to keep the different levels of reality separate.

I did not go to Grief Cottage on Monday because it rained in the morning and in the afternoon Aunt Charlotte decided to rearrange her studio and asked for my help. She wanted to take down the items pinned on her wall-high cork board and then completely clear her two trestle tables and move them to the middle of the room. "I'm going to try some experiments while sitting down." When I asked her about the experiments, she said she didn't want to talk about it. ("In case I fail. So you'll just have to contain your overdeveloped curiosity, Marcus.") She allowed me to dust and vacuum and change her sheets, as I had been doing since her fall. She also talked me through changing a washer on the big laundry sink in her studio, which she used for cleaning up after a day's painting. But after praising my work, she announced in a cordial but no-nonsense voice that I was to stay out of her studio until she invited me in again.

"Maybe I'll finish off my boxes from the garage," I said, anxious to remain in her good graces. The "overdeveloped curiosity" remark was not exactly a compliment. "I need to rearrange my room, as well."

"That's a good plan," she said.

The next box I tackled contained our "linens" on the top, towels and sheets so worn that they went straight into the black trash bag. Underneath those I found Mom's old GED Practice Test Manuals. I started leafing through them, testing myself on various questions, until I became sucked down into not-so-happy memories of our last years together, things I hadn't thought of since coming to live with Aunt Charlotte. I heard conversations between me and Mom that made me wince with shame, and I recalled humiliating instances of our "down-sizing," as Mom jokingly referred to it, with forced courage in her voice.

After she lost her job when the joinery in Jewel went out of business, she returned with a vengeance to her GED hopes. ("It's now or never, Marcus. You must support me in this, *make* me do it even when I'm tired.") Many were the nights I quizzed her out of these practice manuals while she lay on the floor, her legs up against the wall to reduce the swelling in her ankles. First the test-taker had to read a passage "for comprehension" and then pick the right answer from the multiple choice questions below. ("Who were in attendance at Oliver Twist's birth? A. grandmothers, B. doctors, C. nurses, D. a slightly drunk woman and a parish surgeon.") "That was too easy," Mom had said from the floor, "almost insulting." And I had agreed with her: Any moron who had read the passage would know it was D. The way we did it, she would first read the passages to herself silently in a particular area of testing—literacy, math, social studies, science—hiding the questions and answers with a piece of paper. And then she'd lie on the floor with her legs up while I quizzed her. ("Unemployment now has less severe effects than it did in the 1930s. Why?") When she got an answer wrong she would ask me to put a checkmark by the right answer so she could come back and review it. ("I should have known that! 'No countervailing social programs!' With the many social programs that keep you and me afloat, how could I have missed that one?")

From her preoccupied air at supper I sensed that Aunt Charlotte had begun the experiment that was to keep me out of her studio. But now, having discovered the GED practice manuals, I was caught up in my own private quest. The manuals had been given to Mom by the teacher of her first night course back in Forsterville. They were used, but he knew she couldn't afford to buy new ones. ("He was a wonderful teacher, devoted to us. He had been teaching Latin and Greek at a nearby private school until he got fed up and quit. He said his heart would always be with the strugglers rather than the already-haves. But then he got sick and died."

"What of?"

"He didn't take care of himself. He fell into destructive habits and there was no one to guide him out of them. It was such a sad waste. Later the class was moved to another location, to suit the convenience of the next teacher—otherwise she wouldn't come. I kept going for a while, though it was a forty-five-minute commute each way. But the new teacher, you could tell *her* heart wasn't in it. She did it for the extra income. She despised us. She was one of those people who fight their way up the ladder and then have contempt for others trying to follow her. Finally I lost faith and decided to leave well enough alone. I had my good job with full benefits at Forster's. And then you came along. What more did I need?")

XXI.

I stayed up late into Monday night, obsessed with Mom's GED practice tests. I would close my eyes, stab at one of the four manuals, open it to a random page, and test myself on the first question that swam up. In a free market what are some of the ways in which prices can be fixed? What distinguishes the skeleton of a pterosaur from that of a bird? What conflicting impulses can be seen in the democratic ethic? (Correct answer: duty to self vs. duty to society.) When I got one wrong, I would pencil my initials beside the right one. As the night wore on, I entered a manic state. It seemed totally possible that I could pass these tests *now*. Though I always got A's in math at school, the math part of the GED tests would bring down my total score because I hadn't studied geometry or advanced algebra yet. But if I aced the other parts I could balance out the low math score. If I put my mind to it, I might attain high school equivalency without ever going to high school! I could head straight off to college and Aunt Charlotte would have her privacy back and look forward to seeing me on the holidays. She would be proud of me and might even miss me.

When I woke up next morning, it was much later than usual: I could tell from the position of the sun hitting the front of the house. Long gone were the hours of the capering unleashed dogs and the stalwart seniors with their sleeves and sunhats. I lay hating myself for missing my favorite part of the morning, but also struggling to remember the dream I had waked out of. I heard Aunt Charlotte in the kitchen, foraging in the refrigerator, then hopping back to her studio and firmly closing the door (*Keep out until further notice. This means you, Marcus*). I made my bed as soon as I got out of it, a habit begun long ago to save Mom the trouble and to keep our small space looking neat. Now I did it so Aunt Charlotte wouldn't think I was a slob if she decided to take a peek into my—her former—room. Dressing quickly, I wolfed a handful of cereal in the kitchen, swigging it down with milk.

Riding north past the third or fourth yellow trash barrel, I remembered my dream. The whole thing came back in a single whump, like a fist to the stomach. Finally I had dreamed about my mother. It was the first dream in which she was facing me. This was Mom at her best, smiling and opening the door to me. Inside was an apartment better than the ones we'd lived in. It was spacious and filled with light and everything in it was clean and new. My mom looked clean and new, too. She looked refreshed and young, freed of burdens.

"Marcus, I never told you this," she said excitedly, "but I have another son. He's your half brother."

"Was Mr. Harshaw his father?"

"I don't think that's important, do you?"

"Is he older or younger?"

"Older. Oh, Marcus, he's the most wonderful man. He's going to take care of me now. I wish you could meet him, but he's sleeping. He works so hard."

"Is he—in your room?"

"Goodness, no, why should he be in there? He's got his own room."

HOW DENSE PEOPLE are when they reassure you it was "only" a dream. Never in my waking life had I felt such wretchedness as when my refreshed, excited mother, surrounded by the security provided by another, informed me she had a better son sleeping in his own room. In the dream I experienced the castoff's full horror of realizing he has been supplanted and is no longer the main object of someone's love. And then the frantic disbelief ("It's not true, it's not final, I can still win her back!") followed by an agony of hopelessness and the wish to die.

That night last September in Jewel when Mom arrived home triumphant over the life insurance policy she had just bought in honor of my eleventh birthday ("It's twenty-four dollars a month, but now I know you'll be okay whatever happens"), what was my unsporting reply? "Too bad kids can't take out life insurance. If I died first, you could stop cleaning bathrooms."

And then in the winter—which was to be our last together—when she was working day shift at the new Waffle House near the interstate and cleaning the County Housing Authority offices at night, she had prophesied with her forced cheer: "Things are going to get better from now on, Marcus, I feel it." And what was my smartass comeback? "That must mean we've finally hit bottom and there's nowhere to go but up."

Our first year in Jewel while Mom still had her nice job oiling and lacquering furniture at Mountaintop Joinery before it closed, she came home one night in a kind of ecstasy. "Oh,

Marcus, I wish you could have heard the song they just played on the radio. I was so moved I had to stay in the car till it was over. Do you remember Captain Kirk?" (How could I *not* remember Captain Kirk? Wheezer had made me a present of the entire set of the original *Star Trek*. He had got it on eBay for VCRs because that was all Mom and I had.) "Well, he's made a new album under his own name, William Shatner. It's called *Has Been*, and there's this heart-stopping song called 'It Hasn't Happened Yet.' I got chills all over, because he was expressing exactly what I was feeling. *It Hasn't Happened Yet!* He *speaks* the song in his rumbly Captain Kirk voice against this background of haunting music." Deepening her own voice, she chanted snatches from the song: *dreaming of success . . . I would be the best . . . what I might have done . . . falling, falling . . . I'm scared again.*

"Isn't it wonderful what art can do, Marcus? It was so sad, I saw my life in every line, but at the same time it made me feel part of the human family—it made me feel so *alive*."

Later, as things got progressively worse in Jewel, I would resort to those phrases as a teasing form of recrimination. Every time Mom came home and broke the news of another "downsizing" in our lives I would deepen my voice to a Captain Kirk rumble and chant: *falling, falling . . . I'm scared again.* Or: *It hasn't happened yet.* She always laughed, but I could tell it hurt her.

PEDALING FASTER TO get ahead of the rising midmorning tide, I was already talking to the ghost-boy, filling him in on everything that had happened since the last time I was there. ("No wonder she had to go and find herself a better son. Here's what worries me, though. What if—however bad a son I was—I loved her *as much as I am ever capable of loving anyone*? Did you ever feel like this? Did you love any special person when you were alive? Did you ever worry that you weren't capable of loving enough? But it's all over for you. Your life is a complete thing. I envy that. Is it worth it to go on living, knowing I let my mom down and dreading the new school and worrying how long it will be until Aunt Charlotte tires of my company and gets rid of me? Why not save her the guilt she'd feel after she kicked me out? And, I mean, what's the point of 'climbing the ladder' when you know you'll never fit in with the already-haves at the top? Did you think things like this when you were alive?")

A temptation presented itself. Then it morphed into a dare and then into a compulsion, something I knew I had no choice about doing. Today would be the perfect day for me to go up on the porch of Grief Cottage and sit down *facing the door.*

If you have reached the point of wishing your life was completed but knowing you haven't got the guts to complete it yourself, wouldn't the next-best thing be to seek out something that might do the job for you? Today I would face the door of the cottage and stay facing it, inviting annihilation. Surely I wouldn't be the first person to die from fright.

But my plan was aborted when I rounded the last curve of beach and saw the group gathered around Grief Cottage. Charlie Coggins, the realtor, was with two men wearing some kind of summery uniform with shorts. Coggins's weird-looking amphibious vehicle that Lachicotte had helped him assemble was parked next to a white truck bearing an insignia. The men in shorts were looking through instruments on top of tripods, while Mr. Coggins hovered near them. I could either conceal myself behind some dunes and wait them out, or go home before high tide forced me to return by the road. The mood was all wrong now. It would be better to come back tomorrow at my early hour and have the place to myself.

ED BOLTON'S JEEP with its wartime camouflage was parked in front of our dunes when I got back to Aunt Charlotte's house, and there he was in his squashed sun hat crouched reverentially beside our loggerhead site.

"Just checking," he said, knees cracking as he rose to greet me. "All that rain we had yesterday could make a difference to our countdown. Where are you coming from?"

I told him I liked to ride to the north end of the island every morning to sort out my thoughts. "But I got a late start today, and people were already poking around Grief Cottage. There was this realtor I know, Mr. Coggins, and two other men with tripods, measuring things. They were wearing some kind of uniform with shorts and they had instruments on tripods."

"Dark shorts, gray shirts, and blue caps?"

"How did you know?"

"Army Corps of Engineers. Coggins knows he's never going to get rid of that real estate until the erosion experts have weighed in."

"But there was a man from Chicago who seemed interested."

"He pulled out. Nobody wants to start building a beachside inn and have it falling into the ocean before it's finished."

"How do you know all these things?"

"Everybody knows everybody's business here. Our cottage is only four doors south of Grief Cottage, so naturally we keep our antennae on the alert. What's probably going to happen, the Army Corps will do their deformation survey and recommend we invest in geotube bladders. They're expensive as hell, so all us owners at the north end will have to vote on it in a referendum. Coggins will be stuck with those lots unless someone's foolish enough to buy with no guarantee of future shoreline protection."

"What are geotube bladders?"

"They're like great big culverts made of special textiles and buried beneath the high tide line. They're filled with a sand-and-water mixture and can usually block immense waves caused by hurricanes. Note I said *usually*, not always."

"How will the rain change our countdown?"

"It will have cooled the sand. The embryos prefer warmth at this stage of the game. That's why we always detect a rapid rise in temperature with our little thermocouple gizmos when hatching time is imminent. Yesterday's rain may set it back a few days. What's the matter? You look troubled."

"I just wish I knew more about how things worked in the world. The way you do."

"Give yourself a break, son. If you keep on asking questions at your present rate, you'll be a downright sage before you reach thirty."

XXII.

*C*leanup was in full force at the house next door. A team of guys shaped hedges, whacked weeds, mowed and raked the sparse patches of grass on the sandy lawn, hosed down stairs and walkways. One was down on his knees, hand-clipping the overgrown path that led to the beach. Another was planting a last-minute border of hardy annuals. From inside the house came the high-pitched whine of several vacuums going at once.

"That's the life, isn't it, Marcus? You're ninety-five in a wheelchair and won't be going anywhere near the beach but you maintain a full retinue to prink up your paths and grounds and boardwalk so everything will look the same as it did seventy-five years ago."

"Seventy-five years ago?"

"She came to her husband's ancestral beach cottage as a bride of twenty. Ninety-five minus twenty is seventy-five. Lachicotte can furnish you with all the specifics, they're buddies. Could you phone him and tell him she's on her way? He'll want to bake her a pie."

"An oyster pie?"

"No, she hates oysters. Steak and kidney, probably, without the kidneys."

"Will she be coming today?"

"Tomorrow. Her retinue precedes her. As soon as she arrives, she sends her caregiver over with a calling card to let us know she's receiving visitors. The card used to be on a silver salver but now it arrives on a sweet-grass tray made by Roberta Dumas, the current caregiver."

"Will you visit her?"

"She knows my ways. She understands. She respects artists. Roberta herself comes from a dynasty of basket weavers who have examples of their work in the Smithsonian. Where have you been? Let me guess."

"Mr. Coggins was up there with the Army Corps of Engineers."

"What were they doing?"

"I didn't talk to them. But Mr. Bolton from the Turtle Patrol says they're measuring erosion around the cottage. I met him down by the egg clutch."

"How are our little friends?"

"He says yesterday's rain may delay their hatching."

"I've been on this island for twenty-five years and never seen a hatching. What's the term they use? 'Boil up'?"

"Want me to knock on your door?"

"Well . . . why not?"

"Even if it's late?"

"Sure. If I'm feeling up to it, maybe I'll hop down and see it for myself. After all, they have incubated under *our* boardwalk."

I called Lachicotte, who sounded glad to hear from us. "I'd call more often, but I don't want to be a bother (*bah-thah*)." We

made plans to go over to Mrs. Upchurch's early the next afternoon. "You'll appreciate her. She's quite the raconteur. Will
you tell your aunt I have taken the liberty of tuning up her
Mercedes and replacing the tires? It's my little thank-you for
the extended loan."

AFTER SUPPER WITH Aunt Charlotte, I walked down to the
surf and stood on the shiny wet surface mirroring the same
orange light of her big *Sunset Calm* painting that now hung in
the library—and had once been taped as a postcard on Mom's
refrigerator. I was thinking how awful it must be to have
painting taken away from you. It could happen in all sorts of
ways. You could hurt your painting arm, or some fascist regime
could come in and forbid you to paint. At supper Aunt Charlotte
had been telling me about this German painter, Emil Nolde,
who was forbidden by the Nazis to paint anymore when he was
seventy years old and at his peak. For the duration of World
War II, he painted small secret watercolors on Japan paper,
which he hid in his house.

"What is Japan paper?"

"Well, it's not necessarily made in Japan anymore, but it's a
high quality paper made from bark fibers rather than wood
pulp. It's tougher. If you have to paint with water like poor
Nolde, you can build up layers, like in oil. He wrote notes to
the secret paintings."

"What kind of notes?"

"Things like 'Only to you, my little sheets.' That's the one I
like best."

He couldn't paint in oils because he couldn't be seen buying
any, and also if they raided his house they would detect the

smell. During this period of artistic oppression, he abandoned the landscapes that had made him famous and made little watercolors of dreamlike figures and faces on his Japan paper. He called them his "unpainted pictures," and Aunt Charlotte turned on her laptop while we were still eating and showed me the vividly-colored little paintings of surreal or grotesque people, some in lewd and threatening poses, that seemed to have come straight out of his dark regions. I told Aunt Charlotte they made me think of the fiends and fantasies a person had inside of him that maybe he didn't even know he had. "That's very astute, Marcus," she said, sipping her wine. Her face bunched up as it tended to do when she was trying to figure something out. Having impressed her by saying this, I was about to ask how her secret project was coming, but decided to stop while I was ahead. Soon after, she asked me to uncork another bottle and hopped off with it to her studio.

Making patterns in the wet sand with my sneaker, I recalled my extravagant despair of this morning when I had hoped to be scared to death by the ghost-boy. How could a person's moods change so many times in a day? Was it my age, or was it going to be like this from now on? What if a person decided to kill himself in the morning and then woke up dead and realized he had made a huge mistake? Now here I was, the same person in the same body, the same clothes, even, standing in the placid orange light of Aunt Charlotte's *Sunset Calm* and feeling excited about those little turtle embryos under the sand who, if they survived all the intermittent dangers, had eighty to a hundred or more years to go before they could die an old turtle's death and become part of loggerhead ancestral history. Soon they would be bursting out of their shells, flattening out into proper turtle shapes, clambering on top of one another to "boil up" for their dash to the sea—which we would be part of.

For some reason this led to thoughts of William, my ad litem friend, and of our final Vulcan salute to each other at the airport. I wondered what kind of minors he was guarding now and if he ever missed me.

How lucky I was to be assigned to a person who would understand that I needed to see my mother's body *before* it was embalmed so I could truly accept that she was dead. We drove to the hospital in his truck. He had arranged everything with the head of ER, who took us down in the elevator to the hospital morgue. The ER person unzipped the black body bag on the gurney. There she was. It was her and not her. I had been told what to expect. The bone and cartilage of her nose was exposed where it had hit the steering wheel—our Honda was from the pre-air-bag era. Her eyes were open, but the life had drained out of them. The blue irises were now a lusterless yellow-green. Her mouth was ajar, exposing the tooth gaps she was so self-conscious about. She had hennaed her hair recently; it was at its glossiest mahogany-brown. ("At least I didn't die with my roots showing." I heard her exact living voice with its equal mix of self-put-down and resolute humor.)

William and I had gone over burial plans during our drive to the hospital. As an adolescent Mom had read a novel by a famous occultist who had warned against cremation, the reason being that you had to stay in one piece so you could be brought up whole out of your grave. "You might need your bones," Mom said. "It may be superstition, but you find it all the way back in the Book of Ezekiel, so I'd rather not take chances." When we still lived in Forsterville, Mom and I often talked about death and where we would like to be buried. We took walks in a beautiful little cemetery a short way out of town. "If we're still here when I die," Mom said, "I'd like to be buried in this place." But after we moved to Jewel, we stopped romanticizing about graves and cemeteries because we weren't sure how long we'd be staying in Jewel, especially after Mountaintop Joinery closed down and Mom lost her good job.

William took me to the little country cemetery where most of his family had their graves. It was on a hill overlooking mountain ranges stretching as far into the distance as you could see. When the life insurance trust was set up, he said, you'll be able to buy a nice stone with her name and dates. "So wherever you go, Marcus, you'll know you can always come back and find her in the same place."

XXIII.

With the approach of bedtime came the start of a bad feeling. Usually I looked forward to shutting the door to my room, Aunt Charlotte's former room, knowing that nothing more would be required of me until the next day. For at least eight hours I didn't have to be astute or useful or empathetic. I could just fall back on my pillows with childish irresponsibility until I fell asleep.

But this was a new fear that kept me from wanting to fall asleep. It was stronger than my top supernatural fear (could I survive an extended face-off with the ghost-boy without going crazy?) and it was stronger than my top realistic fear (could I survive being sent away by Aunt Charlotte and starting over in another foster home?).

The new fear was that tonight, as soon as I fell asleep, I would dream a continuation of last night's dream. I would be standing in the open doorway of my mom's beautiful apartment and she would have just told me about my wonderful half brother in his own room, and then I would look beyond her and see a door in the rear of the apartment slowly opening. I did not believe I could endure seeing him face-to-face.

To put off going to bed, I made two after-dark trips to the beach. On the first trip, I paced around the dune protecting our egg clutch. I got down on all fours and sniffed. No fresh earthy smell. I shone my infra-red flashlight on the thermo-couple stuck in the sand: no rise in temperature. On the second trip, I sat down cross-legged on the dune and talked to them in the same spirit that Mom would talk to me at night when she was not too tired. She told stories about when I was an infant. ("We used to look into each other's faces. I never tired of looking at you and seeing you look back. You were so new, you didn't have words yet, but I could see your thoughts and moods play across your face.") Or she made up stories about our future prospects, how we were going to prevail.

So I spoke to the turtle embryos about their present secure state of egginess and about their future great voyage. ("It's been programmed into you, so don't worry, your ancestors have been doing it for over a hundred million years. You'll just get out of your egg—rip the shell with your 'egg tooth,' which is that hard little projection on top of your snout—and take care not to get exhausted as you're climbing up because you'll need all your energies for later. It will only be about a twenty-inch climb, and you'll have all your brothers and sisters to step on, as they will step on you in turn, and the whole pile of you will rise like a slow elevator, an elevator made out of yourselves, and then you'll pop your heads through the sand, and we will have scooped out a path through the sand to the ocean. Just follow the path and don't get diverted and crawl up the sides—but if you do, a human hand will be right there to gently guide you back into the groove. It will take you about fifteen minutes to crawl from nest to water, moving at about ten feet a minute. We will escort you the whole way to the water to guard you from the ghost crabs. The reason we can't pick you up and carry you is because you need to do the walk yourselves so you can smell the sand and remember your way back to this beach when you're grown up.")

I did eventually sleep, but woke early into the weird no-light that precedes morning. My first thought was: *I escaped the continuation of the brother-dream.* Then I lay very still to grab onto another dream that was fading away—not a nightmare, not even what you'd call a bad dream, because there were some parts of it I wanted to keep. I salvaged as much as I could, and then quickly made my bed, dressed, snatched some stand-up breakfast, and headed north on my bike. The sky had not yet separated itself from the flat gray of the ocean. I had never been out this early. The empty beach contained not a single living creature.

"It's like a video game," Wheezer had explained to me in the dream I'd tried to hold on to. "But what you need to remember, Marcus, is we're *inside* the screen. Someone else is at the controls." What we had to do, he said, was avoid the "powder-colors." When the game was switched on, whoever was playing on the outside would try to shoot colored powders at us through little holes. Already we could see those powder-colors amassing and waiting to be sent forth from their chamber: thick crusty reds and blues and yellows, like those primitive colors in the un-paintings by the German artist my aunt had showed me on her laptop. If we wanted to stay alive, Wheezer said, we had to keep alert. When the powders hit us, we needed to wipe them off fast. "What happens if some powder gets stuck on us?" I asked. "If *too much* gets stuck on you," he warned in his hoarse little asthma voice, "the colors will *paste you over* and you'll be trapped inside the screen forever." Even though the dream had its scary aspects, it had been nice to be with Wheezer again.

The wind hissed past my ears as I sped north without my helmet, which I kept fastened to the back of my seat. The old people never bothered with helmets on their early morning bike rides. I was anxious to stay within this eerie zone, no longer night but not yet day, until I reached the cottage. It was like the beach was under a spell. The tenuous light through which I rode seemed to wrap itself around me and push me forward to meet whatever I had to meet.

Looking back on that morning, as I have so many times, I calculate that the ten or twelve minutes it would have taken me, pedaling at top speed, to reach Grief Cottage would have given an ordinary summer dawn more than enough time to break through. But as I felt it then, the penumbra stuck to me all the way to the cottage like a faithful cloud cover. It lasted through my dismounting and hiding my bike between two dunes, and it hung above me as I crawled through the sand beneath the wire fence with its warning signs. It was as if time and light and sound had conspired to hold themselves back so that I could receive the full impact of what I saw.

He stood there in the doorway on his own terms, not mine. I reeled with the vividness of him. He was stronger and sharper in substance, and, unlike our last encounter, he didn't slouch or seem to wait passively to see what I might do next. The tense way he braced himself against the door frame, pushing himself outward with both hands (I saw the prominent knuckle ridges between the spread fingers), was that of a figure ready to spring after having been kept trapped for too long.

I saw the long narrow face with indented cheeks, the small raisin-dark eyes lodged deep in their sockets, the pale stalk-like neck, an off-kilter nose that looked as though it had been broken and not properly reset; I saw the wide mouth and the thin lips, and the gangly, slightly bowed legs in jeans, and the black ankle boots. The faded red shirt I had seen before, but this time buttons were left open, exposing the articulated chest of a man.

It felt like turning a corner in a corridor at school and suddenly coming face-to-face with an older boy. He's just there, this totally other being; you're right smack in the center of his attention, and you have no idea where this is going.

Whether daylight had by this time edged out the gloom I don't know, but I remember being thankful for a couple of observations that presented themselves like solid posts of realism for me to clutch onto, as he looked ready to burst out of his door frame. The first thought came in the form of a calculation: If you measured by *an unbroken stretch of time,* he had been in this place longer than all the previous dwellers put together since 1804. The second observation, seeing those knuckly hands braced against the door frame, was a practical question, the kind Charlie Coggins might ask: Why had nobody bothered to replace the door or at least board over the space to slow down the decay? Maybe it was these infusions of practicality that kept me standing there for as long as I did. Was it long enough for me to gauge that I had reached the toleration point of what I could sanely handle? Or had my primal brain propelled me into flight without giving me the luxury of thought?

On this occasion I hadn't even gotten as far as climbing the rotting stairs to the porch. All I knew was that one moment I stood below him in the sand, transfixed by our mutual gaze, and the next thing I knew I was standing far from the cottage, my face turned toward the ocean. The first sound to come back

to me was the thud of my heart racing inside my chest. Then
the sound of surf and birds followed, and daytime was definitely
in control. I knew that if I turned around now all I would see
would be a falling-down cottage and a gaping doorway.

At some point I realized I wasn't by myself at the ocean's
edge. Not far away there was a woman holding a golden
retriever on a short leash. Both of them stood still as statues
facing the breaking waves, as though they were competing to
see which could outlast the other in utter stillness. The dog
wore a dark green vest with a number and an insignia. The
woman was about my mom's age and had her small upright
build and coloring. Only this woman had the means to take
care of herself. Mom would often comment on the ways you
could spot this when she saw a certain kind of woman in a store.
"That's a very expensive look," she would remark about the
woman's hair. "It looks like casual sun streaks, but it's actually a
three-color process."

Suddenly the retriever lunged at an incoming wave and the
woman tightened the leash and murmured something. The dog
sat down and was perfectly still again. This happened several
times. It seemed cruel to bring a dog to the edge of the ocean
and then not let him play in the surf. The longer I watched this
tug of wills between them, the more indignant I became.

Both woman and dog watched me approach. The woman's
look was questioning but not unfriendly. It was as though she
already knew what I was going to ask.

"Why can't he go in?"

"It wouldn't be a good idea. He's in training to be a service
dog. Normally, Barrett is the calmest dog you can imagine,
but when we brought him here, he got excited as soon as
he heard the sound of the ocean, and when he saw the surf he

went wild." She had a Lachicotte-type accent, though not as pronounced.

"Is he for a blind person?"

"No, he'll go to a disabled vet. It's a new program. Prisoners at the Navy brig in Charleston train the dogs. My husband and I are volunteers. We take one dog at a time during weekends and holidays and get him accustomed to new experiences. Distractions and unexpected sounds. This afternoon, my husband is taking Barrett to a firing range, and after that to a children's playground."

"Who named him Barrett?"

"They name them at the brig. Each dog is given the last name of a fallen person in uniform. That's a nice idea, don't you think?"

"Do you know who Barrett will go to?"

"Not yet. That gets decided in his final weeks of training. There's a long waiting list and it gets longer and longer. It's such a strange, awful war over there in Iraq. I never knew there were so many ways a person could get wounded and still be alive."

"Maybe the wounded vet who gets him will live by the ocean and they can go on walks and Barrett can splash a little in the waves."

"That's a sweet thought. Well, Barrett, that's enough beach time for us. It's been nice talking with you. You take care, now."

I PUT ON my helmet for the ride home. The seniors and early exercisers were trickling down to the beach, some unleashed dogs racing back and forth between surf and owner, then bolting off to chase and smell other dogs, activities that would never be part of Barrett's life. And yet he would be loved and needed. He would have a fabulous dog bed in a permanent home. He would feel, in whatever manner dogs felt things, indispensable to his veteran.

My cowardly bolt from the boy disappointed me. I'd had my chance and blown it. This was the fullest he'd ever shown himself, and I hadn't been able to endure it.

What I was sure of was *that I had seen*. I was also sure that I couldn't tell anyone. What I was *not* sure of was whether I was different from others my age. Could another person of eleven have had the same experience? But I didn't believe another person *would* have had this experience. Why not? Here I strained to reason it out. Because the whole series of episodes that had led up to this morning was inseparable from myself, from my history, from my personality. The ghost-boy was related to my life, yet he was also an entity on his own terms. Yet how could that be? How could he be both? Didn't something have to be one thing or the other, either real or imagined? Or could it be that the two things weren't mutually exclusive?

There was no one to ask. What I needed was someone wise and experienced, a mature personality who could take all of my information and give me back a definition, a diagnosis, a concept large enough to contain it all. There were surely such people in the world—only, so far, not in my world. Maybe later there would be a special teacher, like Mom's esteemed night-school teacher who had been so generous with his knowledge until he died, someone I could consult and look up to, who knew things I needed to know and if he didn't know them could show me how to look for them.

XXIV.

I had never met a person as old as Coral Upchurch. I had never met a person of any age remotely like her. Lachicotte had promised I would appreciate her, that she was quite the raconteur, but I certainly never expected to hear the story she told that first afternoon.

Lachicotte came to get me at two o'clock, leaving behind a steak-and-mushroom pie identical to the one he was taking to Coral Upchurch next door. "Preheat your oven to three-fifty and put this in for thirty minutes," he said. "Do not use the microwave or your (*yoah*) crust will be soggy." He had been to the barber and smelled and looked like an older gent who had taken extra pains with his appearance.

During the seven hours since returning from Grief Cottage, I had been pretty busy myself. After a shopping trip to the island store, I had spent some quality time with the turtle eggs and done two loads of laundry. I had been neatening the kitchen shelves when Aunt Charlotte had burst out of her off-limits studio and asked if I had time to wash her hair before Lachicotte arrived. "I wonder if we should cut it first," she said, frowning at herself in the mirror over the sink.

"You want *me* to cut your hair?"

"I don't see why not. Unlike me, you'll have the advantage of seeing the back of my head. All it needs is an inch off."

"Should we do it after we wash it, or before?"

"Before. Just grab a clump and take an inch off. Then grab another clump and do the same thing all the way around."

"What if I mess up?"

"I'd make a bigger mess if I tried to do it with my left hand. Start at the back. You'll improve by the time you get to the front."

I felt uneasy laying hold of my aunt's wiry mop. It was barely long enough to get a grip on. I had cut Mom's hair and she had cut mine, but that was another world from this. Seated below me, humbly baring her neck to the scissors, Aunt Charlotte looked defenseless. I could snip-snip carelessly and brutally and make her look terrible. I could go crazy and stab her in the back. All kinds of worrisome associations ran through my mind. The last time I had *grabbed a clump* of someone's hair, it had been Wheezer's silky roan locks, when I was holding him close so I could better hit his face. Aunt Charlotte's neck was dead white and on the stalky side, like the ghost-boy's. What if I should suddenly blurt, "Listen, Aunt Charlotte, I know how you feel on the subject of ghosts, but I had a sort of hallucination this morning and I need to tell someone." Even imagining such a confession made me cringe. I could hear her alarmed thoughts: *Oh no, when things were working out so well. Hallucinations are not something I'm equipped to deal with. He'd be better off going somewhere else.*

On the other hand, the service I was performing for my aunt was one more way I could be of use to her: cutting her hair and keeping my hallucinations to myself. And after I had washed and dried it, Aunt Charlotte raised her eyebrows at herself in the bathroom mirror and told me I had made her look "formidably sleek."

Coral Upchurch's cottage was in another class from Aunt Charlotte's "renovated shack," as she liked to call it. The Upchurch cottage was one of the old ones, not as old as Grief Cottage, but built in the mid-nineteenth century by a family with money who took it for granted that their descendants would be enjoying it long after they themselves were dust. The kitchen was on the ground floor across from the garage; the main body of the house was above, resting on the sturdy bricked footing columns that supported all the old houses, only these columns were screened by a painted white trellis. Lachicotte imparted all this to me as we walked from Aunt Charlotte's to Mrs. Upchurch's. Her caregiver, Roberta Dumas, sat outside in the shade of the breezeway between kitchen and garage. Her fingers flew, weaving a very large basket. When she saw us coming, she rose from her stool, brushed bits of grass from her smock, and picked her way around a barrier of buckets filled with different shades of tall grasses. She was one of those heavy people who carry their weight lightly. Her skin was truly black, with highlights of blue and purple when she moved out of the shade into the sunlight. She wore a white pantsuit uniform beneath a colorful, flowing artist's smock.

"Mr. Hayes, you always come bearing gifts."

Lachicotte introduced me and handed over the steak pie with the same warm-up directions he had given Aunt Charlotte and me.

"I'll take it up and show her," she said, "so she'll know we're gonna eat well tonight."

"How was your all's winter, Roberta?"

"Well, you know Mr. Billy passed away in January."

"No! How come she didn't tell me when I phoned yesterday?"

"It knocked the wind out of her. She says it's not natural, the parents are supposed to go first. Mr. Billy was just turned sixty-five. He went to get his pacemaker batteries replaced and had a heart attack right there on the table."

"And her not saying a thing!"

"She's still taking it in. When they called her from Washington, she hung up on them. When it commenced to ring again, she told me, 'Don't you dare pick up that phone, Roberta. Some nasty person is trying to frighten me.'"

"But she sounded just like herself yesterday."

"Oh, she's herself all right. It's made her mad, more than anything. Just go up and talk about it normally. She likes to talk about him. She knows he's buried in the family plot in Columbia, but we're almost back to the place where we're expecting his annual visit. The mind is a wondrous thing, isn't it, Mr. Hayes? It hasn't got to stay in just one place at a time."

"What is that imposing object you're weaving?" Lachicotte asked.

"That's my monster. My grandson calls it my Boogie Basket." Laughing, she lifted it from the breezeway floor and set it on her stool, which it overlapped. "They wanted it this size, but the proportions are all wrong. The handles, if I get to them, are going to look like elephant ears. I've a mind to stop while I'm ahead and send word that I passed on."

"A commission, is it?"

She nodded. "They saw it in the Smithsonian book and wanted one just like it, only triple the size. It's one of Granny's models. She'd turn over in her grave if she saw this. Mrs. Upchurch said if I decided not to send it, she'll pay the commission price and we'll use it as our laundry basket."

This struck me as hilarious, because that's exactly what it looked like. I got the giggles and then Lachicotte laughed, and Roberta joined in.

"My aunt just finished a huge painting of these rich people's beach house," I said. "It was forty-two by fifty-six and they wrote her a check too large for her to keep in the house overnight. She said the next thing she painted for herself was going to be six by ten, or maybe even four by six. Unfortunately, she broke her right wrist that same night and can't paint anything for a while."

"Now that's a shame," said Roberta. "I slammed some fingers in a car door once and couldn't work with my hands for six weeks. I about went crazy."

Roberta led us up a flight of outdoor stairs, next to which had been built a ramp for a wheelchair. Inside a screened-in porch a tiny lady sat in the wheelchair awaiting us. As we rose into her sightline, she was taking a last greedy puff of her cigarette before extinguishing it in an ashtray on the glass-topped table next to her.

"What were you all laughing at down there? I thought you were never coming up."

"It was my monster basket. Look, Mr. Hayes has brought us a steak pie."

"Bless you, Lachicotte. Roberta won't have to drive to the store and interrupt her art. And this is Marcus. Welcome, Marcus. This pie smells heavenly, Lachicotte. Come kiss me and we'll dispense with condolences over Billy. I'm still cross with him for breaking ahead of me in line like that. Marcus, why don't you sit in that chair across from me?"

For the second time that day, I imagined how Mom would see a woman who'd had better breaks in life than she'd had. ("Now that simple summer outfit, Marcus, was really costly in its day. And look how well-preserved it is. It's gone back and forth to a quality cleaner for the last forty years. And notice her pampered complexion and the teeth! She's had them capped or veneered, otherwise they'd be yellow from age and smoking. And she's still got all of them! This old girl is a prime example of high maintenance over the long term.")

"I'll leave you all to socialize," said Roberta. "What do we want to have with Mr. Hayes's steak pie?" she asked Mrs. Upchurch.

"Oh, ice cream will be fine," replied the indulged little child-queen of ninety-five, ensconced on her wheelchair throne. Close by her on the glass table, besides the ashtray, were binoculars, a bird book, a carton of cigarettes with a silver lighter on top, a carafe of ice water covered by a drinking glass, and one of those pill containers with slots for a week's supply of morning and evening doses. On our side of the table were two tall glasses, a pitcher of iced tea, two folded cloth napkins, and a plate of unusually flat cookies.

Coral Upchurch's lively old eyes engaged with me. "So you are Charlotte Lee's great-nephew."

"Yes ma'am."

"Oh, please call me Coral. I'm trying to strip down to essentials. If I live much longer, I'm hoping even the 'Coral' will become superfluous. When you reach my age, you want to perform archaeology on yourself, get beyond family names and given names and polite forms of address." Her accent had a Lachicotte base with what sounded like overlays of voice training from somewhere in her past.

"What would be beyond Coral, archaeologically?" I asked.

"That's what I'm trying to figure out! Maybe you'll help me. What would 'beyond Marcus' be like?"

This was a really interesting question. I had to close my eyes in order to think harder. "Maybe not *any* given name," I said. "I mean, for instance, say you had a turtle and you named him Luke. Before he was Luke he was just a turtle. Or, if you wanted to be specific, a loggerhead turtle. And before that—I'm going to have to think about this some more."

"I wish you would. I've never known a Marcus. Plenty of *Marks* but no Marcuses. The only Marcus I can think of offhand is Marcus Aurelius."

"That's who my mom named me after! She loved his *Meditations*. She had two copies of it. One of them was in Greek on the left side of the page. He wrote it in Greek, you know."

"Was your mother a scholar?"

"She loved studying and learning things. She was planning to go to college and become a teacher." I was about to add how determined she was to make something of herself, then remembered I had been through this before with Lachicotte, who had generously suggested that she'd already made something of herself by bringing me up so well.

"Lachicotte told me what a great help you are to your aunt," said Coral Upchurch, "but when you're not being a great help, what do you do to amuse yourself? Have you made any friends?"

Well, I've been spending a lot of time with this boy. He's a little older than me, fourteen, and he's been dead for fifty years.

"I ride my bike a lot. And I've made friends with this man on the Turtle Patrol, Mr. Bolton. This year there's a clutch of loggerhead eggs buried below my aunt's boardwalk steps."

"Marcus has taken quite an interest in our local history," Lachicotte said. "Particularly the old Barbour cottage up at the north end. We went to the library to look up that poor family that was lost during Hazel, but he couldn't find a single mention of them in the microfiche."

"Well, I expect I can tell you more about them than anyone else still living," said Coral Upchurch. "I don't mean the Barbours, who still reside in Columbia as far as I know. And I don't know much about the unfortunate parents, except that the father's cousin sued the Barbours. But Billy knew the son. They were the same age. The boy was kind of a dark customer. Archie, my husband, made us leave the first weekend in October because he thought the boy was corrupting Billy. We usually stayed for the entire month of October. It was my favorite time. I would be by myself during the week, then Archie and Billy would drive down from Columbia on weekends. Archie had his law practice and of course Billy had school during the week. I was quite put out, having to pack up and leave—like we were being evicted or something!—and lose my favorite month just because of that boy."

"Do you remember his name?" I asked.

"It was something simple, like Billy, only of course it wasn't Billy. The family name wasn't one you hear every day, but it was an Anglo-Saxon name. When I remember I will write it down for you. These days, Marcus, I have to put in requests to my brain, as one does at the library, and then a little worker takes my slip and disappears into the stacks. It may take him a while, but he always comes back with the goods."

"How was he corrupting your son? If it's not too rude to ask."

"Billy came back with smoke and liquor on his breath. Archie said it wasn't just any smoke, it was marijuana. You have to understand. Back in that era marijuana was considered the 'stepping stone to heroin.' It was way before the time when doctors started prescribing it to sick people. In the early 1950s the states were enacting severe penalties for narcotic offenses. And the boy was . . . peculiar . . . in other ways. He never went into the ocean. Billy said he never even took off his clothes or shoes. He just walked up and down the length of the island, fully dressed—that's how Billy met him, as he was walking past our house, scowling. That would appeal to Billy's open nature. Billy loved to reach out to scowlers. There'd been some hardship or setback with that family, as I recall, something to do with their house, and there was a problem with the boy as well. The father was employed by a coal company in Kentucky, some low-level management job, not a miner. Some friends of the Barbours knew of their misfortunes and felt sorry for them, and since the Barbours weren't using it in October they offered their beach cottage. I don't know if it was charity, or whether there was payment involved. But the Barbours certainly paid for it later. After the family got washed away in the storm—*Dace!* That was their name, Dace. My little worker just came back from the stacks! The boy's name was Johnny Dace. Now where was I?"

"After the family got washed away," I said.

"Oh, yes, even though no bodies were found, a cousin on the father's side sued the Barbours. The cousin said the father was all she had left, and she only wanted her due. Money changed hands—the cousin even asked that the family's old car and their personal belongings be returned to her!—and soon after that the Barbours sold the cottage. In Archie's opinion, the proper defendant in the cousin's lawsuit would have been Hurricane Hazel. It wasn't the *cottage's* fault. It's too bad, really, that the Daces didn't stay inside it during the storm. That house was built to last. They'd probably be here today. The only part that didn't last was the south porch they say the boy burned down with his cigarettes."

I felt like Barrett the dog on his tight leash, straining toward the beguiling waves. There my beguiler sat, approximately the same distance from me as the waves had been from Barrett this morning, and I wanted to plunge in and immerse myself in whatever she could remember about the boy. My list of questions piled up, but I was on my "company" leash: Lachicotte and I were paying a social call on an ancient neighbor and we each had to take turns telling our news. We had to drink our iced tea and eat the unusual cookies, so thin they demanded you eat more of them. Aunt Charlotte's injuries were described and assessed, her recovery time speculated upon and wished for. Lachicotte brought Coral Upchurch up to date with island news, which at least touched upon the latest developments pertaining to the fate of Grief Cottage.

"The people who bought it from the Barbours should have either restored it or torn it down," said Coral Upchurch. "But they ended up selling to someone else and then Mr. Coggins the realtor, the late father not the son, snapped it up and couldn't sell it again. But I never understood why it was allowed to fall into ruin like that. Most townships would have forced the issue, was Archie's opinion. Every year until Archie died he'd walk up to see the cottage and come back appalled. He said it was a disgrace to the island and made us all look bad. It was Archie who frightened old Mr. Coggins and the commissioners into putting up the wire fence and those warning signs. Otherwise, he told them, you are just shopping for injuries and lawsuits. And even then it took twenty years to force the issue. By that time it had become a genuine ruin. Everyone had long since been calling it Grief Cottage when that fence finally went up."

"It was up when my aunt moved here." A perfectly natural next question would be for me to ask if Billy had visited Johnny Dace at the cottage. "It was Grief Cottage that started my aunt's painting career."

"Yes, she told me that. Please, Marcus, take that last Benne Wafer. It won't make you an old maid. That's an expression left over from my generation, but it only applies to girls. It's a sesame wafer. The slaves brought the spice with them from Africa. Benne is the Bantu word for sesame. Roberta can give you the recipe. She makes trays and trays of those cookies every year after Christmas when her family celebrates Kwanzaa. Do you know what Kwanzaa is?"

I had to admit I didn't know, and thus Barrett and I were reluctantly parted from our beguiling waves while Coral Upchurch filled me in on the first African-American holiday, established back in the sixties, when black people were starting to take pride in their roots.

"YOU COULD SEE her beginning to flag," said Lachicotte, as we walked back to Aunt Charlotte's. "And she kept eyeing those cigarettes."

"I wouldn't care if she smoked."

"Neither would I. I was raised inside a fog of parental smoke. But smokers nowadays have their individual rules of honor. Obviously hers are outdoors only and not in the presence of others."

"Why not in the presence of others?"

"The hazards of secondhand smoke."

"Oh, I knew that."

"It was kind of you to offer to shop for them every day."

"No problem. They eat mostly deli, like Aunt Charlotte and me, and this way Roberta won't have to take the van out of the garage and interrupt her art."

Lachicotte laughed. "That basket sure was a fright."

"Just because people are rich doesn't mean they have taste." A direct quote from my mom.

Lachicotte paused beside Aunt Charlotte's Mercedes, which he'd been driving since he sold the Bentley. "How is she doing?"

"She has some kind of project going in her studio."

"Oh? What kind?"

"It's secret. I'm not allowed to go in there. I think it involves paint but I can't be sure because I can't smell anything through the door. I always used to be able to smell the oils. She spends hours and hours in there every day."

"How is the—?"

"Festering?"

"You read my mind."

"Pretty much the same. It's a bad time for her, she says."

"Well, when we go back to the surgeon in Charleston, I'm hoping we'll hear encouraging news that will make her feel better. Is she having pain?"

"Not that I know of. She made me hide her painkillers and there's still a fair number in the container."

"Well, we may just make it through the summer. If we do, it will be largely thanks to you, Marcus."

"Won't you come in?"

"Thank you, no. I've got things to do, and we've already said hello. One hello is usually enough for your aunt."

★   ★   ★

"TELL ME ALL," Aunt Charlotte said at supper. "I hope it wasn't too boring for you."

"Oh no, I enjoyed it. I liked Roberta, too. She was making an ugly misshapen basket for some people who wanted it extra large. She wishes she could send word that she died so she won't have to finish it."

This amused Aunt Charlotte. She was enjoying Lachicotte's steak pie—heated according to his directions—and putting away her usual amounts of wine. She was in a mellow, receptive mood.

"So, what did *'you all'* talk about?"

"Her son Billy died last winter."

"Really? What of?"

"He had a heart attack at the hospital. He was having his pacemaker batteries replaced."

"Is she devastated?"

"Roberta said it was more like she was angry. She was supposed to go first. She told Lachicotte that her son had broken ahead of her in line. She was in a pretty good mood. Though toward the end Lachicotte noticed she was dying to have a cigarette."

"Depend on Lachicotte to notice something like that."

"She said she'd never known a Marcus before. She asked what I did to amuse myself on the island."

"And what did you tell her?"

"About the Turtle Patrol. And riding my bike."

"That doesn't sound like much. I wonder how you'll look back on this period of your life, Marcus, how you'll describe it to someone in the future. 'When I was eleven, my mother died and I went to live with my peculiar great-aunt on an island.'"

"I don't think of you as peculiar."

"Naturally you have to say that. I've tried to isolate my peculiarities. Being solitary has been a great advantage. At least I don't force my peculiarities on others. I hope I don't."

There was no good reply to this. If I said "You don't," that would be admitting she had peculiarities. So I just said I liked living here on the island. I stopped myself from adding that I hoped I didn't intrude on her solitude too much. That would sound like I was fishing for her to say I didn't, and then to repeat her usual praise about how helpful and thoughtful and astute I was.

As I was tinkering with these moral mathematics, I realized that I was not going to tell her what Coral Upchurch had said about the boy. He had a name now and some character traits (mostly negative ones, except for the walking on the beach). I wanted to keep him to myself until I had time to think about him some more. Ever since I could remember, I had kept a little private zone where I could work out important things for myself.

I had certainly not told Mom everything—a lot of it would have hurt her. In my mandated sessions with the psychiatrist I stuck to safe answers. With Wheezer, up until our rupture, I had left out significant "trues" in my history, allowing him to create his own pictures of how I lived in idealized poverty with my courageous single mom.

But I did tell Aunt Charlotte that I had offered to shop for Coral Upchurch and Roberta every day. "That way Roberta won't have to get the car out of the garage and interrupt her work. They eat mostly deli, like us."

"Sometimes I think you are too good to be true, Marcus."

"I'm not all that good."

I had known as I made my shopping offer that it would link me to their lives on an everyday basis. Coral Upchurch wasn't ready to receive company until early afternoon, but she said she wished I would be her daily visitor. I looked forward to sitting across from her and asking casual questions. And she would send her mental librarian off to the stacks and he would come back with more just-remembered facts about Johnny Dace.

"Actually, I selfishly hope you *will* turn out to be good from the bottom up," said Aunt Charlotte. "It might restore some of my faith in human beings."

XXV.

*T*he dune beside Aunt Charlotte's boardwalk steps had become my meditation post and checkpoint for sanity. Here I could sit in the evenings above the clutch buried below the sand where 110 turtle embryos squirmed in their shells and know that, despite whatever weirdnesses I had undergone through the day, I was also part of the real day that was now ending. And this day linked me to the real days of the ancient world, when the turtles were already old news, and to a future world when I would be dead, when the whole human race might be dead, but these turtles might still be doing exactly what they had always done without any help from my extinguished species.

I felt like the turtles' guest. I wanted to be unobtrusive so as not to upset their progress. As they approached their hatching time, I talked to them in a wise and soothing murmur. I told them stories of what to expect, from the moment each used the little egg tooth on top of its snout to rip through its leathery shell and then stretch its body out straight. ("Remember, you've been curled into a ball for two months, so you'll need to do this. And while you're wriggling around getting straightened out, your body will knock against the shells of your unhatched brothers and sisters and stimulate *their* breakthroughs . . .")

This July was a "two-moon month," Ed Bolton had informed me. Approximately every three years there would be two full moons in a calendar month. We'd had a full moon last Friday and we would have the second one on the last day of July. The second full moon was called a blue moon, which referred to a rare blue coloring, which usually wasn't seen, caused by high altitude dust particles. Tonight's moon was a waning gibbous—*gibbosus* was hunchback in Latin. The curve inside the gibbous moon did look like something hunched. But when the moon shrank to its last quarter the hunch would straighten up. Ed Bolton had given me the turtles and the moon. I would have liked to have been in his high school science classes. He made everything in the natural world sound like it mattered to him—as it would to you, if you saw it right.

How sickening that I had missed Billy Upchurch by one year! He could have answered the really crucial questions. I would have asked him, in gradual increments, what they talked about. Johnny may have told Billy about the Dace family hardship Coral Upchurch had referred to. And she said there had been a problem with Johnny Dace, too. If he wasn't in school in October, maybe he had been kicked out of school. He would have told Billy why he never took off his clothes at the beach, or made up an excuse. And I would love to know why Billy had picked him out when he was walking the entire length of the beach and back, something I had yet to do myself. I would have asked who spoke first. My guess was Billy, who was attracted to scowlers. And did Johnny invite him to the cottage or did Billy invite himself? And when they got there, what did they do together?

If the ghost-boy had lived he would be sixty-five, like Billy, unless he had died before Billy.

I still hadn't become used to the beauty of the island. You are one lucky boy, the foster mother had said, when it was firm that I was going to live with my aunt at the beach. I did feel lucky, though the feeling wasn't free of remorse and guilt. If Mom hadn't died, we would probably still be living in that awful upstairs apartment on Smoke Vine Road with the downstairs landlady from hell. Though Jewel was set in the midst of beautiful mountains, for me its very name would always evoke shame and poverty. Mom had to die so I could get out of Jewel and live at the beach. How sad that we hadn't shared beauty in any of our surroundings. Forsterville (pop. 10,000+) was a piedmont town with a furniture factory and railroad tracks, a few adulterated rivers and streams, and a manmade lake, where prominent citizens had summer cottages, fifteen miles away. The closest to a beautiful setting Mom and I had shared was the quiet cemetery on the outskirts of town with its cypresses and well-tended grass, where we could walk and she could inhale air that didn't smell of sawdust and chemicals and shellac. We strolled among the headstones—many of which bore the name of Forster, the founding family—and played our funeral and burial game. The clothes we would wear in our coffins, the hymns and psalms we wanted. ("We should probably attend church more often," Mom would say. "Then there would be more of a crowd at our funerals. But I don't think God grudges me my Sunday morning sleep-in.") Mom was cheerful and serene when we walked in the Forsterville cemetery.

Things would now be different between the ghost-boy and me. I knew that. Everything in his presence and posture said: *You summoned me. Here I am. Now what are we going to do?* But I had failed the test. I was certain he would not appear to me again. If only I had remembered the rules that were spread all over the ghost stories Wheezer and I used to devour. The living person was either up to the challenge or he was not. If you wished to keep the connection going with the ghost, you had to measure up to the moment of testing. Wheezer and I had often discussed it: if we were ever fortunate enough to meet a ghost, like in one of the stories we loved where the living person measured up, what would we do and say? We were always adding to our rules for ghosts.

"That is, for the ones you feel *deserve* your help," Wheezer once stipulated, "not the other kind." For the worthy ghosts, you had to stand your ground even if your legs were shaking and ask: What do you need? What can I do for you in the land of the living that you can no longer do for yourself? Is there a message you want conveyed to a living person? Is there a wrong that needs to be righted before you can rest in peace? If so, I'll be your errand boy.

"But how would you know the difference between a ghost worthy of your help and *the other kind*?" I asked Wheezer. He thought it over. "Maybe you wouldn't, at first," he said, "until your intuition kicked in. Then you'd feel either sought out or creeped out. If it's creeped out, you'd better cut and run."

But facing my ghost this morning I had felt sought out *and* creeped out. If only I had stood my ground and asked him, What do you want of me? What can I do for you in the land of the living that you can no longer do for yourself? Maybe if I hadn't cut and run I would have experienced an advanced stage of human consciousness.

I needed to ask Ed Bolton to explain more about the problem of time. In school we had been prepped with just enough rudimentary Einstein to unsettle us. Yes, boys and girls, after your brains develop some more you'll have to deal with concepts of time beyond the clock and calendar.

I had been zipping through too many kinds of time to keep track of: waking and dreaming time, outer and inner, since yesterday's dreaming of my mom opening the door of her beautiful apartment and telling me I had an older brother to this afternoon's meeting of a very old lady who was able to tell me the first and last names of the ghost I had seen that very morning.

XXII.

*A*rchie and I were married ten years before we had Billy. We concluded we were going to be a childless couple, and to be honest we had a good old time. We went places we wouldn't have gone if we'd had small children, and we developed an intimacy that might not have flourished otherwise. I was just twenty when I married and quite ignorant and provincial in lots of ways. Archie was eighteen years older and he said it was like having a daughter and a lover all in one package. I'm not shocking you, am I, Marcus?"

"Oh, no. My mom was married a long time before I was born. Her husband was a lot older than her, too. He died before I was born." Not a single lie in those three bare statements. As long as I kept them bare.

"Are you hungry? Roberta has stocked my little minibar over there with nice things."

"I'm not really hungry. Could I get you something?"

"I'm not a great eater, but thank you." Her downward glance at the cigarette carton was barely a flicker.

"I wish you would go ahead and smoke."

"I'd much rather enjoy your company."

"You can enjoy us both. I've been around plenty of smokers." Wheezer's granny could count for at least twenty smokers. Because of his asthma, she did go outside to smoke, or into the bathroom with the exhaust fan turned on. Wheezer and I used to count how long she could get by without lighting up and she maxed out at forty-two minutes.

"Well, I'll keep it in mind. As soon as he walked in the door every summer, Billy would start lecturing me about quitting. And now look, he's jumped the gun on me. I told Roberta I needed to get myself another bad habit so I won't stick around forever. Enough is enough. Besides, I'm fascinated by death. I don't know whether there's an afterlife or not—I'm not a believer in a conventional heaven and hell—but I'm prepared to be surprised. How about you?"

"My mom said the only heaven and hell she believed in were right here on earth. I'm fascinated with death, too."

"At your age? Oh, forgive me. You lost your mother so recently."

"Do you ever wonder if, well, the dead have ways to get in contact with the living?"

"Archie has been gone forty-three years and he speaks to me every day. 'Let me do that,' he'll say, though of course he isn't there to do it anymore. Things I always did wrong, like folding up a grocery bag properly so it would lie flat. And I'll make the extra effort and do it his way. After Billy bailed out on me last winter, I tried to scold him into appearing. I wanted to see him again. Even though the last few years he'd gotten red from high blood pressure, just like Archie. But Billy was drop-dead gorgeous in his younger years. You know what, Marcus, with your permission I will have a cigarette."

I watched the tiny woman transform herself into a forties film star as she attended to the glamorous ritual of lighting up.

"The boy you were telling us about—did you ever see him?"

"The boy?"

"The one your husband thought was a bad influence on Billy. Johnny Dace?"

"Oh, I saw him only once, when Archie and I were looking for Billy on the beach. Archie decided they must have gone up to the Barbour cottage to do bad things, and we were debating whether we wanted to walk all the way to the north end or go back and get the car. Then we saw them walking back toward us and when they got closer Archie said, 'Please don't tell me that sorry-looking lout is Billy's wonderful new friend.'"

"How was he sorry-looking?"

"Oh, ruffianly and sort of . . . paltry. After Billy's great buildup."

"How did he look?"

"We never saw him close up. When Billy spotted us, he leaned over and said something to him and the boy spun around and headed back north. He was taller than Billy—Billy hadn't got his full growth yet—but that might have been because Billy was barefoot and the other boy was wearing shoes."

"What kind of shoes?"

"I couldn't say."

"Could they have been boots?"

"They could have been, I suppose. Billy told us his friend always wore his clothes on the beach, and never went in the water. Billy thought maybe he couldn't swim. Or he might not have owned a bathing suit, was Archie's opinion."

"Did he have on a shirt?"

"I think so, but Marcus, this was half a century ago." She turned away from me to responsibly exhale her smoke toward the ocean. "Lachicotte said you were intrigued by that unfortunate family. I wish I had more to tell you."

"It just seems wrong they were the only ones lost in that hurricane and they're never mentioned."

"Oh, but it was talked about at the time. Billy was quite distressed when we got the news from the Barbours. He kept saying, 'But he'd promised to come and visit me!' Archie said he'd never been glad of anyone's death except Hitler's but he confessed to being relieved we were spared the boy's visit."

The next time I rode my bike to Grief Cottage, I pictured the two friends walking south toward me. Billy Upchurch saying to his friend Johnny Dace when he spotted his parents walking toward them, "Oh, shit, here come my parents." Or did he say, "There's my mom and dad! Now I can introduce you!" And Johnny Dace would have said, "Count me out." Or something more ruffianly. And then spun around on his (shoe? boot?) heel and decamped. It was easier to do it from Johnny Dace's side. Of course he didn't want to meet Billy's parents. He wanted to escape being judged. How did he know they would judge him? Well, ever since he and his own parents had arrived to be charity occupants of the Barbour cottage, they must have felt some of the ways people like the Upchurches conveyed their judgments on people like them. I myself was more of a Dace set down in the midst of Upchurches than otherwise. I simply had more camouflage: my great-aunt was a respected local artist and had given herself the surname of the general of the Confederate army, and I had entered this island community with Lachicotte's seal of approval.

Recent events concerning the figure in the cottage had changed my perceptions. He was now two beings. There was the ghost-boy, the presence that I had sensed behind me on my first visit to Grief Cottage and that I had seen twice since, standing full-length in the doorway. And there was Johnny Dace, short-lived friend (and bad influence?) to Billy Upchurch. And the Johnny Dace who came to the beach with his parents and without a bathing suit.

After my last encounter with him, I altered my routine at Grief Cottage. I still crawled beneath the wire fence with all the warning signs and climbed the rickety stairs to the slanting porch. But I now sat *facing the door*, my back against one of the upright beams that propped up the roof. My old way of sitting with my back to the door had been so he could observe me without feeling threatened. But now I was the one who felt threatened. Better to face the door than to suddenly feel the grip of an unseen hand from behind.

Since I had flunked the test of standing my ground when he appeared to me, he may have, in his ghostly manner, established new rules for my appearances. Rule one: No more "showings" to the visitor. *I* had become the "nervous animal." We had reversed roles. Now he needed to ration his presence so as not to scare me off.

I continued to talk to him, however. I believed it still offered the best chance of maintaining the frequencies between us—if any remained. As before, I opened with the "safe" natural subjects: the ocean and the surroundings we shared, the current phase of the moon, the progress of the loggerhead embryos ("Ed Bolton, the retired science teacher, predicts they'll hatch the middle of next week . . ."). Then I filled him in on my recent routines ("My aunt had to go back and have a metal pin put in her wrist . . . Now she's started some secret project. I'm not allowed to enter her studio . . ."). Then I thought it worth a try to suddenly drop in my visits to Coral Upchurch. ("You never met her, but she's the mother of Billy Upchurch, the boy you made friends with when your family was staying in the beach cottage before the hurricane? Do you remember Billy Upchurch? Now I have to tell you something sad. Billy died this past winter. He was sixty-five. He was having the batteries changed on his pacemaker, that's a device invented after your time, they plant it in your chest and it regulates your heartbeat . . .")

I did feel some kind of agitation in the air between me and the empty doorway. What had set the agitation going? Was it sympathy for Billy or revolt at the mention of Billy's name, or was it exasperation with the tiresome boy on the rotting porch cluttering up the silence with "trues"?

XXVII.

Aunt Charlotte and I were having our one meal of the day together. "His mother told me Billy Upchurch was drop-dead gorgeous. Did you ever see him?"

"Of course I saw him. That first summer when I was fixing up this place he was over here every day of his visit. He was enthralled by all the construction going on. He couldn't stop gabbing with the hunky young men doing the work. He was certainly good-looking. He was very attentive to me, too, though I knew he didn't swing that way and he knew I knew."

"Did his mother know, do you think?"

"I would guess like a good Southern lady she saw only the parts of him she wished to see."

"She wasn't in a wheelchair then, was she?"

"Oh, no. She was all over the place. Then about ten years ago she was going to fly up to D.C. to visit Billy and when she got to the airport she just crumpled and had to be carried out. Her spine had disintegrated. Lachicotte says she can still put herself to bed and doesn't need to be helped onto the toilet. You really are a good egg, Marcus, not only shopping for them but sitting with her every afternoon."

"She's one of the most fascinating people I've ever met."

"Have you known many old people?"

"I forget she's old. We talk about interesting things—she's doing archaeology on herself to get beyond her name and the way people see her. She won't let you call her Mrs. Upchurch and now she's working on getting beyond the 'Coral.'"

"You're making me feel I've missed something."

"I haven't known many old people. Before I met Coral, my image of an old person was our landlady's mother. Her name was Mrs. Harm. That really was her name. And her daughter, who was our landlady from hell, her name was Mrs. Wicket. Mom and I called them Wicked and Harm."

"Why was she a landlady from hell?"

"You really want to hear?"

"Wicked and Harm—who could resist?"

"Well, when we moved into this upstairs apartment on Smoke Vine Road—this was in Jewel, the place we lived before I came here—Mrs. Wicket made this deal with Mom. She would take fifty dollars off our rent every month if I would stay downstairs with her mother on weekday afternoons after school. This gave Mrs. Wicket some time to herself and saved her from having to pay for someone to be with Mrs. Harm until six-thirty, when the next home help came. Old Mrs. Harm wasn't much trouble. She just lay in her bedroom with her oxygen tank and her TV. And she had on a diaper in case—you know. I got used to doing my homework to the sound of TV. It was one of those channels that played the same watered-down music, on and on. I had to go in regularly and check to see that she hadn't yanked her oxygen tubes out of her nose, and I had these numbers to call if there was an emergency. I'm not sure she knew I was a different person from Mrs. Wicket. Lots of times, the home help evening shift was late and I was supposed to stay until she came. So sometimes Mom and I didn't eat supper until eight or even later."

"That is taking advantage."

"Well, there's more. Mrs. Wicket's niece came to visit and Mrs. Wicket told Mom I had earned a little holiday and that her niece would sit with Mrs. Harm in the afternoons. But when we got our next rent bill, it was thirty dollars more. The niece had only stayed four days, but Mom said there was no use wasting time doing the math. It was ungenerous of Mrs. Wicket, Mom said, but she was our landlady and we didn't have a lease. But even when I was back on the job next month's bill was still thirty dollars more. Mom went down to speak to Mrs. Wicket and when she came back she was really upset. The landlady told her the cost of living had gone up and she couldn't spare that thirty dollars anymore. Mom said then maybe she didn't need me anymore, but Mrs. Wicket said, 'If Marcus stops coming I'm afraid I'll have to raise the rent.'"

"This makes me so mad I want to explode."

"It all worked out eventually."

"*How?*"

"Mrs. Harm died and I lost my job, and then we only had to pay the increased rent until Mom was killed. You might say fate worked it out for us. Mrs. Wicket came out of it well because she had some kind of limited income insurance which reimbursed her for the month we hadn't paid and until she found new tenants. My guardian ad litem told me she tried to get the state to reimburse her as well."

"Marcus, it grieves me to think how many more unhappy stories you are sitting on." And Aunt Charlotte did look grieved. She spoke like someone who was hurting because she cared for me. Heartened by this, I was able to recall something else.

"Believe it or not there was a good part to that night. When Mom came upstairs and told me about Mrs. Wicket's meanness, we both flew into a rage—well, a mixture of rage and despair. I really lost it and called our landlady every disgusting name I could think of, and then I started calling down curses, all the horrible things I wished on her, and after a while Mom came over and hugged me and told me that was enough. Then she said, 'Because we are poor, shall we be vicious?' and went to make us some cocoa. At first I thought it was a question she had addressed to me, but when she came back with the cocoa she said it was out of some violent play written even before Shakespeare's time. She hadn't read the play, but this night school teacher she admired so much was always giving them famous quotes that might help them on future tests. And Mom said the quote stayed with her because it gave her a morale boost when she was beating up on herself for being poor. She said maybe it had been selfish to bring me into the world when she had so little to offer, but nevertheless she had wanted me more than anything in her whole life. She said I was her great prize."

AUNT CHARLOTTE AND I had moved outside to the porch. A balmy evening breeze was blowing across the dunes and the tide was on its way out. The sunbathers and families had packed up their things and departed, leaving only strollers and owners walking their dogs. There was no leash-free "dog hour" in the evening, which I thought was a shame. Barrett was probably back at the Navy brig where his prisoner-trainer would be putting the final touches on his skills. I had been down to check on the turtles: the thermocouple stuck in the sand had registered no rise in temperature. Aunt Charlotte had said to leave the dishes for later and hopped on ahead to the porch, calling over her shoulder for me to bring out another bottle of wine. Ordinarily, since she had begun her secret project, she hopped straight back to her studio immediately after supper, but tonight she was being sociable. Maybe she felt sorry for me after my sad story.

"Oh, I forgot," she said when I joined her with the fresh bottle. She had arranged herself to accommodate her casts: the little table that held her bottle and glass on the left where she could reach them, her left leg propped straight ahead on a stool. "Lachicotte phoned while you were next door. He said to tell you he's booked you for the school bus. School starts the third Monday in August. Do you realize, Marcus, you'll be in school before my casts are off."

"We'll have a celebration."

"Let's wait until we're sure I have something to celebrate."

My heart clenched at the mention of school. So far I had stayed on top of the first summer of my new life. Though recent days had been demanding, I had so far been able to handle everything on the schedule: turtle check, followed by early morning bike ride to Grief Cottage, where I worked at building back my credibility with the ghost-boy, then home to do general housework, get the shopping list from Roberta, bike to the store, deliver order to Roberta in the kitchen, a solitary lunch, sometimes eaten on the beach beside the turtles, then laundry—if any. (I did worry about the state of Aunt Charlotte's sheets inside the off-limit studio, but refrained from inquiring.) Next came my afternoon visit with Coral Upchurch, if she was feeling up to it, then supper with Aunt Charlotte, washing up and putting away, evening meditation beside the turtle clutch, unpacking more boxes (if in the mood), then bed, thoughts, dreams, sleeping, and waking to the tides. I was managing everything on the list, and so far keeping enough of a wary balance between inner and outer happenings to stay in the realm people called sanity.

School would be another thing. School would mean judgment again. It was one thing to try to please a great-aunt who was more or less stuck with me, and visit an old lady who fascinated me, and pursue a precarious relationship with a dead boy, but being reminded that soon I would be thrown back into that cauldron of merciless peers made my spirit shrink.

"You know," Aunt Charlotte mused, "the Internet has its upside and its downside. The upside is I can sit in front of my laptop and go room by room through the great museums of the world. I can loiter in front of a picture as long as I please without someone blocking my view or saying something stupid or hurrying me on. I can replenish my wine and art supplies without leaving the house. The downside is that all I have to do to spoil a day is to type 'wrist sprain, stage 3' into that little rectangle on the screen and have instant access to all the less than ideal ways the rest of my life can turn out."

XXVIII.

*W*hen I had been going through airport security before my flight to Aunt Charlotte's—the first airplane ride of my life—the lady in front of me got into an argument with the official who wanted her to open her suitcase. Something inside it had looked suspicious when it passed through the x-ray machine. The suitcase was now open on the counter, and the official asked her to take everything out. "You mean I am to lay out my personal items in front of everybody?" "Yes, ma'am, it will be neater if you do it." "This is highly irregular," she said, "I have never been asked to do this before in my life. I can assure you there is nothing dangerous in this bag. Do I look like a terrorist?" "Please, ma'am, just remove the items and we'll locate the problem." "What if I refuse?" she asked. "Then I can't let you into the boarding area for your flight." He had tuned his patience down a notch. "Very well," she conceded, and in exaggerated slow motion began to lay out the contents of the bag. Faded pink nightgown and worn terrycloth slippers, a yellowing white bra, underpants also in yellowing white, a scruffy stuffed animal that looked like a rat in a red vest, a magnifying glass, a hairbrush with hairs in it, a toiletry bag—"Wait," he stopped her, "Can we have a look in that bag?" "You're running this show," she said with a scornful smile, handing it over for him to ferret out the culprit. "I'm afraid we'll have to confiscate these, ma'am." "Be my guest," she said, repacking her suitcase as slowly as she could. "They are harmless embroidery scissors. Maybe your wife will enjoy them."

I often thought of that lady's things when I was unpacking yet another box from my former life. Laid out "in front of everybody," many of the contents would look embarrassing or mystifying to others. For me, an occasional item in a box would restore a memory; another would shed light into some obscure corner of my past. But on the whole I would be glad when the final box, packed by a social worker back in Jewel, was emptied and stomped flat and put outside for the island's trash collection.

Weeks ago I had concluded there had been no system in the packing of these boxes. If I had been the social worker I would have gone room by room. I would have packed all the books together, all the woman's clothes, the boy's things, the kitchen stuff, the bathroom stuff. After all, it was only three rooms, counting the bathroom. But having grown used to finding toothbrushes and kitchen items packed together, children's books on top of elastic stockings and a shabby coat, I expected to find discrepant bedfellows in each new box.

In tonight's box was Mom's heavily underlined paperback of Marcus Aurelius's *Meditations*, which she always kept rubber-banded with the "serious" hardback that was in Greek on the left side with a stranger's interlinear translation. And under-neath those was an eight-by-ten framed photograph of my coiffed and stylish grandmother, who I now also thought of as

Brenda, the older sister, who had referred to my great-aunt as "Crazy Charlotte." And beneath those was a furry black bear in a gray hoodie—which had reminded me of the lady's rat in the red coat. At the bottom of the box, its sides buttressed by crumpled newspaper, was a toy lumber truck my mom had loved as a child. Once it had carried six-inch logs of real wood, but all but one of them had disappeared by the time it became mine. I had loaded its truck bed with toy cars, or twigs piled like logs, and once, briefly, a live frog who jumped off in a huff and vanished into the shrubbery. Later, the black bear in his hoodie rode in it, sitting sideways against the one remaining log. GASTON & SONS LUMBER was emblazoned on both sides of the truck in gold letters against a background of forest green.

Gaston & Sons Lumber had been founded by Samuel Gaston, my great-great-grandfather, in Cass, West Virginia, and after that I hadn't paid attention whenever Mom tried to take me through her side of my forebears. She must have figured I needed her forebears all the more since for all intents and purposes I was a bastard. For the summer of my twelfth year, which would have been next summer, she had been planning a trip for us to ride the Cass Railroad up to Back Allegheny Mountain, so I could get a feel for the land I came out of. And at a later date, when I had reached a "responsible age," she had promised to tell me about the other side, the side of the man in the photo in her drawer. Regarding the responsible-age thing she had been right. I certainly had failed to be responsible at age nine, when I showed Wheezer the photo in the drawer. Now I was left to guess what age she'd had in mind for the responsible me—not that it mattered now because it was never going to happen.

Marcus Aurelius, who I was named after, had been three when his father died. Later Marcus was to write that he had learned "manliness without ostentation" from what he had heard and remembered about that father. In those days, a father acknowledged a child as his own by lifting the infant up from the hearth in a special ceremony, which I thought was a wonderful idea. Marcus's father had lived long enough to do that. Marcus's mother stayed faithful to her husband's memory. She had always been rich, and died young without remarrying. Marcus remembered her in his meditations as his model for "piety, generosity, refraining from wrongdoing, simplicity in life, and distancing herself from the ways of the rich." I liked that phrase: *distancing herself from the ways of the rich.*

After his father died, Marcus was adopted, raised, and educated by his grandfather, from whom, Marcus writes, "I learned courtesy and serenity of temper." At seventeen, Marcus was adopted by the emperor, whose wife was Marcus's aunt. The emperor had no sons of his own and named Marcus as his successor. Marcus later wrote of his adoptive father that "all men recognized in him a mature and finished personality that was impervious to flattery and entirely capable of ruling both himself and others." I also liked the idea of a mature and finished personality, and wondered if I would have one someday.

When Marcus was forty he became emperor and ruled wisely until he died of the pestilence at fifty-nine.

Alec Guinness's mother refused to tell him who his father was. Later, when he was an old man, he confided to a friend that she probably hadn't known. A snob, she gave him the surname of a famous brewery family on whose yacht she had once been a guest. However, it was a banker who had been sixty-four when Alec was born who paid for his schooling and visited him often in the guise of an uncle. Alec was ashamed of his mother and stayed angry with her all his life. She sent him away to boarding school when he was five, paid for by the banker. Alec loved his school. When he got his first acting job at seventeen, his mother showed up intoxicated at the stage door and asked him for money.

When Aunt Charlotte gave over her bedroom to me she left it so hospitably bare that, as I've mentioned, it took me longer than it should have to realize it had been her room. When I entered it for the first time back in May, I faced a double bed with two views of the ocean, front and side, a table with a lamp on it and a straight-backed chair tucked under it, an empty bookcase, and a bureau with four drawers. Nothing hung on the walls, which had been freshly painted an off-white color that I would discover took on the yellow of clear mornings, a pearly gray on overcast days, and changed into a lavender-blue as it grew dark outside.

On the table that served as my desk were Mom's GED test books, which I had been studying, and the island histories authored by two local ladies who remembered the days when turtle eggs were gathered for fun breakfasts. The bookshelf, which Aunt Charlotte proudly admitted she had carpentered herself, along with the ones in her studio, was too long without a middle support and sagged in the middle. So far I had refrained from displaying any of my possessions above the top shelf, but the Gaston & Sons Lumber truck was the first thing I judged worthy. It was part of my heritage and also it diverted attention from the sag.

I felt conflicted about the black bear in the hoodie; my first impulse was to toss it. Eleven was too old to be holding on to a toy bear, though it wasn't so long ago when I insisted on having him. I was not at my best that day and it hurt to remember it now. Mom and I had been in the new Walmart in Jewel, buying my school supplies. When you were on a budget like ours, you calculated the difference between a $1.99 and a $2.39 box of pencils, and decided that it would be foolish to pay forty cents more just because Batman was on that box. I was accustomed to reading my mother's face and I knew how almost every shopping trip turned into an ordeal for her because she was one of those accursed "crossovers" in society who knew what the best was but couldn't afford it herself. Sometimes she would let resentment get the upper hand and point out to me someone "trash-shopping" in the stores we shopped in by necessity. ("Look at her, she just snatches up something without looking at the price and drops it in her basket.") On that day when I was not at my best, we were already in line at a checkout counter when I noticed a bin full of black bears in hoodies. They had probably been placed there strategically for people like me who were following a parent through the checkout line. I plucked one off the top of the pile and fell in love. He was so soft. He smelled so new. "Isn't he adorable?" I demanded. Mom looked at me rubbing him against my cheek. After scarcely a beat she asked: "Would . . . you like it?"

For now, in honor of my mother, the bear got to ride in the truck. Grandma *alias* fault-finding sister Brenda went facedown into a lower bureau drawer, not the upper drawer that held Mom's tin box with the only photo of my real dad and other cherished items: snapshots we had taken of each other with those throwaway cameras, Mom's supervisor's badge from Forster's Furniture, old Mr. Forster's *To Whom It May Concern* letter, which got Mom her nice first job in Jewel. It was a letter of high praise and must have cost the old man some moments of soul-searching, considering that he wrote it while his grandson was still in recovery from her son's brutal beating.

The two Marcus Aurelius volumes joined the other books on my desk. In the scholarly bilingual hardback, whoever had handwritten their own translation between the lines stopped halfway through the book. Midway down a page of Greek, the penciled interlinear translation broke off at the end of a paragraph.

The same paragraph on the English side of the page completely balked you with its antiquarian twists and turns:

> What then there can be amid such murk and nastiness,
> and in so ceaseless an ebbing of substance and of time,
> of movement and things moved, that deserves to be
> greatly valued or to excite our ambition in the least, I
> cannot even conceive.

The unknown person's penciled translation was simple and clear.

> In all this murk and mire, then, in all this ceaseless
> flow of being and time, of changes imposed and
> changes endured, I can think of nothing that is worth
> prizing highly or pursuing seriously.

XXIX.

*B*efore Aunt Charlotte's accident, I told her I would learn to use her digital camera and take new pictures of Grief Cottage. The plan had been to bring her up to date on its dereliction so she could incorporate it into her future paintings—if she chose to. How my new photos would affect her new paintings I hadn't been sure. Either she would be inspired by more ruination ("How sad! Do you think I can capture this added sadness in pigment?"), or she would be turned off by it ("No, this has gone too far, Marcus. If I painted it like this it would be a Halloween cartoon").

After she came home with her casts, I decided to put off even the mention of it. It would be cruel to hand over a bunch of new photos—assuming they turned out well—to send her rushing off to her studio to see if inspiration struck when she was no longer able to control a brush.

The other reason I had decided against taking the photos concerned the ghost-boy. It might set back our relationship. I had to base my behavior on how I would follow my instincts with living people, and I thought he might feel threatened if he saw me outside, clicking away at the cottage that had sheltered him for fifty years. Was I trying to take something from him? I had heard of those tribes who wouldn't let you take pictures of them because you would steal their souls.

Anyway, that was how I had reasoned up until now. Since I had failed to measure up to our last confrontation, my old precautions no longer applied. His spirit still remained inside the cottage, but he had turned away. Maybe he heard me, maybe not. Perhaps he had removed himself to the collapsing upper floor, where the roof had caved in to make him skylights. He could see and hear the birds without hearing me. The worst had happened to him a long time ago and some part of him had endured. This part had managed to exist without friends and without hope. And then I had weaseled into his space and offered false hope. All the ghost-boy desired now was to get outside the range of any more overtures from the coward-boy and be at peace with what he'd had before.

After making room for the things I had chosen to keep out of the latest box, I revisited my mom's memorials in the tin box. The tin box had been with me since she died—except while I was in the foster home. During that interim, I entrusted it to William, my ad litem. I didn't want the curious foster mom or some nosy child to be rifling through its contents—or stealing something—while I was at school.

First I studied for the umpteenth time the photo of the man Mom said was my dad. I took it into the bathroom to compare my face with his in Aunt Charlotte's only mirror. Did the picture, which Aunt Charlotte said had been cut from a school yearbook, reveal any more secrets since I had last studied it? It did appear we shared the same arched ("quizzical") eyebrows and wide-apart eyes, but that might just seem so because Aunt Charlotte had suggested it. The man's face looked too mature for a high school yearbook, so it must have been college. Compared to his, my face looked undeveloped and embarrassingly open. His face above the coat and tie was still the face of a young man but it had shut down in some way. Aunt Charlotte had said my mouth was like his when I was annoyed, but it was hard to "look annoyed" on demand in the mirror. My mouth was fuller than his and slightly puckered, like someone expecting a kiss. His lips were set in a thin derisive curl as if serving notice to the photographer that this was a crappy waste of time.

Then I reread for the umpteenth time old Mr. Forster's *To Whom It May Concern* accolade to Mom. (". . . this young widow . . . exemplary work habits . . . bringing up a son on her own . . . uncompromising values . . .")

For the first time cynicism raised its ugly head. If I had been the grandfather of a boy who had almost lost an eye, who had stopped breathing, wouldn't I praise to the skies a factory worker whose son had done the deed in order to get her out of town?

Next I looked through the photos Mom had chosen to save from those we had taken over the years. Until now her small collection hadn't excited me much, because she was still in the world and we expected to be taking many more pictures. As it turned out, our bleak time in Jewel had offered nothing we thought worth memorializing on film. The photos she had saved had all been taken back in Forsterville. Most of them were of me: "graduating" from kindergarten in my white cap and gown; standing on a stone wall looking down at her like I owned her; caught studying unaware in my pajamas under lamplight (her favorite). We had become expert with our Kodak throwaway cameras. Learned when to use the flash, when to move someone out of direct sun, when they were overshadowed. The sunshine was never too harsh at the Forsterville Cemetery because we walked there after my school day or in summer evenings after Mom's shift. I particularly liked the one I had taken from the top of the hill looking down on all the graves. It had just rained and there was a glowing mist over the landscape—it looked almost like a painting. There were several shots I had taken of Mom, sitting in front of some upright gravestones at the top of the hill, hugging her skirt close to her knees, her head tilted, smiling shyly to herself.

"Why don't you move over to that weeping angel and stand next to it?" I asked.

"I like it here," she said, patting the ground in front of her. "The view is nicest from up here."

"But *I'm* the one who's supposed to be picking the views!"

To oblige me, she stood by the weeping angel for a couple of shots. But either her eyes were closed or the body language was wrong: she had not kept those pictures. She did look best on top of the hill, though that whole upper section was filled exclusively with Forster headstones.

"Well, of course," she said, when I pointed this out. "They were the first people to get here, so naturally they picked the choicest spot."

THE ISLAND MARKET where I shopped every day stocked those throwaway cameras. If you turned in your camera by five P.M. you could have your photos back by noon the next day. It was popular with islanders and tourists who couldn't be bothered to drive to the mainland for the one-hour service.

I bought two cameras with twenty-four exposures each and set out the next morning with them tucked in my saddlebag. It was too chancy to wait until Aunt Charlotte got her cast off and I had mastered the complexities of her digital camera. The cottage was falling apart atom by atom, minute by minute. I would kick myself if I showed up one morning to find it razed to the ground or cordoned off by a sizzling electric fence. OUT! THIS MEANS YOU, MARCUS. YOU HAD YOUR CHANCE.

For a start I took distance shots of the cottage. Sky above and behind, dunes on either side, roofs of other cottages receding to the south, a wide expanse of empty beach in the foreground. If I angled the lens craftily I could make the wire fence all but invisible. From this distance my subject could pass for a tumbledown cottage rather than a hazardous wreck. I stood at the water's edge, near the spot where I had met Barrett. For a last panoramic shot, I removed my shoes and stepped back into the water up to the line of my biking shorts until I could include the mirrory surf.

As I was wheeling my bike toward the cottage to hide it in its usual spot behind a dune, a figure appeared atop this dune and began a cautious descent. Waving his arms for balance, he partly stumbled, partly slid down the steep incline until he pitched sideways into the waiting spikes of a Spanish bayonet. His sun hat flew off and rolled downhill ahead of him. I was close enough to hear the outraged string of expletives though not the specific swear words. Now he was scrambling to his feet and patting his behind for damage. It was Charlie Coggins, the realtor. He looked around furtively to see if anyone had witnessed his disgrace. I jumped on my bike and pedaled in the other direction so he wouldn't know I had seen. Shit. I should have come an hour earlier.

By the time I approached him openly, walking alongside my bike, he had brushed off his pants, shaken the sand out of his

docksiders, and restored his sun hat to his head. He had his back
to me, surveying his real estate, so I called out a good morning
in order not to startle him.

"It's Lachicotte's young friend, isn't it? You've gotten so
brown. Did you ever tell me your name?"

"Marcus."

I indicated the empty spot in the sand where his strange
land-and-water vehicle had been parked last time. "Where's
your amphibian today?"

"At home in its custom-built hangar. I use it mainly to
impress out-of-town clients. I drove up by the road in the
company car. Took a right smart spill getting down that
blasted dune. You want to avoid those evil Spanish bayonets
at all costs."

"My aunt already warned me about those."

"The artist. Broke her arm, right? Last time we met, you
were going to come back with a camera and take some pictures
for her."

"It was her wrist, but it's still in a cast." No use complicating
matters with the ankle as well. "Today I brought some cameras.
The cottage is getting worse by the day."

"Tell me about it! When I hear a siren at night, you know
what I pray for? That some firebug will have burned it to the
ground before the trucks get there. Every time I come here I
run through my litany of 'why didn't I's: Why didn't I sell it to
the highest bidder before the roof caved in? Why didn't I keep
the empty lot next to it and donate the cottage to the Historical
Society, claim my gift deduction, and let *them* deal with property taxes and hazardous structure policies and erosion engineers' fees until they got fed up and torched it themselves and
had the state put up a nice historical marker? Why didn't Pop

sell it back in the sixties after he bought it from the people who made a mess of the renovation and then ran out of cash? What were we at Coggins Realty thinking? That it was going to magically reconstruct itself one night while we were sleeping, and we'd wake up to find the pristine new cottage as it looked in 1804, with the *shoreline* of 1804, and assessed at twentieth-century value?"

"I thought I'd better get some pictures while it's still standing—so Aunt Charlotte will have something to go by when she can paint again."

"What kind of camera do you use?"

I took my throwaways out of the saddlebag and showed him.

"These do everything you need if you know how to use them. You can get the prints back from the island market overnight. I brought two cameras so I'd be sure to have enough exposures."

"And what pictures were you planning to take?"

"I thought some close-ups from inside the fence—maybe a few from up on the porch."

"I'm guessing this won't be the first time you've crawled under that fence."

"It will be more official now you're here."

"I suppose you expect me to accompany you in your trespassing."

I didn't, but I saw the advantages. If Charlie Coggins trespassed with me under the fence and up on the porch, he would serve both as my buffer and my cover. If the ghost-boy was watching from some new vantage point, he would know not to "count" this visit even if we had still been on good terms. He would know to remain invisible because I came in the company of the realtor who must have inspected this cottage on many occasions over the years. And the bonus was that with Charlie Coggins in tow I could brave the inside of the cottage with no fear of being surprised by more ghost than I could handle.

XXX.

I need not have feared. The ghost-boy was so not there. Charlie Coggins held my cameras while I crawled under the fence, then I held his hat and sunglasses while he shimmied under with some grunts and groans.

I went first up the rickety steps. "I always hold on to this part of the railing. And watch the porch slant, it comes as a surprise."

"I see you've become a pro at this."

On the porch I snapped the front of the cottage with its gaping windows and door. I used the flash since the east side was still in shadow. "I've never gone inside," I said. "But with you here I think it would be a shame not to."

"I haven't been inside for a good long while . . . but for Pete's sake, test every board before you put any weight on it. Lachicotte would have my . . . well, on a platter if you were to get hurt."

I paused to snap some close-ups of the doorless doorway. These were for me in the future more than for anybody else. In my future, when I came across these photos, they would bring it all back: *When I was eleven I saw a boy standing in that space—his hands were braced against the sides—I saw the ridges of his knuckles and his eyes like dark raisins—he looked straight at me—this really did happen.*

As I wound the film forward, I asked Charlie Coggins why they hadn't replaced the door. "Wouldn't it help keep people out?"

"Not when everybody's already been in and removed everything of value. The last door we put in was, let's see, ten years ago . . . fifteen? I'd have to check. Time gets cagey as you proceed in life. The other day my doc asked me could I recall offhand when my last colonoscopy was and I said five years ago. When he looked it up in my file it was eleven."

"What did they remove of value?"

"Faucet fixtures, copper pipes, all the old cypress wood paneling, the wooden latches and the original iron hardware, a toilet . . ."

"A toilet?"

"Not everyone can afford a new toilet. They took the sink, too. Mind you, this wasn't all done in one trip. Just covert truckloads on moonless nights over the years."

"Couldn't you have locked the house?"

"We did. They stole the locks. Before we gave up on doors we must have installed at least half a dozen. Pop was still alive when we put in the last one—whoa, that makes it over *twenty* years ago. Like I said, time can get cagey. Pop said, 'Might as well let in the clean ocean breeze. See what it can accomplish. The whole thing might fall down sooner, quicker, and cleaner.' Of course the Historical Society was still making big noises about fund drives and restoration. But the money just wasn't there. So Pop said put the high wire fence around it with threatening legal signs and let nature have its way. With beach-front values rising we were sure someone would come along and snap up those prime lots and take care of the demolition themselves. Only they didn't and then it was the nineties and then the millennium—and here we are."

We were actually inside. At last I had crossed the threshold. But if I had expected any thrill from Grief Cottage, it didn't come. The room was about as unhaunted as any room could get. It was as though by entering with another person I had canceled its ghost-aura. Sand intermixed with debris had piled high into the room's corners, and cobwebs swagged from its timbers and walls. Droppings from animals speckled the bare floor. A spotlight of sun penetrated a broken place in the roof and revealed the almost transparent skin of a snake. The only other snakeskin I had ever seen had been hooked on a bush in Wheezer's grandmother's backyard. "Look, you can even see where its jaw was!" he cried. "It probably rubbed against that bush to start the process and finally crawled out of its own mouth!"

I rotated in a slow circle, snapping flash exposures. In the middle of the room was a boarded-up fireplace whose mantelpiece had been ripped out. "Yeah," said Charlie Coggins, "that was a lovely mantel, a local carpenter's pride. Wonder where it's living now? Oh, see the blue paint on the facing of the doorway we just came through? I'll tell you a little story about that blue paint. Has anyone told you about Ole Plat-eye? No? Ole Plat-eye is a spirit the Gullahs are absolutely terrified of. Some of them still paint the inside of their doors with this sky-blue color to keep him out. Only it's not always a him, it can be part dog or cow or woman with extra limbs and a big eye hanging down from the center of its forehead. It's one of those completely malevolent and unredeemable spirits."

"Why is it unredeemable?"

"To be honest I don't know. Maybe it's got some unfinished business of the kind that can never be finished. You'd have to ask a Gullah."

"I don't know what a Gullah is."

"Gullahs are the descendants of the slaves who worked in the rice fields down here. They still keep up the old African traditions."

"Did any of them ever live in this cottage?"

"No, they had their own cabins near the owners' cottages. When Pop was selling off the last of those slave cabins in the seventies, I used to see these same blue door facings when we went inside. I painted that blue for the best Halloween party that ever got thrown on this island. Right here in this cottage. Nineteen sixty-eight. Sundown to sunup. The mantel was still here and the toilet and most of the fixtures. We had a band, I was on drums. The girls made a wicked punch. One showoff actually came as Old Plat-eye, with three legs and a disgusting eyeball on a string Scotch-taped to his forehead but we made him take off his costume before he was allowed to pass through the door. Honoring the spirit of the night, my blue paint and all. After the paint had dried, I rubbed it down with steel wool to make it look old, like in the slave cabins. A lot of people still remember that party."

"Can we go up those stairs?"

"I'd rather you didn't. Well, if you're super careful. Last time I went up it was already hazardous, but you're a light fellow. But test *every* stair before you put any weight on it and hold on to the wall. You be the canary in the mine and I'll creep along in your footsteps. You'll find a mess up there. When they were boarding up the south wall after that porch fire, a lot of junk got stashed upstairs and nobody ever took it to the dump."

"You mean the porch fire during Hurricane Hazel?"

"Oh right, you're interested in that family that got swept away. But after the hurricane and the fire, the Barbours sold the cottage and the new owners were going to rebuild it and use it as a vacation home, but then they decided not to and put it back on the market. The next buyers didn't even pretend they wanted to live in it. They were looking for a quick flip. You know, strip it down, clean it out, and resell at a profit. They got as far as bulldozing and leveling the ground where the burnt porch had been and boarding up the south wall. Then they ran out of money and Pop bought it back as an investment. I had to get all this information from Pop's files, seeing as I was only two years old when Hazel hit."

"But didn't they think it was a cigarette that started the fire?"

"Maybe it was a cigarette, maybe not. Folks can't tolerate loose ends—they've got to tie up a story. Pop said the fire could just as well have started *after* the hurricane had passed, because who was paying attention? Everybody was busy picking up the pieces of their own properties."

"It's too bad those flipping people didn't do a better job closing off the south side. Those shingles without any windows in them make it look so blind and sad."

"They ran out of money, like I said. The shingles you see now were a cosmetic afterthought, courtesy of Coggins Realty. I put them up myself. The flipping people, as you call them, had just tacked up sheets of tar paper any old how on the south side of the house before they went belly up. We couldn't leave it like that, it'd put off any buyer, so I found some weathered cypress shingles that would fit in with the rest of the old houses and nailed them up tastefully. I was still in high school, just learning the business—Hey, hey, *hey!* Watch that step!"

He had gripped my arm so hard it hurt. "Look at that! The riser has cracked down the middle. A heavier person could have fallen right through. Son, I'm not sure this is a good idea."

"I'm fine. We'll just be extra careful." We were halfway up now. I was determined to see the upstairs.

He was right. It was a mess. There was nothing you wanted to waste a photo on. It revived unhappy memories of some of the places Mom and I had looked at when we were apartment-hunting in Jewel. "They haven't even cleaned up after the last tenant," Mom would say. "It amazes me how inconsiderate people can be." Nevertheless, I snapped a few pictures so I could finish off the roll and start on the second camera.

"None of these rooms have doors," I said.

"Well, they did when the last people slept in them. Doors are very easy to make off with, all you need is a flat-blade screwdriver. There are places that sell old doors and windows exclusively for fancy prices. The whole layout of this cottage has been compromised. It's more noticeable up here where things went truly awry. Of course I wouldn't point this out to a potential buyer."

"How has it been compromised?"

"For a start, the stairs would have made way more sense on the north side."

"Why didn't the builders think of that?"

"The original builders had a simple, pure plan. Four rooms on one floor with an oceanside porch. H-shaped chimney in the center of the house. It had to warm all four rooms because the rice planters' families stayed into November. Kitchen was to the back, separated from the house by a breezeway. The kitchen had its own chimney. Then came the makeovers of the successive owners. 'Let's build another porch and add a bedroom. Let's add two bedrooms. Let's incorporate the kitchen into the main house. Let's convert the outhouse with its breezeway into an indoor bathroom at the end of a hall. Let's put in an upper floor. Oh, dear, the previous owners have used up the north side with those added-on ground floor bedrooms, so we'll have to break through the roof on the *south* side and put the staircase there.' This may be the earliest cottage still standing on the island, but its vernacular lines have been completely compromised."

He had recounted the compromises so vividly that you could see them piling up, mistake upon mistake, until all that was left was the present ruin we were standing in.

"Are there any cottages left that haven't been compromised?"

"Oh, yes. One's even got a National Register marker—it's been kept up beautifully and added to responsibly. It still serves as a rental house, though the owners are very particular. We are honored to have it on our books. And there's your neighbor's house, which has stayed in the same family since it was built. But the late Mr. Upchurch committed an atrocity, hiding those indigenous brick footing columns behind a painted trellis. And then the old lady had that unsightly ramp built—not that it's her fault she's in a wheelchair. But it can be ripped out easily enough when the time comes. She's a real piece of work. You met her yet?"

"We're friends."

"Ah. Well, then, give her my best regards."

He undoubtedly would have said more about Coral Upchurch if I had said less.

"You can take a picture of the oceanfront room, but you're not going in there. Before the fire, there was a nice dormer window on the south wall, but it was so damaged they sheared it off when they were taking off the burnt porch. Okay, take a photo, but do *not* step into that room. I want to get you out of here without falling through any floors. As you can see, the other upstairs rooms are so piled with trash they're not worth a photo. I hadn't realized how far gone these floors are. Let's see if we can make it downstairs without any broken limbs and we'll finish our cottage crawl with a look at the kitchen. Happily, none of the owners covered over its lovely brick floors, from the days when people still cooked in their fireplaces, and so far no thief has come up with the right tools to dig out those bricks. You won't find any more bricks like those unless you visit the brick collection at the Charleston Museum."

XXXI.

*W*hat's a colonoscopy?"

"Something you won't need for a while. Who's having one?" Balanced on her right foot, Aunt Charlotte was extracting a container of yogurt from the refrigerator with her left hand, which already had a banana in it.

"Charlie Coggins, the realtor, was using it to explain how time plays tricks on you when you get older. He thought he'd had one five years ago but it turned out it was eleven."

"Where did you run into him?"

"I went up to Grief Cottage to take some photos for you. He was there, and we went on a tour inside the house. He called it our cottage crawl."

"You went *inside*?"

"Yeah, the upstairs is pretty bad. I pretty near fell through a stair when we were going up."

"*Marcus!*"

"No, it was fine. He was right there to grab me. I took two rolls for you on those disposable cameras. I can pick up the prints tomorrow. You'll have them when you go back to painting your best sellers."

"If I ever regain my full range of motion."

She must have been on the laptop again, trawling for dire wrist stories.

"You will."

She met my optimism with a sour look. "But here you are, just in time to peel my banana and uncork a bottle of wine. Oh, my bed linens are already in the washing machine—they can wait until there's a full load. I've already put fresh sheets on."

"You managed alone?"

"One-armed people have to learn to make their beds."

"How is your . . . private project coming?"

"I'm either onto something or deluding myself because I can't do real work. A colonoscopy is when they insert a tiny camera into your rectum and send it up through your intestines to look for polyps—or worse things. I've had one. If you want, you can watch the procedure on a TV screen while they're doing it."

"Did you watch?"

"Naturally. I'm the visual type. It looked like the inside of a soft, pink tunnel, going up and up, with little craters and bumps along the way. No alarming bumps in my case. If you'll uncork that bottle of wine for me, Marcus, I'll be off to my obsession or delusion—or whatever it is."

WALKING NEXT DOOR to the "compromised" Upchurch house to get Roberta's list for my ride to the island store, I debated whether those old brick footing columns would look better "uncompromised," without the white latticework in front of them. But I decided the latticework made the house look more solid and neat.

"No list today, Marcus. We're going to Myrtle Beach this afternoon to get her hair and nails done, so I'll do my shopping at the Piggly Wiggly," Roberta said.

"Is there some special occasion?"

"Tomorrow is around the time Mr. Billy arrives."

"But—how—?"

"How we going to handle it? Like the inchworm does." Roberta made a spritely humping movement with the back of her hand. "One inch at a time. She's no fool, she's just taking it slow. She knows he's not coming, but she wants to reverence the occasion in her own way. She hopes you'll be visiting tomorrow at the usual time."

"But, how should I act?"

"The way you always act. She'll do the rest."

BIKING TO THE island market, I racked my brain for tempting meals I might make for Aunt Charlotte. As I considered the options within my range, I was aware that the real problem hovered above me like a sneering gremlin, biding his time for a pounce.

Aunt Charlotte didn't care about eating. Since I had come to live with her, neither did I. We had more interesting matters to attend to. That weird unlit morning when the ghost-boy had showed himself to me in the doorway of Grief Cottage, I had breakfasted on a fistful of dry cereal before I hurried north on the spellbound beach.

Mom and I had enjoyed our meals. Supper was usually our only one together, and though she was worn out from work, that was our time for conversation: *conversation* meaning the kind of talk when people tell their day, complain, and make plans for the future. Aunt Charlotte and I didn't really have conversations. Our exchanges were more like brief Q & A's ("Where did you run into him?" "How's your project coming?"), or requests for things (mostly her requests since her accident—like haircuts and peeling bananas and opening bottles . . .).

"At last!" shrieked the gremlin, nose-diving through space to sink his claws into my back. "You finally said *bottle!*"

Eight cases were delivered to our door at intervals. I carried them in, made a stack in the pantry, and unpacked each case as the necessity arose. Ninety-six bottles allows you three a day for thirty-two days. If you ran out before then, you ordered the next eight cases. There were never more than eight cases, but since I had arrived in mid-May, the deliveries had become more frequent. She ordered mostly Bordeauxs and Burgundies and always chatted, more than usual for Aunt Charlotte, with whoever was on the other end of the line at the Myrtle Beach wine store. She could make it sound like she was having regular guests, who knew the difference between Bordeauxs and Burgundies and why, if you did order Beaujolais, it had to be from a good year.

I had been telling myself that when she got her casts removed she'd taper off. But, now that I thought about it further, she'd always had an open bottle in reach. She always drank when she was painting, which was almost all the days I had lived with her. The only time she had stopped cold had been for a few days after the second surgery when she was afraid to mix painkillers with alcohol. So, what was the problem? She had been doing this for years and turning out paintings and enjoying her solitary life. Why should she stop now?

Maybe it was just my problem. It was all about me. I was afraid if she started drinking more bottles a day, stumbling and falling on a regular basis, maybe really damaging herself, she would be declared an unfit guardian and back I would go into the system.

Yet I shrank from the thought of confronting her: "Aunt Charlotte, do you think maybe you ought to slow down a little with the wine?" I knew her sour look, which I had received as recently as today. "Marcus, just open it," she would say. And I would open it. She could also kick me out of her house for being a pain. ("He was a nice boy, but he became judgmental. Like Lachicotte. My life was no longer my own.")

The "monthly stipend" would of course be taken from her, but she had lived without it all these years, and there would be family court and lawyers and maybe the court would appoint a trustee to manage the funds—I didn't know all the legal details, and also I was in another state now where they had their own rules. I would be sent to another house, not a relative's since there were no more relatives—or, if there weren't any vacancies, an institution.

I stopped here. I would have to trust the fates that she would avoid another disaster between now and getting her casts off. Maybe she'd finish her secret project and go back to taking orders for her paintings. What power did I have to change an old and comfortable habit? I wondered what Lachicotte had said in former days when he "nagged" her . . .

"Congratulations," mocked the gremlin straddling my back. "You're not the brightest bulb in the drawer, but you finally saw the light."

I had carried Lachicotte's card in my saddlebag ever since the day he gave it to me. Once I came close to using it, but then decided it would be disloyal to call him from the pay phone outside the market to tattle about Aunt Charlotte's "fermenting."

I called his work number first and a pleasant woman answered. "Vintage Motors, how can I help you?"

"Is Mr. Hayes there?"

"He's out at the moment. Would you like his mobile number?"

"I have it on his card. Thank you."

"Would you like to leave any message?"

"No, thank you. I'll try the mobile."

"Hello," said Lachicotte's recorded voice. "You've reached my voice mail. Please leave your (*yoah*) number (*numbah*) and I'll get back to you as soon as I can."

I was still trying out phrases that could convey my message discreetly when I was cut off.

What would I have said? "This is Marcus. I need some advice. Aunt Charlotte is—Aunt Charlotte is—"

"You're off the hook for now, but I'm still here," conceded the gremlin. He was behind me but, unlike with the ghost-boy, I knew how he looked. The reptilian skin, the pitcher ears, the grinning saw-teeth. Wheezer and I had spent hours expanding gremlin traits beyond the simpleminded possibilities offered by movies. "Don't you feel," Wheezer said, "that there must be an advanced model of *mogwai* more imaginative and intelligent than Gizmo and, to balance things out, a much scarier and evil model than Stripe?" "Why does there always have to be a *balance* between good and evil?" I asked. "Because those are the rules," said Wheezer. "I didn't make them. There always has to be a baddie to balance out the goodie. And if you have a more complex and interesting goodie, you need to make an equally complex and interesting baddie."

As I approached the market entrance, I saw a fit, sun-browned boy about my age loping toward the door. He wore a helmet like mine. With a jolt I realized he was my reflection in the glass door. When had this happened? When Charlie Coggins said it was probably safe for me to precede him up Grief Cottage's hazardous staircase, I had wondered how he could call me "a light fellow." But he had been right. Someone called Pudge had been nowhere near that staircase.

"Do you want duplicates?" asked the man when I handed over the disposable cameras.

"Will it cost more?"

"A dollar more a roll."

"I'll just have the singles then."

I SHOULD HAVE asked for the duplicates, I thought, biking home. Then I could have mailed any good ones to Charlie Coggins as a thank-you. But I was still living in two worlds and perhaps always would be. The world in which you forfeited having Batman on your pencil case to save forty cents, and the world in which you could afford to pay two dollars for extra copies of pictures because of a dead mother's trust.

XXXII.

ut don't go trying to use the same route twice. Indeed, don't try to get there at all. It'll happen when you're not looking for it. And don't talk too much about it, even among yourselves. And don't mention it to anyone else unless you find that they've had adventures of the same sort themselves . . ."

HOW COULD I have forgotten the Professor? There he had been, lying at the bottom of one of my boxes all this time, with his sage advice about commuting between reality and the supernatural and *the importance of keeping it to yourself.*

I had unpacked the final box from my old life this afternoon after putting away the groceries, checking the turtles' thermocouple (no change), doing the laundry, including my aunt's sheets and pillowcases, and tidying the bathroom. Inside the last box were the usual candidates for the black trash bag: first aid stuff, including our eye cup, some outdated medications, Mom's Ace bandages she sometimes wore at night for her varicose veins, and the little bottle of arnica the dentist had given her to rub into her gums after a tooth extraction. Clothes I was already outgrowing last summer had been folded and stacked carefully, as though the boy who unpacked this box would be the exact same size as last year. And there on the bottom, wedged beside a pair of sneakers (also getting tight last summer) was my boxed Narnia set, which cheered and saddened me at the same time. We had devoured these books, my mom and I, reading them over and over again, aloud to each other and by ourselves, discussing the characters, and figuring out the meanings.

I was sprawled in the hammock with all the books in my lap, thumbing through them at random, letting the illustrations recall the stories, when footsteps approached up the rarely-used outdoor stairs to our porch. It was Lachicotte Hayes, carrying a paper sack in the crook of his arm. "I brought y'all some tomatoes. I used the rear entrance so I wouldn't have to knock and disturb anybody."

"She's in her studio. I haven't seen her since I got back from the market."

"It was you I was hoping to find. Oh, *The Lion, the Witch, and the Wardrobe.* I read that to my niece when she was young. I don't know which of us enjoyed it the most."

"The niece I met at the library."

"Yes, Althea. We were out condo-shopping for her when you called."

"You knew it was me?"

"My receptionist said a young man phoned but didn't need the mobile number because he had it on my card. Then when I checked my voice mail, there was a silence until the cutoff."

"I couldn't think of an appropriate message to leave."

Lachicotte transferred the sack of tomatoes to the stool Aunt Charlotte used to prop up her broken ankle. "Do you fancy a walk on the beach? My father used to say if you went a whole summer without getting your toes in the ocean you were either too busy for your own good or getting too old for your own good. And here is July half over."

LACHICOTTE SAT DOWN on the lowest step of the boardwalk, rolled up his pants cuffs, removed his shoes and socks, tucking a sock into each shoe, and placed them neatly beneath the step. I did likewise: I hadn't been barefoot on the beach since I'd got my bike. It occurred to me as I placed my sneakers next to his docksiders that a passing stranger observing these side-by-side shoes might assume that some father and son were taking a walk on the beach.

The tide was ebbing, leaving a generous expanse of glassy surf where you could walk and still make contact with the incoming wavelets that broke over your feet.

"Are you liking it here, Marcus?"

I was glad he kept walking straight ahead and not looking at me.

"I like it, but it still feels weird to realize my mom is dead. I'm not sure I can explain it, but often it seems like she's more alive than ever. I think about her more than ever and I keep seeing new sides of her."

"You explain it perfectly (*puh-fectly*) well. After all the human noise and conflicts have stopped, the absent person has more room in your heart to spread out and be herself. My mother's been gone ten years and I know her much better now than when we saw each other every day."

I felt it was probably time to say something about being grateful to Aunt Charlotte for taking me in. "But I like living here at the beach. Before I came here I had never even seen the ocean. And I love my bike. And Aunt Charlotte is very good to me. She doesn't preach or pry or interfere. She lets me do pretty much as I like and goes her own way."

"That she does. The first time I met your aunt was at the hardware store. I was putting back some items on the shelf that I had decided not to buy and she came up and asked could I help her. 'I'll try my best,' I said. She said she was laying ceramic tiles in her bathroom and was tempted to buy the more expensive brand of sand grout, but was it worth it? What did it have that the others didn't? I read the information on the can aloud to her. It was mildew and mold resistant, but for best results you needed to finish it off with a water resistant sealer. 'Is the sealer really necessary,' she asked, 'or are you just trying to sell me the extra product?' At that point the owner, who is a friend, came over and made some jokey remarks about my fancy foreign cars. Then he turned to her and asked if he could be of service, and she realized I was not a salesman."

"What did she do then?"

"She looked mortified. Like she'd been forced into violating some taboo. She apologized to me very formally and went her way. But I was left with the sense that she held me responsible for letting her make the mistake."

I had no trouble imagining my prickly aunt reacting like that. "Did she buy the grout?"

"I don't remember. I felt like an oaf. Soon after, I learned she was new to the island and was renovating an old place known as the Rascal Shack. Young bucks had used it as their drinking club for as long as anyone could remember."

"What was she like then?"

"Much like she is now. Straightforward, laconic, a loyal friend—once she decided you were worth it. Lean as a string bean and handsome in an imperious sort of way—she still is. Her hair was dark then and she may have worn a little lipstick in those days."

"I'm not sure I know what *laconic* means."

"Sparing of words. She wasn't like any woman I'd ever known. To a Southern boy like me, her straightforwardness was exotic. No guile, no gush. The next time we met she was working as a receptionist for the local vet and I had brought in my dog to check out a limp she had developed. All the signs indicated bone cancer, and the options were heart-sickening. I came out of the examining room shattered. When I got to the desk to settle the bill, your aunt glanced down at what the vet had written while I was digging out my credit card and hoping I could make it out of there before I broke down. 'Mr. Hayes,' she said, 'why don't you and Dinah go on home?' She did not look at me once. 'We have your address, we'll send the bill.' Then she turned her back on me real fast and looked very busy with some filing."

"What kind of dog was Dinah?"

"Oh, she was a wonderful mix. Shorthair, the color of butterscotch, long, long legs. The vet said he thought she was part golden retriever, part German shepherd, and possibly some greyhound. When she ran on the beach, she scarcely touched the ground. She used to ride everywhere with me, sitting up straight in the passenger seat. She rode like that on our final trip to the vet, although I could tell it hurt her to sit."

"Was my aunt there?"

"There was someone else on the desk that day. But she came by my shop soon after. She said she was sorry about

Dinah and I showed her some of the automobiles in their various stages of rebuilding. She said she wished she could take a class in auto mechanics, she was sick and tired of being clueless about what went on inside her car. Did I know of any class? I said I could teach her better than any class. She wanted to know how much I would charge, and I told her it would be my pleasure. And then she offered to work for me part-time as payment."

"But what about the vet?"

"That was a part-time job, too, but it wasn't long until she came to me full-time. For a while we went into the taxi business as partners. She ever tell you about that?"

"It was a success. She was able to paint full-time after she got her share of the proceeds."

"Painting was the best thing that ever happened to her. You are the next best thing."

"But I'm not really—" To distract from the break in my voice, I veered away from him and stamped and splashed in the shallow waves until I got control of myself. "I'm not doing such a good job taking care of her. Like you said, being her guardian. That's why I called you, but then I couldn't think of a suitable message just to leave on someone's voice mail."

"Well here I am. You don't have to leave any message."

"She spends all day shut up in her studio. She's working on that secret project I told you about. She said it will either amount to something or she's just deluding herself because she can't do real work. I'm not allowed to go in there even to change the sheets, which I've been doing since the accident. The thing is, I'm still in charge of uncorking her wine and the number of bottles keeps increasing. I thought about saying something to her about cutting back, but I knew she wouldn't appreciate it. I was wondering if you ever said anything like that to her and how it went over."

"It didn't, other than shrinking my welcome mat to the size of a lady's handkerchief. Usually people with harmful habits don't want to be told about it. They have to come around to it themselves."

"But what if they don't come around to it until it's too late?"

"I'm working toward that, Marcus. I'm thinking this out as I go."

"Oh, sorry."

"The project, as far as you know, involves painting?"

"I saw some traces of paint under her fingernails when I was cutting them the other day. Not a lot. She has this separate laundry sink in her studio where she always washes up."

"Well, look here, next week we're going back to the surgeon in Charleston. She'll have new x-rays and we'll have more information. Knowing him, he'll say he can't tell for sure until the cast comes off. And then there has to be rehab: squeezing tennis balls and so on, slowly building back the use of that wrist. She's not the only one who's been scouring the Internet for scaphoid stories, only I'm on the lookout for the positive outcomes. After we've been to the surgeon, we'll see how her spirits are. If they're tolerably hopeful, let's let her complete her secret project. It's possible, you know, things will take a turn for the better. Have you known any folks with addictions, Marcus?"

"Well, Mom didn't drink. She wasn't against it or anything, but she was too tired after work, and also wine and beer cost money. My best friend's grandmother was a smoke addict. The longest she could go without lighting up was forty-two minutes. We timed it once. And our landlord in Forsterville had to attend an AA meeting every morning before he went to work so he wouldn't fall off the wagon. And the man in Jewel who had hired Mom for his mountaintop joinery business just before it went bankrupt—he became a meth addict and the next time Mom saw him his teeth were all rotted and he kept picking at sores on his face. Oh, and Mom had this night school teacher in Forsterville she admired, he really cared about his students, but then he overdosed on something and died. She said if he had gotten the proper help in time he might still be alive. I never met him, this was before I was born. So I guess you could say that I've never been close to anyone who had an addiction. But what if Aunt Charlotte doesn't get the proper help in time?"

"That's not going to happen, now we're on the case. There are places to go for treatment."

"But she'd have to go away, wouldn't she?"

"For a while, yes."

"Then I'd have to go somewhere else, too. I'm a minor and I'm not allowed to live alone."

"We can find someone to live with you, like Roberta Dumas lives with Coral Upchurch. But let's wait to hear the surgeon's opinion next week. My first wife liked to say that the only thing in life you could absolutely depend on was change. And sometimes these changes can be for the better."

"But not always."

"No, not always. I'm not denying that."

XXXIII.

ystery solved," Ed Bolton said, cheerfully hovering above Lachicotte and me as we sat on the boardwalk step, putting on our socks and shoes. He had dropped by in his World War II jeep for a routine check on our turtle clutch. "I recognized your sneakers, Marcus, but I couldn't for the life of me figure out who belonged to the docksiders. Good to see you, Lachicotte."

"Ed. How's my favorite jeep?"

"A-OK thanks to you."

"Still not sorry we replaced that tub?"

"Only thing I regret is that I didn't capitulate a whole lot sooner. I was under some notion that the old rusty tub was what kept it authentic. Marcus, their temperature's way up. Tonight may be their night."

"But when I checked it earlier there was no change."

"You remember how much earlier?"

It was before I did the laundry and unpacked the final box from Jewel. "Maybe three hours ago?"

"Even more auspicious. That means it's risen fast. Listen, Marcus, would you be able to babysit this clutch, say, for the next hour until I can get some other volunteers here? If there's any change in the sand just phone my beeper."

"What kind of change?"

"The sand collapsing inward would be the first."

"Does that mean they're coming out?"

"No, they usually boil up within an hour or so after sunset, when the sand's cooler. But it could mean they're getting ready. Tonight would be favorable. Early crescent moonrise, tide coming in so they won't have to race so far. You ever seen a boil, Lachicotte?"

"I never have. If I didn't have to drive up to Sumter to let a customer test-drive an automobile, I'd love to stick around. As it is, I should have been on the road an hour ago. Marcus, we'll be in touch." Fixing me with a "you-know-what-I-mean" look, he hurried off, brushing his trousers as he went. It was because of our walk, I realized, that he was an hour late.

I told Ed Bolton that I would have to go back to the cottage and leave my aunt a note.

"You go on, Marcus. I'll stay here till you come back and make calls to volunteers on my mobile. We should probably go ahead and set up the sound system and shovel the path. If I'm right, there's a backup of hatchlings under there right now, waiting for the sand to cool. It's exciting, isn't it?"

"What's a tub?"

"What? Oh, the jeep you mean. See the bottom frame that rides above the wheels? When it's sitting by itself on the ground it looks like a tub. Lachicotte was after me for fifteen years to put in a new one. But I was afraid if I replaced it I'd lose my direct connection with the past. As it turns out, all I lost was a lot of rust."

★ ★ ★

Dear Aunt Charlotte,

I will be down at the turtle clutch. Tonight may be the night! They usually come up after sunset as soon as the sand cools down. Chicken salad and cucumber salad in fridge, also a tomato from L's garden that I cut up in wedges for you. Uncorked bottle in the usual place.

Marcus

I WONDERED IF some subtle change in my behavior would give me away as having "told on" Aunt Charlotte the next time she laid eyes on me.

I left the note on the table. I had considered shoving it under her door in case she decided not to come out to eat. After all, I had said I would let her know if the turtles showed any sign of boiling up. But what if she were to see it as soon as I slipped it under? ("You can always knock, Marcus. You don't have to go creeping around sliding notes under doors. What's the guilty look for?")

I had anticipated having the next hour all by myself with the turtles. Just me and the peaceful fading light and the wash of the ocean and a more or less empty beach. I was going to be the herald of the long-awaited event, the lone witness to that first little hole in the sand. I might even see a little head pop up, decide it was still too early, and disappear. And then the other volunteers would eventually gather in the cooling dusk, one or two at a time. In my scenario Ed Bolton would be the first to return. He would announce to each new arrival: "Marcus here's been watching this nest like a hawk. As soon as he spotted that hatchling scout, he phoned my beeper and I was on my way. Marcus actually *saw* the little fellow poke his head up, look around, and go back to tell the others it wasn't time yet!"

But during the short time I had been up at the house, Ed Bolton must have been working his mobile nonstop. Because very soon after he had headed away in the jeep to collect digging tools for the hatchlings' path to the sea, other volunteers started appearing over the dunes. They must have parked their vehicles near our house. Yet it was still daylight, no sand had collapsed inward, nothing out of the ordinary had sent me rushing off to the house to telephone Ed's beeper. Some of the volunteers said Hello, or Hello, you must be Marcus, but most of them went straight to their tasks, which must have been prearranged. They were mixed in age: retirees like Ed Bolton; middle-aged ladies in knee-length shorts; younger men, some still in work clothes; and a sprinkling of teenagers.

Two ladies carefully pulled out the wooden stakes and rolled up the orange plastic fence surrounding the clutch. A man knelt near the nest and inserted something down in the sand while another man set up an amplifier on a pole. The teenagers were marking out a path for the hatchlings' crawl to the water.

"But what if it doesn't happen tonight?" I asked the friendlier of the two ladies, one of those volunteers who had greeted me by name. "Then you'll just have to put the fence back up again."

"Oh, Ed has a second sense about these little guys. He said the temperature was way up within the last three hours and there's likely a backup of them under there right now. Here comes Ed now, you can ask him."

The sun had just set and a pinkish haze was forming to the north out of which the jeep was bouncing toward us. At first, I took the waving straw sticking up on the passenger side as some kind of broom, a tool Ed was bringing to scoop out the turtles' path to the sea. But as the jeep came closer, I saw it was the straw-colored hair of a person. Not till I saw him slide out of the jeep did I see it was a boy, taller than I was, light hair cut short on the sides with a fringe swept over the forehead. He wore an orange T-shirt with a large white paw print on the chest, khaki cargo shorts, supersonic-looking gray-and-orange sneakers, and a huge black watch on his wrist. His face was sunburned; the rest of him, not so much.

"Marcus, this is Pickett, he's staying with his grandparents, our neighbors, until his school starts. Pickett, this is Marcus, who lives in that cottage behind the dunes. Marcus, I've told Pickett to stick close to you and you'll fill him in on our drill."

Pickett did not strike me as the kind of boy who would stick close to anyone, or pay much attention to a peer "filling him in" on anything. So far he hadn't looked at me once, but when I said "Hi" he echoed it, looking me over with a languid glance.

"You two could help shovel out the path," suggested Ed, "if you're so inclined. Pickett, go and get that rake and scoop shovel we brought."

"WHAT GRADE YOU going to be in?" I asked as we set to work. I had offered to take the shovel and let Pickett follow along with the rake.

"My school doesn't have grades. I'll be in second form. That's eighth grade."

"Oh, so will I!"

"Funny, you look younger."

"Well, I skipped a year."

This earned no comment. "How wide am I supposed to rake this path?"

"Maybe a little wider? But leave a little mound on each side so they won't be wandering off."

"Such a big deal for a few turtles!"

"It's hardly a *few*. There are a hundred and ten eggs in this one nest. Loggerheads just happen to be the world's largest hard-shelled turtle and they're threatened with extinction. They've been doing this race to the sea for forty million years. *We've* only been around for the last two hundred thousand."

He heard me out, grinding the toe of a sneaker into the sand. "So what did they do for all those million years before we were on the scene to rake their paths for them?"

"They were on the way to *extinction* before this conservation thing got going. People were eating their eggs for breakfast and making jewelry out of them, and . . ."

"Just kidding," he said, like you would to a child who had gotten overemotional about something. "You live here all year round?"

"I live with my great-aunt. My mother died last winter."

"Oh, sorry."

"Why did you want to come, if I'm not being rude."

"Excuse me?"

"I mean, you don't seem very interested in seeing them hatch."

"Oh, the turtles. Ed said I might enjoy it. And I might. The grandparents don't exactly rock. He's glued to the presidential race, she's in the kitchen dreaming up another spicy dish, and by midafternoon they're both in the bag."

We dug and raked in silence for a bit, each thinking our own thoughts. I could not imagine what his were, and didn't want to try. At my new school there would certainly be a Pickett or two: shifty, withholding, sizing you up, putting you down. The whole ordeal of assessment starting all over again.

It may have been my disappointment, but all the other volunteers seemed wrapped in a congenial bubble, calling to one another, all working toward the same purpose, while Pickett and I were outside the bubble, deadlocked in a contest for—what? Supremacy? Survival? Why had Pickett been foisted on me? Ed Bolton had been my friend and mentor: through him I had grown to love the turtles. And now, because he thought the grandson of some neighbors might "enjoy it," he had separated us from the turtle community. Was his ache for his dead pilot son so enduring that he went around collecting boys to be nice to?

The light faded from the sky, except for the new crescent moon on the rise. The volunteers became vaguely distinguishable figures moving about in the gloaming. The lingering quality of the not-quite-darkness reminded me of that morning when daylight held itself back until I could reach Grief Cottage and see the ghost-boy braced in the doorway, waiting for me to make the next move.

Then the tempo of activities increased; voices rose, calling back and forth. Volunteers gathered around the base pole where the amplifier was set up. A woman snuggled belly-down beside the nest and stuck her face in the sand.

"Listen," said Pickett, "I need to use your bathroom."

"Why don't you just go behind the dunes?"

"I need to take a dump."

"Can't you wait? I think the boil is about to start."

"No, I can't." He was holding his gut. "Just tell me where your bathroom is in your house and I'll make a run for it."

His going alone was out of the question. What if Aunt Charlotte was in the kitchen and this strange boy barged in, demanding her bathroom?

"No, come on, I'll show you. Let's hurry."

As we were running up the boardwalk steps, Ed Bolton cried after us: "Boys! Where are you going? It's about to happen!"

"He needs to—we'll be right back!"

"Oh, freaking Christ, I'm not gonna make it," moaned Pickett.

"Go straight through the kitchen and turn left. The bathroom's at the end of the hall." I pushed him ahead, and he wobbled as fast as he could with his ass tucked in. The back of his orange T-shirt said Clemson Tigers. If he hurried, how much could we miss? Wait, little turtles, hold on till we get back.

My note to Aunt Charlotte was still on the kitchen table. The bottle of wine was gone.

"Go!" I said. Immediately following the slam of the bathroom door a violent explosion resounded. I could envision its far-flying brown discharge hitting every nook and cranny inside the toilet bowl. In my mind I was already cleaning up: toilet brush, Mr. Clean for the splatters, followed up by Pine-Sol to cover the odor.

The toilet flushed, and then reflushed. Water ran. Pickett emerged, having taken the time to wet-comb his bangs. "Sorry about the stink in there."

"It's okay. Go on back to the beach."

"Aren't you coming?"

"There's something I need to do. Go on ahead."

"You're sure?"

"Yeah, I'll be out in a minute."

The cleaning scene followed. It was like having a nightmare turn into an exact replica of the way you had imagined it ahead of time.

MY EYES HAD to readjust to the dark of the beach after staring at the white toilet bowl under bright light. The volunteers, most of them squatting, had spread out on either side of the path Pickett and I had helped to make. By the time I reached the group, my night-vision had kicked in and I could see a swarm of dark little creatures scrambling over one another and racing toward the ocean as fast as their flippers could carry them.

A hand gripped my shoulder. "Ah, Marcus, you missed the boil," Ed Bolton said sadly.

"I know. But I had to." A tear slid down my cheek but it was too dark for Ed to see.

"Well, don't worry. There'll be another one next year."

"How many came out of the nest?"

"We've counted ninety out of a hundred and ten. That's a good crop. Some don't make it. They get out of the egg before they've absorbed all the albumen and then they're too weak to survive. Why don't you go join Pickett—he's over there helping to guide the strayers. Just the gentlest touch with the back of your fingers to get them back on track. Like this." Ed Bolton demonstrated, lightly pressing his fingers against my cheek.

The last person in the world I felt like joining was Pickett, who was absorbed in preventing would-be delinquents from scuttling up the sandbanks on either side of the path. The titanium dials on his wristwatch glowed in the dark as he knelt in the sand, conscientiously rerouting the scuttling little newborns back onto the path.

"Aren't they awesome?" he exclaimed as I sank to my knees beside him. "Look at them haul ass! A minute ago they were crawling out of their hole. I actually *saw* the first one come out—the scout. Its little flipper broke through the sand first, then its little head, then the other flipper, and I swear it looked like it was scoping things out—and then it scooted off for the ocean. Then all of them just started *pouring* out, this living mass of prehistoric creatures. It was totally awesome!"

XXXIV.

"Marcus, are you okay?" It was morning and Aunt Charlotte was outside my bedroom door.

"Uh-huh."

"May I come in?"

"Yes."

She hopped in and leaned against the door frame. "Were you sick last night?"

"You mean the smell in the bathroom?"

"No big deal. It happens to all of us." The whites of her eyes were netted with little red veins and she looked haggard.

"It wasn't me. It was this boy. We were down on the beach with the Turtle Patrol waiting for the boil and he said he couldn't hold it any longer."

"I saw your note. Did the boil happen?"

"Yeah, but I missed it."

"You missed the whole thing?"

"No, but I missed the boil, when they're bursting through the sand. Pickett said it was awesome. When I got back, I helped escort some of them down to the water."

"Pickett, I take it, is the boy."

"Ed Bolton brought him. He's staying with his grand-parents."

"Wait a minute. How is it that Pickett saw the boil and you didn't?"

"Because—" I turned away from her to hide my distress. "I needed to stay behind and clean the bathroom. It was pretty awful."

"Oh, Marcus, I am so sorry. Look, would it be all right if I sat on your bed?"

"It's your bed, but sure."

She hopped the necessary steps and I felt the mattress sink with her slight weight. "Damn it, Marcus, I am just so sorry."

Tears trickled unseen into my pillow.

"You were looking forward to it, I was so excited on your behalf that you were going to witness this amazing thing in nature. You waited for it, you tended their nest so faithfully, I would look out my window and there you would be, sitting down there on the sand, hugging your knees, like you were encouraging them to grow—and then *because you cleaned up after a stranger* you missed the boil. No good deed goes unpunished, does it?"

I couldn't answer because I wasn't in control of my voice.

"Oh, Marcus." Her uninjured left hand fastened on my turned-away shoulder. "What are we going to do with you? You are too thoughtful for your own good. How am I going to protect you?"

I held my breath and bit down on my lower lip to keep from losing it completely.

Then she withdrew her hand and expelled the dry Aunt Charlotte-y rasp that served as her laugh. "They must have been beyond malodorous," she said.

"What?"

"Pickett's awful leavings."

"They were pretty bad." I giggled and she went into another rasp. "What time is it?"

"After ten. Which is late for you. I was starting to worry. I've got a nasty headache. I overdid it last night."

"On your project?"

"No, on the Cabernet Sauvignon. When you go to the store will you pick up another bottle of Extra Strength Tylenol? I seem to have run through the last one."

★ ★ ★

SHE HAD MENTIONED the wine herself. Would Lachicotte count that as a "change for the better"?

I felt really bad as I rode my bike to the market. It was over, the thing I had looked forward to all summer—and I had missed it. "You waited for it, you tended their nest so faithfully . . . and then *because you cleaned up after a stranger* you missed the boil." "You'll never believe what I saw," Pickett would tell the "second form" kids back at his school. "These awesome little turtles . . . they've been doing this race to the sea for forty million years, while we've only been here for the last two hundred thousand." Aunt Charlotte had looked out her window and watched me sitting in the sand. Somehow I had never imagined her stopping her work to look out the window at me, but she had: "And there you would be, sitting down there on the sand . . ."

"How am I going to protect you?" She had sounded like someone aching on my behalf. In all the time I had lived with her, she had laid a hand on my shoulder exactly twice. But now I considered the possibility that we would maybe end up protecting each other.

My photos were ready. Before I did the shopping I went back outside to the bench and looked through them. The ones taken from the beach were okay. Aunt Charlotte would see the cottage at a distance in its early morning light, and then in gradual stages approach its present day wreckage. She could pick and choose her level of disintegration: picturesque abandonment or hazardous finale, or somewhere in the middle. The ones I had taken on the porch were poorly lit but distinct enough to remind me if I came across these photos in my future that I really had seen the ghost-boy braced in that doorless doorway.

The interior shots were a huge disappointment. Every picture I had taken inside the house was murky. You couldn't even make out the original fireplace whose mantel had been stolen, and Charlie Coggins's sky-blue paint to ward off Ole Plat-eye showed up gray. The picture I took of the upstairs room he wouldn't let me go into seemed to have suffered a double exposure. It was also on the murky side, except for a slash of light cutting right through the center of the boarded-up south wall. I was glad I hadn't ordered duplicates: the realtor wouldn't show these to anybody.

I looked for a little present to take to Coral Upchurch later today. There was a souvenir section in the market, but the only thing that caught my eye was a plastic ashtray with a picture of a pelican sitting on a pier. But who wanted to extinguish their cigarette in the middle of a pelican?

★　★　★

"YOU LOOK VERY nice," I told Coral. She really did. She wore a white dress with a white lace shawl that matched her freshly-styled white feathery hair. Her nail polish matched her coral necklace. A fragrance that I guessed was her perfume floated subtly in the air.

"Thank you, Marcus. It's a special day."

"Yes, ma'am, Roberta told me. What time did he usually get here?" I had thought this up in advance.

"If he was flying, he arrived in the late afternoon, because that was the best flight from D.C. He landed at the Myrtle Beach airport and had a rental car waiting. If he was driving down, it all depended on where he stopped the night before and whether he took the direct or the scenic route. One time he arrived before daylight and waked me with a breakfast tray."

"That was nice of him."

"It was, though I prefer to be groomed when he first sees me. But he was so pleased with himself that morning he probably overlooked what a fright I was."

"What did you two do while he was here?" In the deep pocket of my cargo shorts the Grief Cottage photos awaited the right moment to nudge us onto the Johnny Dace subject, but it was way too early in the visit to bring them out. Today a lace cloth covered the porch table and our china and silver were more elaborate. Even the ashtray had undergone an upgrade to a light-green cut-glass crystal, one that matched the crystal pitcher holding our iced tea. The pelican ashtray would have been out of place. In the center of the table was a porcelain cake stand painted with little cupids playing their flutes to branches full of birds. The cake, Billy's favorite prune-and-bourbon cake, was still in the oven below.

"Well, when I was still on foot, we always went to Brookgreen Gardens. Billy never could get enough of Brookgreen Gardens, even as an adult. You must get someone to take you, Marcus. There are gorgeous flowers and sculptures and boat cruises and a zoo and walkways through woods with rare birds and two-hundred-year-old trees and even alligators. They issue passes that last a week because there is too much to do in one day. As a child, Billy had to be dragged away, and even when he was in his fifties we had to go back and refresh his memories of it. And let's see. We ate out a lot, even after my wheelchair confinement. Billy liked the local cuisine. And when I took my afternoon nap, he would drive across the bridge to Charleston and shop for antique furniture for his place in Washington."

"What was it like, his place?"

"Oh, Marcus, I never got to see it! We had been planning my visit year after year and something always interfered. And then finally we got everything right. Billy made all the arrangements, I had a first class ticket, and I was waiting in line at the airport to check my bag when I collapsed on the floor. From then on I was in a wheelchair. My spine had given out. I won't bore you with details. It's the great disappointment of my life. For years and years, Billy had been saying, 'Mama, when are you going to come up here and see how I live and meet my friends? I want you to get to know the *Washington me*.' Now I will never know the Washington Billy."

"What did he do in Washington?"

"He had a highly responsible job with an insurance company that takes care of armed service personnel and their families. He loved his job. This isn't always true of artistic people like Billy. They feel somehow *thwarted* if they're not directly connected to the arts. But he never did. He went right on taking voice lessons and collecting old furniture and going on his little jaunts to France and Italy. He had a beautiful rich tenor voice. People were always asking him to sing at their weddings."

"Lachicotte's mother has been gone ten years and he said he knows her better now than when he saw her every day. He said when all the human noise and stuff are out of the way the absent one can spread out and be themselves in your heart. Maybe that will happen with Billy and you."

"Oh, Marcus, I can't think of anything I'd like more. How I would love for Billy to spread out and be his whole self in my heart! We know so very little about the people we are closest to. We know so little about *ourselves*."

"How is your archaeology on yourself coming along?"

"Oh, you remembered that. What was I saying when we last discussed it?"

"You wanted to get rid of family names and social stuff and strip down to what was below Coral. Or no, you said *beyond*."

"I think I like your *below* better. Well, I've hit one or two cul-de-sacs since then and now I am coming to terms with my findings."

"What are *cul-de-sacs*?"

"Just a fancy French way of saying dead ends. What am I when I get past being a particular daughter, wife, mother, neighbor, friend? What would be left of the essential me without any of my roles? That was the first dead end I reached. Maybe nothing will be left, I thought; I *am* my roles. Even when I'm dead I'll be in the role of 'Mrs. Upchurch's remains' to my undertaker. When people remember me, it will always be in one of my roles. I must say, that took the wind out of my sails."

"Why?"

"Well, you've gone on your archaeology dig and you've found some nice coins and jewelry and pottery and you think, oh, if I've dug up all this already, the best of all is going to be at the bottom! But then when you get to bottom there's nothing there but dirt."

"But you said that was the first dead end, so there must have been a second one."

"Well, here's what came next. I just couldn't accept that there was nothing more to me than who I am in relation to others. What about this consciousness that inhabits my body and nobody else's, the unrepeatable part of me who experiences everything in the world from its one-of-a-kind viewpoint? After all, every tree in the forest has its one-of-a-kind experience of its own tree-ness. And then I thought about Billy, how he said 'I want you to know the *Washington* me,' and that's when I came to my second dead end, which was not exactly a dead end but a cause for sorrow. I realized that below all our *mes* that become known to others is a self that nobody else can ever fully know. No self can ever share its entire being with another self, no matter how much love there is between them. And that made me cry. I had a really good long cry. And after I dried my eyes, I thought, well, what have I got left? And all I had left at the bottom of my digging was love."

I was debating whether or not to tell her that love wasn't such a bad thing to find at the bottom, which might have evoked the same bitterness Aunt Charlotte had shown when I had assured her that her wrist would regain its full range of motion. Roberta's solid footsteps ascending the outdoor stairs beside the "unsightly ramp" deplored by Charlie Coggins saved me from making the choice.

"Here it is." Roberta slid the fragrant cake from its plate onto the waiting stand. "Four generations of prune cake. That's right, isn't it, four?"

"Four indeed. The recipe came down from Archie's great-grandmother. At first it was baked in ordinary cake pans, then Archie's mother received a Bundt mold as a wedding gift and ever since it's been baked as a Bundt cake. The icing was always made with rum until one day they didn't have any rum in the house so she substituted bourbon, and so this is the cake Archie and Billy grew up on. Roberta, did the tea roses arrive?"

"They're in the kitchen. I just have to cut the stems and shake in those little packets and we're good to go."

"Marcus, I'm going to show you Billy's room before you leave. You'll remember, won't you, Roberta, it's the apple-green vase."

"I'll remember, Miss Coral."

"SHE DOES THAT 'Miss Coral' thing to punish me," the old lady said once we were alone again. "I shouldn't have reminded her about the green vase. Of course she remembered. Marcus, help us both to that cake. Don't be shy. Just pick up that cake server and take the plunge. Make mine a thin slice, make yours a double."

"Why is it a punishment?"

"I was being lady of the manor, so she backtracked into the bad old days of disparity. We Southerners have a different history, Marcus. It will take a while for us to blend in with the rest of the country. I won't see it in my lifetime, but Roberta Dumas and I have made our little start."

She had said "I am going to show you Billy's room *before you leave*," and with that deadline impressed on my mind I brought out the pictures as soon as she lit up her first cigarette in my company, explaining about Charlie Coggins showing me the inside of Grief Cottage.

"The distance shots are best," I said. "They're for Aunt Charlotte when she starts to paint again. They show its up-to-date damage and she can choose how much of it to put in her pictures."

"I see what you mean. The shots with the other houses in them are nice. Oh, poor Archie, I can't see these pictures without thinking how upset he got when he walked up there every summer and saw that thing still standing. He finally shamed them into putting the fence around it—or did I already tell you that?"

"You may have."

"At my age the short-term memory betrays you more than the long-term one does."

"The indoor shots are terrible," I said, spreading them out. "Too dark, and the colors don't show."

"I'm surprised Charlie Coggins allowed you to go inside. It can't be safe at all."

"Did you—were *you* ever inside?" My preplanned takeoff question.

"No, Archie and I were not great socializers. His island time in *this house* was too precious to him. The Barbours were more the rental type of owner than those who kept their houses strictly for their own families. They rented out right through the season, sometimes through October. Those unfortunate Daces were the exception, which of course the Barbours came to regret."

Bingo!

"I think I told you already," she went on, "the Barbours got sued by some cousin who said Mr. Dace was the only kin she had left, and they paid up."

"Did Billy ever go inside the house with . . . his friend?"

"I expect he must have. Because he reported things the parents said and did. It may have been while he and Johnny were spying from their hiding place."

"Was it in the house?"

"As I recall, you got there from the outside, but the people inside didn't know you were so close. Mind you, Billy told me some things he didn't tell Archie, and that was probably one of them. The parents were out of their element at the beach. The family was from Kentucky, and they'd had some bad luck, which I think I told you before. They were afraid of the ocean and huddled together in one of the Creekside rooms. The father went fishing every morning with the folks who fish from the creek, and the family ate fish and cornbread and some rice and beans they'd brought with them. Billy said Johnny hated his parents. They were too old and wouldn't let him do anything. He got so hard to manage they put him in this delinquent home several times. Then they would all cry and reunite and try again. Before they came to the beach, Johnny had been suspended from school. Billy told me—this was later, after the hurricane, when everyone had heard about the family's disappearance—that he had been going to send Johnny the bus fare so he could run away to Columbia. They had it all planned. Johnny would go to public high school with Billy. Lord knows where they thought Johnny was going to live! Funny, I had forgotten about those plans till you stirred up my memories with all your questions."

CORAL UPCHURCH SHOT her wondrous machine into action for our excursion to Billy's room. What a great ride it would offer if you were sure of getting out of it again. Its *sissing* sound rose in pitch the faster it went, and it took sharp corners better than we did.

Billy's room was everything someone like Billy—or what I had come to know of him—would feel entitled to. The ocean was right outside the sliding doors, which were open to let in the breeze. The bed was made and turned down with crisp linens. There was a chintz-covered armchair with matching hassock and the prettiest writing table I had ever seen. I would have said more if I hadn't used up too many superlatives on the cake. On the desk was a framed studio picture of a young man with flowing hair and perfect features. Everything in his countenance testified to expecting nothing in life other than unqualified admiration. "Billy's about twenty in that picture," said Coral. "Isn't he handsome? That's an antique Provençal desk, Billy had it shipped here direct from France." On the desk was the apple-green cut-glass vase full of pale orange roses in bud.

"I'll leave y'all to yourselves," said Roberta Dumas.

"Before you go, tell Marcus what we did with your Boogie Basket," Coral said.

"Thanks to her I sent back my commission money to those folks, and now we have ourselves a great big sweet-grass laundry basket," said Roberta, laughing softly as she went.

XXXV.

The period of time following my afternoon with Billy and Coral Upchurch and leading up to Aunt Charlotte's return date with the surgeon had a mournful feel. Some things were drawing to an end, other anticipated things had not happened. For me it was a time of flat days and anxious thoughts. The sun rose later and set earlier. It was as if the summer knew that its best days were gone and was giving in without a fight. I continued my morning rides to Grief Cottage, wearing my helmet and ducking my head as I hurried past the final few cottages in case Pickett happened to be looking out. There was nothing going on with the ghost-boy, no sense of my being seen or heard. My visits to the cottage were so blank that I began questioning the relationship I'd had with him before going inside with the realtor. It was as if Charlie Coggins's sky-blue paint to ward off Ole Plat-eye had driven away my ghost. I still talked to him, updated him with alluring trues ("Billy Upchurch's mother said he invited you to run away from home and go to school with him in Columbia . . . she said you two had a hiding place where you could spy on the people inside . . . I missed the turtles' boil because I had to clean up after this boy who left a mess in our bathroom, but I did get to see them racing for the ocean . . .").

Not a flurry in the air between us, no vibrations of either interest or disgust, just a boy by himself on a rotting porch disturbing the peace with his human noise.

Ed Bolton had apologized. ("The boy was at loose ends and I thought it would be exciting for him. But you got the short end of the stick.") Ed had returned to Aunt Charlotte's dune to clean out the nest and count the little corpses and unopened eggs and carry them away to the sea turtle conservators for research. ("I'm sorry, Marcus. And Pickett was mortified, for what it's worth.")

I missed talking to the turtle eggs and sorting out my day. Their presence had been an aid to my meditations.

Coral Upchurch had overtired herself with Billy's "welcome home" celebration and had taken to her bed. I still went over daily to get their list, but there wasn't much on it. I asked Roberta had I done anything to tire her. "No, she's getting down to her real grieving. Lord knows it's about time." Roberta was weaving an elegant bread basket of modest size.

Aunt Charlotte and I still had our evening meal together, though she ate less and less and I opened more bottles of wine. Sometimes when she asked me to open another one, she gave me this measuring look like she was seeing how close she was to goading me into "nagging" so she could counterattack with her "Just *do it*, Marcus."

I told her about Coral's "welcome home" for Billy. And about her collapse at the airport, which kept her from ever seeing how her son lived in Washington and meeting his friends.

"Did it ever occur to you that she might not have wanted to see how her son lived in Washington and meet his friends?"

I said no, it hadn't.

"People have so many ways of shooting themselves in the foot to avoid facing something."

These days her supper talk bristled with this kind of caustic observation. After that one, I asked myself if her kitchen mishap had been a means of not facing up to something. And if so, was she aware of it?

Lachicotte took me to his barber for a haircut—I had asked for this after meeting Pickett. The barber wanted to know how I would like it, as it was too long for him to make out the "line" of my last haircut (which the foster mother had given me). I said short on the sides and in back but leave a little fringe brushed sideways at the front. You could dislike someone and still admire their hairstyle. Then we went shopping for school clothes, which I knew how to do, so Lachicotte sat on a bench outside the store while I let Mom's taste guide me through the Boys section. Trendy is soonest out-of-date. Wear your clothes, don't let them wear you. They should fit your body, not be tight or baggy or out to make a statement. Go for the well-made things—as far as your budget allows. When I summoned Lachicotte so he could pay with his credit card, to be reimbursed by Aunt Charlotte, he said he'd expected me to spend more. I felt sad Mom wasn't around to see how well I'd done.

While trying on clothes in the dressing room, I had scrutinized myself in the full-length mirror and pretended to be others at school watching me come down the hall. The beach and the bike riding had definitely improved the basic shape. Stripped down to my underwear I examined myself front and back from haircut to feet. I was not the boy that my mother had last looked upon. I was definitely on the road to manhood. Was this something to look forward to?

What had I looked forward to this time last year when Mom and I had been shopping for back-to-school things? If the patch of black ice had been somewhere else instead of under of her tires what would we be doing right now? We would probably still be in our upstairs apartment in Mrs. Wicked's house on Smoke Vine Road. I would be *pudge-wonk* going into eighth grade, looking forward to my new books and lessons and building up my defenses against peer assaults. Mom would have two or more jobs to offset our loss of income from the death of Mrs. Harm and still be gamely assuring me that our life was going to get better. If all went as planned, we could be going to college together in five more years.

Aunt Charlotte received parcels from the art store in Charleston. She asked me to slit them open with the serrated kitchen knife. I had made the mistake of pulling out the contents of an early parcel, some packs of paper labeled with oriental writing. "Ah, my Japan paper," she had said breezily, snatching it from my hands. After that she stood guard as I opened the parcels so I couldn't peek inside, then hopped off to her studio clasping them to her chest. She gave me the task of answering the messages on her website. "Just the ones that seem serious. When in doubt, ask me." I was relieved to find some promising inquiries, mostly for paintings of Grief Cottage. One lady asked if the artist would be willing to paint a boy into the foreground if she were to provide photographs of her grandson.

"Send a brief reply that the artist doesn't paint people," said Aunt Charlotte.

"How should I sign it?"

"'Marcus Harshaw, Assistant to Charlotte Lee.' Next someone will be asking for me to paint that Confederate ghost into the foreground."

The art store deliveries, the inquiries on her website, the fact that she spent all day, except for speedy bathroom hops, shut away in her studio with the Japan paper and whatever else had arrived in the parcels: these I took as very positive signs she was getting on with her secret project *and* preparing for resumption of business as usual with her right hand.

Two days before the trip to the surgeon in Charleston, Aunt Charlotte asked me to trim her hair and then wash it. I was halfway around her head, "grabbing small clumps" and snipping, when she said, not for the first time, how handsome I looked with the new haircut. She went on to relate how I had impressed Lachicotte on my back-to-school shopping trip. "He expected you to spend twice that amount."

"Mom and I had to make every dollar count, so I guess I was trained well."

"So much needless want and suffering. All to escape a monster. If she had stayed at home and finished high school and kept inside the lines of Brenda's bourgeois groove . . . but I should be careful about wishing in retrospect. If she hadn't run away, you wouldn't exist."

I followed her line of thinking, though I shied away from contemplating my nonexistence. The line led back to her devil incarnate father who was my mom's grandfather, who had caused them both to run away. I longed to know more, but how much more would be more than I needed to know? It was like in my dream when I asked the sunburned man what was in the trash barrel in front of Grief Cottage and he laughed and said, "I could tell you but then I'd have to kill you."

"Well, Marcus, you've made me svelte for our trip to Charleston," she said after I had cut, shampooed, and blow-dried her hair. Coasting on the good feeling between us and remembering her anguish on my behalf about missing the turtle boil, I said I was really looking forward to it.

"You're not going, Marcus. It's just for a meeting with the surgeon. There won't be time for fun and shopping with Lachicotte."

"But I thought—"

"You thought what?"

"You've always said *our* trip to Charleston. Even Lachicotte—"

"Well, 'our' in this case meant Lachicotte and me. It's not a family outing."

Did I pick up a disparaging twist on the word "family"?

"All you'd be doing would be sitting in the waiting room with Lachicotte."

"Yeah, I'd probably be in the way."

"I'll level with you. If it's unpleasant news I don't want to have to put on a cheerful face. I'd rather be driven home in silence and feel as bad as I like."

"But *I* wouldn't—"

"Enough, Marcus. This is the way I want it."

MY DAILY LIST was no longer full. No more turtle eggs to watch over and keep me company while I ran my reality check at the end of the day and concluded I was still sane. No more boxes to unpack. No afternoon visits with Coral Upchurch, who was getting down to her real grieving. Someone had taken over the sunburned man's route. Had he gone back to college (if he went to college), or had he done something to cost him his job? I still had my housework and grocery shopping. I biked faithfully to an empty Grief Cottage every morning and some afternoons. I was like those characters in movies who are determined to keep faith with the old schedule while the loved one is away or off fighting in a war.

After Aunt Charlotte had set me straight on who was going to Charleston, I looked for things that needed doing so she wouldn't think I was "moping." I cut the tags off my school clothes and ran them through the wash several times so they wouldn't shout "I'm new!" when I was coming down the halls. I missed having the boxes to unpack, but at least I could clean the garage where they had been stacked. Then I worried that Aunt Charlotte might interpret this as a ploy to make her change her mind about the trip. But she was pleased when she saw it and said it had never looked that neat. Then she repeated that thing about me being too good to be true and that I was restoring her faith in humans. It occurred to me that it would take some pressure off if she could accept that I was not as good or as strong as all that.

Since she hadn't asked to see my Grief Cottage photos, I hid them away in the same place where (at her request) I had hidden her container of painkillers. Either she had more important things on her mind or she was superstitious about seeing the photos before she was certain she would be painting from them again soon.

XXXII.

"Marcus, where did we store that walker I brought home from the hospital?"

"It's in my closet."

"Would you get it? I don't want to lean on Lachicotte more than I have to."

The day of the surgeon had arrived. I helped Lachicotte guide Aunt Charlotte and her walker down the front steps and get her settled in the passenger seat of her own car. "Why does it smell so good?" she asked.

"I had it detailed for you," Lachicotte said.

"*Detailed?*"

"A place just opened, it's their specialty. You leave it all day and they recondition it inside and out. Steam-clean the carpeting, wax the leather, the whole enchilada."

"How nice to be reconditioned inside and out. How much do I owe you?"

"It's a thank-you for letting me drive it."

"You already thanked me with four new tires."

"Then think of it as another thank-you," said Lachicotte.

"Be good, Marcus. Not that I need to tell you that. We should be back by late afternoon."

It smelled so good because she had remembered her car smelling of vomited-up shrimp. They would probably have an early lunch in some nice restaurant. Maybe there would be a shrimp dish on the menu and Aunt Charlotte would say it reminded her of the day I arrived and reveal some specifics, charitably adding "But poor boy, he was mortified." Then she would say, "I'm not hungry, I'll just have a salad and a glass of red wine. But Lash, why don't you have one of the specials?" It would be her first outing this summer without me tagging along as "family."

The rest of the day stretched ahead like an endurance test. It was too early to go next door and see if Roberta had a list for me. I had missed my early morning bike ride to Grief Cottage in order to be around when they left for Charleston, and now it was late morning, the beach filled with shrieking children, the light wrong. I prowled around inside the house, imagining a less honorable version of myself crossing the threshold of my aunt's forbidden studio. Having washed the few breakfast dishes by hand, I was elated when I looked down at the floor and saw scuff marks and sand on the kitchen tiles: overlooked remnants of Pickett's ass-tucked scramble for the toilet? A really good floor scrubbing was needed. Kneeling and applying the hard-bristle brush in serious circles recalled the day we had been cleaning house for the Steckworths' visit, when Aunt Charlotte had dropped to her knees and scrubbed with a fury. ("It's either that or kill someone.") Then she had ordered me from the house. ("Just *go*, Marcus. Don't make me ask again.") This was after she'd learned from me that Mom, like herself, had run away at sixteen to escape a worse situation.

After I finished the kitchen floor, I mopped the hall, cleaned the bathroom, and tidied my own already-tidy room. Following that, I took the trash out.

As I was closing the lid to our bin in front of the house, a silent ambulance with its red revolving light turned into our street and stopped in front of the Upchurch house.

Roberta was beside the ambulance before the two men had finished unloading the stretcher from the bay. She led them quickly up the outside stairs. She hadn't looked my way. Soon they returned, this time bearing the stretcher down the ramp, probably for a less bumpy ride for the tiny figure covered with a blanket. All you could see above the blanket was the breathing apparatus clamped to her face. They loaded her into the bay and, after a short consultation with Roberta, slammed it shut and drove off as noiselessly as they had come, red light revolving. Roberta still hadn't looked my way, so I ran after her as she headed to the house.

"Roberta! What *happened*?"

"They're thinking pneumonia. Her breathing was all wrong when I went in this morning."

"Pneumonia in the *summer*?"

"You can get it any time. Healthy people carry the bacteria without it hurting them. My guess is the beauty salon. The hairdresser could have coughed on her, or the lady under the next dryer. But it's no joke at her age. She was running a fever and I wasn't taking chances."

"Will she be all right?"

"Pray God, Marcus. We've been together since she got in that wheelchair. It's—it's a *friendship*." Tears rolled down her cheeks.

"Do you need anything at the market?"

"No, I'm going to pack her some necessities and drive them over to the hospital and wait until we know something."

"Tell her I said please get better."

"I surely will. She has enjoyed you so much."

I crossed the immaculate kitchen floor and stepped out on the porch. The shady hammock was not inviting before afternoon. Out of habit I went down to the dunes and sat in my old meditation spot. The absence of the turtles' nest made the spot as forlorn as the unhaunted doorway of Grief Cottage. Why had Roberta said, "She has enjoyed you"? Why not "She has *been* enjoying you"? Before the sun went down today, it could easily become "She *enjoyed* you."

It had been like watching some tiny extraterrestrial creature carried respectfully out to the ambulance by some large humans. Just some helpless little bumps under a blanket with an oxygen mask perched on top. I had not seen a single human part of her, not even a wisp of white hair. Now she wouldn't get to finish her archaeology on herself. No, she said she had finished it and down at the bottom found only love. But now I would never be able to tell her, "It's not such a bad thing to find love at the bottom."

I was losing the casing that held me together. I could feel it coming loose, like that boy's cheek melting down the side of his face back at the foster home. I drew up my knees to make a smaller, denser package of myself, and buried my face in my hands. When Mom was alive she would say, "Marcus, when you sit like that with your knees drawn up and your face covered, I want to die."

Well, you did die. I waited for you to come back and you didn't. Whereas I'm still here, coming loose from my moorings, getting ready to fly apart.

The corpses of the hatchlings and the eggs that never opened had been taken away to be studied. It might have been better to be one of those eggs that never opened. No pain, no fight, no terror. Just a kind and curious person in a lab, gently cracking your egg, looking inside to see how your remains might benefit future hatchlings.

When you start feeling sorry for yourself, the foster mother told us, make a list of all the good things you're grateful for. What were the good things of this summer? My bike, my room by myself, the ghost-boy until he shut down. Lachicotte, Coral Upchurch, Aunt Charlotte.

For Wheezer, a "true" was a story that had really happened to someone, the more shocking and sensational the better: Van Gogh slicing off his ear and handing it to a prostitute; Wheezer's brilliant uncle who read Latin and Greek and died shooting up inside a trailer full of rats.

Wheezer also had a term for a person you could always count on to be thinking of you and missing you, no matter where you were. Wheezer called this person a "sure." Like rare marbles, we displayed and discussed our sures. Each of us had only one. ("But, Marcus, lots of people don't have *any*.") The cigarette-smoking grandmother in whose house Wheezer lived was his sure. His mother and father, even his big brother, all of whom lived in other places, were not. ("Weeks can go by without any of them giving me a thought.")

My mom was my sure. "And who knows?" Wheezer had said. "Maybe one day we'll end up being each other's sures."

Fool that I was, I had been on my way to considering Aunt Charlotte and Lachicotte as my potential sures. And maybe even Coral Upchurch, since she no longer had Billy in this world.

If that patch of black ice had been a little to the left a little to the right of Mom's tires, we would still be sleeping in the same bed; there was only room for one bed in the apartment on Smoke Vine Road. I wondered what age I would have had to reach before she said, "Marcus, you're getting to be a big boy, let's go see if we can find a sofa-bed and squeeze it into a corner and pay for it on the installment plan. I may not be able to afford an extra room, but it's time you had your own bed."

What if the time never comes? I sometimes caught myself thinking as I lay beside her. And then I would try not to think the next thought: *How will I ever get away from her?*

"I'M NOT STAYING around to think any more 'next thoughts' with you," my gremlin from the causeway suddenly piped up. "I am an evolving gremlin, trying to improve myself. *You* are going in the opposite direction. You'd be more suitable company to the others."

"What others?"

"The evil baddies that balance us out. I've called in a cutting-edge baddie, fresh off the assembly line. Here he comes now. I'm out of here!"

MAYBE I'D HAD my meltdown, after all. Here I was, running from the beach at midday, fleeing a *gremlin*. I didn't want to meet Cutting Edge or even glimpse him out of the corner of an eye. I slammed the kitchen door behind me and wished it had Charlie Coggins's Gullah-blue paint sloshed all around its frame. To put an extra door between us, I shut myself in my room.

What help was in here? I picked up the black bear in the hoodie and rubbed him against my face. I looked out my window at the line where the ocean met the sky. Out there I had felt I was melting away; now my skin felt like it was growing too tight to hold me. The tension was unbearable. I was sweating and heaving but nothing came up. The awful things I didn't want inside me kept expanding.

I opened Mom's tin box with its sacred contents and plucked out Aunt Charlotte's container of painkillers from its hiding place. I had never taken anything but aspirin. Maybe one pill would kill enough physical feeling to tide me over until they got back. Now to wash it down. In the kitchen, on an impulse, I grabbed an opened bottle of wine in its usual hiding place and swigged down the pill, drinking from the bottle. The wine tasted murky and sour. How could she put away glass after glass of this? If I were to become a serious drinker I would choose something light and clear that worked really, really fast. I walked a circle around the kitchen, then another and another. How long did a painkiller take to kick in? It wasn't that my thoughts were "racing," but that every time I started to think any thought my mind recoiled from it. Every subject I approached had some kind of pain or horror attached to it.

I turned on Aunt Charlotte's laptop and checked for new e-mails on her site. No promising inquiries, no inquiries at all. I deleted the junk mail.

"Did you think," said a voice I can only describe as *crumbly*, "did you *really* think you could keep me on the other side of a measly door? I'll tell you something you won't want to hear. You can't keep me out because I'm one of the cutting-edge models. We work from inside. And I don't mean inside the house. I mean inside of you. The upside to this, the only upside, is that you don't have to see me or imagine what I look like. I am beyond looks. I am inside you so I can camouflage myself in your looks."

XXXVII.

"hat's behind that door?"

"I'm not supposed to go in there."

"Who says *I* can't? And since I'm inside of you, you'll have to come with me."

The painkiller must have reached my bloodstream because everything felt . . . not *better*, but a remoteness now muffled the unbearable anguish. Soon they would be having their early lunch in Charleston; they might be at the table already. ("This shrimp dish on the menu reminds me of the day Marcus arrived . . .") They would take care of each other. He would get her to a recovery place in time. They would be each other's family without the commitments. They would become each other's sures. But now this didn't hurt as much as it would have a short while ago.

"Go on, turn the knob. Good boy. Or I should say bad boy. So this is the forbidden temple. What have we here?"

A neat and organized studio. Giant easel pushed out of the way to the same spot where she had ordered me to move it. Laundry sink (where she had talked me through changing the washer) clean, but with paint rags hung to dry on its sides.

The wall-high cork board from which she had told me to take down samples of famous landscape paintings she admired, rough drawings of clouds, postcards of her own paintings, and some write-ups about her in local papers, was filled with tacked-up little paintings, all the same size. ("I have a particular fondness for four by sixes, about the size of my palm," she had told Ron Steckworth the day they carried away their forty-two by fifty-six. She had held up a palm to demonstrate.) I measured my palm against the paintings on the corkboard. My hand was already the size of hers.

"What is it?" asked Cutting Edge. "Some kind of comic strip?"

"Why would you think that?"

"Because, dumbass, the story goes from left to right, then drops down and goes left to right again."

"What makes you think it's a story?"

"Because I'm a speed reader and I've already scanned it. Wow, your aunt is one obscene lady. And so clumsy and crude for someone who passes herself off as an artist."

"She injured her right hand. These are painted with her left hand. Also I think she painted them with her fingers. Except for those first drawings."

"Filthy Auntie!"

"I wish you'd shut up."

"Mum's the word until slowpoke has stumbled through the story."

The few ink drawings before the paintings started were so badly done they were embarrassing. It was like someone with a shaky hand had been struggling to keep control of the pen; like Aunt Charlotte's left-handed signature that day she wrote Lachicotte that left-handed check for my bike. And even for that, she said she had been practicing all day.

But despite their clumsiness it was obvious what she had set out to draw: a figure of a little girl standing before a man seated on a bed. The strange thing was that the trembliness of the lines made the figures appear to be slightly moving. The little girl was standing close to his outspread legs. Drawn on a bigger scale, he bulked over her like a sitting giant. Her outer hand loosely held a doll by its arm and her other arm reached out to the man. In the first picture, this arm stopped at the wrist, but in the ensuing drawings there was a hand that moved nearer and nearer to the man's crotch. Then splotches of color began to be painted over the ink lines until the lines disappeared. The rest of the board was tacked up with progressive paintings of the two figures. A suitcase materialized beside the bed and the doll had been dropped on the floor with floppy legs outspread. The man sprouted a green penis that curved upward. At first you could see its green tip like a small mushroom until gradually it was obscured by the girl's bowed head being held in place by the seated man's large hand.

She had used lots of pink and green, the girl being pink and the man green, though there were other colors, too. She had piled paint on top of paint and the man and girl mutated into less human images, grotesque figures in a bad dream, the man's head becoming anvil-shaped and sprouting stubby green horns, the girl's face widening into a sinister grimace. Where had I seen this crusted-over paint style, these grimaces before?

You could see the little paintings getting sharper as she gained control of those left-hand fingers. On a paper halfway down the board she had finger-painted some blue words, edged in yellow: ONLY TO YOU, MY LITTLE SHEETS.

That's why the pictures looked familiar. It was what the old German artist resorted to after the Nazis had forbidden him to paint: watercolors piled on top of each other on heavy pieces of "Japan paper": his "Unpainted Pictures" small enough to be hidden if necessary.

"I need to get out of here," I heard my voice saying from a hollow place inside my ears. As I was uttering the words, my floaty mind reached out and brought back Wheezer's voice saying the exact same thing that day in our apartment when he was handing back the forbidden photograph.

"Such lengths you humans go to color up the evil inside of you," crowed Cutting Edge. "How many green penises did *you* count?"

"Shut up!"

"I kept my trap shut till you spoke first."

"I'm out of here!"

"Oops, watch it! Oh, too late. Oh, dear, dear, dear. *Now* what are you going to do?"

I had knocked against the trestle table where Aunt Charlotte had left a small work in progress, which I had overlooked when we came in. One of the plastic glasses still filled with colored water slopped over onto the painting, which started to bleed. I ran for the paper towels and he followed right behind. Or from deep within.

"You're done here, you know," Cutting Edge observed, as we re-entered the violated studio.

"What do you mean?"

"I have to spell it out for you? You've trespassed, you've overstayed. You're not 'too good to be true' anymore, you're too bad to be wanted, even by Filthy Auntie. *Especially* by Filthy Auntie. When she sees you've discovered her filthy pictures she'll never want to see you again. We need to hot-foot it out of here. You need to be somewhere else before she sees what you've done. What's ruined is ruined. Oh, ruination, we crown you king."

The little painting-in-progress I had ruined was the girl sitting alone on the bed where the man had sat. From out of a black background, a giant green mask was starting to emerge. The glass I had tipped over was unfortunately the one that held black water.

"You're just making it worse with all that dabbing, stupid. Besides, what could you possibly tell her when she gets home? 'Oh, Filthy Auntie, a weird wind blew up out of nowhere and I heard noises in your studio and I went in to see if anything was damaged and I saw the knocked-over glass. I did my best with paper towels and I didn't look at anything else in the room, I swear.'"

"Do you ever shut up?"

"I'm programmed to keep my mouth running till yours stops."

"But if mine stops it means I am dead."

"I was waiting for you to catch up. So here's the plan. Leave Filthy Auntie a nice note. Don't go on too long and don't get theatrical. Thank her for taking you in. Say you *aren't* too good to be true—you are harboring a cutting-edge baddie— no, dumbass, don't write that second part, just stop at you aren't good anymore. Then close with 'I've decided to go somewhere else.'

"Now I'm going to tell you something you won't want to hear. She'll be alarmed at first. But she'll be relieved to have you gone."

"You're probably right."

"I know I'm right. Give up and let me run things. Now you're going to pocket the rest of Filthy Auntie's painkillers and take along a bottle of water. Then get your bike—that's right, put on that helmet. Don't want shit-boy to spot you riding past his grandparents' house and saying 'freaking little loser, he's gone and copied my haircut!'

"Tell me, Marcus, now we're out on the beach, pedaling north on your usual route, don't you feel you're headed in the right direction? Isn't it a relief to finally face your awfuls? You aren't wanted, you weren't wanted, and you're not going to be missed. You weren't wanted back when Mom kept checking her panties and it didn't come. Then when you were about the size of a bean, she panicked: 'I can't do this, not by myself, scraping it out would be kinder than bringing it up poor without a father.' But when you had swelled to the size of one of those little hatchlings she realized she'd left it too late and submitted to her penance.

"And do you really think when Filthy Auntie received word she was your only kin she ran down to the beach and danced for joy at the prospect of sacrificing her solitary life, not to mention her only bedroom?

"Wait, there's worse to come. We haven't got to the thought you were trying not to think, the thought that was too much for poor Evolving Gremlin and sent him wailing back into the ether. Pedal a little faster. No use trying to arm yourself against it because it's already written on the fleshy, bumpy insides of your pink soul. However, I'll keep up my cutting-edge standards and tell it aloud in my crumbly voice."

"Not yet, please!"

"*Please* isn't programmed into my vocabulary."

XXXVIII.

I'll hang out with you on this squalid porch while you swallow your medicine. We'll think *the next thought* together while you're swigging down the pills. How many did Filthy Auntie leave you? There are seven in the bottle and you swallowed one back at the house. That should cover it. No, no, no, don't cram them in your mouth, swallow each individually and wash it down with water. You don't want to ruin everything by choking up and vomiting. You're such an easy little vomiter. Now, are you ready for that contemptible next thought? The one that takes all the prizes?"

I buried my face in my hands as Cutting Edge spewed out the contemptible thought. I did feel like vomiting, but kept it down.

"So now you know the worst about yourself. And you know what you have to do now."

"No one would want to go on living after hearing that."

"You get the idea. I've done my job. Off to the next client!"

"Aren't you going inside the cottage with me?"

"I'll level with you. Do you know what DNA is?"

"Of course I know what it is."

"The thing is, I share some DNA with Ole Plat-eye. I might self-destruct if I passed through those blue-painted portals. You're on your own when you go through that door."

At first the dead silence inside Grief Cottage felt worse than Cutting Edge's voice. At least he had been company.

I prowled around the cobwebby front room waiting for the pills to take effect. A surge of dark clarity washed over me. I understood what I was going to do now and why it had to be done. I also understood that if I had anything to say to Johnny Dace I'd better get going because my time was ebbing.

"I don't expect you to appear. I don't expect you to respond in any way. But I have to tell you that you got me through the summer. I sought you out and you were there for me as I was for you. You were my *sure*. You were my lifeline, if that doesn't sound too weird.

"Just in case you are listening and wanting to hear the rest of the story in whatever way ghosts want to hear the rest of the story, I'll bring you up to date. This morning my aunt went off to Charleston to find out if her wrist is healing. Strange to think I'll never see her again. Then you know I told you about Billy Upchurch's mother? Well, an ambulance came and took her away. They think it's pneumonia, which is no joke for a person her age, and she'll probably be gone by nightfall. Now I'm like you, I don't have anybody. It's really lonely without the turtle eggs. The hatchlings are well on their journey now, though some of them have already been eaten or caught in the shrimping nets, others didn't have enough energy left over for their ten-mile swim to reach the open ocean, and others never made it out of their egg yolks.

"There are so many things I wish I knew about you. About you and Billy. Where was that hiding place you showed him?

"You will have to be my eighth grade friend. You'll be the boy I suddenly come face-to-face with when I turn a corner in a corridor at school. I have seen you, the long narrow face, the raisin eyes deep in the sockets, the stalk-like neck, the nose that looked broken and not reset right, the bowed legs in jeans and the black boots. You were braced in the door frame, pushing yourself outward with your hands. I was close enough to count the knuckle ridges on your spread fingers. You had unusually large hands.

"Have you ever had a thought as contemptible as this? It's a wonder how I managed to forget it until now. When my mom went out to get our pizza and didn't come back, I got hungry. The smells of our landlady's supper wafted up through the heat register and I got hungrier and hungrier and finally wolfed down some cereal and hated myself—and Mom—for spoiling my appetite. I watched the movie. I watched the whole movie. A lot of it I didn't pay attention to because of this separate track running in my head. The separate track had already killed her. I was at the point in the track where I was fantasizing what would happen to me after she was gone. And I could see possibilities spread out in front of me. I didn't think of Aunt Charlotte that night, my scenarios were more on the line of myself, Marcus, alone, with Mom gone. Independent and alone. People would walk softly around me and ask me what I wanted to do.

"Then I yanked myself off that track and felt despicable for letting the scenario progress as far as it had. By this time in the movie, the old lady had helped them steal the gold with no one the wiser, including herself. At that point I got scared. I worried that I might have already killed her by thinking these thoughts. I got a blanket and a pillow and lay down in front of the TV with the sound turned off. When she got back she would find me on the floor still in my clothes and feel terrible for taking so long.

"And then I really did fall asleep, and was waked by the state troopers knocking on our door.

"I think I can go to sleep now, here in Grief Cottage. But not in this cobwebby room. I want to be where you are. Please show me. Put your hand on my shoulder and when I stand up just push me from behind. I want to sleep where you sleep."

I almost left it too late. I was half asleep when I felt the pressure on my shoulder. How could I ever have dreaded his touch? I wobbled and almost fell when I stood up, and I tripped going up the stairs. ("Hey, hey, *hey!* Watch it!" Charlie Coggins had cried.)

How peaceful it was going to be when all this chatter stopped.

I felt the palm of his large hand guiding me up the remaining stairs, then steering me to the right and to the right again, over the threshold of the oceanfront room Charlie Coggins wouldn't let me enter.

I was somewhere in the middle of saying, "I have seen you and felt you and that's enough. I'm glad your voice never joined the rest of the human noise—"

I may have reached the "I am glad"—then there was a splintering and a falling followed by a crack that brought horrible pain and my weak shout from the bottom of darkness.

XXXIX.

efore I ever walked through the doors of my new
school, I was known as "the bones boy." And all through
the school year I was called "Bones." ("Hey, Bones . . .") The
nickname trailed me into high school, then faded as more
and more people came along who knew nothing about how
it had originated. I sort of missed being Bones because the
name had evoked awe and respect and some notoriety. But it
had certainly done its job, airlifting me out of the realm of
merciless peers before any of us had a chance to lay eyes on one
another.

I said "walked" through the doors of my new school, but I
should have said "swung through on crutches." (Spiral break of
the tibia, requiring a plate and eleven screws.)

"Do you know what a realtor's worst nightmare is?" Charlie
Coggins went around saying to the news media. "When they
find human bones under one of his properties."

"You were still under your self-administered anesthesia,"
Lachicotte said, "when the paramedics were putting your leg
into alignment. But the firemen had to come and knock out a
wall so the paramedics could get to you. And there you were,

doubled up in that cramped enclosure. They had to stabilize your breathing first (*fust*) before they moved you. The next problem, at the hospital, was what kind of anesthesia to give you for the surgery when the Percocet you swallowed was still meandering through your bloodstream in dribs and drabs. So they opted for the spinal block."

Concerning the subjects of Aunt Charlotte's painkillers and Aunt Charlotte's breached studio, silence reigned. Maybe each of us was waiting for the other to go first, but it felt more like an unwritten restraining order that the three of us had tacitly agreed upon.

I was still on crutches and into regular sessions with a psychiatrist in Myrtle Beach when the painkiller subject got brought up. Lachicotte's former second wife who had become a therapist had recommended this psychiatrist as being excellent with children and adolescents. Lachicotte drove me to these sessions as Aunt Charlotte had not yet resumed driving. Both ankle and wrist were healing, though she would later insist she never did recover full range of motion in her right hand. On one of our drives to Myrtle Beach, Lachicotte suddenly spoke up. "I had to report the container in your pocket, Marcus. For a scintilla of a moment I considered keeping it quiet. But that wouldn't have been in anybody's best interests. You understand, don't you?"

"What's a *scintilla*?"

"A touch, a dash, next to nothing."

"I think you probably did right."

I was more resentful of what I considered "the worst" betrayal Lachicotte had been guilty of while I was still in the hospital. Yet I knew that eventually I'd have to forgive him for that one, too.

★ ★ ★

IN MY SESSIONS with the psychiatrist, I had made up my mind
that everything was going to be on the table, even my true feelings when I was beating up Wheezer—everything except for
my sightings of the ghost-boy. Since Johnny Dace's remains had
been discovered, I had a second reason for keeping the secret.
Formerly, it was because I didn't want to be thought crazy and
sent away. But if I were to tell about our relationship *after* his
bones became public property, I would be seen as a boy who
was making up things to get more attention for himself. As
Aunt Charlotte had put it, back when we had been discussing
the "man in gray" who was said to walk the beach before a
hurricane: "People see what they want to see. Or imagine they
saw. And others *say* they saw something in order to sound
psychic or special."

Predictably, the psychiatrist encouraged me to talk about
my mother. In order to get the awful part out of the way, I
described the scenario I had been creating on the night of her
accident, and how when I finally remembered it as "the thought
I didn't want to think," I hadn't wanted to live anymore. The
psychiatrist was a lady of about Aunt Charlotte's age, whose
disposition was a lovely mix of alertness, humor, and respect.
Her filigree earrings swung along with her shoulder-length
gray hair when you made her laugh. She wore nice clothes and
shoes and spoke with a sanded-down version of Lachicotte's
accent. As I completed the story about my awful scenario, I
noted, as good students do when they have pleased their teacher,
that she was excited by the start we had gotten off to. *This is
exactly the right material for us to be facing together*, I could see her
thinking.

This is not meant to be condescending to the woman who helped me so much. Having chosen her profession myself, I know all too well how cautiously we must treat our young patients, how we are taught to follow diagnostic guidelines until we can glimpse the individual beneath the presenting material. We start all over again with every new patient—or we should.

The "pleased teacher" being "played" by the student was the perception of a boy whose sessions with an earlier psychiatrist had taught him a few strategies for protecting his secrets. Because he still lives in me I am perfectly aware how cunning an eleven-year-old boy can be when it comes to withholding information. Being super-cunning requires handing over *another* secret in place of the one you want to keep buried.

She was just what was needed and she was in the right place when I needed her. Her most lasting gift has been the little notebooks. She told me to go out and buy a small notebook, small enough to fit in my pocket, and to write things in it that were important to me.

"Anything that strikes a chord. A line a day, or nothing, or as much as you want. Anything that strikes you as worth saving for yourself. A passage from something you read, something someone said—write it down when it's fresh and don't censor yourself. No one's going to see this little book but you. And when you have filled up all its pages, go out and buy another one. Store them in a secret place."

"Can it be just thoughts I have?"

"Absolutely. And also," she smiled, "the thoughts you *don't want to have*." By then she had glimpsed the individual beneath the presenting material.

★　★　★

"YOU KNOW THE words a realtor never wants to hear?" Charlie Coggins loved explaining to reporters: "*Secure the site.* That's right, those three little words: *secure the site.*

"But in this case I gave the order myself. I was early on the scene, thanks to Lachicotte Hayes phoning me on his mobile from the spot of the accident. 'Right now the fire squad's knocking down a wall to get to him,' Lachicotte said, 'so you'd better come.' By the time I arrived the medics were getting the boy's breathing stabilized before they set about moving him. I knew just what had happened. He had gone and done exactly what I'd told him not to. He went into that upstairs south room and fell right through the floor. The 'wall' the firemen had been knocking down, on the south side of the house, wasn't a true wall, just a boarded-up makeshift with some shingles nailed on top, so they had an easier time than they expected. The boy fell through the upper floor and landed in a small enclosure beneath the staircase and beneath part of the south upstairs room. Nobody knew this enclosure existed; even I didn't, until our helpful Historical Society kindly obtained the old plans for me. Originally it was a wood storage closet built into the south wall, so you could load in firewood from an outside opening and then fetch it from a door inside the house so you didn't have to brave the elements. Rice planter families stayed though November and it was cold by then.

"Then, when later owners decided to build the south stairs and the upstairs room, they nailed up a partition to close off the wood closet from inside. They removed its lift latch because it stuck out and then whitewashed over the door.

"Then, when Hurricane Hazel hit us in 1954, the south porch burned down for reasons still unknown. The rest of the house stood up just fine. New owners, interested in a quick flip, sheared off the burnt porch and boarded up the south wall. That's the quote-unquote 'wall' the firemen knocked down. After my dad bought the cottage from the flippers, who had run out of money, he sent me over to nail some vintage cypress shingles over that unsightly makeshift wall.

"Like I said, when I got there the medics were still stabilizing the boy's breathing, they hadn't moved him yet, and when they did that's when we all saw what he'd been lying on top of. I say *lying*, but the skeleton was in a cramped sitting position and the boy had fallen right on top. It looked like he was sitting in the skeleton's lap.

"Then everybody began speculating. Folks can't tolerate loose ends—they've got to tie up a story. So it was, Are these the remains of a *murder victim*? How long have they been buried in there? Is the perpetrator still alive? My first thought was, Oh, _____, now I'll be stuck with this property until the victim is identified, and maybe even until the murderer is apprehended! But then I recalled going through the house with this very boy not long ago and him talking so much about the boy that got lost during Hazel. That's when I was almost positive I knew who these bones belonged to. In that case, the sooner I got it confirmed the better, and that's when I said, 'Nobody touch or move any of those remains till we get the forensics people here.' So in this case it was the realtor who gave the order to secure the site. By the way, the inside door to that old wood closet is preserved in fine shape. It's got its original eighteenth-century lift latch and strap hinge, and even the old wrought nails. I'm going to make a gift of it to the Charleston Museum."

★   ★   ★

"SHE MUST BE really mad at me," I said to Lachicotte when I was emerging from my semi-conscious fugue in the hospital.

"Why do you think that?"

"Because, why isn't she here?"

"She wasn't sure you would want to see her."

"Why not?"

I really could not think why. It would be weeks before all the events (both inner and outer ones) of that day were reclaimed. The first memories to swim up were the bike ride with Cutting Edge hectoring me all the way to Grief Cottage . . . then a blank . . . then pain cracking inside me . . . and another blank . . . then being carried across sand in daylight with voices calling back and forth against the sound of the ocean, and me thinking as they carried me, *Please don't drop me on one of those Spanish bayonets.*

"Well, that note you left her," Lachicotte said.

"What was in it?" I didn't remember writing a note.

"You thanked her for taking you in but said you were no longer a good person and you were going somewhere else."

The words sounded familiar, but why had I written them?

Then I remembered they had gone to the surgeon that day. "How is her wrist?" I asked Lachicotte.

"The news was guarded but good. This surgeon never gets overenthusiastic. Most surgeons don't. Your aunt is deeply concerned about you, Marcus. She cares about you, more than she shows. The last thing she wants is for you to feel you have to stay with her when you'd rather go somewhere else."

I was puzzled. "Why should I want to go anywhere else?"

★ ★ ★

AUNT CHARLOTTE'S SECRET project, dubbed *Filthy Auntie's Pictures* by Cutting Edge, and the events leading up to my invading her studio, would be one of the later memory sequences to return. When I did remember and apologized for disobeying her, she simply nodded and then formally invited me into her studio, much as she had that first time when she wanted "everything to be aboveboard" about my trust and about the "nice monthly stipend" she would receive.

In the same matter-of-fact monotone she presented me with a "shrink-wrapped" version of her demon-father's violation of her childhood, beginning when he took her and her doll on business trips when she was five and ending when she ran away at sixteen. ("That's enough now. With your super-active imagination, Marcus, you can fill in the rest." She didn't add, "Besides, you have the memory of the little paintings to help you picture the scenes.")

The paintings were never mentioned. They truly did become her "Unpainted Pictures." I have no idea what she did with them. The corkboard once again bore its former items, tacked up in their former spots: details from landscape paintings she admired, sketches of clouds, of the ocean, the postcards of her own paintings, and gallery announcements and local press cuttings. She asked Lachicotte to move the big easel back to its old spot and would I mind, until her casts were off, changing her linens again and giving the studio a good sweep and dusting in preparation for her return to work.

THE OPENING ENTRY in my first pocket-sized notebook (those Moleskine ones with the elastic band and sewn spine had just come on the American market) was the old professor's advice:

Don't mention it to anyone else unless you find they've
had adventures of the same sort themselves . . .
—*The Lion, the Witch, and the Wardrobe*, C.S. Lewis

And many notebooks later, when I was in medical school, I
recorded this treasure:

It could be said of all human beings that at times when
instinctual frustrations lead to a feeling of hopelessness
or futility the fixing of the psyche in the body
becomes loosened and a period of psyche and soma
unrelatedness has to be endured. [. . .] The idea of a
ghost, a disembodied spirit, derives from this lack of
essential anchoring of the psyche in the soma, and the
value of the ghost story lies in its drawing attention to
the precariousness of psyche-soma existence.
—"Dwelling of Psyche in Body," *Human Nature*,
D. W. Winnicott

"Yes, the anchoring of the psyche in the body is very precarious," I wrote on the following page. "What I was sure of at the
time was *that I had seen*. What I was *not* sure of was whether I
was different from others my age. If so, was I super-sensitive to
the uncanny or was I going insane? Could another person of
eleven have this experience? Or was this my experience alone
because the ghost-boy was inseparable from my history, my
personality, my needs? I knew he was related to my life, but he
also appeared to be an entity on his own terms. How could he
be both? What I needed was a mature personality who could
earn my trust, comprehend my contradictions, and help me
form a concept large enough to contain them."

* * *

"I CAN'T BELIEVE you didn't tell me!" My leg was in its cast. I felt perfectly fine. Why was this my fourth day in the hospital?

"Well, I am telling you now," said Lachicotte patiently.

"But it's too late! They've moved everything. I found him—I was the one who fell on *top* of him, for God's sake. And you're just telling me all this *now*?"

"You were unconscious when we found you, Marcus. We didn't know if you were going to make it."

"But I didn't get to see him."

"You can still do that. The remains are at Johnson's funeral home. I'll take you over when we get you discharged."

"But I'll never see the way he was when—"

"They took lots of *in situ* photographs before anything got touched or moved. Charlie Coggins had the presence of mind to secure the site. You can look at the photographs. And the bones will be laid out in their anatomical order."

"Why is he at the funeral home?"

"The forensic team finished their work on him there. It was relatively quick. Dates and times matched. They concluded he was hiding in that enclosure, probably from the hurricane, and then the fire started, perhaps from his cigarette dropped on the porch, and he died from asphyxiation while waiting out the hurricane. When the cousin arrives, she will be the one to decide where the remains go."

"What cousin?" I couldn't believe the unfairness of it all. I was the one who found him and then they went ahead and did everything without telling me!

"Well, she's that cousin of Mr. Dace, very old now, the one who settled out of court with the Barbours fifty years ago. The

Barbour family was able to provide her old address and it turned out she was still living there. Her DNA matched up with the remains and now Charlie Coggins is flying her in from Louisville at his expense."

"Why is he doing that?"

"She says she won't be at peace till she sees the boy. Or what is left of him."

"Lachicotte, I *need* to see him. This is *important*. Can't you get that surgeon to discharge me?"

"It's not the surgeon who's keeping you here, Marcus. They need to make sure you're not a danger to yourself before they sign you out. If you had swallowed a few more of those tablets, we would be making arrangements for *your* burial, too."

So again I was trapped in my old situation. The wheels of the law had to turn first. Nevertheless, I felt robbed, betrayed. This was far worse than missing out on the hatchlings' boil. Unfairly, I measured Lachicotte against William, my ad litem, who had immediately understood I needed to see my mom's body before it went to the undertaker.

"Can you at least tell me *how we looked* when you found us?"

"How you looked?"

"How *we* looked. After the firemen had knocked down the wall, and you first saw me and him. What did you see?"

"I saw only *you*, Marcus."

"But what about him?"

"You were as much as I could take in. We didn't know if you were going to make it."

"I can't *believe* nobody bothered to tell me."

"Well, I do have some good news. Your friend Coral Upchurch, who's on the floor below you, is recovering. She's going home tomorrow, weak but on the mend."

*   *   *

IT WAS THE kind of human interest story everybody loves. Long ago mystery solved—and on the fiftieth anniversary of Hurricane Hazel, when the mystery had begun. A local boy falling on top of a skeleton boy who had been sitting cramped in a forgotten closet in an abandoned cottage built two hundred years ago. It had all the elements. It had "legs," as the newspeople say. It had staying power. Today I can tap in "Johnny Dace" and see those *in situ* images photographed by the forensics team. There are his bones huddled upright in a corner of a forgotten closet, waiting to be found. I was identified as the boy who discovered him. Marcus Harshaw, age eleven, a resident of the island.

We buried him in the cemetery of Lachicotte's church. Coral Upchurch was present in her wheelchair, attended by Roberta Dumas. The DNA cousin, in her eighties, took the spotlight—for a while. Her life had clearly been lived at the other end of the spectrum from Coral Upchurch's and she had not held up as well. But she could still walk and talk and had some faded Polaroid snapshots of Johnny Dace in her purse. She blossomed under the attention of the newspeople until the discrepancies in her narrative piled too high and toppled. The Polaroids were of a much younger Johnny, a frowning child who was too much for his parents to handle; they had sent him off several times to a facility for wayward youth, but kept bringing him home to try again. In a later version of the cousin's, he was a smart, sweet boy if you knew how to handle him and had been like a son to her. Finally, in her toppling version, Elvis himself had passed through Louisville and told Johnny Dace, "You could pass as my double." But the problem was that

Elvis had only begun his career the year Johnny Dace went missing in the hurricane.

That was when Charlie Coggins murmured to her that there was just enough time before her departing flight for him to show her the cottage where her only remaining kin had spent the last fifty years. Refusing the realtor's offer to pay for transferring the remains back to Kentucky, she signed papers releasing him to be buried on the island on the condition that she would not be liable for any of the funeral and burial expenses.

Before Johnny's burial, Lachicotte took me to the funeral home to see his remains. He was five-feet-eight-and-a-half, had bow legs, and large hands. I had hoped to check out the broken and badly repaired nose, but the nose was gone. They allowed me to run my hand along the long tibia bones.

WE ORDERED HIS stone from the monument place Lachicotte's family always used. It was down the coast, near Georgetown, and we drove there in a 1936 Bentley Derby touring car Lachicotte had just taken on. We had the top down, or rather Lachicotte was having a new top made, and my hair whipped in the coastal wind the way Pickett's did when he was arriving in Ed's Jeep to destroy my evening. The steering was on the right side of the Bentley and we'd moved the passenger seat back all the way to accommodate my straight-leg cast.

At the monument place, a very tan young woman in shorts and a T-shirt was at work outdoors chiseling a stone for a monk who had died in 1904. After Hurricane Floyd had flooded the monastery in 1999, she explained, all the monks' remains had to be dug up and relocated to a new cemetery built on higher ground. New stones were needed because marble crumbled when you tried to move it. "This is the longest order we've ever taken on. Eighty-one stones! We've been working on them for almost five years. We have to do it between other jobs, but the abbot said that was fine, because monks were taught to live in a different kind of time anyway."

Lachicotte was fascinated, and so she took us around to the back where some finished stones were stacked on wooden trays, waiting for delivery to the monastery. All the stones were the same modest rectangular size and carved exactly alike. IHS at the top, then underneath the monk's name, below that, his dates of birth, profession, and death.

"What's IHS?" I asked.

"The first three letters of Jesus's name in Greek," she said, and Lachicotte obligingly spelled out the name for me: I-h-s-u-s.

We had gone back and forth about choosing the appropriate stone to lie on top of Johnny Dace's grave. Aunt Charlotte and Lachicotte and I were dividing the cost among us.

"But if we just put his birth and death dates, it'll look like any old boy who was born in 1940 and died fourteen years later," I reasoned.

"Yes, but when in doubt, less is usually more," said Aunt Charlotte. "We want to stay away from the maudlin."

"What's *maudlin*?" I asked.

"Smarmy, sentimental, melodramatic, like for instance, 'Lost in Hurricane Hazel, 1954, Miraculously Found, 2004.' That still doesn't tell enough and it uses far too many letters."

"Let's think what he would want," Lachicotte finally suggested, "if he were here (*he-ah*) to give the order himself."

By the time Lachicotte and I headed south in the Bentley Derby to the monument place, we had settled on the simplest information.

"That's probably enough," I said. "When Mom and I used to discuss our funerals and burials, she said all she wanted on her stone was ALICE HARSHAW, and her dates. She didn't even want her family name on her stone. I still haven't decided."

"Decided what?" Lachicotte asked. "What you want on yours?"

"No, I haven't ordered Mom's stone yet. My ad litem back in North Carolina is going to take care of it when I decide. The money's all set up to pay for it. All I have to do is say what I want on her stone."

The young woman at the monument place sat down with us and made some sketches. JOHNNY DACE with birth and death dates. She showed us the possible fonts on a chart. We both liked the name in square capital letters. "It looks like a Latin inscription," said Lachicotte.

"I wish we had something more," I said.

"Like what?"

"Well, like those monks have. Something above themselves to watch over them."

"There's always the good old STTL the Romans put on their gravestones," said Lachicotte. "*Sit Tibi Terra Levis*. It means 'May the earth lie lightly upon thee.'"

"I love that! It's perfect—especially for him."

"Latin was the one thing I loved at my boarding schools," Lachicotte said.

"But maybe we should just have it in English, so people around here will know what it means."

"We can do that," said Lachicotte.

"And you know what? I think it would be the right thing for my mom's stone. Only maybe both the Latin and then the

English underneath. My mother had a special thing about Latin."

"You can do that, too," said Lachicotte.

★ ★ ★

AUNT CHARLOTTE WAS to become what she called "an intermittent recoverer." At first she tried to limit herself to a bottle and a half a day. She did her hand exercises religiously and began to paint again, though according to her not ever with the same range of motion. The publicity surrounding the Johnny Dace remains brought her a flurry of new commissions for paintings of Grief Cottage. She worked from my photos, and from her memory of her earlier paintings. The cottage was demolished soon after the publicity died down, and Charlie Coggins quickly relieved himself of the two lots to an eager buyer. Then the new owner's neighbors, which included Ed Bolton, advised the man to call in erosion experts before he started building. The experts found that the north tip of the island was dissolving at such a rate that any structure he built would probably be washed away by 2025.

Aunt Charlotte tired herself fulfilling the new commissions and when she was back up to three bottles a day, she let Lachicotte and me talk her into going on a month's retreat at a very nice recovery villa in Savannah. Lachicotte moved in with me, making my breakfast, driving me to school, and leaving the toilet seat up. After that she made it through a two-year dry spell, during which she built an addition onto her cottage: a bedroom and bath and a north-facing deck where she could paint outside without people spying over her shoulder and making stupid remarks. After she had her "deck-studio," her painting underwent a significant change. Small canvases, though not as small as four by sixes. You looked at them and thought, "Oh, she's become an abstract impressionist." But if you kept looking long enough you thought, "No, wait, that square of grays and lavenders is a close-up of a cloud after sunset, the way it looks when the artist has penetrated the mass and shape of its vapor. No, wait, that's the surf at high tide, the way it looks when the artist has gone beyond the outline of the waves and is among the droplets."

We lost a third of my trust in the crash of 2008. Aunt Charlotte continued to draw her "nice stipend," which she deposited straight over into my college fund. "Look at it this way, Marcus. When we were in clover, I was able to draw on my old savings to build my addition, and you got four years with your expensive psychiatrist. We're going to be okay. Whatever happens, you've proved yourself smart enough to walk away with a hundred scholarships, and my 'droplet and vapor' paintings, as you call them, aren't doing half bad. People can live with them. I like them myself. They're both soothing and strange, and they enlarge beautifully on aluminum prints. A lawyer in Columbia bought six of them for her office."

Lachicotte's sudden death in 2013 sent her back for an extended stay at the villa in Savannah. In exchange for reduced rates to cover her stay, she gave art lessons to other guests, demonstrating the therapeutic values of painting with the non-dominant hand. ("You will uncover all sorts of things about yourself," she promised her fellow recoverers. "Your unpracticed hand will waver and wobble into places your controlling hand would never let you near.") It turned out she hadn't needed to barter, as Lachicotte had divided his worldly goods between "My dear niece, Althea," and "My good friend, Charlotte Lee."

"Just like Lash . . . typical, typical," Aunt Charlotte would rage or lament on my visits to the villa—by this time, I was in pre-med at the state university. "I mean, he was old but not that old. If it weren't for his foolish need to please everything that crossed his path, he had some vital years left in him. He had no business switching cars with that boy, just because the boy wanted to drive the Jaguar."

The "boy," a young man in his twenties, was supposed to follow Lachicotte to Hilton Head in his own car and take him home after they had delivered the Jaguar. "I'll never forgive myself," the boy anguished. "I just wanted to drive that beauty for the final stretch, and at the rest stop before the bridge, Lachicotte handed over the keys and said, 'Remember. You're still driving on the right side of the road, but now the steering wheel's on your right, as well.' And then he jams on the brakes of my car to keep from running over a dog and crashes against an abutment. I saw the whole thing through the Jaguar's rear-view mirror. I'll never be able to look through a rearview mirror again without reliving the whole thing: that brown dog streaking across the road and Mr. Hayes's wild, crazy turn straight into the abutment."

"That boy reminds me of those witnesses being interviewed after a disaster," Aunt Charlotte would say. "It's all about *the witness* who saw the tragedy." And she would then mimic a witness's plaintive voice: "'I was sitting in the outdoor café having my cappuccino and planning my sightseeing for the afternoon when suddenly this building right across the road from me explodes! It was close enough to make my table shake and little pieces of ash fall into my cappuccino . . .'"

I could hear Lachicotte as he handed over the keys: *"Remem-bah, you're still driving on the right side of the road but the steering wheel's now on yo-ah right as well."*

In fact, I could hear Lachicotte a dozen times in a day, saying things I knew he would probably say if we were sitting next to each other in the car or walking on the beach or eating supper together. I will go on hearing him for the rest of my life. He makes fresh observations, suitable to the occasion, and my ear-memory still registers his pitch of voice, his speech rhythms, his modest-warm mode of delivery. He is one of the permanent figures of my dream life.

Coral Upchurch lived another eight months after surviving pneumonia and is buried next to Billy in Columbia. She left me the antique Provençal writing desk, which is my nicest piece of furniture. Roberta inherited the Upchurch house in Columbia, which she sold to pay for her grandson's college. The Upchurch family beach house, compromised by Archie's trellis hiding the old brick footing columns and Coral's unsightly wheelchair ramp, was bequeathed by Mrs. Upchurch to the island's Historical Society, which soon restored its vernacular integrity. The William Upchurch Community Center is rented out for special functions, the proceeds going into the Society's coffers. To celebrate my graduation from college, Aunt Charlotte gave me a party on Coral's smoking porch.

When I came home to Aunt Charlotte's during college and medical school breaks, we would make our pilgrimage to where Lachicotte was buried next to his mother.

"Damn it, Lash," Aunt Charlotte would scold his grave. "Why did you think you had to look out for everything on legs and wheels?"

Though another time she said to me: "Isn't it strange, Marcus, that after someone dies you like to recall the very traits that used to drive you crazy."

"I miss him a lot," I would say.

When we visited the cemetery, Aunt Charlotte usually remained on a shady bench near Lachicotte's grave while I walked over to the newer part of the cemetery to visit "your friend," as she called him.

I followed new rules for these visits to Johnny Dace. I wouldn't have dreamed of plunking myself down beside his stone and choking his eternal stillness with my living chatter. He was no longer the missing dead boy crammed into a forgotten closet. His bones were at rest, laid out flat in their anatomical order until they crumbled in their own time and became part of the island's soil. And I was no longer the boy who needed the lifeline of a silent listener who had showed himself, on two occasions, as an entity on his own terms.

"IT'S SO SAD," Aunt Charlotte was to brood at a later date. This was after I had started my residency and was seeing patients, some of them the same age I had been when Aunt Charlotte met me at the airport and shook my hand and said, *Well, Marcus, here we are.*

"What's so sad?" I asked.

"When we don't realize how remarkable someone is while they're still with us. Then after they're gone we wish we had told them, but when they were around *we didn't know yet.* Does that make any sense?"

That was when I told her about the day I had met Lachicotte. "You were still in the hospital after your accident and he was taking me to buy a bike before we picked you up. We were driving across the causeway and I was telling him about my mom and I said that Mom had planned to take the high school equivalency exam and go on to college. I said, 'She wanted to make something of herself.' And he was quiet for a minute and then he said, 'I would say she had already made a great deal of herself by bringing you up so well.'"

"That sounds exactly like something Lachicotte would say."

"Yes, well, it went right over me that day, but later when I thought about it, I felt such sorrow that I had never understood this when she was alive and how it would have pleased her if I had said something like, 'Mom, you are a real warrior, I'm so proud of you.'"

Aunt Charlotte looked at me. "Then you do know what I'm talking about."

The island in late May, fourteen years later, supper hour.

"WELL, MARCUS, HERE we are."

"That was the first thing you ever said to me."

"Was it?"

"When you met me at the airport, you said, 'Well, Marcus, here we are,' and shook my hand."

"What a memory. I remember nothing, other than being scared."

"Of what you were taking on?"

"I was scared you were thinking, 'Oh, no! I have to live with *her*?' Even now I'm not sure I'd want to know your first impression of me."

"'A thin serious lady all in white, with beaky features and a Roman centurion haircut. When you shook my hand it was such a relief not to be hysterically hugged. Your turn, now. What did you think of me?"

"Marcus, you're the one studying to be a shrink. Don't you know when any two people meet both are thinking, 'What does X think of *me*?'"

"You must have had some impression. What kind of boy did you see when that airline attendant was leading me to you?"

"I'm not sure. Well, let's see. Maybe that you weren't as much of *a little boy* as I'd been expecting. I had no experience of little boys. Though I'm not sure I even thought that much. It may be something I'm adding in hindsight. I guess I was mostly worrying what you thought of me. Sorry to disappoint you."

"You haven't. When people think they're making something up about the past, they're often remembering."

The island, early next morning.

"WELL, IT'S TIME to be on my way."

"It's hardly daylight, Aunt Charlotte. Savannah is only a two-hour drive."

"I know, but I get antsy before a trip. I feel neither here or there."

"You're sure you don't want to take along a sandwich and a banana?"

"No, I've got my bottled water and a package of that boring trail mix. I want to make it inside the gates of the recovery villa without falling off the wagon."

"Maybe I'll replace those damaged shingles on the ocean side."

"Marcus, the shingles can wait. You've been slogging nonstop as long as I've known you. Middle school, high school, college, medical school. Now you have ten free days before your residency starts. Why not relax and see what it feels like to do nothing at all?"

"I'm not sure I could handle it. You sure you have all the materials you need for your painting classes at the villa?"

"You loaded them into the car yourself. Now let's exchange a hysterical hug and I'll hit the road. A person my age drives better earlier in the day."

She stuck her hand out of the driver's window, fluttering her fingers in a playful farewell as she turned left onto Seashore Drive. I stood at the curb, watching her little silver car out of sight. When her vintage Mercedes gave up the ghost after Lachicotte's death, she went out and purchased a new Japanese compact along with an additional 75,000-mile warranty that included pickup when it needed service or misbehaved and a rental car delivered to your door. ("This ought to see me through to the end. I never go anywhere except for shopping and my periodical recovery jaunts to Savannah. Lachicotte couldn't stand new cars, but he doesn't have to know.")

I feel neither here or there, she said as her excuse for leaving so early. After she was gone, I kept rerunning that fluttery farewell out her window. It reminded me of the dismissive finger-wave from her stretcher as the medics were carrying her out the door. ("Be a good boy, and be sure to lock up front and back.")

"You can tell when a person has already left you behind," explained a young patient I had been treating under supervision. "Even if that person is right in front of you, you know they're only pretending to be with you and that makes it worse." At fifteen, she had attempted suicide three times.

"Why not relax and see what it feels like to do nothing at all?" Aunt Charlotte had suggested. Still rooted to the curb, I contemplated how I was going to get through the rest of the day and felt the onset of a terror I thought I had outgrown.

I hated it when these *clusters* started to form. One unwelcome subject sought out its counterparts—farewells, people leaving and never coming back, ambulances—like the silent ambulance with the revolving red light turning into our street and taking away Coral Upchurch. And then *those* counterparts attracted similar old hurts and horrors until you were trapped in the nucleus of the cluster. This cluster, I knew, was labeled LOSS in big black letters. I knew this much, thanks to therapy and training, but simply *knowing* it didn't protect you from reacting to it over and over again. Until one day you resolved to sit down in the middle of the nucleus, fold your arms, and invite the cluster to do its worst. And if you survived that, you could look around and see what was left in its absence.

I followed my feet back to the cottage. What they wanted next, it seemed, was to perform a house check. Kitchen in order, bathroom left neat; Aunt Charlotte must have wiped the sink and floor dry with her used towels and dropped them in the laundry basket.

My room was so full of my boyhood self that I felt the urge to report back to him and keep him apprised of our progress. ("Well, medical school is over, now comes four years of residency in a new place, and after that, if we prove ourselves worthy, a fellowship in child and adolescent psychiatry. That gets us into our thirties, but thanks to your skipping that grade back in the bleak Jewel era, we're still a year ahead of ourselves.")

My aunt had left the door to her studio open. It was arranged and tidied as if expecting an imminent tour: "The Painter's Empty Studio." The big easel had been wheeled away from the center, the trestle tables with their tubes of pigment and containers full of brushes moved flush against the walls. (Lachicotte's Coronation tea caddy was still home to the precious sables.) Pinned along the top of the wall-high cork board were Aunt Charlotte's blown-up photos of tidal pools recorded on low-tide evenings over the period of a month. Below were her pastel sketches on Japan paper of the shapes and colors left in the sand. ("I want to see how far I can get toward *pure design* while still remaining faithful to what nature left behind.")

In the "new wing," as we still called it twelve years after it was built, she had made her bed. I had been half-hoping she hadn't, so I could justify running a small load of laundry, just the sheets and towels.

("Marcus, the sheets and towels can *wait*.")

My feet having completed their house check, I was at liberty to go back to bed and start catching up on four years of lost sleep as a medical student, or to walk down to the beach, which, sad to say, no longer offered the unrestricted pleasures of my boyhood.

Our beach had not held up as well as Aunt Charlotte's cottage. Nevertheless, the ocean remained its old self, calming you with its predictable rhythms, taking its ancient watery breaths as it did millions of years ago when the little loggerhead hatchlings made their mad dash for its deep waters.

"The ocean is going to be just fine and the beaches are going to be just fine," explained an unwelcome scientist at a contentious meeting when the island residents were at their most divided. "They will go on together perfectly well. There will always be beaches, but the ocean will move the beaches *to new locations*. The only losers will be the property owners fighting a hopeless battle to make nature stand still." He was booed down and the twenty-three timber groins went up, jutting out perpendicular to the shoreline from the north to the south end of the island. Gone was the wide swath of unencumbered beach as far as you could see, where walkers could walk without going around the regularly spaced four-foot-high beams. Except at very low tide, bicycle tires sank in the sand. Eleven-year-old Marcus would have had to rely on Seashore Road for his daily visits to the ghost-boy.

I sat down on "our" groin, placed a few feet beyond Aunt Charlotte's boardwalk steps in approximately the same place the

Turtle Patrol had relocated the loggerhead eggs the first summer I was here.

The tide had started to go out, but the waves still covered most of the beach. Aunt Charlotte had left so early that there was a good hour left for unleashed dogs to chase one another into the surf, get good and wet, then streak up to shake water and sand on their owners hugging the dry space up by the dunes. Dogs on the beach brought back Barrett, the service dog I had met on the same morning I had seen the ghost-boy poised to leap out from the doorway. Barrett would be an old dog now, his wounded warrior preparing sorrowfully for the loss of him. The warrior himself, approaching middle age, had years more to live with his handicap and his war memories. Would he be given a new dog? Or maybe both Barrett and his warrior were already dead.

The phone in my back pocket buzzed once. Who at this hour was sending me a message?

It was Charlie Coggins:

Fellow wants you to call him, said it's important. He found my name in all those Grief Cottage news stories and phoned our office to ask if I knew where you were. Here is his contact info. Said you'd remember him as Shelby's older brother. I hear good things about you when I run into your aunt, which is not often.

Below were the home phone, cell phone, and street address of Andrew Forster. It took me a minute to realize Andrew was Drew and Shelby was Wheezer.

A man picked up the home phone.

"Is this Andrew?"

"He's still asleep. Can I take a message?"

"Oh sorry, I didn't realize it's so early. I'm all turned around today. This is Marcus Harshaw, I'm calling from—"

"Wait, Marcus, give me your number in case we get cut off. I'll go wake him. We've been trying to locate you."

"Marcus? This is Andrew, Shelby's older brother. Thank you for calling back. Do you remember me at all?"

"Yes. Wheezer always called you Drew."

"Hey, I forgot his little friends called him that! We've been trying to find your whereabouts, Marcus. First we found an article you wrote in a psychiatry journal, and Shelby said he would gamble on that being you. Then we found those old news stories—about you discovering the buried boy on the South Carolina island—and we decided to contact the realtor who was quoted. Listen Marcus; Shelby—Wheezer—isn't doing so well. Lymphoblastic lymphoma, Stage Four, if that means anything to you. He had a high response with the initial chemo and we had high hopes he was going to make it, but he had an early relapse and—well, now it doesn't look so good. It's too late for a bone marrow transplant and we've made him comfortable at home. He's been talking about you a lot. Where are you right now?"

"I'm on that same island in those news stories. Where are you?"

"Same old town, Granny's old house. You know it. Granny's gone, but we're all living in her house."

"There are a few things I need to take care of here, but then I could come."

"That's what we were hoping for. But, look, Marcus, don't leave it too long."

"I could get away from here by noon."

"You mean you would come *today*?"

"If I left at noon I think I could be there in late afternoon. What's the street address, I don't think I ever knew it."

"We're Number One Maple Avenue. It's at the top of the street. You'll stay with us. There's plenty of room. Oh, and when you get as far as Asheboro? Why don't you call to let us know you're close. That'll give us a good half hour to get him up to speed for your arrival."

"Will you tell him I'm coming?"

"I surely will, as soon as his nurse gets him bathed and set up for the day. Then he'll have something to look forward to."

Getting a sick person "up to speed" for a visitor could mean anything from disconnecting a catheter or an IV so the person could move around without dragging a pole, or taking injections or pills to block pain, or to keep you sharp and awake for short portions of time. It was useless to try to guess. I would know soon enough.

The route from the island to Forsterville was largely interstate, cutting northwest through salt marshes, coastal plain, up into the piedmont, and right into the foothills of the Appalachian mountains, but what I saw was mostly the asphalt in front of me and signs naming the towns that I was not going to see. "It is still possible to go the back roads and get an idea of how people lived," Mom had said when we had been planning our trip to West Virginia so I could see my roots, at least on her side. "The back roads take longer, but we'll take all the time we need." I had traveled this interstate route before, when I had gone back to see to the stone for her grave.

THE BIG WHITE Forster house at the top of the tree-lined street looked down at a nondescript car packed to the gills with belongings laboring upward in second gear. ("We're Number One Maple Avenue," Drew had said.) Wheezer and I had always taken the back route to the house to avoid the uphill pedaling. Why this surge of anger and worthlessness at the sight of the house on top of its green hill? I was expected, I was wanted; wasn't I an equal player now?

"They got here first," Mom had explained when we had taken our afternoon walks in the Forsterville Cemetery. "So naturally they would choose the highest lots to be buried in." Her favorite spot was at the top of the hill. My best photo of her, which I carried tucked in my wallet along with the headshot of my unknown father, was of her sitting beside one of their family gravestones, leaning a little sideways, so her cheek grazed the edge of the upright stone. I had wanted her to pose next to a weeping marble angel farther down the hill, and she obliged me, but the body language between them was terrible. Then she had returned to her usual gravestone. "The view is better up here," she called to me.

MY OVERLOADED CAR crackled around the circular white gravel driveway of the front entrance. Waiting in the open doorway was a gaunt, elongated person still recognizable to me as the complete little man in first grade. Wearing jeans and a polo shirt to match the Carolina blue baseball cap tipped low over his forehead, he leaned into the door frame, his unsupported side steadied by a cane. In eager silence he watched me unfold myself from the car and make my way toward him. Before I had reached the steps, I could feel myself entering his realm. Whenever we had been separated as boys, even if for only a few hours, he would beam that "I-own-you" gaze at me when I came back. He was now sending me this gaze from under the baseball cap. I was close enough now to take in the skeletal cheeks, the bony shelf of his clavicle, the stick-thin upper arms;

I also saw the effort it was taking him to stand upright, even with the help of door frame and cane.

"I knew you'd come, Marcus. All we had to do was find where you were. Now you can hug me if you like."

I embraced the emaciated frame, taking care not to upset his balance. My tears wet the front of his shirt, which smelled fresh from the dryer. "Whoa," he said in his new adult voice, "go easy on my bones. I've lost forty pounds. Now step back and let me look at you, Marcus. Funny, I always assumed *you'd* be the tall one, but even in my sorry state you only come to my shoulders. Listen, before we go inside, I've made some house rules. You are *my* company. When I'm awake, we'll catch up on important things. Any *medical* information will be left for the others to relate while I'm asleep. I have it all planned, and it will be perfect if everyone will do what I say."

SUPPORTING HIMSELF AGAINST me on his cane-free side, he led me through the shadowy formal living room, which had been off-bounds to children, and onto the screened porch, where his grandmother had escaped for her smokes. There, seated in chairs, were three people who clearly wanted to give the impression they had simply been relaxing together and not waiting on tenterhooks to see if he could accomplish his solo welcome of me.

The two white men with pleasant faces and balding heads came forward and greeted me, Andrew clasping my hand warmly in both of his and introducing "my partner, Bryson, and this is Tobias, Shelby's resident nurse." The muscular black man in green scrubs bounded forward to shake my hand and in a passing, fluid motion slid his arm effortlessly around his patient, relieving me of the weight.

"Not so fast, Tobias," Wheezer said. "I'm not done yet. Marcus, how long can you stay?"

"I have ten days before I start my new job. No, nine. I used up one of them today. And it's an eight-hour drive to get where I'm going. Then I'll need a few days to unpack and get organized. I could stay here three days."

"Is that counting today?"

"Counting today."

"And you'd leave on the morning of the fourth day? Then here's the plan. Tobias will carry me off for my injection after which I'll snooze, and Drew and Bryson will get you settled into your room and feed you, and then you and I will meet up later in the evening, when I'm usually at my best."

I was to sleep in Drew's former upstairs bedroom, which I had never been inside. When we were boys he had kept it locked when he was away and when at home he shut himself inside and turned up his stereo, except for meals. The bed had been temptingly readied, the counterpane turned down, and a gentle breeze brought the scent of an unknown flower through the open windows.

"We used to hear your jazz and blues coming from this room," I told Drew.

"You probably remember me as Gloomy Gus."

"No, I figured we must annoy you, two loud little boys. You were so much older than us—"

"It's hard to realize I was once that unhappy wretch. This room was always given to the oldest son, or just the son if there was only one in the family. It was Granddad Forster's room, then it passed on to my father's older brother, our ill-fated uncle who threw away his life—I expect Shelby told you about him."

"The brilliant uncle who died of an overdose?"

"That's the one. Shelby was born too late to meet Uncle Henry, who was the most lovable and fascinating human being in the world when he wasn't drinking—or later when he was on the hard stuff. I remember when I was about six, Uncle Henry was reading a book, oblivious to everybody else in the room, and I wormed my way into his lap and asked him to read it to me. 'But you wouldn't understand it, Drewie,' he said. 'No, I will, I will!' I insisted, so he wriggled me into a more comfortable position and started to read aloud in this beautiful, mysterious language. After a while, he said, 'Do you want me to go on?' and I said I did. 'You understanding it okay?' 'Not every word,' I told him, 'but I love it.' This made him laugh and he went on reading until I got interested in something else and climbed down from his lap. Turns out he was reading something in classical Greek, which he often did for pleasure, the way you and I might curl up and read a detective novel."

WHEEZER AND I did not "meet up again" that first evening. "He overestimated himself," Tobias told me. "When he heard you were coming, he got all excited and wanted so many things done. He would have done it all himself if he'd had the strength. He's a perfectionist and he likes to be in charge."

"He was like that when he was six."

"This is one of those forms of lymphoma there hasn't been a lot of research on."

"It's a relatively rare form, which usually strikes the young. I met several children with it during my oncology rotation."

"You're a doctor?"

"As of one week tomorrow. I just graduated from med school and I'm on my way to my residency in Nashville."

"Way to go. Congratulations. I've made up my mind to go on for further training myself. After Shelby doesn't need me anymore. I'm still deciding between physician's assistant and nurse practitioner. What do you think?"

"The pay scale for PA is higher—well, depending what doctor you go to work for. But if you want to be your own boss and have more contact with patients, nurse practitioner would be the choice. I know 'Physician's assistant' sounds more important because it has 'physician' in the title, but . . ."

"Isn't it the truth. What something's *called* can sway you before you rightly know what it is."

DURING THE LONG evening that Wheezer slept through, Andrew and Bryson updated me on Forsterville and on themselves. Forster's Fine Furniture had gone out of business back when Mom and I were still enduring the indignities of Wicked and Harm on Smoke Vine Street in Jewel.

"Forster's downfall can be summed up in three words," Andrew said. "'China is cheaper.' We held on longer than most, but it was swift and merciless when it hit. It killed Grandpop. His factory was his family, his preferred family, actually. His employees were his children, his preferred children. He handed out the severance checks himself, crying the entire time, and then came home and collapsed. We buried him five months later. There were occasional renters, who ended up doing more damage than good, until finally someone left a coffee machine on and burned down an entire wing. By then, Granny was gone, having got Shelby through his disaster—this was before the cancer, but since it's not strictly a medical subject, he'll probably want to tell you himself—and Bryson and I had taken the marriage vows twice, first a civil service in North Carolina, and then the following year, when it became the law of the land, we had a ceremony here at the house. Shortly after that, we were walking around the empty factory, inspecting the abandoned machinery, debating whether we should sell to someone who wanted to gut it and turn it into condos, when Bryson had his idea. We could make it into a museum. Today's public doesn't want too much reality, Bryson said, they're happier with simulations and reenactments. They like their reality broken into manageable pieces and then stylishly arranged for them as an entertainment. So that's what we're doing. Bryson even got us a state grant, and the building was already on the historical register, which helped. We're both accountants, that's how we met, but Bryson has all the creative savvy. It's going to be a Furniture Factory Museum, with rental spaces for custom-furniture makers if they're willing to ply their craft while people watch. And woodworking courses, with credits from the community college. And we've sent out a call that we're buying fine old pieces made at Forster's, and we've already got some in hand: the idea being that we'll hold contests for woodworkers to duplicate these pieces, the way painters sit in front of old masterpieces and copy them. And we're having an old film digitalized—it's the factory workers doing their various jobs and talking about it. Grandpop had it shot back in the early nineties, and the museum-goers will watch that first in a comfortable screening room."

"My mom was at Forster's in the nineties. I wonder if she's in it."

"We'll send you a copy, let's make a note. Wouldn't that be something?"

The second day, the first full day I was to be there, Wheezer stayed in bed without his baseball cap. They had made the downstairs sunroom into his bedroom and Tobias had the guest room next door. A hardly visible stand of fine hair was making a comeback on Wheezer's scalp.

"Come here, Marcus, I want you to feel it."

I sat down on the edge of his bed and ran my palm respectfully across the new growth. Naturally I thought of the last time I had touched his hair, gathering it into a silky clump so I could hit his face better.

"Bryson says it feels like petting a baby rabbit. How does it feel to you?"

"I've never petted a rabbit. Maybe putting your hand down on new grass?"

"Let me guess. Drew and Bryson have got as far as touching on 'Shelby's disaster,' then one of them said, 'No, no, that's outside of our medical guidelines, he'll want to tell you about that himself.'"

"How did you know?"

"I lie here and read people's minds. Drew is so at one with himself he goes whole stretches forgetting he exists as an individual. He plans the meals, pays the bills, and thinks up more things for them to do at the Furniture Factory Museum. Bryson goes around plotting happy little surprises for Drew. Tobias wonders if he'll be able to register in time for courses in the fall, then feels guilty for having the thought, and rushes in to bring me a fresh glass of shaved ice or a smoothie and ask if I want a backrub."

"Are you sure you're not just imagining what they might be thinking because you know them so well?"

"Oh, either way, Marcus. My point is, the mind doesn't use one-thousandth of its powers. It can be all over the place simultaneously and go down roads you didn't even know existed.

I've learned that through being sick and all the drugs that go with it and from my coke and heroin era and even when I tried and failed to kill myself."

"Oh, Wheezer."

"Yes, that was my 'disaster.' However, I hate to say it, Marcus, but when you're high you get glimpses of other ways your wonderful mind can operate. That's one reason people keep doing drugs. Do you remember how we'd tell each other 'trues'?"

"I certainly do."

"You used to *do research* in order to dig up stories to shock me. Van Gogh handing his sliced-off ear to a prostitute. That's what I was leading up to, telling you a true about the awful year I spent with my mother. I'd flunked out of college here, so in a rare moment of motherliness she invited me to live with her in Boca Raton and try the local community college. Well, to keep it nice and short, I dropped out after a couple of months and went to work for a contractor. Basic grunt jobs, like climbing on a roof and removing old tiles, doing coffee runs, picking up supplies, but I loved the outdoor work and I loved the paycheck. The contractor had a sixteen-year-old daughter named Cricket, who brought him lunch every day on her bicycle; she was too young to drive. She was a user and a dealer, still in high school, very small and smart and irresistible, she was an awesome little creature, and we fell in love and she introduced me to her wares. Then one night when we were together she didn't wake up from an overdose and when I woke up I was devastated. It was clear she was dead, and I tried to join her. But I cut the wrong way. If you ever get serious about cutting your wrists, do it lengthwise, not crosswise. But you'd know things like that, being a doctor. Anyway, Mother said she'd raised one queer and one junkie and she was packing it in. Actually, she *hadn't* raised me, but I was too despondent to contradict her. Granny came and got me and brought me back to life in this house and then died. Drew had paired up with Bryson by then and they'd started work on their Factory Museum. I went to work for the contractor they hired to do the renovations. As I said, outdoor work suits me and I would still be at it if I hadn't come down with this children's cancer."

"The cutoff age for it is usually around thirty, though I met one man in his sixties who had it."

"Did he survive?"

"To be honest, I don't know. It was at the end of my oncology rotation."

"How much longer do you have to go to school before you can hang out your shingle?"

"Four years of residency, which includes two of general psychiatry and two of child- and adolescent-specialty training. After that a two-year fellowship. It seems long, but at least I know what I want to do and am on track to do my chosen work."

"I wanted to read your article we found in that psychiatry journal—I forget its title, it had *supernatural* in it, but in order to read it I had to join something first and time was running short. We still had to find you."

"It was called 'Psyche and Soma in the Human Child: the Supernatural Episode.' Actually I co-authored it with my supervisor, otherwise it probably wouldn't have been accepted. I'll send you an offprint as soon as I unpack my boxes."

"You always were so smart, Marcus."

"You were the best friend I ever had. I spent part of first grade watching you so I could learn how to please you. And I never stopped dreaming about you. I still do. You are a permanent member of my dream theater—there are only about ten people in the entire repertory."

"I don't know whether to ask this or not."

"Go ahead."

"You may be sorry."

"No, please. Ask it."

Wheezer raised himself to an upright position, wincing a little from the effort, and took a dramatic deep breath. "Okay, here goes. What did I do, or say, that day I came to have lunch at your apartment, that made you try to kill me the next day?"

"It was something you said at school."

"What? I know I must have done something, but I can't remember."

"It was about my mom. About us sleeping in one bed. Next day you told your other friends, 'Marcus is his mother's little husband.'"

"I said that? And this was at school the next day?"

"Yes."

"Funny, all the times I've tried to remember, I was *sure* that whatever I did took place at your apartment. Didn't I come for lunch?"

"Yes, but you didn't stay. You left in a huff before my mom returned with the pizza."

"I don't remember *any* of this! Why did I leave in a huff?"

"I had shown you this picture of a man Mom kept in her drawer. I said it was my father and she was going to tell me his name when I was old enough to be responsible."

"Why don't I remember any of this?"

"We all have these blank spots. Sometimes it's because we repressed it, other times it's because another memory shoved it aside. You took the picture and shook it in its frame and said, 'Someone cut this out of a book.' And then you said, 'You two are crazy. I need to get out of here.'"

"I didn't stay for lunch?"

"No, when Mom came back with our lunch, I told her you'd felt an asthma attack coming on and had rushed home to get your medication."

"You know what's funny? I never had another attack after *your* attack. You're probably the last person in the world who calls me Wheezer. So did she tell you later who your father was?"

"No. As I told you, she died in that accident when I was eleven, so I never knew. But not knowing doesn't torture me as much as it once did. I was lucky enough to make friends with a man when I went to live with my great-aunt, and he became a sort of fatherly stand-in. He's dead now, but he stayed around long enough for me to get an idea what having a father would have been like."

"Well, you'll have to tell me about it because I've never had the experience. I don't know if Drew told you, but all those years my father was traveling for Forster's Furniture he had a second family in Roanoke, Virginia. Married and children and all and this was before Mother divorced him, so he was a full-fledged bigamist for a while. I didn't learn about this until I was in my teens. I used to fantasize driving up to Roanoke and introducing myself to my half-siblings, but I never got around to it. What would have been the point? I haven't even told my mother about my present state. She'd feel obliged to rush up from Florida and make a bedside appearance and Drew and Bryson would have to feed her and she'd say something mean to hurt their feelings. But look, you were born in Forsterville, your mom worked at Forster's Furniture. I mean, we all assumed your father was Mr. Harshaw because that's what your mom said, but it must have been someone around Forsterville."

"Whoever it was died before I was born, that much she told me."

"Do you still have that picture?"

"It's in my wallet upstairs."

"No, don't get it right now. We need to make the most of my waking time. But maybe Drew being so much older, he might recognize the face. Shit, my mouth feels like a sewer and I have so much more to ask! Would you go and find Tobias—he's probably doing laundry—and tell him I could use a lemon swab?"

"I can do it. Where are the swabs?"

"No, Marcus, the inside of my mouth is not pretty. I can't let you see it."

"I'm sure I've seen a lot worse. Besides, I'd like to do it for you. I promise I'll do a good job."

"They're in the top drawer of that bureau. They come in individual packages. Will you also promise you'll be here when I wake up—in case I fall asleep?"

ANDREW AND BRYSON were off to the Furniture Museum and asked me to go along.

"He usually sleeps for hours," Andrew said.

"Well, but I promised I'd be here when he woke up."

"Understood," they said.

"MARCUS, I WANTED to say about Cricket—it was the total thing and we both knew it. Just because she happened to be sixteen—I mean, I was only six years older. That's not a lot. Have you ever loved someone totally like that?"

"When I was fourteen, I fell in love with my therapist. She was fifty-one."

"What did you do?"

"I brooded and anguished and dreamed up scenarios where I saved her from danger or her husband died, or left her. I finally broke down and told her. And she said it had a name, *transference*, it happened a lot in therapy and if handled correctly it could sometimes turn corners. She said, 'We can do one of two things, Marcus. I can refer you to someone else, or we can work through this ourselves—within the bounds of therapy.' And we did that. I still loved her afterward and probably would still love her if I were to meet her today."

"And that's all? Your therapist when you were fourteen? Was there anyone after that?"

"I shared a house with another med student for a semester. It started off—well, it started off in a passionate ... *collision* ... that's the best way to describe it. So I asked her to move in with me and after the passion dried up we were nothing but roommates who shared the rent but didn't like each other very much."

"So you've never known the total real thing?"

"There's still time. The loggerhead turtle doesn't reach sexual maturity until he's in his thirties."

Forsterville, the last full day.

"MARCUS, I'M GOOD for the whole day. Tobias has given me a shot."

"A steroid? You'll probably pay for it later."

"I don't mind. You said last night you had saved up a true for me that you'd never told anyone."

"I couldn't have. They would have thought I was mentally unbalanced and sent me away for treatment, or they'd think I made it up to seem clairvoyant and 'special.' It's about that boy—well, that skeleton I fell on top of. The one in the news stories that led you to me."

"Were you more grossed out or freaked out when you felt him under you?"

"I was out cold. I didn't learn about him until I was in the hospital. But I need to start back at the beginning of that summer. I was eleven, my mother was dead, and I was sent to live with my great-aunt on a small island in South Carolina . . .'"

I WAS SURPRISED, and frankly let down, to realize that the entire story of Grief Cottage had taken less than twenty minutes to relate to Wheezer. How could that be? I had gone chronologically through those summer weeks fourteen years earlier, bringing in the necessary side-stories, the lost family in the hurricane, Coral Upchurch's memory of seeing Johnny Dace on the beach that one time fifty years before. I had been careful not to exaggerate the ghost-boy's manifestations to me: that first time on the porch when I felt invisibly watched from behind; then the two visual showings in the doorway; and the final time when I had taken the Percocet pills and felt his large hand on my back guiding me up the stairs of Grief Cottage.

"Wait, let's go over this again," said Wheezer. "That first time, when you fell asleep on the porch and then woke up and felt someone watching you from behind, was that before or after your aunt had told you about the missing family?"

"It was after."

"Okay, now, I'm going to play devil's advocate. The first time you saw him was in what you say was dazzling afternoon sunshine. Are you sure the dazzling light wasn't playing tricks on you?"

"No, he looked like a real person standing in the doorway. His face was in shadow because the dazzling light was behind him, but he was looking at me and he had on a red shirt."

"Okay. Now what about the big showing? The morning you got there before sunrise and everything was crepuscular and spooky, and he was braced in the doorway ready to spring out at you. You saw his red shirt again, unbuttoned this time, and his broken nose and the expression of his mouth, and his bow legs and jeans and boots. Right? And then later Mrs. Upchurch told you he never undressed at the beach and he was wearing some sort of footwear that might have been boots. Am I accurate so far?"

"An accurate devil's advocate."

"But then! Then everything changes. You go to the mortuary and see the bowed leg-bones. The nose was gone and the clothes were gone, but it turns out this *was* the remains of Johnny Dace, the boy lost in the hurricane, and now there's the DNA to prove it. It seems to me, Marcus, that somehow you were able to make contact with his spirit. It's like he needed you and you needed him and there was some kind of collapse in time and you were able to save each other. He got out of that cramped little closet and is laid peacefully to rest, and you are still here instead of being laid out underground yourself. It's got something to do with how time interacts with spirit, only you're going to have to figure it out for both of us. I think you do have special powers, Marcus. I give you permission to try them out on me."

"What do you mean?"

"Look. If you could reach a boy you never knew, a boy *who'd been dead fifty years*, why, reaching *me*, as close as we have been, will be a piece of cake."

TOBIAS ENTERED, BEARING a tray with a protein smoothie and a glass of shaved ice. He suggested his patient take a rest to conserve his energy for my farewell dinner that evening. Wheezer had asked for the dinner, and was planning to show up for it fully dressed and on his feet. Making ready to assist Wheezer to the bathroom, Tobias suggested I take a little walk outside in the sunshine, "and maybe you could use a little rest yourself."

I hadn't been outside the house since the first night, when I reparked my car and carried in my overnight bag. As I embarked on my assigned walk, I realized suddenly how drained I was. It was like coming off duty after a twenty-four-hour stint at the hospital. Seeing patients face-to-face, concentrating on their needs, you put yourself on hold, only to be confronted at the end of your rounds, cradling your pent-up umbrage like an ailing pet. *Now. What about me?*

Circling the backyard once, twice, a third time, I tried to recall how this patch of land had looked and felt when I was a visiting child. I passed the row of boxwoods where Wheezer had seen a snakeskin floating from a branch. ("Look, Marcus, you can even see where its jaw was! It probably rubbed against that bush to start the process and finally crawled out of its own mouth!") Or were these the same boxwoods? Shouldn't they have been more mature by now? In acute self-consciousness I performed this memory ritual in Wheezer's backyard: Now I am looking at the same boxwood or a replacement of the boxwood where the snakeskin floated; now I am remembering how Wheezer's grandmother stood under that tree, her back to the house, puffing her cigarette; now I am approaching the path where Wheezer taught me to ride Drew's old bicycle: ("If you'd just stop *thinking*, Marcus, and ride!")

Eventually it dawned on me that I didn't have to continue this forced-march down memory lane. Before a trip she felt neither here nor there, Aunt Charlotte had said, and I, too, was in that sort of antechamber between what was ending and what had not yet begun. I sank down on an outdoor chaise whose canvas pillows bore a faint scent of mildew and fell into a sort of half-sleep in which I was floating above a MapQuest aerial view of all the miles I had to drive tomorrow between Forsterville and Nashville.

WE MADE IT, all of us—well, almost—through my farewell supper. Drew, Bryson, Tobias, Shelby, and Marcus. Wheezer, dressed, arrived with a cane on his own steam, Tobias hovering close behind. He had left his head bare, with its rabbit fur exposed. Drew did salmon and vegetables on the outdoor grill. There was wine for those who wanted it, iced tea for those who didn't. And a silver bowl with fresh-cut fruit waiting for dessert. Beside my plate was a book-sized gift wrapped in white-and-gold paper.

"You have to open it now," ordered Wheezer. His face had gone ashen and he had sunk down in his chair.

It was one of those too-beautiful leather notebooks with Italian endpapers, the kind you postpone using, or never use, because you don't want to spoil it. "It's from all of us," Wheezer said. "Everyone's signed the card, but I went ahead and wrote the first entry inside."

While I am writing this, announced his familiar childish script at the top of the first page, *we are still together under the same roof, on the same earth at the same time. As for later, don't forget!*

There was more.

While we were serving ourselves fruit, Wheezer went limp in his chair. "Listen, Tobias, I'd better lie down." Tobias all but carried him away.

"Listen, Marcus," he said later, when we had joined him round his bed. "Show Drew that photo you were telling me about. He's so much older he might recognize the face."

I went upstairs, returned with the wallet, and handed the picture over to Drew, who took one look and raised his eyebrows.

"I think I do know this person, but I want to be sure. May I borrow this for a minute, Marcus?"

We heard him rustling around in the formal living room nobody used. A book dropped. Drew cursed and sneezed three times in succession.

"Someone needs to dust those shelves once in a blue moon," he said, returning with a book under his arm. "Okay, I've checked it out. This is the picture of Uncle Henry in the 1976 Harvard yearbook. That was his sophomore year, the year he dropped out. Only someone cut it out of the yearbook."

He opened to the page.

Under the cutout space was the name *Henry Arthur Forster, Jr.*

"And look," said Drew, "Marcus's photo fits right in the space. Now, would someone please tell me what this is all about?"

"Marcus will have to tell you," said Wheezer in a near-whisper, his eyes excited, feverish, "and it's going to be an interesting ride. Look, guys, I need to snooze for a while and when I wake up I'll be good as new. Then I expect to hear everything everybody said, and I mean *everything*."

ACKNOWLEDGMENTS

GRIEF COTTAGE HAS been enriched significantly by the close readings and rereadings of my editor, Nancy Miller, who has now seen me through six books, and my agent, Moses Cardona, who is all a literary agent should be—and more. Nancy is a master of her craft who has a sharp eye for what is not there yet. Moses, besides being my champion, possesses the rare gift of seeing right into the heart of a story and helping me see it, too.

Thanks to Katya Mezhibovskaya for creating a jacket design that expresses the mood and story of *Grief Cottage* so perfectly.

Thanks to Evie Preston for her guidance and encouragement.

Thanks to my astute "tough reader" of many years, Robb Forman Dew, and to her son Jack Dew, who offered an invaluable suggestion concerning the ghost.

Thanks to Lynn Goldberg, who asked the right question at the right time.

Thanks to Ehren Foley at the South Carolina Department of Archives and History for providing details about two-hundred-year-old beach cottages and their floor plans, and for his enthusiasm and cordiality.

Thanks to Lee Brockington of Hobcaw Barony for putting me in touch with the right sources. I kept her sumptuous volume, *Pawleys Island, a Century of History and Photographs*, with Photo Editor Linwood Attman, near to me throughout the writing of *Grief Cottage*.

Professor James R. Spotila's passionate guide, *Saving Sea Turtles*, introduced me and Marcus to the fascinating journey of the loggerhead turtle.

And thanks to my sister, Franchelle Millender, who invited me to share a beach cottage with her on the Isle of Palms in South Carolina, where *Grief Cottage* was first conceived.

Aunt Charlotte's island is drawn from both Pawleys Island and the Isle of Palms.

Grief Cottage
Gail Godwin
Guide written by Zoe Gould

The following questions are intended to enhance your discussion of *Grief Cottage*.

About this book

After the sudden death of his mother, eleven-year-old Marcus is sent to live with his Aunt Charlotte on a small South Carolina island. A recluse and unaccustomed to house guests, Charlotte leaves Marcus largely on his own to acclimate to his new life. Marcus is fascinated by Grief Cottage, the island's most notorious home and the frequent subject of Charlotte's paintings.

When a hurricane ripped through the island fifty years earlier, the boy and his parents who rented the cottage were swept away and their bodies were never recovered. Marcus becomes obsessed with uncovering their identities after he encounters the ghost of a boy slightly older than himself in the doorway of the decrepit home. Marcus builds his new life around the routine of visiting the cottage each morning, attempting to catch another glimpse of his undead friend. But the ghost is not so forthcoming; Marcus is slowly drawn further and further into the fatal history of the cottage. Tasked with rifling through his own past as well, Marcus attempts to reroot himself with the help of a cast of local characters, a nest of turtle eggs, and a ghost that won't let him go.

Far from a traditional ghost story, *Grief Cottage* is an examination of the psyche as it experiences wonder, grief, and loss.

For discussion

1. Consider the novel's epigraph: "Not everybody gets to grow up. First you have to survive your childhood, and then begins the hard work of growing into it." Childhood and survival are central themes for this novel. Charlotte, Marcus, and his mother all had traumatic childhoods that influenced their behavior as adults. What tools do each of them employ to help them survive? What does it mean to "grow into" one's childhood? Who in the book is a good example of that?

2. The turtle migration is a central fixture in Marcus's new life; he convenes with the eggs each day, monitors their temperature closely, and is devastated when he misses their historic sprint from nest to ocean. Before the migration, he explains to them, "The reason we can't pick you up and carry you is because you need to do the walk yourselves so you can smell the sand and remember your way back to this beach when you're grown up" (151). Why are the turtles a source of comfort for Marcus? Compare and contrast their ancient ritual for survival to Marcus's own journey toward growth and safety. How does the turtles' journey serve as a foil for the other characters' attempts at survival?

3. Because of his relationship with Johnny's ghost, Marcus often feels as if he straddles the line between sanity and insanity. He thinks, "The ghost-boy was related to my life, yet he was also an entity on his own terms . . . Didn't something have to be one thing or the other, either real or imagined" (156)? Discuss Marcus's question: Is it possible for something to be both real and imagined? In your opinion, does Marcus actually see a ghost in Grief Cottage or is he merely hallucinating an imaginary friend of sorts? How

does this ghost story in particular challenge our preconceived notions of the boundaries of reality?

4. The past and present are at constant odds throughout the novel: Marcus's confidant Lachicotte is enamored with restoring the antique; the turtles prepare to embark on an annual, ancient tradition; and Marcus finds himself obsessed with the fate of a family who inhabited the island over fifty years ago, only to develop a present-day relationship with the ghost of their teenage son. What point, if any, does the novel make about the function of time? Does the novel advocate for attempting to preserve the past or for letting it go? How do the characters reckon with, honor, and run from their pasts?

5. Despite receiving praise from his aunt, Marcus is constantly wracked with anxiety that she will find him unsatisfactory and send him away. When Charlotte leaves for surgery, Marcus has a mental breakdown and is tormented by "Cutting Edge," a malicious voice urging him to take his own life. Cutting Edge taunts Marcus with his worst fear: "You aren't wanted, you weren't wanted, and you're not going to be missed" (269). Discuss this part of Marcus's personality. How does it impact his life and relationships? Why does Marcus feel unwanted despite reassurance? In your opinion, what is the seed of his insecurity?

6. Before his overdose is complete, Marcus races to see Johnny's ghost at Grief Cottage. He thinks, "You were my *sure*. You were my lifeline" (271). Explore Marcus's inexplicable connection to Johnny's ghost; in what ways are the boys similar or different? Why does Marcus feel closer to Johnny than any of the living friends he has made so far? Marcus

believes that "since ghosts didn't have living brains, the work must be done by the living person. The living person had to offer his brain as the dwelling place for the ghost" (133). Why does Marcus give himself to Johnny as a place to dwell? Likewise, why does Johnny choose Marcus as his host?

7. Discuss the significance of Marcus's friendship with Wheezer. He often remembers fondly their boyhood closeness but is still haunted by Wheezer's accusation. When Marcus returns to visit Wheezer years later, how has their relationship changed? How has it stayed the same? When the two friends catch up, Marcus learns that Wheezer also attempted suicide in his younger years. What brings each of these two boys, who have very different backgrounds, to the brink of death?

8. Charlotte begins painting a secret project when she loses the use of her right hand. Under the influence of Cutting Edge, Marcus sneaks into her studio to find "Only to you, my little sheets," an intimate and grotesque set of paintings about her abusive past. Later, in rehab, Charlotte tells her art students "your unpracticed hand will waver and wobble into places your controlling hand would never let you near" (290). How does her discomfort allow her to come to terms with her own ghosts? How does this logic apply to other aspects of the novel? Who else benefits from their discomfort, and how?

9. Marcus grows up to become a child psychiatrist. In his studies, he is struck by the following passage: "The idea of a ghost, a disembodied spirit, derives from this lack of essential anchoring of the psyche in the soma, and the value of the ghost story lies in its drawing attention to the

precariousness of the psyche-soma existence" (282). Why is this precariousness important? What does it teach Marcus about his childhood self? In what other ways can a ghost story, with its emphasis on the supernatural, teach us about human existence?

10. Marcus and his elderly neighbor Coral Upchurch have a special bond over the loss of their loved ones. Ever since the death of her son, Coral Upchurch has been attempting to undergo an "archaeology on herself": "What would be left of the essential me without any of my roles" (243)? How does Marcus attempt his own archaeology on himself? What are his roles throughout the novel and how do they evolve? He believes that love is the answer to the question of everyone's essential role. Do you agree? Discuss all the roles you play in life; who do you become if your roles disappear?

11. "I realized that below all our *mes* that become known to others is a self that nobody else can ever fully know. No self can ever share its entire being with another self, no matter how much love there is between them" (244). Even though Marcus makes strong connections with his island neighbors, his experience with the ghost of Johnny Dace is the most impactful. Is Marcus connecting to Johnny, or to himself? Do you agree with Coral? Explain why or why not.

Recommended reading

Anything is Possible: A Novel by Elizabeth Strout; *Giving Up the Ghost: A Memoir* by Hilary Mantel; *Eva Trout* by Elizabeth Bowen; *Lincoln in the Bardo* by George Saunders; *Sing, Unburied, Sing* by Jesmyn Ward